Leron saw that Sibby had joined him in the cave and she, too, was stretching out her hand. He cried out for her when she touched the bird's white breast, but her tears were only for the Kermyrag. He lifted his great head slowly, and one dazzlingly bright bloody tear fell onto Sibby's hand. She drew it back with a silent cry and touched it to her lips. As she did so, Leron looked up into the wings, which were suddenly bursting into greater and more golden flames than before. Among the arched and curling feathers of fire, he could see Tredana, his city, burning also. It seemed his whole future life was drawn on a small scrap of paper, which turned up at the edges and flamed and crumbled into ash. As he thought this, the fires around him dimmed, and they were alone in the dark room remote from the Kermyrag.

Leron looked up from the table. It was empty. The Zene-drim and his treasures were vanished; there was no food or wine. Sibby's scarred hand was still pressed against her lips as she met Leron's gaze, then they both turned to where Yoseh had been sitting. His chair was empty, and the dust in its seat and on its arms was thick and undisturbed . . .

Other fantasy titles available from
Ace Science Fiction and Fantasy:

- Daughter of the Bright Moon, *Lynn Abbey*
- The Face in the Frost, *John Bellairs*
- Peregrine: Primus, *Avram Davidson*
- The Borribles, *Michael de Larrabeiti*
- Idylls of the Queen, *Phyllis Ann Karr*
- Journey to Aprilioth, *Eileen Kernaghan*
- 900 Grandmothers, *R.A. Lafferty*
- Swords and Deviltry, *Fritz Leiber*
- The Seekers of Shar-Nuhn, *Ardath Mayhar*
- The Door in the Hedge, *Robin McKinley*
- Jirel of Joiry, *C.L. Moore*
- Silverlock, *John Myers Myers*
- Witchworld, *Andre Norton*
- Tomoe Gozen, *Jessica Amanda Salmonson*
- The Warlock Unlocked, *Christopher Stasheff*
- Bard, *Keith Taylor*
- The Devil in a Forest, *Gene Wolfe*
- Shadow Magic, *Patricia C. Wrede*
- Changeling, *Roger Zelazny*

and much more!

THE BROKEN CITADEL

JOYCE BALLOU GREGORIAN

WITH DECORATIONS BY THE AUTHOR

FANTASY
ACE BOOKS, NEW YORK

An Ace Book

Published by arrangement with Atheneum

ISBN: 0-441-08099-5

First Ace Printing: January 1983
Published simultaneously in Canada

Manufactured in the United States of America
Ace Books, 200 Madison Ave., New York, New York 10016

For Douglas, With Love

As the years turn (a curious Carousel),
We'll watch the painted horses rise and fall.
This ride's for you: come take your turn, and
    look—
Here is a ring for you to catch: this book.

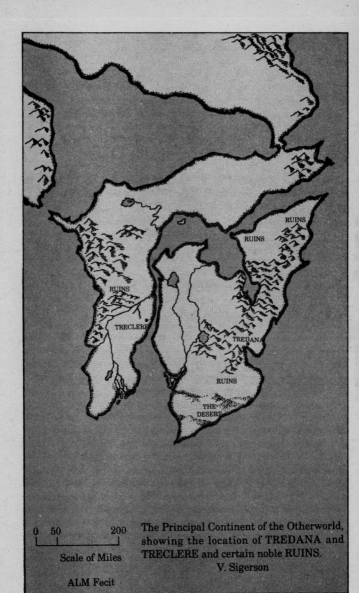

The Principal Continent of the Otherworld,
showing the location of TREDANA and
TRECLERE and certain noble RUINS.

V. Sigerson

0   50   200
Scale of Miles

ALM Fecit

Contents

THE BROKEN CITADEL

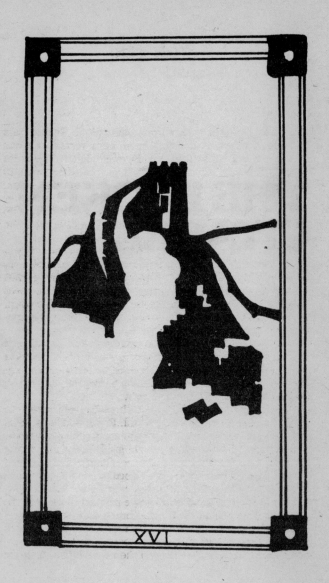

XVI

Prologue

Always Sibby walked home from school alone. She had said that she preferred to be alone for so many years that it was now one of those things that equally well might or might not be true. The walk could take anywhere from fifteen minutes to an hour depending on how much she wanted to get home. For the streets on West Newton hill take unlikely turns as they cross over the remains of great Victorian estates, cutting up the parks with their enormous mansions into little suburban house lots; and Sibby had many routes.

One house in particular drew Sibby like a magnet. It was five stories high, a dark roof raised above thick old oak trees on its own high hill. The windows of one wing stood at least three stories tall, and the mysterious room behind them was always dark. Sibby had first noticed the place long ago when, one day in second grade, she took a shortcut through its gardens.

Grey stone statues of men and goat's feet and half-dressed women stood there among the overgrown bushes. The next year, in third grade, Sibby had learned to recognize the figures as famous Roman works. But the feeling the garden gave her had never changed, it was creepy.

Now Sibby was eleven, and in fifth grade—old enough to know better, as her mother often said. It was an afternoon in September, overcast and smoky with burning leaves, and she was cautiously walking around the great house wondering how to get in. She tried the front-door handle, but a twisted wire sealed with lead had been wrapped around it, and it was locked. "Maybe I can get in through the cellar," she thought, but the recessed cellar windows were painted black, and she could imagine behind them a cavernous dark strange basement. "I bet the back door's locked, too. But in books there's usually a French window open, or something . . ." The windows were locked, but by the greenhouse Sibby had a stroke of luck. A few panes hidden by the laurel bushes were broken, and leaning around carefully she could undo a long window section from the inside. It slanted out and she pulled it up as far as possible, with difficulty worming her way up and under its rusty projection. "I hope I don't have to get out in a hurry," she thought, "and thank goodness there's a table here." As she scrambled onto the rough potting table, the warm sour smell of the disused hothouse hit her, but she hardly noticed. She ran to the inside door and took hold of the brass knob, afraid to be seen from the street. She clicked it around, her heart hammering. Then she was in.

A dark paneled hall stretched before her, with a closed door on either side halfway down and worn red carpeting underfoot. The room on the left was like a museum, dark and as smelly as a science lab. It was filled with glass-topped tables and things in jars. There were no chairs. Sibby backed out quickly, wondering what kind of weird people could want a place like that in their house. The room on the other side of the corridor was better, a game room, but not very cheerful. Sibby looked curiously at the massive oak pool table that stood in the center of the room, and wondered at the hollowed-out elephant's leg that held six pool cues and an umbrella. There was a faded rose velvet sofa by the fireplace, and in front of it, on a folding wooden table, a big pack of cards was spread out. They had vividly colored pictures on them, captioned in strange round writing that Sibby couldn't read. The top picture was of an old man holding a lamp, and underneath she could see part of a broken tower standing empty on a hill, and under that a dragon pierced by a spear. The cards were dusty, and Sibby, remembering fingerprints, didn't touch them. But a moment later fingerprints were forgotten as she curiously pushed the mother-of-pearl button set into the wall. There was an irritable reverberation deep in the house and Sibby jumped. None of the maid's buttons worked in her house. She hurried into the hall, closing the door noiselessly behind her.

At the end of the corridor the carpet stopped abruptly, because the high-ceilinged front hall had an inlaid floor of black-and-white marble. "Just like a checker-board," thought Sibby, and jumped two spaces. "And what fantastic windows! I wish we had some in our house!" She craned her head to look up the dark curving stairs, which passed two ranks of brilliant stained-glass windows, the lower group yellow and the upper crimson. More stained glass framed the door to the front entryway, and a strong smell of furniture polish filled the hall. Sibby crossed the red and yellow patches of light and opened the door on the right, across from the deep dim archway that led into the cavernous living room.

This was the room with the tall windows she had seen from the outside, a library. It was a library with two—no, three—tiers of wrought-iron balconies passing around its three stories of bookshelves. In front of the high windows at each level the balconies were joined by little iron bridges. There was a smell of mildewed leather and old paper, and books were absolutely everywhere. Sibby looked at the tall windows guiltily. It was getting late. She really shouldn't stay. But she had never been able to resist books. She began to drift around the lower shelves, skimming the titles. She'd hate to miss anything exciting. A set of Dumas, a sequel to *Lorna Doone*—there could be anything with so many books. A short fat travel book caught her eye, wedged out of place in a set of reference books. She loved stories about adventures in strange countries. The book was bound in brown leather and had a ribbed spine. The title page read: TRAVELS TO TREDANA WITH AN ACCOUNT OF THE MYSTERIOUS CITY OF TRE-CLERE, *being the Report of hitherto Unrelated Adventures in a* REMOTE LAND, *by V. Sigerson, noted Traveler and Lecturer.* THE HAGUE, *1892.*

None of the names were familiar to her; she wasn't even sure where The Hague was, although she knew she ought to know. The frontispiece, a map, was even more baffling. It showed a completely unfamiliar continent or island, which according to the legend must be half the size of North America. Only two cities were shown, Tredana and Treclere. Sibby knew there was no place on earth a continent that size could be hidden unknown to her: after all, she was in fifth grade. "The big lake is a little like Lake Superior," she decided. "but even if there were five lakes instead of two, the shape would still be all wrong." With a sigh she replaced the book where she could easily find it again. It was getting dark, and she would have to hurry. "At least I can look up Sigerson and Tredana in the encyclopedia," she thought as she hurried out. They didn't have very many books at home unless you counted her father's law-books, but there was a new encyclopedia bound in white leather in the living room.

For no good reason she stepped only on the black squares as she went back across the hall. She stepped also across the yellow rectangle of light that still lay in her path. Then she paused, startled. "Sunlight?" She looked to see it pouring down the stairs, lying in a shaft on the polished treads and glinting on the dark brass carpet rods. All around her it was nearly dark, yet sunlight blazed in through the window on the landing.

Her heart in her mouth, Sibby ran up the first few steps and knelt on the window seat. The yellow and white window had been open recently, for an ivy tendril had been caught in its closing. On it, unconcerned, was an inchworm making a careful meal. "Excuse me, worm," she said, and opened the clasp. The window sprang out through the rustling leaves and Sibby gasped with pleasure. Here was no yard with trees, no sidewalk, no familiar street, but an incredible tumble of jagged rocks, bright in the afternoon sun with a fresh breeze blowing. She did not stop to consider but jumped out quickly through the ivy tangle onto the stones, which sloped away in all directions. She could smell the sea, and when she turned there was no window in the bushes behind her. Her heart pounded, first with fear and then with a strange delight. She laughed and spread her arms to the wind, sucking it in through her mouth. She felt, for some strange reason, as though she had at last come home.

An extract from Vasili Sigerson
TRAVELS TO TREDANA WITH AN ACCOUNT OF THE
MYSTERIOUS CITY OF TRECLERE

PROLOGUE

A close friend of mine has often remarked on the simplicity of apparently complex problems, once they have been examined through the lens of logic and deductive reasoning. Sadly, the case of the nonintellectual or mystic matter does not admit of so easy a solution, and on close examination may prove increasingly knotty and difficult to undo. Such a case is that of my observation of Tredana.

Although Tredana is not of our world, I entered and left easily for the good reason I was never there in reality. In spirit only, under the guidance of the Dalai Lama, as outlined briefly in the foregoing chapter, I visited that strange city and observed the people there. Although unaware of my presence, they know of our world, I found, for them the Other-world; and travellers have been known to them before. Indeed, once a group of mystics left there for our world and never returned; when in our own history this may have occurred, or at what geographic point the entrance was made, I cannot say. Still, it is of interest to observe that the door, or bridge, is not exclusive of direction.

The next most interesting fact for me was the parallel I saw there between our own culture and their independent one. For example, the hereditary principle of kingship is like that of the ancient princes of Kiev, existing not within one line but within the entire royal generation, passing from father to nephew, or cousin to cousin, as the case may be, entirely determined by primogeniture. Strange to say, this system includes the female children as well, and queens are as common as kings, the percentages of birth being roughly equivalent. One might assume much chaos to be the result, but apparently this is not so in their world.

THE DRAGON

XII

Chapter One

By the time Sibby had scrambled down through the rocks and reached the beach, she was sore and scratched, and her dress had ripped in two places. She was sweating freely despite the cool breeze, and the library dust on her hands had ended up all over her face. She ran across the clean sands, past the high-tide mark, and plunged her hands into the lapping water. It was icy cold and choppy with whitecaps. The brown sands, littered with shells and dried seaweed, were as familiar and reassuring as a Cape Cod beach; but the emptiness was not familiar. Always in her own world even the emptiest day had at least the faraway drone of an airplane overhead; here there was nothing but rocks and sea and sand. The air smelled good, and it was a pleasure to take off her oxfords and walk along the dampy firm edge of the beach, scummy with foam.

Sibby had always been a good walker, and enjoyed it, although her mother often accused her of dawdling. Not that her mother liked to walk. Even when they were together, shopping in town for example, her mother never wanted to walk. She would run for a cab and say, "Sibby, for God's sake can't you hurry up? He won't wait all day!" Sibby stepped along now quicker, setting her own comfortable fast pace. The only other time she had really been on her own was when she had flown to London last summer, to visit her married sister. "Now I'm really an unaccompanied child," she thought, and giggled.

For the first few hours, Sibby's feeling of freedom and pleasure held. But then the sun began dropping down toward the horizon, it was getting colder, and she didn't have so much as a candy bar in her pocket. She was beginning to feel the first vague shadow of apprehension, when she saw an uneven place in the damp sand ahead: the print of a small horse or pony. "And these other marks could have been made by a person," she said, speaking out loud for company. "They

must be pretty recent, or the water would've covered them."
She sat down and put on her shoes, brushing off most of the
sand with the edge of her sweater. Then she hurried along in
the direction of the tracks. There was a stitch in her side and it
was almost dark before she saw, far ahead, a gleam of fire
among the rocks.

For a moment the breeze shifted and Sibby could smell
food cooking. Her stomach twisted in knots. Never before
had she been so tired and so hungry. It was not until she was
quite close that the obvious problem occurred to her. What
would she say to whomever she met? She had slowed to a hes-
itant walk when the tall figure of a man appeared from behind a rock, almost making her jump. He was middle-aged
and bearded, dark-skinned with black hair, and he wore a
sheepskin tunic over a woolen shirt and kilt. With his leather
boots strapped crisscross to his legs, he looked like an illustra-
tion in one of Sibby's old picture books, but he was real and
he spoke in an unfamiliar accent. Or maybe the language
wasn't English. But she understood it.

"Name your name, outlander, and show me weaponless
hands."

Sibby raised her hands above her head, like a cowboy. She
swallowed and said in a small voice, "Sibby Barron. I'm—
I'm unarmed."

"Well, child, if child you be in truth, state whence you are
come and to what purpose travel here."

"The trouble is, I don't know. I didn't mean to come—it
just happened." Sibby suddenly felt on the verge of tears, and
it made her angry and incoherent. After all, this was her adventure. She could feel her voice rising in pitch, and she knew
that if she spoke again she would sound like a baby, so she
stopped talking and clenched her teeth. A second figure came
from out of the gloom as she stood there, a young man holding a torch. He was wearing a long dark cape pinned in front
with a round silver brooch, and a triangular canvas bag was
strapped over one shoulder. In the torchlight Sibby could
make out dark curly hair and friendly eyes.

"So, Gannoc, you have found one of Dansen's long-
sought seafolk. But what a shabby water sprite." (The torch
moved closer.) "And what a young one. Even the underwater
people cannot mean to let their children wander unattended!
Tell me, child, whence are you come?"

Sibby threw up her chin. "I just said I don't know how I got here, and I'm not a child, I'm almost twelve [this was not quite true], and my parents do so let me go out unattended. I'm even old enough to fly by myself!" Sibby was thinking of her trip to London, but her words had an unexpected effect on the two men. Gannoc looked at the younger one with a question in his eyes, then gently turned her about with one hand on her shoulder.

"And yet I see no wings," her murmured softly. "Can Dansen's marvel tales be true after all? Or is this some outlandish plot to trick our confidence?"

"Child," said the other gently, "if you can fly alone, why tarry here? Why not rejoin your kindred who must even now be grieved for your sake?"

Sibby looked from him to the man called Gannoc, hearing them make fun of her but seeing only concern and wonder in their faces. She wanted to say that her kindred probably didn't know she was missing, but the strangeness of the afternoon and their questions was too much for her. To her great surprise, she fell into tears, and sobbing tried to run away. Strong hands took her by the shoulders and swung her up into the air. Gannoc, preceded by the young man with the torch, carried her unresisting toward the fire.

In the camp a tall handsome woman rose from the fireside and took Sibby in arms as strong as Gannoc's. Sibby stifled her embarrassed sobs against the woman's breast, and as soon as she was quiet the woman had her sit beside her, pulling a heavy cloak up warmly around her. She offered her a bowl of soup and smiled. "Here," she said, "eat this. I am Mara, the wife of Gannoc, and I never poison children." Her teeth gleamed in her dark face, and Sibby, noticing her gold earring, wondered if she were perhaps a gypsy.

"Thank you," she said. "I'm sorry I was so silly. I'm really not afraid of you."

Mara smiled again. "Good," she said, and turned to her husband. "And it will be well for you, Gannoc, if you do not try to frighten her out of her wits tonight! She's just a child. Time enough for questions in the morning." As Mara matter-of-factly arranged a bed for Sibby, talking of commonplaces such as the weather, Sibby suddenly relaxed and began to feel sleepy. She must have traveled miles. More, if you counted the whole way from Newton to here. Wherever "here" was.

She'd find out in the morning.

With the sun's rising, she woke to find breakfast almost ready, and some ponies she had not noticed in the dark already saddled for travel. She was alone, for Mara and a strange man were over by the fire, cooking. Still drowsy, she stretched and changed her position, listening to them talk. "He thinks she may be a sign," said Mara, and the other nodded. "After all, how could an ordinary child appear in the middle of this vast wilderness? We have traveled more than a month and seen nothing but seabirds and coneys."

"How indeed?" murmured the other, tasting from his wooden spoon and then stirring more vigorously. "But I doubt she is one of the winged company, in that she lacks the vital essentials. Nor does she have gills as Erlandus describes the water folk possessing. But see, she awakens. Come, eat, my dear, for we must be on our way and you will need strength. Even gods must eat, is a saying in our city."

Sibby found herself looking up into a kindly face, framed between a tightly fitted skullcap, embossed in gold, and carefully trimmed whiskers. Unlike Gannoc and the others, he was dressed in a discreet brown velvet gown, with embroidery on the sleeves and collar. His soft hair fluffed out from under his cap and there were ink stains on his fingers.

"I, my dear, am Dansen, a man of learning with I hope no ignorant prejudice against outlanders. You, I believe, are called Sibbybarron?"

"Sibby is enough."

"Honored," he replied, and nodded courteously. There was an open writing case strapped to his belt, fitted with little bottles and with quills.

Since no one was paying attention to her, Sibby got up and ran down to the beach. She plunged her hands into the foaming cold and dashed it on her face. She tried to untangle her short black curls and, giving it up as hopeless, returned to the fire. Gannoc and the young man were there, beginning to eat. The triangular case he had worn the night before was open on the beach beside him. Sibby could see the top of a small harp protruding from it, made of dark wood and inset with silver wires. Completing the group was an old man so huddled in his cloak that Sibby almost took him for a pile of clothing. When Sibby looked at him, he turned and smiled, his face wrinkling around his one good eye, which blazed a startling blue and made the sunken pouch where the other had been more noticeable.

"One Eye will talk with you later on," said Mara, as she handed Sibby a piece of bread and a steaming cup. Sibby choked on the unfamiliar mulled wine, but it warmed her immediately. "By afternoon the sun will have aroused him."

"I've questions that cannot wait so long," said Gannoc. "By your leave, sir"—this to the young man—"I must ask the child some questions. She's slept well and fed twice and I see no reason to delay further. I feel you mean no harm, child, but as leader I must know. Who are you, and whence are you come?"

Sibby no longer felt shy. "My name's Sibby Barron, as I told you last night, and I'm really only just eleven, not almost twelve. And I guess I must come from another world or something. I live in West Newton, on Lenox Street. That's in Massachusetts, in America." They all looked at her uncomprehendingly, so she hurried on. "I was in this empty house, and I went through the window and found myself on the beach, miles back, instead of in the yard outside the house. At first I was glad because I've always wanted an adventure, but then I got worried about being all alone out here. When I saw your tracks, I followed and you know the rest. You're the first people I've seen. What's the name of this country?"

The young man, ignoring a motion from Gannoc to keep still, spoke with authority. "You are on the northeast coast of the lands claimed by the sovereign city of Tredana, claimed but not taken since they are yet barren and without value. We are travelers from that great city, come on a journey to the ruinous north on a private matter."

"Tredana?" cried Sibby. "But that was in a book in the house I told you about. Tredana and . . . and Treclere?"

"Treclere?" asked Gannoc, suddenly suspicious. "And what know you of Treclere?"

"Only that it was on the map with Tredana. I was puzzled because I'd never heard of either place, and yet the country looked so big. I thought one of the lakes looked familiar but that was all."

Now it was Dansen's turn to interrupt. His eyes gleaming, he asked in a trembling voice, "Did you say a map? A map of this country? You held such a map in your hands?"

"Yes," said Sibby, "I told you." She added curiously,

"Don't you have one? You live here!"

"Dear child, had I such a map I would feel my life's work complete. Truly you are of good omen for us, and will be of inestimable help to us in our travels."

"You accept her story, then?" asked Gannoc. "This tale of other worlds is a strange one. Easier to believe in water folk."

"I disagree," said Dansen. "The ancients tell us, if I read them aright, that such things may happen. What of that Prince of Vahn, who, descending a well, found himself in another country where hid the giant whom he sought? And the famous story of Arleon's wanderings, after the fall of Treglad? He traveled to stranger lands than Vahn. Then, too, there are doors that open for the Zenedrim in Tremyrag, bringing him guests from other worlds, or so we all have heard. To say nothing of the evil arts of the Deathless Queen."

"But," said the young man, "here is no Prince of Vahn, no Zenedrim, and, thank Vazdz, no Deathless Queen. Unless this is some trick of Simirimia's to lull us with so innocent-seeming a stranger."

"A foolish trick, then, to make so mysterious an appearance. Perhaps One Eye may enlighten us later. For the moment, since we can hardly leave a child alone in the wilderness, I say welcome her and gladly. As Milecta says in his *Maxims,* 'The Unexpected Teaches Best.' " And Dansen smiled kindly on Sibby, who was beginning to feel awkward.

She smiled back and said, "I'd love to come with you. But where are you going?"

The young man suddenly relaxed and smiled, which made him look much nicer. "If we are to travel together, you should know something of us. Gannoc and Mara you know a little already. Dansen is a scholar who hopes to record our journey, that future generations may profit by our discoveries. In days to come, One Eye will be our guide, since in his youth he was a famous traveler. When Prince Armon of Tredana fell in battle against Simirimia of Treclere, it was One Eye only who escaped alone to tell us of the tragedy, an army of two thousand Horse and Foot, utterly slain. He is familiar with the wastes that lie before us; he has crossed the sands and become blood brother to a great chief of the desert people, the Karabdu; he has journeyed westward as far as Vahn and northward even to Tremyrag."

There was a pause, and Sibby asked shyly, "Are you an explorer then? Or are you looking for something, like a—a quest?"

The young man nodded gravely. "Yes, child, this is something like a quest, although I am only a singer, a maker of songs and stories, and no great explorer." He smiled at Gannoc who had raised a warning eyebrow. "Many years ago, when I was a child, One Eye spoke the prophecy that has brought us here. Later his words were confirmed for me by one who can see the future, a great leader of the Players. She saw in her cards what One Eye had seen in his dreams, and the words she spoke were so compelling I felt I could avoid my fate no longer. So now that I am twenty-one I have set out to find my future." He paused again, then smiled at Sibby's expectant face. "The words will not mean much to you, perhaps.

> Riskless remain at home, and you will see
> An idle life, inglorious destiny.
> Boldly go forth, and your own pain will prove
> The righting of great wrong, the risk
> of everything you have.

Gannoc believes this is a silly challenge, but he and my other friends have kindly agreed to accompany me, for the sake of an adventure and, of course, in hopes of rescuing the unhappy prisoner of Glass Island, which would be a great wrong righted indeed if we can but accomplish it."

"Who is the prisoner?" asked Sibby, interested.

"Dastra, the daughter of the Deathless Queen, that is, Simirimia of Treclere. They say Simirimia was told in a dream that her daughter would bring her death, and for this reason has had her shut up in a tower, built on an island of glass, dark as night and slippery as ice. It is further said the whole island is so ringed with spells and mighty demons and terrible dragons that none may approach. This I mean to test, if it is granted we find the place."

"If," said One Eye, and Sibby jumped, because she had thought him asleep.

His eye was still closed, and since no more speech was apparently forthcoming, Sibby spoke up again. "Please, you say you are a singer. Do you have a name, also?"

He smiled. "Yes, I am called Leron."

Gannoc broke in brusquely, with a sudden smile. "I suggest we have had enough of confidences for the nonce, and that we be on our way before the sun has quite passed its zenith."

Leron smiled at Mara. "See that the child has a warm tunic and cloak from our stores. I will go and bring in the goats."

As Mara pulled the warm sheepskin over Sibby's head (it came to her knees), Sibby saw Leron returning from some small pasturage higher in the rocks, driving before him two black goats and two spotted kids. They seemed strange company for such an adventurous journey, but Sibby reflected they were probably for milk. She was glad to see that the pony saddles were deep and made of wood with thick leather quilting. It would be hard to fall from them. Instead of a bridle and bit, each pony had a leather thong wound about its nose and a long rein passed back over its left shoulder. Sibby watched Mara, and, like her, wound the rein around her left hand, which she then let rest on her knee. Leron finished tying the goats to the last of the three pack ponies, and then they started off.

THE PRISONER PRINCESS: A SONG
by Leron, son of Mathon Breadgiver, Prince of the house of Tredana and Governor of Villavac. (In the sixteenth year of his age)

I wake to the chill rain falling
and hear my lady weep;
Her hair is silver as moonlight
Her cries disturb my sleep.

Alone on her glassy island,
She thinks her cries unheard;
But her grief has flown into my heart
and nestles like a bird.

O Dastra, I am coming
to rend your chains apart;
and you shall freely wander through
the gardens of my heart.

Chapter Two

They soon settled into an easy pace, and Sibby almost drowsed as she trotted steadily across the first of several long gravelly stretches. From time to time Dansen would stop and look at the sun through a small brass instrument that he called a ddimry and make a few hurried notations. Then he would push his pony to a brief canter and rejoin the others.

The following days fell into a pattern, and after a few days Sibby found herself less stiff in the evening, and soon her body moved easily to the pony's motions. Evenings were best. The seaweed fire would die down and crackle softly. Then Leron would take out his harp and polish the wood with a piece of soft leather. The thirteen strings were carefully tuned, and he would sing. He had a nice voice, deeper than you would expect. In this way Sibby learned about the glories of Tredana and of its great heroes; of the fierce desert tribesmen, the Karabdu; and always, like a cloud on the horizon, vague murmurs of the evils of Treclere. She heard how Prince Armon had been forced into fatal battle by Simirimia, and how his body had never been returned for burial, a thing contrary to all usage and custom. And she often heard of Dastra, the silver prisoner of Glass Island, for on this subject Leron's talent was inexhaustibly fertile. He pictured her pining the long melancholy years of her confinement in a variety of arresting and moving songs.

The more Sibby heard, the more she understood that people in this world took their dreams seriously. If you talked about them at breakfast, no one would tell you to shut up and eat. It wasn't just One Eye's prophecy and the fortune-teller's cards that had made Leron set out on this journey. The final straw had been a dream he had had himself, on the eve of his twenty-first birthday. It had been told to him then that, if he cared to risk it, the daughter of the Deathless Queen could be found on a journey north, and a great enchantment broken thereby. And even though his friends had thought he was being foolish, it was only the danger they minded. No one thought the reasoning was bad. They all believed in dreams.

For her part, Sibby tried to tell the others about her own life, such as it was. She could describe important things, like cars and TV, but she didn't know how they worked so she couldn't really explain them. To them her stories sounded like Dansen's wonder tales, and were greeted with the same polite interest. Dansen she disappointed. She had looked at the map too briefly to be able to describe it to him. The size she did remember, though, and he was amazed to find his country so extensive. "I shall have to revise my thinking, child," he said, absently patting her hand, and he made a few more notes in his journal.

During her second week of travel, Sibby plucked up her courage and asked Leron about his harp. It was a special one and had a name, Telyon. She had been dying to touch it and was delighted when Leron explained the instrument to her, showing her how to play a simple tune. Every evening afterward she practiced, and the others smiled and said she showed remarkable talent.

In this way the weeks passed, and the days began noticeably to shrink. Nights were very black and clear, and sometimes in the morning there was frost upon the ground. Sibby's shoes, considered sturdy in her own world, began to fall apart, and Gannoc made her high leather moccasins similar to those the others wore. Each day the wind from the sea blew more bitter, and in the distance, away to the west, mountains came into prominence, jagged and dark blue against the sky, with white peaks shining.

All the while Sibby continued observing her new friends closely, saying little, but watching and listening. She had long ago learned in her own family not to bother people with questions. It only made them mad at you. But the little fragments of talk began to fit together in her head, and without having to ask she learned that they were looking for a wasteland, the ruins of an old city, where someone was supposed to meet them, a guide. Sibby was especially eager not to bother the others because she had realized that the obvious thing for them to do, once they reached a settled area, would be to leave her behind. And she didn't want to be left. She wanted to see Leron find his destiny. It sounded exciting. So she listened and hoped and tried to be helpful and there matters stood. Until they met the dog.

He was a large, dark brown dog, in feature something like a bear, and he appeared one morning without warning. One Eye suddenly seemed to come awake, and held out his hand. "Welcome, Calab. We had hoped to be in time." Calab looked slowly around the group, staring into their eyes in turn, then walked to One Eye and briefly touched his muzzle against the outstretched hand. One Eye turned to the others. "This is the guide of whom I spoke, back in Tredana. Calab can lead us to the Lady of the Rock, Rianna of Treglad. In his company our way is assured and our going safe. Ever he has conducted me through rock and ruin safe to the Lady; and if he chooses, so shall he now conduct us all." Calab cocked his head slightly after the fashion of ordinary dogs while One Eye spoke, then slowly walked around the group, testing the air by each. By Sibby he paused and snuffed deeply; then, wagging his tail he thrust his head against her for a moment before turning away. Just outside the group he sat down, with his back to them, and waited. "It is a good sign," said One Eye. "He will lead us. We must all make ready to follow."

Quickly they gathered their goods together, covering the fire with dirt. As soon as they had mounted, Calab, without looking back, began to trot in a northerly direction. They followed him single file. Dansen as usual was taking note, and he muttered furiously as he tried to write while jiggling awkwardly in the saddle. Leron looked back over his shoulder at Sibby. "It seems Calab was pleased to see you. Your coming to us may well have had some purpose, shortly to be explained."

"One Eye said he told you before about Calab. Were you really expecting a dog to meet us?"

"We were, but with all respect to One Eye, some of us had private doubts. We thought it best to wait and see if his words proved true. Now if all continues to go aright, we should shortly come into the presence of the Lady of the Rock. Since Calab has welcomed you, it is clear you are also expected. Her wisdom is great, and it is not for me to describe her. Soon you will see for yourself." Sibby nodded silently.

Around them the air brightened and seemed to thin as the morning grew older. Calab's course turned slowly inland, and by eleven o'clock the sea was left behind and they were in a vast plain. The ground was broken and uneven, with clumps of stone and small eruptions of strange foamy-looking rock, which Sibby could recognize as volcanic. It crumbled and crunched underfoot. Sibby thought she could see the suggestion of buildings and towers in some of the more intricate formations; she looked back to speak with Dansen. "Dansen, what is this place? Why do the rocks look so strange? Some of them even look like buildings." Dansen looked up from his notes blankly, then smiled at her in sudden recognition and stuffed the papers into the breast of his gown.

"It is written by the ancients that here once stood the greatest city of all, Treglad," he said in his usual careful manner. "Her like shall never be seen again by the race of men now living. Brydeni writes, I think with good authority, that here the first tribes of wandering hunters came to rest and to build and to prosper. Treglad came to be a strong city and, outgrowing the need for walls, spread out peacefully among her gardens and canals, fearing no attack. But some great corruption began to fester in the souls of her people, until finally Vazdz caused the earth to vomit, and all good and all evil together were buried in streams of boiling rock and smoking ash. Travelers from Treglad (for they were a learned people and much given to exploration) returned to find their city vanished, and in its place steaming rubble. Their songs of lamentation have come down to us, but are deemed too sad for singing. Many died of grief; others joined together and made their way to the outpost villages, Tredana and Treclere, and these they builded up after their several fashions. That was more than thirty generations ago."

"So it isn't just imagination . . . those really were buildings. Did everyone really leave? Nobody tried to rebuild the homes?"

"I have heard rumors of a small people living furtively here among the ruins. One Eye in his travels saw nothing, but in my grandfather's time several accounts were written of them. Skotla suggests that certain children might have escaped the destruction of their homes and grown up to a savage existence in the wild. But there is also the possibility that the occasional traveler here, distraught, with his mind full of old tales and legends, has seen what was not there in the moving light of his campfire."

Sibby glanced around her with a new awareness. By now

the sun was almost directly overhead and the shadows had all been gathered close in by the base of each fantastic ruinous mound. Her thoughts full of Treglad as it must have been and of the dwindled race now said to inhabit its ruins, she knew her eyes were seeing more than was there. She was glad when Calab silently stopped and they dismounted to rest the ponies and to eat.

As before, Calab sat with his back to the group, facing northwest and communicating nothing. Gannoc and Leron milked the goats while Dansen helped Mara prepare the maize for chowder. One Eye drowsed in the sun, wrapped warmly against the wind; and, unnoticed, Sibby wandered off to investigate a long ribbed stone formation. It was, she discovered, a row of empty houses, joined and roofless and curiously melted together. She stepped through the first distorted doorway and stood a moment inside, breathing heavily. Her mind was racing with strange images, and she suddenly recalled the house in West Newton where all her adventures had started. The feeling she had had in that dim mansion somehow was the same she had here in this little roofless room with dark ash swirling around her feet. She shook her head to clear it and moved on.

Lunch was ready when she returned. "Did you find anything of interest over there?" asked Mara.

"I don't know. Those rocks are really a row of old houses, or rooms, anyway."

"Well," said Mara, practically, "best not to search too deeply here."

"Yes," added Leron, "after all, we are guests here, having no business except with the Lady, to pay our respects and ask her advice. And besides, should you in your exploring find another unlooked-for passageway and leave as suddenly as you came, we should all miss your company."

He smiled at her very kindly, and Sibby dropped her eyes for a moment, pleased and confused. In some ways her new friends were more of a family than she had ever known, but she had no words to tell them this. "I think if I found a window now, I might not jump out in such a hurry," she said finally, and smiled back at Leron. As they were packing up to continue on their way, Sibby impulsively squeezed Mara hard around the waist, as she would have liked to have done with her own mother, and Mara smiled and hugged her in return.

They continued through the afternoon as they had all morning, jogging single file amid the crumbling crusty earth, Calab trotting tirelessly ahead. Dust rose in dark red puffs around their horses' feet, and after an hour or so the air was so thick they each had wrapped kerchiefs around their noses and mouths. Leron coughed and shouted hoarsely ahead to Gannoc. "Poor country for an ambush, I think."

"Indeed, sir," Gannoc called back, "I had been thinking what a pretty target we must make."

"I wager no enemy could approach without becoming as good a one."

Gannoc's reply to this was never made, for as Leron's words died away the shadows at the foot of a mass of twisted stone rose up and silently stood by Calab in a semicircle. They were small men, shorter than Sibby and even darker than the Tredanans, their strong bodies streaked with red, black, and white clay, and bits of feathers and stones hung round their necks. The surprise was complete, but no hostility was intended, for the men had left their short spears stacked by the rock. Calab was greeting them with grave friendliness. One Eye had roused himself when they stopped, and now he rode forward, pulling his kerchief down below his chin with slightly shaking fingers. One of the small men stepped forward and touched his throat with his left hand; then, reaching up gently, touched One Eye's neck with the same fingers. One Eye made the same gesture, and they both smiled and said a few words softly in a strange language. Sibby was torn between interest in them and a longing to watch the changing expression on Dansen's face, whose amazement was comic.

The old man turned toward the group. "Meddock greets us in peace from the Lady, and says we have come in good time. He and his kinsmen will free Calab for his other duties and personally lead us to the chamber." He spoke clearly but heavily, and Sibby began to realize that he had conserved his strength for this moment. As One Eye fell silent, Leron rode forward and, dismounting, touched his throat as he had seen them do, stretching out his hand. One Eye nodded approvingly, and Meddock greeted the young man as he had his old friend. The other warriors took up their spears and surrounded the travelers like a guard. At this, Calab stood up and shook himself, casting one last glance over the group. He turned and ran away to the west with surprising speed, and was soon small in the distance.

Sibby turned to Dansen, who was nearest. "Do you know why he's left us? I thought he was our special guide."

One Eye answered without looking at her. "Calab is guide to many, willing and unwilling. Many wait impatiently to begin their journeys, because he has delayed for us. Others breathe more easily for the seeming respite. You here are among the very few who will follow Calab twice, both now and again at the end of all our futures. Would he might stop for me in earnest."

The back of Sibby's neck pricked as she looked after the disappearing figure of Calab, but too much was happening for her to wonder long. With six of the wild men on either side and Meddock as their leader, they were all heading at a rapid jog toward a low hillock of rubble that looked like the base of a fallen tower. Two walls spread out and crumbled into the sand on either side of it like ragged wings, and Sibby did not like the way its door gaped dark and open like a mouth. But Sibby was not in the lead, and when Meddock entered that open mouth she had to follow with the rest.

It was larger inside the arch than she had expected; dimly before her she could see the ruins of a circular stair that led up to a broken piece of roof and down she could not see where. Meddock signaled that they were to dismount here and go on alone; in a solemn silence the ponies were tethered and the small warriors squatted around them on their haunches to wait and to watch. Sibby had somehow expected that One Eye would go first, or Gannoc, but it was Leron who took the lead. He stood at the head of the stairs, looking down, and waited until the rest had gathered; then he stepped down into the dark.

The warm close air enveloped them as they descended. Sibby, between Gannoc and Mara, did not like to breathe its alien smell too deeply, as she carefully felt out the worn crumbling steps in utter blackness. Ahead she could hear Dansen muttering as he helped One Eye to keep his balance. The stairs were too narrow for two to walk abreast, so Dansen was a step ahead with One Eye's hand on his shoulder. For many minutes it seemed they continued thus, until she stepped down hard onto level ground. They were at the end of a narrow corridor, apparently, at the further end of which showed the faintest of lights. Sibby almost gasped at what she took to be a soft touch on her ankle, before she recognized the sensation as a soft puff of dust. It lay several inches thick on the floor of the passage and completely muffled the sound of their footsteps.

The light at the end of the passageway was diffused in a small chamber shaped like a beehive, empty except for an oblong of marble like a tomb, before which stood a brass lamp on a three-legged stand. All light came from the lamp, a tall blue flame. Leron went down on one knee and the others did likewise, so Sibby joined them awkwardly. As they knelt, a quiet voice spoke in their minds, remote as starlight.

"You are welcome in my house. I know what each would ask, and I will answer for the love borne me by one of you." As Sibby watched, a flickering image formed behind the flame, the insubstantial sketch of a woman, restlessly fluctuating in shape as oil moves on water. Her bare white arms gleamed against the vague stuff of her gown, and the long dark curling hair merged with the shadows.

"Gannoc," she said, "you need not fear this journey to be folly, for a good end will be won though it will be long in the winning. Your prudence and that of Mara is an estimable quality, but in one thing you may forget your caution. Within your present company, the prince may reveal himself and fear no evil for it." Gannoc and Mara had knelt hand in hand; as the Lady finished speaking to them they raised their eyes to her shifting image.

As she looked from them to Dansen, she suddenly glowed with color and her figure seemed perceptibly to solidify. She smiled on him, and her now distinct face was calm and lovely. "It seems your thoughts are full of my city," she said. "You are one of my chief rememberers. In this undertaking you have set your feet on a path of learning, and that wisdom which is your first delight awaits you in the end. Never fear to change your opinions. Truth lies not in books but in your heart. And remember always to share, for hoarded knowledge is abominable, being of no use. And forget not the city of Treglad." Like a changing expression, her features dimmed and wavered for a moment. "Now depart, you three, in peace with my blessing, for I have to speak further that which is not for your ears."

In silence they rose to their feet and left, not even pausing to brush off the soft clinging dust. As they went, the Lady's image flared up and shrank like a guttering candle, spreading out wide and then uneasily contracting. "Rise, Prince," she said, and it was clear she spoke to Leron. "Here is no need for you to kneel." Leron rose unwillingly, his head still slightly bowed in respect. "Power I have yet, but no control of anything, and as my city is forgot, so too I fade and dwindle."

Leron answered, "My respect is not for power alone nor should it be, for then I might worship who knows what; my respect is simply for the Lady of the Rock, worthy of all honor in any case."

"The answer honors the speaker as well. I have three things to tell you. First, that you will find a guide when you return to the world above. He will lead you far, to Glass Island and beyond, and farther still, even to your choice and destiny. Second, I will warn you that this enterprise will unleash a serpent more terrible than any beast of flesh and blood yet seen by you, and you will be happier when that beast is no more. Third, and most important, there will be three times when to this child's speaking you would do well to listen. Even the greatest of princes should not think it shame to be instructed by a child." At this, Sibby raised her eyes, startled, and found the Lady looking at her. A white hand, momentarily bright against the shadows, was stretched toward her.

"My child, you little know how great was the need for your coming. By the very name you bear, so shall you speak the truth when it is most needed, and also by your name shall hidden matters be brought to light. Sibyl you are and Sib shall be, and I promise you much enlightenment, enlightenment and attainment, but I cannot promise any happiness. Here is my seal on that." She stooped over Sibby and the white hand was pressed lightly to her throat. "Be brave and trust in the truth as you see it." Sibby almost cried aloud as the air in her lungs seemed to burst into flame, the heat radiating outward through all her veins. A great content followed, however, and she almost drowsed as the Lady turned to One Eye.

All this time he had knelt with his head bowed and his face hidden in his hands, the white hair hanging almost to the ground. Now he raised his face and his one bright eye seemed to reflect the blue flame of the lamp; a terrible grief and joy was in his face. Lovingly the Lady spoke, and very softly. "O Arbytis, Arbytis, faithful even now. I had not thought to speak with you again." She held out both her hands to him, and Sibby in recollection flinched. But One Eye took them eagerly in his own, pressing them to his face and then his breast, while tears ran down both sides of his face. "For your sake I would have Calab lead you on your last journey, but for mine I am glad that he has not. Yet I see how heavy the years hang on you. You should not have come now that weariness can only breed further pain, yet offer no release."

Still holding her hands, he answered, "My Lady Rianna, should the peace of death be offered me tomorrow, I would not accept unless it was to your honor. True it is I came on this mission for the sake of Leron, whom I love, and for the ruining of Simirimia, whom we abhor; yet it is also true I would have come for no reason but my oath." His voice was trembling with passion as much as with age, and once more he bent his head over her hands.

"You have kept your word to me faithfully for thirty generations, Arbytis. Yet the price you have paid, and still pay, could make me wish it otherwise."

One Eye's response was lost in a sudden uprush of wind that sounded like beating wings and pulled the Lady's hands from his grasp. She cried aloud, her voice for a moment as living as a mortal woman's. "Ah, Arbytis, you stay too long. Once more Vazdz comes between us." The light dimmed, and her voice grew smaller. "Though I am forgot and dissolve into air, you I will always remember. May you find peace soon. Go now, all, with my blessing."

Somehow Sibby rose to her numbed feet, and silently she helped Leron raise the old man from his knees. He straightened without their assistance and stepped forward toward the lamp, which burned clearly in the chamber the goddess had deserted. He touched his fingers to the flame, and after touched his throat, murmuring strange words as the tears dried on his face. Then they silently turned and went out into the dark tunnel.

LAMENT FOR TREGLAD
traditional: translated from the original by Brydeni

The sky will not be blue again
The sun will not be warm again
Waters will not run sweet again
    Here was Treglad:
    Now nothing remains

Cold the northern wind forever
Dark the starless night forever
Hard the barren earth forever
    Here was Treglad:
    Now nothing remains

Treglad: in our thoughts waking
Treglad: in our hearts sleeping
Treglad: on our lips dying
    Still Treglad:
    Though nothing remains

Chapter Three

As they stepped out into the upper world, the light made them blink and shake their heads. Leron said nothing to the others who were waiting, he only smiled at them and stood by One Eye to help him mount. By the time they were ready to ride out, One Eye had recovered himself and spoke. "Meddock has invited us to pass the night with his people, delaying our departure till tomorrow dawn. I urge you, my prince, to accept their offer."

Leron said, "Please thank him for me, and accept for us."

As they set out in constrained silence, Leron held his pony back, next to Sibby's, and spoke with her quietly. "You must forgive me, child, if I was not completely open with you before this. I think we have both heard much to surprise us."

"I understood why you didn't tell me everything. And anyway, I was beginning to guess you were—well, important, from the way the others treated you."

"The art of the mime is among the very few neglected in Tredana. Those wandering performers, the Players, act with such skill and charm we have become lazy and are notoriously poor at such pretenses. But the lie was not too great, as I also am a maker of songs."

"Of course I know that! But can you tell me anything more about the Lady? Or are you supposed not to talk about her?"

"Her acceptance of you has been complete, and I am sure she will not be angry with me for sharing the little that I know. When Treglad was a great city, the Double Goddess was worshiped with fire at many temples, and principally at Ornat, the great temple. The Double Goddess was two and one at the same time, and you will understand better if I say that the city was as the body, the goddess the spirit. Eventually the half that became Simirimia called on Vazdz and acknowledged him her master, but Rianna would not submit, although he caused her city to be destroyed and set Simirimia free to pursue her own destiny. So Rianna has lingered on in the ruins, her power growing fainter as her city disappears from the memories of mankind. Until today I had not realized that some few men, such as Meddock and his company, are yet alive to worship her. They are few in number and not much civilized, however. What moves and amazes me most is that which we both witnessed there at the end."

"Do you know why she called him Arbytis, and what she was talking about?"

"The story of Arbytis is one I know well, a song I dislike to sing because it is so sad. I cannot believe that this old teacher of mine can be he, and yet it must be so. It explains much. . . ."

"What is the story? I've never heard it."'

"Of course not . . . I was forgetting. It has been told for many years in Tredana how the High Priest of the Double Goddess refused to worship Vazdz when he came in power to destroy, but shielding the eternal flame with his body swore a great oath never to forsake his trust. And although the Goddess was split in two, and Ornat, which means 'closed circle,' was broken, he defied Vazdz to his face. They say he cried, 'Were I to live forever, yet would I perform my office and worship at the shrine of Ornat. Though thou wert ruler of all and she who remains as nothing, I would continue to serve her. I would turn my back on the sun and face the cold wind ever for her sake, nor rest long in any spot where there was peace but not her presence.' And they say Vazdz promised him that it would be as he had said. Never again would he rest in peace, nor could he look forward to death and a final rest. He would prove his oath by doing, and be fated to wander the ages, aged himself, until he renounced his words and accepted Vazdz as his lord. And this he has not done as yet, though near ten hundred years are come and gone . . . yet I cannot believe it . . . One Eye . . . Arbytis!"

"There's still something I don't really understand," said Sibby. "I mean about Vazdz. You and the others swear by him. How can you do this if he was the one who destroyed Treglad, and made the Lady fade away, and has tortured One Eye for so many years?"

"I see you do not understand. Vazdz is chief among gods. What may he not do if he wish it?"

"But it was wrong—it must have been. Dansen said there

was evil in Treglad, but I think his histories must be wrong. You've seen the Lady, and One Eye and Meddock. Why you just said yourself that it would be wrong to worship power alone, and that's what you're doing. Can't you see? And these are your friends who've been hurt."

"Child, child, all this took place thirty generations ago. It is not for us to question the gods, and even if it were, it would not be possible to roll back the years. It has happened and must be accepted, though we may regret it. Doubtless it is all for the best and part of some plan whose pattern we know not."

Sibby was so angry, tears started from her eyes. "How can you talk like that! You are like all grown-ups, and I thought you were different. Everything's always for the best, even when you know it's wrong!"

Leron drew back, hurt, then smiled down at her. "I am curious to see this world of yours sometime, where apparently men think nothing of arguing with the gods. It is not like that here, where we respect them. If you are wise, you will dwell no more on the matter."

Sibby shook her head, not trusting her voice, and turned away with smarting eyes. Leron started to speak again, thought better of it, and pushed his horse to a faster pace, moving into line ahead of her.

The sun had almost set when they arrived at Meddock's village. Their way led down into a cluster of ruins, where one whole section of the city still partially stood, a maze of narrow uneven alleyways and courtyards enclosed by broken, leaning walls. Before they had reached the center, the alley became a narrow path, and they had to dismount. Gannoc and Leron quickly tethered and fed the ponies and goats, leaving them in a large courtyard filled with various livestock. Here Sibby saw cattle and poultry, and other less familiar beasts, something like deer, but heavier.

In the central courtyard a woman met them, Mellas, the wife of Meddock. Like the other women they saw, she was dressed in skins, her long hair separated into twenty or thirty dark braids hanging about her shoulders. She wore a necklace of golden leaves enclosing berries made from carved gems, evidently a relic of the old city and sign of her position.

The news of their coming had preceded them, and the compound to which she silently led them had a fire already lighted, warm furs laid out, and water ready for washing. Two rooms opened on the little yard, and in each there was a pile of dried wild grass for bedding. Treasures scavenged from the ruins of Treglad were much in evidence: cracked ivory bowls with delicate carving set in twisted brass holders, small statues, and in the yard a weather-rounded marble bench. There were traces of once-bright murals on the inner walls of each room.

As soon as they were ready, Mellas led them back into the great central courtyard. On one side, two floors of a large fallen house remained intact, and from this building Meddock appeared, dressed in furs with fresh clay on his cheeks and forehead. As before, he singled One Eye out and had him sit between himself and his wife in a place of honor. The rest were ranged along the sides of a deep pit filled with glowing coals, and food was brought. The smell of roasting meat and burning fat filled the air.

While Meddock and One Eye exchanged a few words, Dansen listened intently, then hesitantly spoke. Meddock's eyes lit with surprise, he answered, and Dansen responded. He turned to the others with excitement. "Their speech! With some difficulty I can understand it! It seems a debased form of the Old Tregladan tongue, which has been preserved for us in fragments by the early chroniclers."

One Eye looked up under heavy brows, his eye bright and amused. "It is the Old Tregladan that they speak. Scholars have caught the meaning but not the sound; since they were content, I saw no need for correction." At this, Dansen immediately pulled some papers from the breast of his gown and opened the writing case that hung at his belt. Throughout the meal he continued taking notes and carefully framing small sentences, which were greeted politely despite the obvious amusement that his pronunciation created.

When the meat was done, it was forked from off the fire by two cooks and skillfully arranged on a large copper platter, then covered with hot brown wheels of bread the size of dinner plates. Following One Eye's lead, each took a piece of bread and filled it with slices of meat, the last so hot it burned their fingers. Sibby sucked her hand and found the taste greasy and delicious.

No one spoke while eating, but treated it as a serious business to be performed quickly and with dignity. But as soon as the food was gone and bowls of water had been passed for drinking, soft conversation started up.

Sibby began to feel sleepy. She snuggled into her fur robe and leaned her head on Mara's shoulder, her eyelids drooping and jerking awake again as she watched Meddock on the other side of the cooking pit. The fire had been allowed to flare up, and the bright flames danced over the different faces and cast black shadows behind them. A jumble of impressions floated through Sibby's mind . . . smoke smell . . . soft scratchy furs . . . cold night air . . . crackling fire . . . and, further back, Calab and the Lady of the Rock. Gradually the crowd fell silent, and Meddock began speaking; Dansen translated softly while he spoke, occasionally corrected by One Eye, whose head was nodding with weariness but not sleep. Mara put her arm around Sibby, and Dansen's whispered interpretation came vaguely to her as her mind drowsed and wandered.

They were telling stories, stories about the beginning of time and the first men to walk the world. Half asleep, Sibby heard about the Great Mother's three children, modeled of dust and baked and set upon new legs to discover the world. The first was almost unfinished, pale and raw, and he was sent to the desert to finish baking, the first of the Karabdu. The second was baked too long and sent to the northern ice fields where the cold would soothe his skin, and he was the first of the black Zanida. The third was an even brown in color, and his race built Treglad. They talked on and on, describing the days before death came and the sorrows that came after, the pains that they endured when the Great Mother went away and the Great Father ruled instead. They learned to conquer and kill for the Great Father, and Treglad prospered. Here the story paused, and Sibby was almost asleep when a new voice took up the tale, and she realized that it was One Eye.

He told how the people of Treglad looked into their hearts and saw the need for something more than glory. They cleaned the great temple of Ornat with sand and water and lit a lamp of pure oil upon the altar. And they called, each night for seven years, for the Great Mother to return, setting free all their slaves and prisoners with promises not to conquer or to enslave or to kill again. And after seven years the Double Goddess came to them, she who was two yet one. She told

them that her mother was gone forever, but she would care
for the city as long as they believed in her. Under her protection Treglad flourished for forty generations, and in peace.
There was a long pause, then One Eye added slowly, "But
Simirimia, jealous of Treglad, secretly plotted with the son of
the First Father, Vazdz, and left her sister for him. But that is
another story." He stopped speaking, and tears formed in the
corners of his eye and where his other eye had been. Sibby realized she must have been asleep, for she suddenly found herself being raised from the ground by Gannoc, while Mara
wrapped the furs around her legs. She was going to tell them
she was awake and could walk to bed, when suddenly it was
daylight and she was awake indeed, warmly wrapped and lying next to Mara and Gannoc in one of the small painted
rooms.

While Sibby helped Mara and Gannoc and Leron pack up
their few things and tidy the rooms, One Eye sat on a bench in
the courtyard, dreaming in the sun, with Dansen near him on
the ground. Dansen was sorting through his notes from the
night before, making little piles of paper, which he weighted
with stones to keep from being blown away. As usual, he was
talking excitedly to himself, and he did not notice when Meddock, Mellas, and a young boy came through the gate.

They had brought cold meats and bread for breakfast, and
they sat down and ate with them. One Eye turned to Leron.
"Meddock would have us take his son for guide. His name is
Lelu, signifying 'small.' Sixteen years ago Meddock journeyed with me to Treclere, and because he returned thence
uninjured, he feels he owes a life to me, and his son believes
likewise. This I do not believe, but it is for you to accept or
reject, since it is your journey and since it was to you the Lady
spoke concerning our trip."

Leron considered a moment. "I would not lead anyone
into danger who was not willing. Yet I am sure this must be
the guide of whom the Lady spoke. Ask Lelu for me if he will
truly be happy with us; if so I will gladly accept his company
and promise to return him safe home if it lies within my
power."

One Eye spoke, and Lelu's face lit with pleasure. He
opened his mouth carefully and said, "Thank you," so musi-
cally it sounded sung rather than spoken. Meddock's wife
smiled proudly at her son's accomplishment, while Meddock

turned his head away to conceal his pleasure. Lelu spoke
again, "My name is Small. What is your name?" Since he addressed no one particular, Leron answered and introduced
the others.

An extract from Skotla
CONCERNING THE HISTORY OF THE WORLD

*. . . And it has been further rumored that some escaped de-
struction in those times by reason of their tender age and innocence. It is said Vazdz in his mercy spared certain children
knowing that, freed from the corrupting influence of their elders, they would come to worship him as indeed all men
must, acknowledging him in their hearts the Lord of Light.
And they lived in the wilderness, prospering after the fashion
of the wild beasts, not caring for the morrow nor remembering the day before, and in their hearts the unnatural doctrines
of their ancestors were repudiated, and they made no images
but worshiped only Vazdz. And thus they were saved and
taken by Vazdz into the heavens, and truly no man can tell of
seeing them with his own eyes. And so may we all come to
that happy estate, becoming one with the True Light. . . .*

Chapter Four

By the time they had reached the courtyard where the animals were kept, Lelu, or Small, as he called himself, had managed to explain it would be wisest to leave the ponies behind. The way ahead was treacherous, he said, and the footing uncertain; they would make better time afoot. The People would give them two of their own pack beasts to take, one for their stores and the other for One Eye to ride.

These were animals Sibby had noticed the evening before, resembling reindeer but with gentler faces and more oddly twisted antlers. Their fur was golden brown, thick and heavy. They were called ganoose, and one could carry as much as three ponies could. The ganoose that One Eye was given to ride had a yearling calf at heel; and since the mother had milk to spare, the goats were also left behind.

The villagers gathered to see them off, and Meddock and Mellas kissed their son before performing the ritual of touching. Dansen said good-bye to Mellas in this fashion and murmured to Leron over his shoulder, "The act signifies 'my life for yours.' With such as Meddock I feel that the formula is no mere formality." Leron nodded assent, and said good-bye in his turn.

Sibby had not had such a good walk since the first day on the beach. She set out happily, easily keeping pace with Leron and Small. Leron was friendly as usual, but a little on his dignity; the argument of the day before was not quite forgotten. The rest followed at a short distance. All morning it seemed they strode directly into the wind, while the sky, which at dawn had been clear, slowly filled with clouds. The dusty plains were left behind, and during the morning the footing became rocky and treacherous, and their pace grew slower. Then they stopped to eat and rest at midday, the sky became darker, and the first few flakes of snow began to fall.

Sibby had always enjoyed snow, but she had never before

been out unprotected in furious weather, at least not for long. They set out into the rapidly growing swirl of snow, and her discomfort increased. She fell back and walked between Mara and Gannoc, bending head down into the wind. As they forced their way on, snow froze on their tunics and cloaks, coated their hair and eyebrows, and made the rocks slippery underfoot. Only the ganoose walked on matter-of-factly. Small explained, raising his voice against the roaring wind, that good shelter lay some two hours ahead of them, so no halt was called.

The two hours lengthened into three, then four, while their pace grew slower and slower. The storm became a raging blizzard, and drifts several feet deep formed across their path in places. It was almost dark when the shelter was reached, an earth cave hollowed out in the middle of several large boulders. The ganoose were left outside, where they philosophically turned their tails to the wind and drowsed with lowered heads, warm in their furry coats, the calf hidden beneath his mother's belly. Inside, Small quickly kindled a fire where its smoke would be least annoying, and soon it was warm and close in the cave.

They slept early, huddled together for warmth, and Sibby hoped she would not have to wake up for a long time. She could not have been asleep long, however, when a fearful bellow outside the cave brought her awake with a snap. She saw Gannoc and Leron already on their feet, hurrying to join Small by the entrance. The three took brands from the fire and plunged out into the roaring night.

Soon they returned. "What is it?" Sibby whispered.

Leron smiled, but he looked pale and worried. "Some animal, Gannoc thinks a panther from its tracks, disturbed our beasts. They are uninjured, however, and the predator has fled. Go back to sleep. All is safe."

But Sibby noticed as she drowsed again that the three men had arranged themselves by the mouth of the cave; and in Leron's hand she could see the gleam of a dagger reflecting the firelight.

Next morning Leron was up early and went out to look for tracks. But the storm had smoothed them before blowing itself out. As the rest came reluctantly from the cave, they were greeted by a calm and windless day, very chill and bright. As the sun rose higher, the sky deepened into a rich summer blue, and as far as the horizon a thin glitter of ice covered everything. Sibby almost gasped with delight. Walking was not so delightful, however, even with the ganoose to break trail. Under its glassy surface, the snow was unpredictably deep, and in places the jagged ice crust cut their leather shoes or their hands when they stumbled. They still made poor time, although not as poor as the day before.

Noon did not melt the ice; the air became brighter but no warmer, because their way led up a gentle slope. Its whiteness made Sibby's head ache, while the unremitting climb told on the back of her legs and neck. They continued their slow climb for three days, crunching through the sparkling snow with their breath burning in their throats and hanging in front of their faces in smokelike puffs.

The top was reached before noon of the fourth day. Leron made a weary push and reached the crest, scanning the horizon eagerly with one hand shading his eyes. "See, comrades!" he shouted exultantly. "See what lies ahead!"

Sibby toiled up after him and squinted at the distance, but her eyes were not as sharp as Leron's. She could make nothing of the vague darkness she saw, but Gannoc saw better and smiled at Leron, pleased for his sake. "Indeed, my lord, the Salt Lake lies before us, and not a myth at all. We must trust now that the island be not too far distant, for Dansen has often told us that the early travelers mistook the lake for the sea in its immensity."

Dansen, puffing a little, nodded his head. "Erlandus was the first, I think, even before Brydeni, to write of the lake's fabled proportions. Which makes me wonder, lord, how we proceed. It would be a pity to follow the shore, weeks perhaps, and in the wrong direction."

"Small thinks he knows how to find the island. So you may rest easy on that head, Dansen." Leron looked around, and found them all assembled. "I hope that our way shall now prove more easy, being all downhill!"

Leron's hope was ill-founded. If the climb upward had been difficult, the descent proved twice as hard. The ganoose slipped and floundered in the drifts, and the rest did no better. Sibby got so used to slipping and falling she hardly noticed when she lost her footing, except for the bruises. Only Small managed to maintain a good pace, and he was constantly forced to stop and wait for them to catch up. Distance

in the snow proved deceptive, moreover, and that night when
they made camp, the lake seemed only a little nearer. There
was no shelter, so Small had to show them how to dig holes in
the snow for sleeping. They all huddled together in one,
wrapped in furs, the ganoose standing patiently between
them and the wind. As Sibby fell asleep that night, she saw a
pair of unblinking green eyes regarding her from the outer
darkness, and her last coherent thought was to wonder why
she had never before noticed the color of the ganoose's eyes.

Soon after the group had settled to sleep, the moon rose
round and full, and in its clear light Sibby awoke to a confusion of cries and snarls, and the bellowing of the ganoose. She
tried to see what was happening, but the furs covered her
head. When she had finally struggled clear, she saw the fields
as clearly lighted as day, with a fierce battle taking place.
Mara and Dansen were bending over a dark shape in the
snow, some yards away from the shelter past the noisy, plunging ganoose. Gannoc with his dagger and Small with his spear
were trying to be of aid to Leron, who was rolling in the
drifts, his arms around some powerful, savage-sounding
creature. As Sibby stumbled nearer, she saw it was an immense panther, muscles rippling under a shiny black coat.
Foaming jaws were fastened on Leron's upraised arm and
throat, and curved claws ripped at the front of the tunic. As
Sibby watched in horror, the panther laid open Leron's right
sleeve, and blood began to drip onto the dagger he held in
that hand. Gannoc and Small were trying to help, but they
obviously feared their blows would go awry. Finally, after
what seemed an endless period of confused sounds, thumps,
and snarls, Leron brought his weakened arm down full force
onto the panther's neck, making a jagged tear just under the
ear: the effect was stupefying.

The panther's snarl turned into a high-pitched scream of
anger and pain and, incredibly, its shape wavered for a moment, and it seemed that Leron clasped a tall dark woman in
his arms, her mouth and hands tearing at his breast. Blood
showed plainly on her white neck and shoulder, but a sudden
cloud covered the moon and her shape dissolved into
shadow. Leron sank to the ground, exhausted and alone.

They ran to him, but he shook his head. "I'll be all right,"
he gasped. "Look you to One Eye."

Dansen had the old man covered with furs, and Mara,

holding his head, called to Gannoc, "Quickly, rekindle the fire and heat some water. We must bathe this wound and make a healing drink."

Sibby knelt by her and saw that One Eye's face had been opened from under the inner edge of his eyebrow to the corner of his mouth, and the blood still flowing soaked his beard and hair. She helped Mara tear a piece of cloth from the bottom of her cloak, which was too long anyway, and they made a rough bandage. One Eye was conscious but seemed unable to speak; the blood on his face showed black in the brilliant moonlight, and he lay breathing raggedly through his open mouth.

As soon as the water was hot, Mara dampened a cloth and laid it, steaming, in the cold, on One Eye's face. She gently wiped the blood away and gave a start of horror. For fresh blood was welling up under his eyelid as well as in the gash along his cheek. Gently, she bound a pad of cloth in place, and then helped him to drink some broth that Dansen had prepared.

Only then, still pale and controlled, did she turn to Leron, whom Gannoc had been attending. She dressed his scratches and tied up the one deep gash in his arm, which fortunately did not seem too serious. While she was doing this, Sibby knelt by One Eye, grasping his hands, not knowing why the tears ran down her face. At length in a hoarse and shaken voice, he broke the silence. "I am thankful, Leron, that you have not taken needless hurt. I thought the lady must tear your throat away, but you struck in good time. It was the iron in your blade and not its edge, I think, that did undo her. The demons Simirimia sends are not of earth and cannot bear its elemental touch."

They looked at him in surprise. "Forgive me, sir," stammered Leron, "but are you then acquainted with this demon? She let her shape shift only at the last, and until that time I thought her a very panther. It was as a panther she struck and dragged you down."

"True," said One Eye. "And she would have fled, having gained her desire, if you had not foolishly attacked. But it was bravely done nevertheless, though what the outcome shall be, none can tell. To answer you, I did not know her then as I do now. For now I see as gods do, but not as men can." He raised his hand and undid Mara's bandage; under it the blood had already thickened. "You had best call me by my rightful name, Arbytis, which some of you know already. I fear that 'One Eye' can serve me no longer." He suddenly became aware of Sibby's hold on his hands, and of her tears. "Child, never weep for me. I always survive." He spoke without bitterness. Presently, his strength restored, he allowed himself to be helped back to their dug-out shelter, and of all the group he was the only one who slept again that night.

Next morning confirmed his statement: Arbytis was truly blind, One Eye no more. Small took his hands and pressed them to his own eyes. "I will be your eyes," he said, and from that moment he was inseparable from Arbytis. They continued downhill in a greatly saddened mood, and the lake looming large along the horizon did not cheer them as it had before. By evening they had reached the frozen flats that surrounded the water to a distance of perhaps ten miles, and camped in expectation of crossing on the next day.

Next morning, as they approached the shore, a cutting wind and the strong sea-smell of salt greeted them. Small had led them well. They reached the lake just at the narrowest point, where in earlier days Treglad had built a bridge. Crumbled walls still ranged along the southern edge of the straits, and parts of the old bridge's foundations showed dark against the dull grey water. Leron walked to the water's edge and stood staring, lost in thought, at his wavering reflection. Then he straightened his shoulders and spoke in a firm voice. "We can eat and rest in the guardhouse ruins yonder. You shall be out of the wind there, while Gannoc, Small, and I see how we may cross most comfortably."

For an hour or more, Leron and Gannoc considered the problem, wading out into the chill waters of the lake to examine the strength of the structures still remaining. As soon as Arbytis had been comfortably settled, Small joined them in their probing. It was he who solved the problem by suggesting that the two ganoose be used to drag stones from the ruins into the shallow water, there to be wedged into the gaps left in the broken bridge. They spent the afternoon at this labor.

By late in the day, clouds had filled the sky and the wind blew ever more sharply, and long before sunset Mara had forced the men to stop working and come dry themselves by the fire. They sat wrapped in furs while their clothes dried, and after sunset the temperature had so dropped that the edges of their shirts farthest from the blaze were frozen stiff. After dinner they sat in weary silence, with little enthusiasm for the next day's adventure. Arbytis was leaning forward, the heels of his hands pressed against his eye sockets and his fingers dug into his hair. He began to speak in a low voice. "I can see them sitting here. . . . They built their fire here where ours is now. They sleep on the floor, and in the corner their weapons are stacked." Sibby looked up sharply and peered at the one remaining corner of the building, as though the weapons of old Treglad might still be there, quietly rusting. Arbytis went on, talking as if there were no one else there. "Strange . . . their captain has the look of a man I knew once. But he was old then, and that was near nine hundred years ago." He stopped speaking and remained motionless for some minutes.

Dansen nervously commented, "Many writers have noted the peculiar virtue certain old buildings retain, of raising before the present visitor visions of past inhabitants. Though some, it must be admitted, ascribe these images to romantic imagination."

Arbytis shook his head and laughed. "Dansen," he said, "dear scholar, this is no freakish turn of mind. I am beginning to see clearly that which has never yet been seen by men, as once in the distant past I read futures in the Book of Ornat; and what will come of it I cannot tell." Not long after, they settled down to sleep.

THE SONG OF ARBYTIS
traditional: recast into the Tredanan tongue anonymously

No man living can be happy
Pain may strike before Death does
Even as he walks with Calab
Gods may crush him to the ground.

Listen to the tale I tell you
How a High Priest honorèd
Fell beneath the flaming blade of
Vazdz. He once was counted happy

Holy blessed and *fortunate.*
Arbytis! *before his face*
The people knelt to *hear the words*
Their Lady spoke *through Arbytis.*

Fair Treglad *the mighty city*
Vazdz struck down *beneath his wings;*
Snakes and worms *hold holy day*
Within the fallen *temple there.*
And Arbytis *is struck to dust*
His death denied him *through the years*
Meaner than the *meanest beasts*
He ranges the *unsheltering world.*

Consider no man *to be happy*
Envy none his *fortune, fame*
Pain may strike *before death does*
Gods may yet *come crush him down.*

Chapter Five

The men had done their work well, and the next morning the company crossed dry-shod. If it had been cold before, on the lake's northern shore it was almost too cold to breathe. As they walked, their muscles seemed on fire. Time seemed frozen also. Afterward, Sibby could not have told how many days or weeks they followed the lake shore westward, scanning the blank and featureless water for sign of the island prison.

As it happened, Arbytis in his own way saw the island first. One morning as they walked along, shortly after breakfast, Leron turned to feel Small's touch on his shoulder: Arbytis wished to speak to him. He walked back to where Arbytis sat on his ganoose, his blind face raised to the pale watery sun. Arbytis turned at his approach and, leaning down, placed his fragile hand on the prince's shoulder. "Soon we shall reach your island," he said. "Beware, my Leron, lest you find more than you seek. I see something amiss, but the image is unclear. Be careful."

With a rare gesture of affection, Leron briefly kissed the hand that touched him. "I will heed your words," he said. "But in truth I am grown impatient for this island. It is the proof of many a prophecy."

"Be careful then, that it prove not your downfall." Arbytis spoke softly, and Leron did not seem to hear.

They walked on another two hours, perhaps less, and then they all could see it plainly. From the angle at which they looked, the island appeared domed, like an old and shrunken moon made of grey glass and half submerged in greyer waters. No barnacles or vegetation clung to its slippery sides, and for the first time Sibby wondered how they intended to rescue the princess from such a place. The tower was also glassy, fused of the same substance as the island and broken only by two windows, like close-set eyes, near the top. From where they stood, the whole was very tiny and distant, and after they had looked their fill, Leron impatiently set out. They pushed on at a rapid pace until they were opposite the island, and there they made camp. Leron's first concern was for Simirimia's fabled spells, but everything appeared remote and calm. Gannoc was more matter of fact.

"The island lies some two miles or more from shore. I assume we must construct a craft, unless you intend to swim."

"We shall not swim, Gannoc. And with luck we need not paddle. Look at the water more closely." Gannoc approached the shore and bent over. Then he started with surprise and touched it with his fingers.

"Frozen, my lord? But is this possible? A salt lake?"

"By Glass Island I should think anything possible."

"But what if this be a trick, sir? A trick to lure us into a freezing grave?"

"If any be lured it shall be myself alone, Gannoc. I have risked your life and that of Mara quite enough. Here I set forth unaccompanied."

"By your leave, sir, and without it if necessary, I shall not abandon you here. The king your father would be most displeased."

Leron laughed and clapped him on the shoulder. "I doubt if the king will ever hear of your failure, if we fail. We shall test this lake's strength after we have eaten."

That afternoon Leron and Gannoc walked onto the water cautiously. Mara refused to watch, but turned her back to them, poking the fire and biting her lip to keep from snapping at Dansen, who wrote on, oblivious. The men gained the island without incident, only to find its sides unscalable. The substance was pitted and marked with lines and flaws, like a great grey agate, but there were no handholds. Furthermore, it was so cold that some of the skin on Leron's left palm was pulled off when he touched it lightly. And they saw no signs of life in the tower, although they called loudly to it.

Mara implied, as she bandaged Leron's palm, that it served him right, touching so enchanted a place. Sibby was curious. "Didn't you know your skin would stick if you touched the cold stone with your bare hand?"

"In truth," he said, "I have never felt anything so cold."

"I have, at home. You never touch the inside of a freezer, especially if your hands are wet. You stick."

Leron grinned. "I know that now! But I am not sure how I will climb this island without touching it."

Sibby thought a moment. "If skins were wet, I mean animal skins, wouldn't they stick, too?"

Gannoc looked up with quick interest. "The child has a good idea. We could wet skins, and if they fasten on, construct a sort of ladder ahead of us as we clamber up."

Leron took Sibby by the shoulders and kissed her forehead. "Truly you were sent by a kind fate. I have a feeling your wit has solved our problem."

The rest of the afternoon he spent with Gannoc and Small, going through their stores and taking every bit of hide that could be spared. Dansen contributed the soft wrappings from his instruments, barely concealing the pain it caused him. Small's skillful fingers fashioned from these bits and pieces a long wide strip with braided handholds all along its length. Before they finished, it was dark, and lights shone in the windows of the tower. The legends were true. Leron lay down to sleep eagerly, that the sun might rise the sooner on the day that would see him right a great wrong and fulfill a prophecy.

Shortly after dawn, Gannoc and Leron set out for the island, and Sibby followed with some kindling. Small carried two skins of warmed water and a kettle, and when they reached the island he quickly lighted a small fire and began to reheat the water. While Gannoc and Leron soaked the skins, Sibby set out cautiously around the island's perimeter. The nearer she got to the south side of the island, the less firm the ice felt beneath her feet. The air was perceptibly warmer. She hoped there would be no sudden thaw, and hurried back to warn the others. But when she got back, it was as cold as ever. Leron and Gannoc had already managed to attach about ten feet of ladder to the island, and Small was at the top, easily balancing, reaching down for the next piece.

While Gannoc and Leron worked, they did not go unnoticed from the tower, although they did not know it. Dastra had spent the morning as usual, seated before her long mirror combing her hair. It was long enough to sit upon and a pale silvery blond in color. But from time to time she went to the window and cast appraising looks at the activity below. Simirimia had warned her that many might try to rescue her and be destroyed in the process, but these men, the first she had ever seen, were making good time and seemed to have been undisturbed so far. She reflected it would be even more amusing to be rescued than it would be to see them destroyed, and turned to her mirror to try the effect of a long blue gown with white fur trimming. She had no one to judge her beauty by, except for Verissa, who lived with her and was old; yet her private conviction was right, for she was very lovely.

Thinking of Verissa reminded her to check and make sure she still slept. Last night when Dastra had heard the men call up to her, she had quickly gone to the inner garden where Verissa usually sat and read. She made sure that Verissa did not go near the windows all evening. Playing games and talking and singing with a stringed instrument, Dastra had kept her occupied until well past midnight, and now, as she had hoped, Verissa stayed late asleep.

Fortunately for Dastra's plans, the ladder of skins was completed soon after eleven o'clock. At the island's base, Leron turned to Gannoc with pleasure. "Now shall I venture up and find if my dreams have led us aright." He smiled at Sibby. "I pray you shall soon have a royal sister to bear you company." Sibby smiled back, wondering why the prospect seemed so unappealing.

Leron scrambled to the top and stood below the tower a moment, breathing heavily. He looked up at the windows and felt a great lump in his throat. For there, carefully draped against the side of the embrasure, was the most beautiful girl he had ever seen. Her long silvery hair floated down around her shoulders and she was becomingly draped in blue velvet and fleecy white fur. She smiled at him and leaned forward with an appealing gesture. "I pray you, sir, be careful and quiet. My evil mother has so jealously imprisoned me that the least sound might bring her demons upon you. I will endeavor to come down." Dastra cast a quick look over her cushioned and carpeted chamber. It came to her that she was actually being quite kind to Verissa, to leave her in such luxury, which her humble birth did not merit. She smiled complacently at her own generosity and tied a rope of clothing to the heavy bedpost.

As Leron watched, delighted at her bravery, Dastra slid down from the window. Her rope being a little short, he had to catch her in his arms as she fell the last few feet. She was a light and sweet-smelling burden, and he was aware of a desire to kiss the hair that floated across his face. However, he set

her down politely and helped her button her fur cloak under
her chin. Then he went down on one knee and bent his head.
"I bring greetings from my father, Mathon Breadgiver, Lord
of Tredana. I am Prince Leron, and I offer you in my father's
name a refuge in our city from your mother's wrath and most
unnatural punishment." Dastra smiled as she ran her eyes
over Leron's tall, well-knit frame. She stretched her hands
out prettily and raised him from the ground.

"Please do not kneel to me, my lord. I, Dastra, am yours to
command, and only wish to commend your bravery."

Leron flushed with pleasure, and then, unable to speak,
led her to the edge of the island. He showed her how to manage the ladder and watched her descent closely, while Gannoc
stood ready to catch her in case of a mishap. Then he hurried
down after, and presented her to the two who waited there.

Gannoc greeted her with courtesy and reserve. He had
served many noble youths and two princes, and had a distrust
of young and beautiful girls whatever their rank. As for
Sibby, she tried to be as warm as she knew she should be.
Here was the poor prisoner princess, cut off from human society all her life in a desolate waste. But instead of a pathetic
figure, Sibby saw only a girl like other girls she had known,
older girls in school, who acted so very strangely whenever a
boy appeared. In Leron's presence, Dastra was beginning to
glow like a candle.

As they walked to shore, Dastra held on to Leron's arm to
keep from stumbling, explaining that in her tower she had
never had a chance to move about much. As they crossed, she
explained a great deal; in fact she never really stopped talking. Sibby realized it must have been very lonely all those
years in the tower, so she tried not to interrupt.

When they reached camp, Mara warmly hugged the princess, exclaiming at her beauty. Dastra kissed her sweetly in return. Introduced to Dansen, she marveled at his spread-out
papers and journals. "I had not thought such scholars existed! Perhaps you will be good enough to help me mend my
sadly thin education." While Dansen smiled with pleasure she
turned, light as a butterfly, to the corner where Small sat with
Arbytis. "What a wonderful little creature! What does he
do?" Leron, blushing for her, introduced the son of Meddock and then presented her to the old man. Arbytis, who
had seemed asleep, raised his face to Dastra, and at the sight

of his closed and sunken eyelids she covered her mouth with her hand and shrank back. She recovered herself, however, and stretched out her hand as though he should kiss it. He merely nodded his head, slowly.

"I bid you welcome, lady. Surely this is a happy day for you after so long alone, without even a handmaiden to attend you."

Dastra flung back her head. "In truth, it is as you say. I am filled with gratitude to you all, who have made this trek for my sake." She turned away, and all eyes followed her. Only Sibby noticed the pain that crossed Arbytis's face.

An extract from Gannoc
A GUIDE TO THE SCHOOLING OF PRINCES

. . . It is truly said, amongst those who would counsel kings, that the trick lies in the manner of speaking as much as in what is said. He that is wise will refrain on occasion from giving advice, good though it may be, in cases where the giving of it may engender anger or a wounding of the pride. For a prince is but a man, though a man appointed by the gods to rule other men, and as a man it is his right to make mistakes, and better he should do so than lose his trusted friends and advisers. Like the lone mountain peak, the prince lives an elevated life apart from his fellows, and may forget his own indiscretions; but also like that peak he is isolated, and though he forgives not the friend who wounds him, yet he suffers the more that loss of companionship. Above all, be faithful and discreet. . . .

Chapter Six

That afternoon, council was held as how best to return to Tredana with Dastra. It seemed obvious that she would be safest there. Small spoke first. "We have little food," he said simply. "Must go south."

Gannoc agreed. He turned to Dansen. "Do not your chroniclers tell of warm lands always summerlike, nearby the southern shores of this same lake?"

Before Dansen could reply, Small said excitedly, "Yes! The place where animals go to die! My people know of it."

Leron frowned. "If animals die there, might not the same befall us, too?"

Dansen shook his head. "It is called a graveyard more by virtue of its peace than danger. Some geologic property of the marshes keeps the climate warm despite the season. We would be wise to head there."

Arbytis spoke, quietly. "He speaks truly. Across this lake the marshes lie in steamy summer heat. But to reach them is another matter."

At this Sibby spoke up and told them of her walk around the island. Leron nodded. "Plainly we must retrace our steps a little and attempt a crossing somewhat east of here. I feel that Simirimia, expecting rescue from the south, kept that side of the lake from freezing fast. There too, mayhap, her dragons and demon guardians lie. At a distance of some thirty miles, we may yet cross in safety."

No better plan was forthcoming, so next morning they began to return eastward. There was some difficulty at first, because Dastra declared herself quite unable to walk more than a few steps at a time. Leron, however, gladly took some of the burden from the ganoose onto his own shoulders, that she might ride. Gannoc shook his head but said nothing, and Mara smiled at him with understanding.

After two days or so of traveling in this fashion, Leron decided that they might strike out across the ice in hopes of gaining the further shore. The ganoose bellowed and balked at this, but followed the calf, which Gannoc dragged onto the ice by main force. There were no untoward occurrences, but that night not even Arbytis slept well. As Sibby dozed and woke, she was supremely aware of the cold black water moving sluggishly a few feet beneath where she lay. Two days more brought them in sight of shore and, as they had hoped, it was green.

Once they had seen this they pushed on at a faster pace, hoping to sleep on land that night. Disturbingly, however, cracks began to appear in the ice, and the air was grown much warmer. They could smell the lake coming alive again under the ice. That afternoon Leron called a halt, and stood scanning the far shore. Gannoc joined him. "Look, Gannoc. Do my eyes deceive me, or does some rocky cape indeed jut out from shore into the ice?"

Gannoc looked where he pointed. "I think you are right, my prince. With luck we shall not get a wetting after all."

Leron ran to tell Dastra the good news, and she leaned from the saddle and clasped his hand in fervent thanksgiving. "No one could have led us better," she said softly. "You have saved me again, dear Leron." She called the good news to the rest of the group, and as she looked round her eyes swept over Sibby without noticing her. Sibby clenched her teeth, and they set out again.

There were a few dangerous moments before they got safely onto the rocky ridge, for the ice around it was breaking up into sun-softened chunks. And once on solid rock they had to move carefully, for the top was quite narrow and treacherous to walk on, its sides sloping down steeply into the lake. The weather began to resemble a brisk spring day, and a breeze from the glades ahead brought wet green earthy smells. Sibby raised her eyes from the path to look curiously at an enormous and glistening black boulder standing half submerged to the east of them, then looked again a second time and gasped.

A long, attenuated, graceful neck rose dripping from the lake, and the small calm head atop it gazed at them dispassionately. Some weeds hanging from its jaws moved slowly up and down and disappeared into the sides of its mouth. It did not move or blink as Dastra's shrill scream split the peaceful air and sent hundreds of heavy awkward birds flapping upwards from the marshes. Leron was pale and resolute. "The Lady spoke the truth. There can be no serpent in all the world more terrible than that. Simirimia did not leave her daughter quite unguarded after all."

Gannoc, pale also, took his arm. "Surely, my lord, this beast can mean no harm. I doubt it can move with speed, considering its bulk. Mayhap we can pass on and disturb it not."

Dastra's eyes flashed. "Your rescue is sadly incomplete, my lord, if you leave my mother's evil guardians alive to track us down and bring our ruin! That great worm must be killed if we are to be safe!" She tossed her head. "Besides, I would have its head for a remembrance of your valor and a reminder of the danger whence you brought us."

Sibby broke in excitedly, ignoring Dastra's words. "No, no, you don't have to worry. I know what that is, we used to have them in my world, and they're not dangerous at all, really they're not. It's a dinosaur, a brontosaur, and all they ever do is stand in the water and eat plants. Really!" She turned to Dansen for a confirmation, and he smiled at her.

"We have no names for them in this world, child. But no one ever wrote that they were dangerous."

Gannoc looked at her curiously. "How do men deal with them in your world? Just pass them by?"

"They all died a long time ago. I think it was because they couldn't walk, or something like that. The lakes dried up and they died."

Dastra sneered. "A pretty piece of hearsay! As though a great beast like that could not move, and quickly, too!" She shrank back. "See, it comes at us even now! Make haste, I beseech you!"

The great reptile, tired already of the small figures on the cape, had plunged its head with a roar of water back into the lake, grubbing for another mouthful. It turned a little as it did so, and they all could see plainly its large and powerful tail swish slowly through the lake, entangled with weeds. It was the height of two men and the length of ten. Leron made his mind up quickly. "First, we must all get safe ashore. Once escape is possible for you, I shall go back and kill the worm if I can. If not, then Gannoc is your leader." He turned at Small's touch on his arm, and shook him off gently. "I have no time to speak with Arbytis now. Later, Small."

Ashore, Leron quickly undid the cloth that protected his weapons from dirt and rust. He took his sword and dagger both and left his cape behind, for the air was beginning to feel like early summer. Sibby, in anguish, dragged at his arm, trying to speak and almost in tears. "Do you fear for me, child? Tell Dastra I shall assuredly bring her this monster's head."

"No, Leron, you mustn't! Please! I know that he won't hurt you; it would be terrible to kill him just because he's big! It doesn't make sense—it isn't like you! I'm sure that isn't what the Lady meant. I know this isn't a dragon or anything bad. I know it!"

Leron pinched her cheek and smiled in a grown-up way. "Your tender heart does you more credit than your sense, child. What else can such a monster be but an emissary of Simirimia?"

Sibby suddenly remembered something, and blurted, "You must listen to me! The Lady said there would be three times you should listen!"

Leron smiled again and turned to go. "And are you sure this is one of them? You have indeed given good advice in the past, or I might never have rescued Dastra from her tower. But it was to me that the Lady spoke concerning this dragon, and now I go as she advised to destroy it." He waded out into the lukewarm shallow water, holding his weapons high, while Sibby choked and swallowed. She became aware of Dastra standing near her, smiling, and ran back farther to where the others stood.

Dastra stood by the water's edge, her hands clasped on the bosom of her gown. She was breathing rapidly through her mouth, and from time to time she wet her lips with her tongue. When Leron turned, she smiled encouragingly. As he drew near the beast, it once more flung up its head, and the water surging around Leron almost knocked him off his feet. He bravely lunged, however, and managed to stick his sword some little distance into its leg. Pain slowly communicated itself to the monster's sluggish brain, and it tried to turn away. Again, the water swirled around Leron, and then the mighty tail swept him under. He struggled up and stabbed at the great belly, which glistened hugely above him. The brontosaur stupidly turned and tried to see why its side was hurting so. Leron countered this seeming attack with a shrewd thrust to the throat, and blood flowed out over his arm and shoulder. With a terrible whistling sound and glazing eyes, the brontosaur heaved around toward shore. Almost falling onto its knees, it plunged through the weeds and sucking mud, breasting one of the many small channels that led into the lake from out of the great green marshes. Leron, stumbling, followed after, trying to prick it away from the company on shore. The beast ignored them, however, and lurchingly blundered into the protecting swamps. Dastra picked up her skirts and, forgetting her delicacy, hurried after; the rest followed at a distance. The dying reptile floundered deeper and deeper into the glades, and as they followed, the heat became unbearable. There was a stench of rotting vegetation and the marsh sucked hungrily at their feet; the air was steamy and the light was green. No sky could be seen.

Suddenly they were aware of a great quiet. The stream had opened out into a still, small lake, thick with weeds. As the brontosaur stumbled into it, brown mud surged up, and its blood, still gushing, formed in a pool on the pond's overgrown surface. The beast fell forward on its knees, and the small head, large as a pony, fell at an awkward angle. The lidless eyes looked blankly up at the dim leafy ceiling while the head rocked slowly, half floating, on the water.

Then Sibby cried out in pain and horror, for Leron was stumbling over to where the beast lay in its last agonies. He looked down for a moment into its face, then stabbed hard several times. Blood bubbled distressfully in its nostrils, and with a slow inevitability its huge bulk slipped sideways into the water.

As Leron stooped over to rinse the blood from his weapons, Dastra's voice rang out, sweetly. "Well done, my lord! But you have forgotten my trophy!"

Leron straightened slowly, and Sibby could see there were tears in his eyes. He walked calmly to shore, however, and looked at the princess a moment. Then he bowed and handed her his dagger. "You may take whatever prize please you," he said, and, walking over to Arbytis, knelt before him. "I think you were going to tell me that the beast meant us no harm," he said, and suddenly dropped his head in the old man's lap and began to cry in earnest. No one said anything, but Dastra bit her lip in vexation, flinging the dagger from her with distaste.

An extract from Erlandus
OF NATURAL THINGS

. . . And it is not to be supposed that the inaccessible central regions are devoid of interest to the naturalist. From earliest times, those who have had occasion to traverse the dread marshlands have told of monstrous reptiles twenty times the size of a man. One, whose veracity cannot be doubted, tells of seeing what he mistook to be the bare ribs of a large ship hung with green moss and slime, wrecked at an angle in one of the streams that led to the great salt lake, but further investigation proved the ribs to be of bone, not wood, and the skeleton that of an enormous reptile. He took one of the teeth and kept it by him, that he might authenticate his tale at a later date, but in the ensuing months it was mislaid he knows not where. That he and other more recent travelers have seen no living beasts makes one wonder whether they have some natural predator as yet unknown. . . .

Chapter Seven

After the killing of the dinosaur, it seemed to Sibby that some of the easy friendliness that she had missed returned. Although Leron still made excuses for much of the princess's behavior and was oblivious to some of it, her spell was slowly fading. As they made their steamy sticky way southward through the marshes, he once more found time to talk to Sibby and help her with the harp.

In one thing the princess amazed Sibby. No matter how hot it became, she looked as fresh and uncrumpled as though she had just gotten up and had a bath. Her hair never looked limp and dirty, nor did it curl up tightly in the humidity. Sibby's hair had grown considerably and she had both problems. Finally she had Mara braid it up very tightly and she did her best to forget it. That this talent was a major part of Dastra's charm and power was obvious. At night they would sit around, tired, sweaty, disheveled, and muddy, with Dastra an elegant blue-and-white flower in their midst. Sibby gave up trying to like her after a while, but Dastra didn't seem to notice.

Eventually, the sluggish river that they had been following led them out of the swamp into flat fenlands. As they continued south, walking upstream, the water ran colder, clearer, and more sweet; to the east, rich, rolling meadowlands appeared, although the west bank continued swampy. They kept to the east side, savoring green grass and clean spring weather. They were finally able to wash themselves and their clothes, and the difference to their spirits was marked.

Leron explained that this region was part of the unclaimed empty land midway between Tredana and Treclere. Soon they would make their way east to the mountains and pass around them and thence home. They were thus relaxed and in good humor, following the river up a gentle hill toward a deep lake where it had its source, when they became aware they were not alone in the wilderness. A small fire flickered up in the hills, on the shore of the lake where they intended to camp.

Gannoc as usual counseled prudence; there were other places to camp. Arbytis agreed, although he could give no reason for his advice. But Dansen was curious to meet other travelers and perhaps compare notes, and Dastra especially looked forward to meeting strangers. So they made their way to the lakeshore, Gannoc walking ahead to announce their coming and assess their probable reception. Five men, dressed like hunters, got to their feet in apparent surprise as he approached. He introduced himself as a traveler from Tredana, and the men immediately relaxed, explaining that they themselves were Tredanans, trappers from Villavac. They greeted the rest of the group with pleasure, and that night there was a merry dinner party and singing and friendly conversation.

There was a moment's fright when Dastra carelessly addressed Leron by his rank and not his name, but as no one noticed, the incident was passed over and forgotten. The trappers had fresh wine with them and healths were freely drunk. Sibby lay down that night with a humming head, and she was not the only one.

A little before dawn, Sibby woke and saw the others still sleeping heavily. She looked again and realized that the trappers were gone, and in panic saw that they had taken the ganoose with them. She shook Leron by the shoulders, and he struggled awake. "Leron, you must wake up! They've taken the ganoose! We're alone!" He sat up suddenly and looked around him, then jumped to his feet and walked to where the beasts had been tethered. The stakes were still there, but the lead ropes had been cut with a knife.

Quickly he roused the others. "There is no time to waste," he said. "I fear that I have led us into a trap. No doubt even now those hunters are on their way to alert Simirimia's forces, secure in the knowledge we cannot move far without our stores and pack beasts. But we shall give them a merry chase. No, Gannoc, there is no time. Let me speak. To you I entrust the safety of the princess: conduct her home to my father. Vazdz willing, I will join you. If you all set out now, around the lake, you may reach the Tredanan shore by afternoon and thence cross in safety to the mountains. I do not think Simirimia will venture that far east. If necessary, you may trust yourselves to the Karabdu, our cousins, who are reputed to be men of honor after their own fashion."

"But," ventured Gannoc, "what of yourself, my lord?"

"I must stay with Arbytis, of course, and see him safe away," answered Leron with surprise. "Shall I leave him to enjoy the Deathless Queen's hospitality once more?"

"But, my prince, if they should capture you!"

"I know, I know, you could not face my father! Well, you may tell him from me that I have no intention of being tamely taken. But my duty is to Arbytis, who cannot move so quickly, and also to Lelu the son of Meddock, who would never abandon him. Dear Gannoc, remember, Arbytis was the first source of this quest of mine: it is somewhat fitting that the risk of which that prophecy spoke should concern him."

Gannoc grasped Leron by the shoulders, as though to shake him; then, his mouth working with emotion, he swiftly bent one knee. "It is as your grace commands." He turned and swiftly gathered the others for flight.

Arbytis raised his voice slightly. "I thank you for your concern, my Leron, but I do not think this sacrifice is necessary. This is a risk you can easily avoid. Why stay? They cannot kill me, and life has no further terrors for me. I do not like what I see, if you should come before Simirimia. Go, and take Small with you." But Lelu shook his head.

"I stay with you as Meddock said. My life for yours. I will not go."

Leron looked at his impassive countenance. "You see, dear Arbytis, he stays as I foretold. If it will make you any happier, I stay for his sake and because of my promise to Meddock, not for you."

He turned and saw the others waiting. Dastra was pale with fright; he kissed her hand. "I trust we shall meet anon in my father's house. Gannoc, my dear, keep her safe. Dansen—" (here he embraced the scholar) "—see you make copies of your journals in the future. I hope you can reconstruct your records in Tredana. I have confidence in your memory as I have in your honesty and love of truth." Mara he hugged and kissed. "Reassure your husband that he is right to obey me in this. And if my father snaps at him, then tell him from me, respectfully of course, that he is a fool if he gets angry with the best servant a prince or king could ever have." Finally, he turned to Sibby with a smile. He took Telyon from off his shoulder. "I fear this will be a useless encumbrance to me. Take it for me, if it does not trouble you, and if I do not come to claim it, then keep it as a remembrance." He kissed her cheek. "Be assured we shall all meet again." He waved his hand to them in farewell. "Now go, and do not delay further!"

It seemed to Sibby a dream in which they hurried away around the lakeshore. Leron's kiss on her cheek and Arbytis's farewell clasp on her hands seemed printed on her flesh. She thought of Small, gravely touching his throat in good-bye: he really meant it, "My life for yours!" She sobbed and caught her breath, hugging the harp tightly to her.

Throughout the day they did not pause to rest for more than a few minutes at a time. Even Dastra did not complain; she urged the others on in her fear, scrambling and slipping in panic as they forced through the bushes. By late afternoon they had reached the far side of the lake, and perhaps five miles distant across its calm water they could see the small beach where they had slept the night before. Even as they watched, a glittering cavalcade of armored horsemen rode out on the sands. Small parties detached themselves and spread out along the shore, and it was not very long before they could see a horseman returning in haste with good news for his captain.

When the prisoners were brought up, there was no doubt who they were, although faces were unclear at that distance. Leron was taken, and with him Arbytis, the High Priest of Treglad, and also Lelu, son of Meddock, chief of the People. Gannoc led the small party eastward, there being no time yet for tears.

Mathon Breadgiver, Lord of Tredana
Privately to his JOURNAL

. . . It being the first day of the seventh month since my dear son left, I spent the day no more happily than can be expected. I dreamt last night a black bird with green eyes did take him up in her claws and bear him away to the west, and

*ever since awaking I have been heavy in my heart, unable
even to enjoy my dinner (memo: I must speak to Sentell
about fresh crabs for next week), and I am troubled for his
safety. It seemed further in my dream that he was speaking
with my dear wife's brother, who was lost to us near seventeen
years ago when Leron was but four or five, though in my
dream they were of an age and alike in their beauty. I thank
Vazdz my sweet Leriel has not lived to see her son follow her
brother, and can only pray I am wrong and will wake to see
my son returned and the city rejoicing. Now, concerning the
banquet tomorrow . . .*

THE KARIF

VII

Chapter Eight

That night they did not dare to light a fire; they had nothing to eat and only stream water for drink. Gannoc and Mara withdrew into themselves, while Dansen, usually so unemotional, was plainly on the edge of tears. Dastra seemed to have forgotten the day's events already, but she soon realized that no one was listening to her complaints and withdrew into a sulky silence. That night Sibby slept with Leron's harp clasped tightly to her.

Often things look better in the morning, but next day this was definitely not true. Fortunately, there was much to do, and as long as they were busy there was no time for thought. Gannoc set some traps and began working on a bow and arrows, for he said there was no point in going on if they had no food. By nightfall they had a weapon besides Gannoc's dagger, and they had eaten rabbit stew. But only Dastra showed any appetite, and she did not eat as much as she would have liked because there was no salt or seasoning. The second evening, all in all, was as cheerless as the first.

The third day they made good time, striking out east and south across rich, rolling bottomland, following the cover of a winding stream, beside which trees grew thickly. They caught two fish, and Gannoc identified some wild vegetables that were safe for eating. For a moment this seemed to rouse Dansen from his distressed silence. "In early times," he said, "this weed was held to have magic properties and be unsafe for human consumption. But travelers among the Karabdu found it much used in the desert and prized for its flavor, and so began its cultivation among civilized men. It is said that. . ." His throat tightened with remembered emotion. "I forget the rest," he muttered, and turned his head away.

Gannoc put his hand on Dansen's shoulder. "You have never forgotten a word you ever read, dear scholar. Why be ashamed of your tears? We both have watched him grow from boy to man, and continued to teach him though he knew it not. We both have loved him. See, I weep for my prince openly." And Dansen, watching Gannoc cry, fell into tears himself and they embraced each other.

Dastra was scandalized. "Verissa always says that tears cannot mend so much as a broken saucer, much less a broken heart! We may have lost our companions, but at least we are still safe! I pray you do not let us fail now through weakness."

Sibby looked at her curiously. "Verissa?" she asked. "Who is Verissa? I thought you spent your whole life alone."

Dastra covered herself easily. "When I was a small child, of course I had an attendant. I have only been alone these last ten years."

As this seemed likely, Sibby thought no more about it, but Mara looked worried for some time afterward.

A few weeks' easy traveling brought them at length to the edge of the great mountain range. They were thinner and somewhat dispirited, but enough time had passed so that they could talk of Leron and Arbytis and Small without breaking down. There was no gap in the sheer jagged walls before them, and Gannoc explained that they must turn south and pass below the mountain chain, to Villavac and thence home to Tredana. This route would lead them across the edge of the desert where they might encounter the Karabdu, but he was not inclined to fear these wild tribesmen. Although they often held raids on unwary villages and carried off goods, they were also said to be generous to their guests and most willing to act as guides through the desert. Besides, Leron had recommended them as likely to be trustworthy.

A gentle rain began that night, pattering on the leaves above them and hardly wetting them at all. It continued all next day, however, and they had to leave the trees, which had been their cover, behind. As they turned southward, they entered a desolate area. The soil was hard and split into many little cracks, and the rain made a slippery surface but did not penetrate very deeply. Walking was soon quite difficult, and they were all soaked to the skin by afternoon. A little past noon, Dastra suddenly turned away from the rest of the group and stumbled over to the steep cliff on their left. She sat down on a rock and defiantly spread her draggled skirts out around her. "I refuse, I absolutely refuse to go another step." She looked at Gannoc angrily, her lower lip trembling.

"You promised Leron you'd take care of me, and I know I'll die if I have to go any further today. I wish I'd never been rescued! I wish Verissa were here with me! She wouldn't let you bully me and make me walk in the rain and get cold and tired! I wish I'd never left her!" And she began to cry for the first time since she had joined them, choking and sniffling with her hands covering her face.

Sibby could hardly believe her ears. "You mean you left someone behind in the tower? You mean you weren't alone? And you never told us?" She felt sick to her stomach.

Mara put an arm around Sibby's shoulders, pushing the damp hair out of her eyes with a motherly gesture. "We guessed, Gannoc and I, that this might be so, and yet we did not like to think it. Dastra, I think it is a little late to mourn the absence of your serving woman. The only good I can see in your action is that undoubtedly the poor woman's case is easier than ours here, although I myself had rather be uncomfortable than lonely. Now cease your crying and come along: it is no drier sitting than walking."

But Dastra shook her head. "I am a princess! The daughter of the Queen of Treclere! You shall not order me around any more!"

"Princess indeed!" cried Mara indignantly. "This little one here is more a princess than you. You do not have the spirit of a—of a milkmaid!"

Gannoc added, "Although it goes against the grain to say it, yet I must agree with my wife that you do not conduct yourself as befits your rank. You are quite right that I promised Leron to care for you, and little though you may think of him now, I will hold to my word if only for his sake."

But Dastra refused to move, sitting in the rain with water trickling down her small proud nose and her silvery hair unusually dark and sleek against her head.

Since it was hardly feasible to carry her, Gannoc finally sighed and decided that they would go no further that day. They sat around wetly on various rocks, somewhat sheltered by the cliff, and talked, but their conversation was as limp as their spirits and their clothes. Gannoc took Dansen and went out a little way to find game; they shot a small animal something like a rabbit but with round ears, and skinned it in cheerless silence. Mara somehow managed to light a fire against the cliff side, using kindling they had carried wrapped in a cloak, and so they ate a warm dinner that night.

As Sibby slept, dreaming of warmth and dry clothes, a terrible roaring came into her mind. It seemed a great fire in her dream, but the sound grew louder and woke her up. The noise was real, deafening, and ever increasing in intensity. She looked around her and saw the rest awaking slowly. "What is it?" she cried and looked where Dansen was pointing, frozen with horror. She suddenly knew what it must be to die, for coming down the cliff face toward them was a solid wall of water, carrying boulders and large trees in its current. She had a glimpse of Dansen, his hands stretched out as though to stop the water before it struck, and as the flash flood rolled over their camp, she had a sight of Gannoc also, holding Mara to shield her with his body. Dastra she did not see, but there was no time for wonder: the water hit her, and she knew no more.

When Sibby woke she knew she was alive because her body hurt her so. She was lying spread out on the ground and she was somehow dry and warm. Then she realized that the sun was shining, no, blazing down on her and all around the ground was steaming. She tried to move, and the pain of sitting up made her burst into tears, but she knew that if she could sit up at all there was a chance she'd be all right. When she looked at her legs, she changed her mind, however, because her left foot was turned outward as though she were double-jointed, and she was not. Nevertheless she tried to get to her feet, and was almost glad when she fainted, because she hurt so much.

When she came to again, she thought she must be dreaming, for Dansen was looking down anxiously into her face. He was real, however, and alive, though very ragged. His hair stood up all over his head, released from the cap he always wore, and his gown was split and tattered. He was holding her hands, and when she smiled at him he kissed them and said in a trembling voice, "My dear! Thanks to the gods you are alive. I had feared I might be called on to make your bier."

"Are . . . are the others safe too?"

Dansen looked grave. "I pray they are, but here there is no sign of anyone but us. I have been awake some hours, and although I am able to walk, the broken ribs I have sustained make it difficult to wander far. Indeed, they make it difficult merely to breathe. But my injuries are nothing. We must look to your leg and see what may be done. I wish I had spent more time in the study of medicine!"

He had enough knowledge to diagnose Sibby's problem. Her hip was dislocated, and he would not be able to set the joint right without assistance. Among the debris left by the flood he found a stick that Sibby might use to support herself, and she staggered weakly to her feet and hopped a few steps with it. He smiled encouragement, and she noticed the pain in his own eyes.

"Shouldn't you have a bandage? When my father broke his rib skiing, he had one wrapped all around his body." When Dansen merely nodded, she knew his pain must be considerable, for he didn't ask her what skiing was. He helped her tear a long strip from his gown and then she wound it as tightly as she could around him. It was not a marvelous bandage, but it did ease the pain. Leaning together for support, they set out, southward by the sun, having no idea where the waters had left them. Dansen was sure they must reach the desert soon, however, and hoped the Karabdu would aid them.

One good thing happened as they started out—Sibby saw a familiar triangular case lying not far from where the waters had dropped her. She had been holding Telyon when she slept and apparently not let go. Within, the wood side of the harp was broken, but it looked as though it could be repaired, and Sibby took the case gladly. It was a keepsake from which she would not willingly be parted, had it weighed three times what it did and been twice as big.

They had little progress that day, and the featureless plain around them offered no food or shelter. Grief, despair, and pain made that night the worst Sibby had ever spent, and she could not tell whether she wept for Leron, the future, or the pain in her body. Dansen held her in his arms as tenderly as a mother, despite the pain it caused him in his ribs; at last they slept, exhausted. Next day they were both giddy and weak, yet Dansen insisted they continue walking, in hopes of finding a stream or shelter.

By this time thirst was a torture, and the heat intense. Finally Sibby fell on her right knee, her stick slipping from her hand. "I'm sorry," she said, "I have to rest for a minute." She looked up through tears in her eyes to see Dansen looking not at her but at the horizon.

"Vazdz may intend us to live after all," he said. "I think I perceive a rescue coming toward us." She struggled up and, following his gaze, saw a cloud of dust billowing up on the horizon, growing larger as it approached. Soon she could see figures within it, three horsemen dressed in voluminous robes, scarlet and turquoise and white.

Dansen put his arm around her shoulders for reassurance as the three galloped up, foam hanging from their horses' mouths. A few yards away they slid to a halt, and the white-robed leader sprang down lightly, tossing his reins to one of the others. Sibby knew she was looking at one of the fabled Karabdu, and despite her pain and fatigue she looked at him with interest. He was very tall and sparely built, with strong hands and high cheekbones; his fair hair had receded at the temples and he had cynical blue eyes. They looked directly into Sibby's with a quizzical expression, and as she noticed the yellow ring around the iris, her own eyes widened with surprise.

He laughed at her expression. "It is the imprint of the sun," he said, "and marks me Karif to the Karabdu. I bid you welcome to my lands." And he swept his arm in a wide gesture, indicating the distant circular horizon. "Are you of the party that traveled with Leron, Prince of Tredana?"

Dansen, who had been eagerly absorbing every visual detail, looked at him sharply. "We had that honor," he said. "And before he fell into misfortune, he recommended us to your people if we needed help, and indeed I do not see how our case could be much worse. We throw ourselves on your mercy and pray you will conduct us to the Tredanan lands, for the respect of Mathon Breadgiver and the peace between your two countries. And," he added, as realization struck him, "how did you know we were of the prince's party?"

The Karabdin chief laughed again. "I met with another of your group yesterday, and although she assured me she had been alone except for the prince and some servants, I thought it best to see with my own eyes what guests lodged in my lands. And here you are. I am Ajjibawr, and I welcome you travelers from the Empty Regions." He looked at them more keenly, and little wrinkles formed at the outside corners of his eyes. "But you are in pain as well as in tatters. It will not do to keep you standing here. Ab'Bakr, I require your horse."

The red-robed rider swung down obediently. With casual

strength, Ajjibawr lifted Dansen to the saddle and nodded to Ab'Bakr to mount behind. He then sprang back on his own mount and, leaning over, lifted Sibby lightly to the horse, and held her before him. The sand swirled up around as they wheeled their horses, and then the three riders, with their new burdens, galloped back in the direction from which they had come.

Despite the intense pain shooting through her leg and the spinning sensation in her head, Sibby could almost enjoy the ride. How different this was from the little jogging ponies they had ridden on the beach. Ajjibawr's horse, a dark iron grey, moved smoothly across the hard-packed sand, great muscles rippling rhythmically in his shoulders. His white mane, incredibly long, whipped Sibby's face. Ajjibawr guided his horse with his legs, and held Sibby securely with a light clasp on her waist; she looked at his hands, so much whiter than her own, with wonder, for memories of her own world made her expect a desert horseman to be dark.

It did not seem long before they had crested a hill, behind which lay the tents of the Karabdu in a narrow valley where a stream ran and some trees grew. There was a brief pause before they plunged down the slope at breakneck speed and halted in the center of the settlement. Attendants gathered around them as they dismounted, and Ajjibawr turned to an old white-bearded man with heavy eyes and a curved nose. "Ibsina, you will tend our guests' hurts. When you have made them comfortable I will return." And he swept away without a backward look, leaving Dansen and Sibby surrounded by curious faces.

Ibsina signaled his attendants. "Please come, O guests," he said gently. "I am said to be skilled in medicine, and it is clear you can use my services."

An extract from Dansen
LIFE AMONG THE KARABDU
Introduction

. . . They were not always the tribal people they are now. This was indeed their origin, but for a space of more than

three hundred years they held sway as the mightiest of known peoples, and their capital was a thing of wonder and beauty, carved from the living rock in their secret valley. They had nine kings, the first and chief of whom was Dzildzil, he who heard Vazdz speaking in the desert and taught his people to obey Him. But their city is now more desert than their lands, and they move with the seasons from place to place. For it happened that in the reign of the last king discord fell among them and brother fought brother in bloody rivalry. A chief among chieftains arose then, named by them the Karif, and settled their differences, and he decreed that they must return to the old ways and leave the city forever, and this they did. Truly their poet writes when he says:

> *As horse with speed*
> *As light with sun*
> *Must land and Karabdu*
> *Be one.*

For nineteen generations now the Karabdu have lived in harmony with themselves and with the desert, in accordance with this ancient truth. . . .

Chapter Nine

Dansen had warned Sibby that putting her leg back into joint would be very painful, but even so she was not prepared for it. Fortunately she fainted, and although this was embarrassing, it made the operation easier for her and for the two men who were working under Ibsina's direction. By evening she was quite comfortable, although weak from shock, and was able to talk with Dansen who had been tightly bandaged and was now regaining his strength with rest and food.

Outside, the wind whistled and the tent creaked around them, its ornate poles and braided ropes shifting from side to side while the silk-embroidered heavy woolen sides breathed in and out. Dansen looked up from his dinner cheerfully, and carefully picked an errant grain of rice from his beard. "Truly, this is a most fortunate chance that brought me here, to see the storied Karabdu with my own eyes and hear their words with my own ears. Someday it may be that Dansen's *Travels* will rank with the famous writings of earlier ages. If only they will bring us news of our companions rescued like ourselves, all will be well indeed."

"Ajjibawr said that someone was here. It must be Dastra. But by now his men might have found Gannoc and Mara, because they must have had as good a chance of escaping alive as we did, don't you think?" As Sibby spoke, she knew she didn't believe it herself, but neither she nor Dansen could face the possibility of having lost the rest of their friends.

"We can only hope and pray so." As Dansen spoke, the flaps of the tent were thrown back and two men entered, standing on either side and bowing almost to the ground. Ajjibawr strode in between them, making a small gesture with his hand that they were to leave, and they backed out hurriedly. They almost collided with a servant who was carrying a brass tray laden with brass pots and china cups, who swore at them fluently in an unintelligible language. Ajjibawr pointed, and he immediately stopped cursing, bowed, and set the tray in the indicated place.

As soon as the tent flaps had fallen again, Ajjibawr walked to the tray and poured a thick black liquid into the cups, which released the wonderful odor of coffee. Sibby had a sharp but distant vision of breakfast back at home, the smell of coffee and bacon.

Ajjibawr came to where they reclined on pillows and rugs, a cup in each hand, and his tall figure blotted out the light of the swinging lantern. "I rejoice to see you so well," he said courteously. "I beg you to set a seal on my hospitality by partaking of drink as well as food. It is written that he who has eaten and drunk under one's roof becomes as a brother and inviolate from attack, and I would have you two feel secure in the company of myself and my people."

"No such seal is necessary to reassure us," responded Dansen, "but we accept the courtesy gladly."

Sibby took her cup and sipped cautiously—it was strong and terribly sweet, and she decided that she rather liked it. Ajjibawr returned with his own cup and sat down on the floor by them, and for a moment there was silence. Then Dansen spoke again. "This morning, my lord, you spoke of another of our company whom you entertain here. May we have news of her, and of the search for our other two comrades?"

Ajjibawr set his cup down on the rug. "When I heard from Ibsina that you were concerned for the loss of two further companions, I sent Ab'Bakr and his brother to search, for I trust them as I do my own hands. I regret to say that they returned but a few minutes since, having seen no sign; and I hope you will believe that they were thorough. It may be Vazdz has written that you will not meet your friends again in this life. If this is so, you will assuredly feast together in paradise."

Sibby felt her coffee rise in her throat, and her eyes swam. Dansen controlled his voice and simply said, "We thank you for all your help. But what of the Princess Dastra?"

A curious expression flitted across Ajjibawr's face, and his thin mouth twitched. Before replying, he took a small ivory box from his sleeve and opened it with a flick. It seemed to contain tobacco, and Sibby was surprised to see him delicately sniff a pinch up into one side of his nose. He sneezed slightly and rubbed a long finger reflectively against his nostril. "I fear that here we tread on soft sand," he finally replied. "When Osmin, the brother of Ab'Bakr, discovered the lady in question, she was walking unattended along the cliff foot, and she told him that she was the only survivor of a murderous attack by the Trecleran queen's armies. Osmin naturally asked what had provoked this attack, and she would give him no satisfaction. Thus he brought her to me, also claiming, as indeed it was his right, that she become his fifth wife according to our customs." Sibby looked up, startled. "However, when she explained that she was the affianced wife of Prince Leron, now a prisoner and his servants dead in the fighting, I promised her for the sake of my respect for King Mathon to return her safe to Tredana. And yet a small doubt pricked me, and I went looking and found you. So now another doubt also pricks me, and here I would crave your aid. Is she indeed the prince's promised wife, or may I reward Osmin as he feels he deserves?"

Without a moment's hesitation, Dansen answered, "In this matter she told the truth, so I beg you do not hinder easy relations between your people and the Tredanans through hasty action. The sun or the perils of the flood may have tampered with the princess's memory, but in this essential fact she speaks truly. I would further beg as a favor that we may visit her soon."

Ajjibawr smiled cynically and rose to his feet. "I think you are a loyal servant to the prince, and I like you for it. Truly, you are free to see your princess any time you wish, and I will arrange that you all may lodge in adjoining tents. But tonight I will follow Ibsina's advice and leave you here undisturbed." He bowed his head slightly and made to go, then paused at the door and spoke. "I will tell you one thing, however: the Karabdu fear no power, not Tredana nor yet Treclere, and had I wished I might have given this princess to Osmin were she fifty times the wife of a king. But in truth I think better of Osmin than that." And the flaps fell together behind him as he left.

There was a short silence. Then Sibby said, hesitantly, "You just said that to save her, didn't you? She isn't really going to marry Leron!"

Dansen looked at her with kind understanding. "If we all return in safety to Tredana, and Leron comes home again, it would be surprising if they did not marry. He has risked much to save her, and while I do not think it has been spoken of, yet am I sure they both intended such an alliance. And still my mind misgives me. We owe her safety to Leron, yet I feel he might be happier in the end if she were to marry elsewhere."

Sibby moved restlessly against her pillows. "And Ajjibawr thinks the same about Osmin! I hope when I grow up people don't talk like that about me!"

Dansen smiled. "When you grow up? You are beginning to grow up already, although you may not know it. It is a most interesting thing to watch, the change from a child to a woman." Sibby was embarrassed by this, but Dansen's next words gave her an even funnier feeling. "It is said," he mused, "that among the Karabdu they marry at age twelve. By their reckoning, Dastra must be almost too old for consideration. Unless you have a fancy for desert life, child," and here Sibby was not sure if he joked or not, "best not grow up too quickly whilst we are here."

Sibby had much to think about that night, and yet she fell asleep quickly, exhausted by the past few days and the pain in her hip. Next morning attendants brought them each new clothing: for Dansen, a gold gown made of finely woven wool with an embroidered leather vest to wear over it, and for Sibby a white silk dress with a long woolen jacket striped red and green. She had never had a silk dress before, and its softness was delightful. A woman helped her brush out her hair and put it up on her head, which made her feel very grown up. While Sibby tried to keep the short ends from curling around her face, the woman held the polished brass mirror for her. Sibby was so surprised and upset by what she saw that she had to clutch at the comb to keep from dropping it.

The face in the mirror was not hers. It was darker, thinner, and older; she looked more like a girl in junior high than a fifth-grader. She took the mirror from the other's hand and held it close, studying her face. She had not looked at herself for more than six months; but the change looked like years. Where her face had been round before, there were hollows under the cheekbones, and her skin was deeply tanned. Long hair was looped up on her head where short curls had been before, and her eyes were serious. As she looked at herself, shivers chased up her spine, and she looked from her face to her hand where it held the mirror and had another shock.

When had her knuckles appeared? Surely there had been dimples on the back of her hand the last time she looked, but now her hand was angular with clearly marked joints. Never before had she been particularly aware of her body; now the silk dress seemed to be clinging to her in strange ways, and she was aware for the first time in her life of the skeleton beneath the flesh, her collarbones and wrists and the way her hips curved. She was still confused, her heart beating hard and blood drumming in her ears, when the curtains parted and Dastra walked in.

Dastra was more beautiful than ever, wearing a new silk gown patterned in blue and green, her silvery hair wound up along the back of her head with one ringlet down on her shoulder. Dansen nodded to her politely. "We rejoice to see you here well and safe. It made us much easier in our hearts to know you had escaped the terrible flood."

Sibby, recovering herself, tried to make a friendly smile, and in return Dastra looked at them with arched brows. "I was never in danger from the waters. That night, after the insults of Gannoc and Mara, I was determined to make my own way to Tredana. After watching the terrible retribution of the flood, I decided not to mention their cruelty to me, since they were already punished for it by the gods."

Sibby's mouth fell open with surprise, but Dansen only nodded. "Doubtless the gods deal fairly with all in their own time," he said. "Furthermore, you may rest easy on the matter of your engagement to the prince. I reassured Ajjibawr, who for some reason was beginning to doubt your ladyship's veracity."

Dastra looked surprised. "Of course I am! Did you ever doubt it?"

Sibby broke in hotly. "Of course we doubted it! I don't care what Dansen says about its being expected—that still doesn't mean you were really engaged."

Dastra smiled a smile that barely moved her lips. "It was not only expected, but accomplished. You, child, do not know what was spoken of privately between the prince and myself, evenings after you were asleep."

Dansen put his hand on Sibby's shoulder and was beginning to speak when once more the curtains parted. Ajjibawr's two servants came in and bowed, as they had the night before, and Ajjibawr strode in between them. Today he had a purple robe thrown over his long white gown, and the cloth which the Karabdu wore covering their heads was draped loosely about his neck. He looked around the little group, and it seemed to Sibby his mouth twitched.

"It is a good thing for friends to be reunited," he said at last, and as before he gestured to the servants to wait outside. He turned to Dastra. "I can well understand how eager you must have been to see your lost comrades, but I will request, and if necessary require, that you not walk about my lands unattended. I have given you one of my female servants for your own, and in the future she is to accompany you everywhere. It would not contribute to Prince Leron's honor among the Karabdu if it were to become known that his promised bride walked around as freely as a young girl."

Sibby expected Dastra to object proudly, and was surprised to see her lower her eyes and look at Ajjibawr through her lashes. She thrust out her pink lower lip and said, "But you know I would do anything to please you, my lord. I have no wish to cause any trouble to you who have been so generous."

Ajjibawr's eyes lighted with appreciation. "I know well your intentions," he responded, and turned to Dansen. "Ibsina tells me you are a man of learning. I have the privilege of three such among my people, and I am sure you and they would profit by association. It will be a matter of some weeks before I can spare the men necessary to conduct you to our borders, and in the meantime I will gladly grant you the use of our records and writings."

Dansen beamed. "It is a pleasure to find the hospitality of the Karabdu as open as it has been reported." Ajjibawr nodded. "You speak gracefully. I think you will not find it hard to master the Karabdin language. And that is a study I recommend to you, for in no other tongue may the niceties of polite conversation be so exactly expressed."

Finally he turned to Sibby. "I am afraid I cannot offer you much amusement, child, but pray accept the freedom of my encampment. There should be much here to interest a curious mind." As Ajjibawr left, it struck Sibby that there was a lot to be said for not being grown-up after all.

Ajjibawr had been quite right about his encampment. Sibby found it fascinating. She visited the men who baked bread in round stone ovens, and the shepherds who tended flocks out past the tents. One of the shepherds, a man named

Musta, was very kind to Sibby and let her hold a kid that was only a few hours old. She also visited with the women who were weaving rugs on looms that were set on the floors of special tents set apart. They showed her how to tie the knots and clip the wool, and Sibby never knew that they always had to undo her work after she had left. In camp she also found a maker of instruments, who mended Leron's harp for her and restrung it. She tried to make friends with the children she saw, but they were shy and kept to their own families. She did notice that little girls much younger than herself had black makeup around their eyes and red paint on their lips and hands.

But nothing was of more interest to Sibby than the stables. Although the rest of the camp was quite dusty and the air dry to breathe, all around the stable area boys kept the ground watered down. It was thought unhealthy for the horses to breathe too much dust. The horses of Ajjibawr slept in their own tents and drank a bowl of goat's milk every night. Sibby thought she had never seen any animals more beautiful.

The third day she spent watching them, Ab'Bakr, who was attending the hurt leg of one of his favorite mounts, came over to her. He offered to take her up for a ride, and Sibby was entranced. He only galloped a little way along the valley floor and back again, but he promised to take her again the next evening. But next day his brother Osmin was there and insisted on taking her himself; and soon Sibby had been on rides with most of the young men in the tribe.

One evening, however, she found the place curiously deserted when she arrived. She looked into the largest tent and found Ajjibawr there with his head groom, examining a two-year-old colt carefully. It had been sired by his own favorite mount, and like him was iron grey with a white mane and tail. Ajjibawr looked up. "I heard that you rode abroad every day and decided it was fitting you should have your own mount. Mubassa here will teach you to handle him."

Sibby hardly listened to his last words as she looked at the colt and realized it would be hers to ride. It was undoubtedly the most beautiful horse in the camp. Her long ride along the beach had given her confidence in the saddle, but she knew there was much she did not know. So she listened to Mubassa's careful instructions and gave the colt a handful of grain as he counseled. "Horses love food best," he advised, "and also the bringer of food."

Sibby smiled at this, because she was sure her colt would love her for herself, and mounted cautiously. As Ajjibawr turned to go, leaving her to Mubassa's instructions, Sibby looked down from the saddle and tried to thank him. Then a thought struck her. "You didn't tell me his name!"

Ajjibawr for once showed surprise. "Men and gods have names, child, and also the spirits of the air. Animals do not require them."

Sibby said nothing, but in her heart she had already named the horse Leron. She leaned forward and kissed his mane, and felt the strong muscles in his neck flex under her caressing hand.

THE FIFTH SONG OF VAZDZ
as set down in the book of Dzildzil
(Rassam's translation)

I am the sun: I give light to the world
I am a lamp in dark places
I give you mastery over the world
the maker's fire is my gift.
Without me the rain is as dust, and the earth
is barren without my touch.
I shall stand unchanged when the mothers who bore you
are one with the earth again.

Considering the moon my wife and sister
She who lightens the night
Her light echoes mine; without my presence
she is less than the stars.

Consider the stars, my messengers
They bring my light to earth
and still I am undiminished, still VAZDZ
MOON TAMER   COMMANDER OF STARS
THE ONE TRUE LASTING SUN

Chapter Ten

Once Sibby had her own horse to ride, the days went by all too fast. She still saw the young men who had taken her riding, but now it was on a more competitive footing, as she challenged them to races and exhibitions of skill. They usually won, because she would never push her horse as hard as they pushed theirs. But she didn't mind, since Leron, as she still privately called him, was plainly happy to see her every morning and called after her in the evenings when she left. Sometimes when she was riding on her own, she would make up stories in her head about the real Leron's escape from Simirimia. Occasionally in her stories she would even help rescue Leron, riding up on her horse that was faster than all others. And these stories comforted her.

Dansen, meanwhile, had found his own comfort in books and manuscripts and an exchange of knowledge. Except for evenings spent with Dastra and Sibby, he was with Ajjibawr's scholars constantly, translating legends, sharing historical notes, and learning of their religion. Although Vazdz was acknowledged chief among gods in Tredana, it was here in the desert that he had first been worshiped and his teachings set down in a book by the first prophet, Dzildzil.

They had been in camp three weeks when Ajjibawr invited them to dine at his own table. Before when he ate with them, he had visited them in their own quarters, and they were curious to see how he lived. At dusk his servants came, carrying torches that flared up in the clear desert evening and smelled of oil. The tent to which they were brought was very large, with curtains hung within to divide it into rooms. Rugs were laid along three sides of the front main area, and there were rich tassled hangings and embroideries, and lamps made of pierced brass and silver. In the center was a charcoal brazier, set low on short legs, and by this Ajjibawr stood. As was his custom, he wore white, tonight with a rich red sash and some embroidery at the open throat for contrast.

It was clear that they were to be guests of honor. Ajjibawr set Dansen on his left and Dastra on his right; Sibby was next to her. Once they were seated, others of the Karabdu came and sat around, each bowing first to Ajjibawr. When the mutton and rice was brought, Ajjibawr served his guests with his own fingers and fell to eating with appetite. He spoke to Dansen with his mouth full, wiping his lips with the back of his hand. "I had intended to offer you our chief delicacies, but I was warned in time that the Tredanans do not value the entrails of a lamb as we do."

Dansen laughed and swallowed. "As ever, I must thank you for your courtesy."

Ajjibawr took this to be very humorous, and the tight skin on his temples crinkled in laughter. As Sibby looked at him, she thought suddenly how much she liked him and how little any of them knew him.

Ajjibawr turned to Dastra. "I regret your time here has been so uneventful. In a fortnight, no more, we shall set out for Tredana as I promised. It will be a sad thing for you to see Tredana without your affianced husband there, yet I am sure that King Mathon will greet you kindly for his son's sake."

Dastra fidgeted a little and tucked a gleaming wisp of hair behind her ear. Timidly she laid a slender white hand on the chief's sleeve, and she looked up at him from under her lashes, which were extraordinarily dark and long. "Sir, you speak truly. For me it will be a homecoming that is no home-coming at all, for I fear I have no place in Tredana without Leron, and yet I have no other place to go. And I further feel Leron will not return to his city."

Ajjibawr raised his left eyebrow. "Surely there are others who will make you welcome there?"

Dastra dropped her eyes and moved her shoulders slightly toward him. "You have made me so comfortable here, I would be ungrateful to wish for a better home. But of course there is no place for me here, either." And she pressed her fingers against her eye as though to suppress a tear.

Ajjibawr moved his sleeve away from under her hand. "I had been meaning to ask you where you come from, and now is a good time. You have freely told me to where you go, but little has been said of whence you are come."

Dansen was worried by the question, but Dastra opened

her blue eyes wide and looked up into Ajjibawr's bluer ones. "I cannot tell, sir, for fear of reprisals against those who share my secret. Suffice to say I was a prisoner and most unhappily pent up when the prince set me free some months since. More I dare not venture."

Ajjibawr looked at her eyes a moment, until she blushed in earnest. Then he nodded acceptance and looked past her to Sibby. "Mubassa tells me that you handle your mount with skill. So you may enjoy your last weeks with us, I tell you now that the colt will be a gift to you when you leave, and you need fear no parting from him." Sibby choked with delight, and Ajjibawr went on. "It will be hard for my young men to realize that you feared a parting from your colt more than from them." He laughed at her startled look. "Had you stayed another year, I would have had too many asking for your hand, and I would have been forced to disappoint too many good comrades. Vazdz knows I have as much fondness for women as any, yet it often seems to me a pity that friendships must so often be broken for their sake." He wiped his hands on a napkin and took out his snuffbox.

Sibby hardly heard what he said for embarrassment and confusion, but Dastra's tight sweet voice cut clearly through the humming in her ears. "In that you speak most truly. I have admired your way of living here, the more I see it. It is plain that in the desert an obedient and retiring wife is most prized, one who does not flaunt herself abroad or indulge in rough activities." She folded her hands in her lap, while Ajjibawr sneezed and rubbed his nostril with a characteristic gesture.

"Did I speak truly indeed?" he asked softly. "I was not sure myself. It comes to me that not one of my twenty-eight wives is particularly obedient or retiring, and yet I would not willingly be parted from any of them." And while Dastra tried to recover herself, he turned to talk again with Dansen.

The meats were removed about this time, and coffee and sweets brought in. There were various types of dried fruits coated in honey and sugar and chopped nuts, and Sibby forgot her embarrassment trying the different kinds. Dastra had apparently lost her appetite, and Sibby relished the situation to a certain extent.

She was just finishing a fig stuffed with almonds when there was a commotion outside the tent. The flaps were flung

back and a short, round, angry man came bounding into the
tent, his long robes, black beard, and thick curly hair white
with dust, his hands gesticulating as he swore and cursed. Behind him hurried two of Ajjibawr's men, their hands upon
the hilts of their long curved swords. Ajjibawr rose with an
expression of amused embarrassment and stopped his guards
with a gesture.

"Emr, Tafs, peace! This is our worthy friend from Vahn.
You may leave us."

As Emr and Tafs, confused but obedient, backed respectfully out of the tent, Dansen looked at the newcomer delightedly. "Vahn!" he breathed. The stranger was making a per-
functory bow before the Karif, still cursing and trembling.
Finally, intelligible words came through.

"Outrageous! Outrageous! Friend from Vahn indeed!
Friend? Are friends held captive by armed men? Do friends
have their bales opened, their goods ransacked, their choicest
items of commerce filched, their legitimate business questioned? Are friends made mock of and illegally taxed? This
for friends!" And he made a gesture with his hand that even
Sibby could tell was extremely rude. Ajjibawr only smiled
and shook his head.

"Peace, Varilda, peace. I can see without your showing me
that you have met with my most difficult subject. Your losses
shall all be made good, as well you know. Tell me, how does
Adaba Tayyib these days?"

Varilda sighed and sat down suddenly, and when he spoke
it was in a quieter tone. "Very well, as any man would, suddenly the richer for twenty measures of coffee, three hundred
golden krahs, two bales of nesting silk grubs, and a fine
young donkey only two years old!"

"They shall be returned. Here, eat of this. The eyes are yet
untouched." And to Sibby's fascinated horror, the man
Varilda began eating of the sheep's eyes and other unappealing parts as he continued his story.

"We were but two days into the desert, scarcely out of sight
of the sea, when Adaba rode to us. The wily dog! He told us
he repented of past sins and would conduct us safely here.
Shame cover my head that I believed him." Varilda paused
from eating and ran a greasy hand over his curly hair. The
gold ring in his ear gleamed brightly. "Six days from water he
met with his men, and they presumed—not to rob, no they

are reformed now!—they presumed to hold a levy on my goods, a tax in your name, O Karif!"

Ajjibawr laughed, but there was a look in his eyes that made Sibby glad she was not Adaba. "As you were taxed in my name, so shall you be reimbursed. Relax, now, and eat. I have guests here you must meet."

But Varilda hardly glanced at Sibby and her friends, leaning forward over the tray of food to whisper confidentially, his velvet-covered belly almost touching the heaped-up rice. "There are guests coming here you may not wish to meet. I had meant to tell you first, but my anger with your guards betrayed me. After parting from Adaba I saw them, and they cannot be far behind. A hundred men ride from the west, two days' march from here, and their ensign is the banner of Treclere."

"They have left the Empty Regions? They are in the Land?"

"I have said it. Two days, no more, and they shall be upon you."

"Upon us? I think you are mistaken. If the queen came in force, she would not bring so few. I take it she has come to parley instead. I will be interested to meet the fabled Simirimia." He beckoned his steward. "Begin preparations for a royal guest. Tents for her soldiers, a special one for herself, and lambs to be slaughtered for a banquet two nights hence. You know what must be done." The steward nodded and went out.

Ajjibawr turned once more to his guests, to introduce them to the merchant, and saw for the first time the expressions on their faces. "Do not despair," he said. "There will be no murderous attack within my lands! And mayhap you shall learn of your missing companions and a ransom be arranged for your prince." But Dastra shook her head, genuine tears running down her face.

Dansen made a difficult decision, and spoke. "May we speak privately?"

Ajjibawr nodded, and at his gesture all drew back, even Varilda. "Well?" he asked.

Dansen wet his lips and smoothed his wool gown over his knees. "This lady, Dastra, whom Leron rescued from a cruel imprisonment, was no ordinary captive. From birth she had been exiled upon a northern island by her unnatural mother, this same Simirimia of Treclere. And now she fears, as I do also, that she will be retaken and forced to spend the rest of her years as she did all her youth, cold and alone and friendless amidst the northern wastes."

Ajjibawr looked at their faces, and his eyes paused on Dastra's terror-stricken expression. He spoke to her more kindly than was usual with him. "You have eaten my bread," he said. "You need fear no betrayal. I thank you for your confidences. However long the great queen stays, I give my word, with Vazdz as my witness, that your path shall not cross hers, nor shall she hear of your presence." He looked at the others. "If you wish, you may lie concealed also, but I do not think a scholar from Tredana and a child with him will arouse great curiosity. Now I must beg your leave to go over accounts with Varilda here, for there is some work that must be done before I sleep again. We shall talk in the morning." Servants with torches, as before, led them back to their joined tents, and they were left to their private reflections.

If Sibby had not been so familiar with the daily routines of the camp, she would not have realized how much was being done to prepare for Simirimia's visit. Outwardly there was little change, and people seemed to be performing their usual tasks in their usual ways, but Sibby soon saw that much was being accomplished in a short time. Ajjibawr's camp was efficient and tightly controlled. By evening of the first day, new tents had been set up and made ready, the stables had been added to, and food and fodder provided for man and beast.

Dastra, meanwhile, could not be convinced that she was safe. Dansen tried to sit with her and read words of comfort from the ancients, but she threw her pillow at him after half an hour and said he wanted to see her dead. Even so, he would have stayed and tried to help, but Sibby urged him to go back to his conversations with Varilda; and Dansen, eager to learn more of Vahn, agreed. The second day was worse, and Dastra was looking so pale and sick Sibby finally went to Ibsina for help. He made a sleeping draught, and Sibby, feeling a little guilty, gave it to Dastra toward the end of the afternoon. She was soon curled up on her bed, one hand tucked under her cheek and her hair spread out behind her head. Sibby helped Dastra's maidservant cover her up and told her to stay and watch. Then she was free.

In her own tent, Sibby quickly washed and put on her best

dress, the white silk she had been given her second day in the desert. Her hands were shaking with excitement. Once she had seen Simirimia with her own eyes, she would know what to feel for their captured friends. The Tredanan picture of a Deathless Queen practicing evil arts was very different from Ajjibawr's matter-of-fact acceptance of Simirimia as a fellow ruler. Sibby hardly knew what to think. Tonight at the banquet she would know better.

Outside the curtain that parted her tent from Dansen's, there was a slight cough, and then Dansen entered. He looked at the curtain as it fell back into place and shook his head. "I marvel not that the Karabdin language is a web of polite speeches and suitable answers. It is most necessary in a country where one cannot knock before entering." Sibby smiled at him. His hair had been sleeked back and curved below his ears, his beard was trimmed, and he wore a brown velvet gown that had been made to the pattern of his old one. He looked quite handsome, and she realized he wasn't really very old. There were still ink stains on his fingers, and he rubbed them absentmindedly as he spoke again.

"I have been thinking that it may not be wise for you to be seen by the Trecleran queen. She may wonder that I have brought you along and not anyone else."

Sibby shook her head. "She won't notice me, I'm sure of that. And I have to see her for myself."

Dansen looked at her with understanding. "I, too, am curious to see this queen. I hope we may be wrong in our tales of her. I suppose as long as the princess remains hidden, all will be well."

Sibby explained about the sleeping potion, and the two of them stepped outside to watch the arrival of the party from Treclere.

As a courtesy, Ajjibawr had ridden out to meet Simirimia and conduct her back in person, taking with him only a few men such as Ab'Bakr and Osmin. At first, Sibby could not be sure if the dust they saw on the horizon was Ajjibawr on his way out or everyone returning. But as she watched, the cloud grew larger and continued to grow, rising up against the streaky evening sky. Bands of bright pale color spread out on either side of the swollen sun, and against this backdrop the black shapes of horsemen were framed. For almost half an hour they watched, and finally Sibby could make out the white figure of Ajjibawr near the front, riding as usual on his dark grey. Next to him was a splash of scarlet and green that finally resolved into a billowing silk canopy held by two riders over a chariot that drove between them: Simirimia of Treclere. Sibby could see that it was drawn by three white horses, but the rest was blurred by distance.

Twenty minutes later they rode into camp. Simirimia stood behind her driver, her strong body clearly marked under her thin green pleated gown, which draped from one shoulder and left her arms bare. Gold ropes thick as a baby's wrist and formed into bulls' heads at the top were wound about her arms, and her black hair fell below her waist as straight as rain. Her eyes were green.

When they stopped, she leaped down easily and Sibby could see that her feet were bare, and more gold encircled her left ankle. Her chariot was dull and black, decorated in front with something that looked like a crescent moon, only drawn out and twisted.

Ajjibawr stepped up to her, and they were the same height. As he walked with the queen and her servants to the tent prepared for them, they passed close by Sibby and she noticed something, noticed it with a terrible sinking feeling in her stomach. Where Simirimia's gown came together at the shoulder it was pinned with a circular brooch, and this ornament was silver, not gold. Sibby knew it well, for she had last seen it holding Leron's cloak together at the throat.

MUBASSA YL BAS'ASSAS
Poem from the Karabdin translated, with annotations, by Dansen

Your ribs are more beautifully arched
than a maiden's sleek black brows[1]
Your mane is like water falling
Your skin, soft as the rose.[2]
If you run, the wind lifts your feet
Lightning[3] *cracks at your cry*
Beneath your pounding hooves
the thunder dies away.

Your eye as noble as woman's
Your heart⁴ more pure than hers:
My steed, when I am dead and gone
may my bones lie with yours.

1. *brows*　　In Karabdin, there is one word that may mean either lashes or brows, that is, *mi'la'i*. The metaphor here demands the latter meaning. ("Black" refers to their regrettable habit of painting, and not to their natural complexion.)

2. *rose*　　The desert rose, *julleh,* is flatter than the domestic variety, having six broad pink petals and a bright yellow center.

3. *lightning*　　The word used here, *vazdzunir,* most commonly means fire, but I have interpreted it as lightning because of the thunder reference in the following lines.

4. *heart*　　Among the Karabdu, the stomach, *silebb,* is held to be the seat of emotion and the affections; I have translated "heart" as more nearly catching the meaning, and to avoid seeming ridiculous.

Finally, I must apologize for my weak rhymes, for I thought it best to stay with the meaning as closely as possible, rather than to create too poetic a translation.

Chapter Eleven

That night, at the banquet in her honor, Simirimia still wore Leron's brooch. She was dressed in something grey and floating, like a spider's web, and the fragile fabric was bunched together at the throat with the silver brooch pinned through it. The lamplight glowed on her bare arms and neck while she ate, listening to Ajjibawr but rarely looking at him. Her green eyes were fixed in a sort of trance and she looked ahead of her under half-closed lids. From time to time she would finger the pin absently, running her thumb across the design cut round its edge. Her black hair absorbed the light rather than reflecting it.

Sibby, completely fascinated, could not help watching Simirimia through the evening. Every time she ran her fingers across the brooch, Sibby shivered slightly. Somewhere she felt she had seen a face like Simirimia's, with straight black eyebrows and arrogant cheekbones, but it might have been only in dreams. A face less like Dastra's was hard to imagine.

During coffee and sweets, an entertainment had been arranged in the queen's honor. Three shepherds, Musta among them, played pipes and drums while two young men danced, leaping in the air and moving their bodies with great energy and grace. Simirimia looked through them and beyond, almost motionless. Next one of Dansen's friends, a scholar and a poet, spoke of the nine great kings and of the Karabdu's past glories, accompanied by an old man who kept time with a small drum. Simirimia seemed to smile as she reclined against her cushions, watching nothing in particular. As the story came to an end, however, she turned her head very slowly and looked at the assembled crowd. When her eyes came to Dansen, they opened slightly, and to Sibby they seemed to glow brighter green. For the first time that evening she spoke to Ajjibawr, although she did not look at him. "This is no desert dweller." Her nostrils slowly flared. "I smell Tredana here."

Ajjibawr looked uninterested. "Indeed, this is a visiting scholar from that city, a man most learned in legends and histories."

Simirimia's eyes relinquished Dansen and turned without haste to Ajjibawr. "I am curious to speak with this guest. Arrange it so after dinner." And to Sibby's surprise, Ajjibawr agreed as through he were accustomed to taking commands.

Soon, at Ajjibawr's signal, the tent emptied and the servants closed an inner curtain, which made the area where they sat more like a small and private room and less like an audience hall. Ajjibawr introduced Dansen and Sibby, and then withdrew to speak with his servants. Simirimia leaned back once more and veiled her eyes. Her hand dropped forward, and the fingers closed languidly in a beckoning gesture. "Come here, Tredanan scholar." Sibby might not have existed. Dansen stepped forward and sat down near her, looking her over with frank interest. "Am I as you expected?" she asked, and even as she spoke Sibby felt herself drowsing and angrily shook her head to keep awake. For Simirimia's shape was wavering before her eyes, and her hair now seemed more brown than black, and her complexion paler. Her dress no longer shimmered.

Dansen replied, "Much as I expected. May I say you do not look your age?" Simirimia laughed silently, her head fallen slightly backward, and Sibby saw that her eyes were rather blue after all. She no longer seemed as sinister, and Sibby began to hope for their lost friends.

As though she sensed Sibby's changing mood, Simirimia looked full at her for the first time. Her pupils dilated, and a small frown momentarily appeared between her eyes. "You are young to be so traveled," she said, adding to herself, "and yet perhaps not so young. How old are you, child?"

Sibby said hesitantly, "Almost twelve. Dansen is my guardian. I would be lonely without him." Simirimia barely nodded in reply, but her frown smoothed out. To Sibby she looked almost a different woman, kinder and softer and not barbaric at all. Simirimia looked at Dansen once more and smiled, showing white teeth. "If you search for wisdom and have no fear, you must come to my city. There is much you could learn there, much I could teach you. And I am curious to hear more of Tredana, for several reasons. Remember my words."

And she lifted her hand for Dansen to kiss, which he did, holding it in his a moment longer than was necessary.

There was bewilderment in his kind face, and he looked into Simirimia's face as though he were not sure what he saw. To Sibby, the queen merely nodded dismissal, but then she changed her mind and gestured her back, holding her hand out to take Sibby's. As their palms touched, Ajjibawr came back into the room, and as suddenly as lighting a lamp, color washed over the queen. She was as vivid and dark as ever, and her green eyes glowed with power. Sibby looked into her face and felt her throat contract, for the face before her in some way made her think of the strange face she had seen in her own mirror. She turned in confusion and fled from the tent, barely noticing Ajjibawr's sudden start of surprise at seeing the two of them face to face.

For the rest of the queen's visit, Sibby and Dansen saw little of her. Mornings she spent in official parley with Ajjibawr, sometimes privately and sometimes with her stewards and his officers also in attendance. If she spoke of Leron to Ajjibawr, he did not mention it, and Sibby and Dansen could not ask without betraying their identities. Different diversions filled the queen's afternoons. She was fond of the chase and went with Ajjibawr on antelope hunts and hawking expeditions. A few times Sibby fell in unnoticed with her train, partly to exercise her horse but mostly to watch Simirimia.

Sibby noticed that alone among the hawks Simirimia's killed successfully on every flight. It would rise rapidly into the sky, a small speck against the sun, and the bird would swoop, plummeting like a dropped stone only faster. Then Simirimia would close her eyes slowly and let out her breath and a shrill scream would herald the bird's success. Sibby noticed also that the queen's eyes were definitely green and her hair most certainly black, and she wondered that she could ever have thought otherwise.

The night before Simirimia left, Sibby had a strange dream. In it she was very young, watching her mother dress and fix her hair before going out. As her mother brushed her hair in front of the mirror, she leaned down and let Sibby kiss her powdered cheek, because it was time for Sibby to go to bed. Sibby's mother always smelled good. But her face when she looked down was not hers, it was Dastra's, only older. Then the scene changed and Sibby was asleep in bed. Her mother was moving around softly in the dark. A voice, she was not sure whose, said, "Is this the child?" And another said, "It hasn't worked! She's still here!" Sibby began to cry in her dream, like a small baby, and her mother bent over her in the dark to hush her. But the face was not her mother's face, it was Simirimia's, and Sibby woke up in terror in her tent to find it was almost dawn.

Unable to go back to sleep, Sibby finally went through the curtain into Dastra's tent. Dastra's first fright had given way to pleasure at being protected, and this morning she was sleeping peacefully, as Sibby had expected. Sibby had brought a blanket with her, and she rolled herself in it and curled up against some cushions on the floor. She did not intend to fall asleep there, but Dastra's quiet breathing eased the dream's hold on her mind, and almost before she knew it she was waking up again, this time in full sunlight. Her dream had faded, however, and all she could really remember was the first part. Now she was able to see there was a strong resemblance between her own mother and Dastra, and she was surprised she had never noticed before.

Simirimia left before noon that day. When all was ready, she came out from her tent into the strong sunlight, Ajjibawr beside her. She was dressed as on the first day, with Leron's brooch still clasped on her shoulder. Ajjibawr helped her step up, and as she leaned down from the chariot to say a last few words to him, her heavy hair fell around their two heads like a curtain. Then she gave the signal and her chariot moved forward, under the canopy, and the hundred horsemen followed in order. Soon they were only a dust cloud against the sky.

That night Ajjibawr joined Sibby, Dansen, and Dastra in their tent for coffee after dinner. At first he did not speak, but only took a pinch of snuff, sneezed, and rubbed his nose. He continued to rub his nose while he turned something over in his mind, and then he finally spoke. "As I said, the queen has gone, and you are safe, and tomorrow I will take you on your way." He paused, flicking the lid of his snuffbox open and shut. "There is one thing I do not understand, however, and if possible, I beg you to enlighten me. Why conceal this lady here," and he nodded to Dastra, "and expose this one to the queen?" Sibby felt his eyes on her and looked startled.

Dastra spoke up, amazed at his ignorance. "We have al-

ready told you how it stands between my mother and myself!
I have not been able to draw one easy breath this whole past
week! But monstrous though she be to me, one would not expect her to attack some unknown child, a guest in your
camp."

"Enough!" Ajjibawr looked unusually stern. "It is plain
you do not wish to share your secrets! But I am not blind.
One need only look at this child and the queen together to see
the truth of the matter! It is evident you play some deep
game; but I warn you, Simirimia will not be easily fooled. She
begins to suspect already, and if she chooses to strike, I do not
think you can defend yourselves. The politics of your tiresome cities are of little interest to me, but I think you might
warn this child before you sacrifice her."

Sibby shook her head. "No, no, you're all wrong. You really don't understand. There's a lot I can't explain to you, but
there's no way Simirimia could be my mother!" She laughed
at the idea, in spite of Ajjibawr's seriousness. "I can't explain, really, but it is impossible. You have to believe me."

Dansen added, "She speaks truly, my lord, and you must
not think we meant to trick you. There is no way in this world
she could be of Simirimia's blood; and besides, we rescued
Princess Dastra from her mother's enchanted tower just as we
told you."

Ajjibawr still frowned, but their obvious sincerity made an
impression. He looked again from Sibby to Dastra; and Dastra, forgetting all her wiles, flung up her chin and glared at
him. "How dare you infer," she whispered. "How *dare* you
suppose that I am of common descent, and this little waif the
child of a royal house?"

Her pose restored Ajjibawr's usual good humor, and he
snapped his snuffbox closed a last time and tucked it back
into his sleeve. He rose and bowed to them all, an eyebrow
slightly lifted. "We shall leave tomorrow morning, and I will
conduct you to the edge of the Empty Regions. One thing no
one can doubt, and that is that you," he nodded to Dastra,
"were most certainly reared as a princess. But there is much
here none of us understands yet." And he left them in their
bewilderment.

A TRUE STORY OF VAZDZ
as set down among the Karabdu by Musala yl alaat
(Rassam's translation)

I, Musala yl alaat, had this story from Jallem yl lemas, who had it from Sala yl salassa, who had it from Musta yl talebend, who had it from Bendas yl dasineh, who had it from Zalman, Prince of the House of Dzildzil and keeper of record there: break this chain who can!

It is said that Dzildzil in those times was a godless man, living according to no book and wandering without purpose in the desert. One night as he slept, a flame lit up the sky and a voice spoke, and said, Wherefore do you live like this, acknowledging not your creator and living not according to his plan? And Dzildzil was frightened and knelt and covered his head, saying, Truly, I know not who my creator is, unless it be the earth around me. Then in his dream a flame touched the ground before him, and in the fire he could see the most beautiful man in the world, but his face he could not see. And this figure was the color of fire and had wings of pure gold, and spoke to Dzildzil with the voice of thunder I am HE, VAZDZ, and I require your obedience. And he spoke again, saying, I have revealed myself to you that you may worship me and prosper in knowledge, craft, and power, and I have written a book for you to read. And you will bring the world to kneel at my feet, or you and it were better dead. And Dzildzil awoke and found a book written in fire and bound in gold, and he read it and took it to all he could find, telling what it said, and he was the first messenger from VAZDZ, the first Holy Reader, and the first king of the Karabdu. And all among his people came to acknowledge the glory of VAZDZ, and thus they were not destroyed when the earth heaved and flames consumed the northern city of Treglad. And this is a true story.

Chapter Twelve

As soon as they had eaten the next morning, Sibby went around the camp to say good-bye to all her friends. Much to her astonishment and delight, they all had presents for her. Musta gave her a sheepskin to use as a saddle blanket, and the weavers gave her a flat-woven bridle and reins with a beautiful geometric design in red and blue and white. The instrument maker had picked some early roses from his little garden and had a bouquet for her to take.

No more than an hour after breakfast, they were on their way. Sibby found that once they climbed out of the valley and entered the treeless wastes, it became very hot; the air grew even drier than they were used to, and the fine dust sifted in among their clothes and stuck under their eyelids.

Presently Ajjibawr spoke. "Before sunset we shall have reached the Valley of Dead Kings, and with Vazdz's help the stream will still be running and we shall have a good rest."

Dansen, who had been wiping the dust from his face, looked interested. "The Valley of Dead Kings, lord? Is that where the ancient capital of the Karabdu once stood?"

Ajjibawr nodded. "Now only the kings of the old time remain. The rest of us need pasturage." And his mouth laughed but his eyes did not change, squinted as they were against the sunlight and the dust.

They did not speak again until they stopped for a short rest. Among the food stores were several large melons, and these helped quench their thirst. Sibby felt sorry for Dastra, who was white with exhaustion, but did not say anything for fear of triggering an outburst of self-pity. Instead, she ate her melon in greedy silence and slipped part of her water ration to her colt. The horses of the Karabdu were trained to go without drink for long periods of time, but Sibby did not see the need for enforcing the law too strictly.

As they rode through the afternoon, their way led them

due east, and the setting sun threw long shadows in front of them, black streaks on the yellow sand. Finally, they could see ahead of them an irregular shape against the sky, which gradually sharpened into a group of rocky cliffs rising steeply from the desert floor. This was their gateway, and when they came to the rocks Ajjibawr led them calmly into a narrow dark valley.

As they rode in, it became quite chilly, and Sibby could smell water on stone. Ajjibawr turned in his saddle, a pleased expression barely visible on his shadowed face. "The spring yet runs," he said. "We shall drink deep tonight." They pushed on, and the sound their horses made echoed coldly from side to side of the narrow passage. It was almost dark when the valley opened out into a large meadow of some hundred and fifty acres extent, surrounded by cliffs on all sides. Near where they entered, a stream of water ran down the rock's surface and made a pool before running away into the sand, and by this they all camped. First the horses drank, but slowly so they would not be sick, and then the riders. That is, all except Dastra, who would not wait for the horses and had Sibby fetch water in a cup, because she did not like to use her hands. They fell asleep easily that night.

After breakfast, when Sibby went for a second drink of water, she saw for the first time that where the stream came out of the cliff a lion's head had been carved in the rock, and the water came from his mouth. The lion had wings, which stretched out on either side of his face. Sibby looked down, surprised, and saw that the pool where the water collected was a rock basin, carved with a beautifully scrolled edge, which turned over in one place for the water to run out when it was full. So she looked around her carefully, and soon was lost in wonder.

The entire cliff face as it encircled the valley was carved into doorways and arches and building fronts, covered with intricate ornamentation. Opposite their campsite, an enormous niche had been hollowed out, at least two hundred feet high, and the space was filled by a gigantic statue. On the statue's right hand, the cliff face was broken up regularly into a series of nine wide panels with a small door in each, halfway up the steep cliffside. Dansen joined Sibby and looked at these with a pleased expression.

"What a refutation I shall publish to Skotla, who claimed

there was no such city! If only he were still alive to hear this!"

Sibby asked, "What is that big statue?"

Ajjibawr spoke in answer; she had not heard him come up. "That is the statue of Vazdz, which Dzildzil ordered made in memory of his dream in the desert. He stands there with golden wings, his face covered, as he first appeared to us, holding the crown of the Karabdu in one hand and the holy flame in the other. And on his right hand the nine first kings of the Karabdu lie sleeping. When we took to wandering again, we kept the flame but the crown was broken, and now we are tribe and karif, and no more country and king." He spoke with emotion, but what his feelings were Sibby could not tell.

Sibby could have spent the day exploring the city, but Ajjibawr was anxious to lead them to his borders and be off. So they set out soon after, across the valley floor. Broken columns and pieces of masonry, fragments of inlaid floor littered their route; Ajjibawr explained that everything of value or use had been taken ages since. But even as he spoke, Sibby noticed a blue glassy glint in the short dusty grass by her horse's feet; she got down and picked up an irregularly shaped ring made of glass.

Ajjibawr swung round and took it from her fingers, holding it up to the sun so it shone with a beautiful iridescence. "Once," he said, "we had much skill with our hands, and could turn sand into glass such as you see, glass that can be set into the fire or dropped upon stones without marring. But no longer." He gave the ring back into Sibby's hand and closed her fingers over it. "Keep it as a remembrance if you like." It was too big for her finger, but Sibby carefully put the ring into her saddlebag before riding on.

When they had crossed the valley, they paused a moment at the statue's foot. As Sibby bent her head back and looked up at its enormous bulk, she almost shivered. The massive featureless face was covered with painted inscriptions: the sayings of Vazdz, Ajjibawr explained.

As they looked up, Dansen trotted his horse away to look up at the first of the nine tombs. He called to Ajjibawr, "Is it known what messages were carved hereon?"

Ajjibawr rode to where he was and looked up briefly at the flat tomb face. "The message is known, and is of importance to us all, though Dzildzil meant something else by it. It reads in part,

> *I am Dzildzil, King of the Karabdu, King of the Land,*
> *Rightful ruler of all the Empty Regions, Regent to*
> *VAZDZ and his messenger to all peoples. Here I held*
> *sway, and here too shall my sons, and my sons' sons*
> *even to the last generation. Who reads these words, fall*
> *down and worship VAZDZ, and marvel at his work, who*
> *has raised a nation of wanderers to be the rulers of all*
> *men."*

And Ajjibawr threw back his head and laughed, and his laugh echoed restlessly around the empty valley.

Before Dansen could take out his papers and make notes of the inscription, Ajjibawr had wheeled his horse around and cantered to a fissure in the cliff face between the statue and the first tomb. Wide flat steps were carved there, and up these he rode slowly. The rest followed, and the way led round and round in a large easy spiral, enclosed in the cliff. From time to time there were small windows cut in the side through which they could see the valley floor retreating beneath them as they climbed even higher. At the top, Sibby's horse scrambled onto a ledge, and the view made Sibby's head reel. They were on a narrow platform directly above the statue's head. The geometric shapes of buildings and courtyards could be clearly seen from above, although the walls were gone long since.

Ajjibawr seemed to sigh, then he smiled at Sibby. "It is a sad sight, and yet not so sad. For it was here my people forgot their real creator, the desert, becoming almost like those who live in the Empty Regions."

Sibby looked away from the view which was making her dizzy. "You talk a lot about the Empty Regions. I always thought it was the desert that was empty, but you don't mean the desert."

"No, I do not. For us of the Karabdu the Empty Regions are those that have no desert." And Ajjibawr turned his horse and walked delicately along the narrow ledge, across the niche and into another wide stairway on the other side. This led them down as the first had brought them up. As Sibby crossed, a small wind ruffled her hair, and the empty space seemed to ring in her ears, but she looked ahead resolutely and did not breathe until her colt's four feet were safely on the rock floor opposite.

At the foot of the further stairs, they passed out into brilliant sunshine, for the stairs had brought them through the cliffs and out of the hidden valley. The sun struck hot on their faces for it was not yet noon, and once more there was dust everywhere. They continued thus all day, and camped that night in the open; and it was the same for two days more. Their course now led north, and Ajjibawr said they would reach the edge of the desert before nightfall.

"Where on your borders do you take us to, lord?" asked Dansen.

Ajjibawr smoothed back his long fair hair slowly, and spoke with his eyes on the horizon. "I will bring you to a point not eight miles south of Villavac, and there, if he has our message, will await a guide who is of your city and yet a true friend to my people as well. He and one other are the only two outsiders who have lived among the Karabdu as brothers."

At his words, Sibby's memory stirred, and she wrinkled her face in concentration. Something Leron had once told her . . . it came to her. "Was the other an old man, an old man with a beard?"

Dansen looked at her with quick understanding, and Ajjibawr showed his surprise clearly. "Yes, what do you know of him?"

"Oh, if only I'd remembered before! You could have talked to Simirimia about him! Arbytis was one of the two who were taken with Leron. It was because he was old and blind that Leron stayed and was captured, because he wanted to try to protect him!"

Ajjibawr looked into her eyes, and his eyelids dropped a moment. "I can see you tell the truth. Here is a heavy thing to learn, a heavy knowledge to carry. I have given and received favors of my brother's jailor, though I knew it not. Yet as surely as our blood has mingled, I will not leave him a friendless prisoner." Ajjibawr straightened and spoke more briskly. "I will take you on your way with all possible speed. For it seems I soon may have another journey to make, and this time westward."

As Ajjibawr had said, they reached the desert's edge before night. It was almost dark when they saw far ahead a warm yellow light like a lantern. The faint uneasy sounds of sheep were carried to them on the breeze. As it grew darker, an occasional sheep would blunder up out of the dark and bound away in front of their horses, and the noise of the flock grew louder all around them. At length the light could be seen near at hand, shining from the window of a small house. Ajjibawr held up his hand for the rest to halt, and rode a few steps forward. "Hand of my hand, brother of my blood, is it you?" he cried, and within the house the lantern was taken up and a tall man came to the door, the light held high in his hand.

"Brother by blood, it is truly I," he answered in a deep voice and came forward.

Ajjibawr swung off his horse and the two embraced, and then Ajjibawr led the tall man to the rest of the group. "This is the true friend of whom I spoke, Rassam to the Karabdu but Herrard to his own people, and a keeper of sheep by trade." Ajjibawr laughed as though at a private joke.

"Herrard!" cried Dansen. "Herrard of Villavac! Is it you indeed?" And he leaned down from his saddle, peering ahead into the dark.

Herrard stepped up with the lantern, then shouted with pleased surprise. "Dansen! I thought you safe among your books in Tredana! How do you come to be here?" He clasped Dansen's hand warmly shaking it up and down for several minutes.

"It is too long a story for tonight," replied Dansen, "but you shall hear it soon."

Ajjibawr interrupted them. "Rassam," he said, "I must leave you now. I thought to stay the night, but I have had heavy news and must act upon it. Our brother Arbytis is in need of succor, and it may be I can help him. I see Dansen is your friend; he can tell you more." He looked up at Dastra. "Farewell, lady. I wish you well and a happier future than you have had past." Before she could answer, he spoke to Sibby, holding up his hand in good-bye. "So long as you have your horse, I know you will remember the Karabdu, and I hope for longer. Mayhap we shall meet again, by the grace of Vazdz. You are always welcome amongst us." Sibby bent down and hugged him, and her face brushed against his shaven raspy cheek. He smiled at her and turned to Dansen. "You will be able to tell Herrard everything. Although it was bad fortune brought you to us, I cannot regret your visit." He swung up into his saddle and briefly clasped Herrard's hands in farewell. Then he pivoted his tired horse around on its hind legs and urged it southward, followed by Ab'Bakr and Osmin and also the six others. Sibby felt empty to see him go.

There was silence, then Herrard spoke. "Come in where it is comfortable. I will put your horses in the pen and join you presently."

They dismounted and stretched their tired muscles, then Sibby sleepily followed Dastra into the cottage and Dansen came after ward. Talk could wait until morning.

THE EMPTY CITY
traditional: written anonymously by a Tredanan traveler
annotated by Skotla

Great the king	*who built this city*
Giants worked	*at his command*
cutting temples	*from the cliffside*
hollowing halls	*from solid stone*

Thirty times	*a tall man's height*
stands the statue	*he raised there*
Scorpions bow	*before his feet*
Grey wolves sing	*before its face*
. . . (ms. fragmentary)	
water from	*the lion's mouth*
fills the bowl	*and drowns in dust*

It is evident that he who wrote this poem describes a vision rather than a real city, since no such ruin exists in our world, as many travelers can aver. There is real truth in this poem, however, for all is vanity without the True Light and he who builds and calls not on Vazdz in the building accomplishes nothing though he thinks his work a mighty monument. Thus the wild beasts make mocking worship of the pagan's vaunted images, and thus the water from the lion's mouth, signifying temporal power, drowns in the dust of eternity, for he who dies without Vazdz is dead indeed.

Chapter Thirteen

The next morning both Sibby and Dastra slept late. There was a little loft at one end of the cabin's one large room with a ladder leading up to it, and Herrard had sent them up to bed as soon as he saw how tired they looked. When Sibby woke, she was aware of sunshine and birds singing, but no voices. Except for Dastra, the cottage was empty.

After lying still a few moments, she got up and carefully climbed down backward. There was water for washing by the front door, bread and cheese on the table, and wine in a crock on the floor. The front door stood open, and the outside air was warm and smelled beautiful. She was eating her second big piece of bread and cheese when she heard Dansen and Herrard returning. Herrard looked solemn, but he smiled when he saw her. "Up at last, little lady? I have been hearing much of you this past hour. And of your royal friend." He smiled at these last words and Sibby smiled with him. He was a big tall man with a square chin and light brown hair. "I only wish that happier circumstances had brought your visit. As it is, we must go straight to Tredana that you may tell of the peril in which the prince and his two friends stand." Herrard's mention of Leron began to cloud Sibby's fresh morning, but at that moment Dastra awoke and gave her something else to think about.

Dastra, who was daily becoming more tiresome, if this was possible, complained that she had not slept well. She complained about the Karabdu, and about breakfast, and she complained that they couldn't stay and rest. Only when Herrard explained the need for haste in cryptic fashion, briefly mentioning Mathon's nephew Ddiskeard, next in line to the throne, did Dastra show some slight interest.

While Dastra ate, Sibby listened to Dansen and Herrard talk, then interrupted them. "Have you been friends a long time? And what about the Karabdu? And Arbytis?"

Dansen set down the mug with which he had been gesturing. "Years ago, child, when we were young, though not so young as you . . ."

Herrard interrupted, "Twenty-eight years ago, exactly."

Dansen nodded. "Twenty-eight years ago, Herrard and I studied of the same teacher, together in Tredana. He did not find the same satisfaction I found in learning, however, and he set out to see things with his own eyes."

Herrard shook his head and laughed. "I did see many things, and most important perhaps was that I met Arbytis and learned his story. It was after the doomed Tredanan march on Treclere that he became One Eye, and it was I brought him back to the city and introduced him to Dansen, although not as Arbytis. For I knew he had special knowledge and memories that would prove useful to the prince in his growing."

"I knew his life and travels only in part," added Dansen. "I had no knowledge of his tie with the Karabdu until Leron mentioned it, no more than I had of yours."

Herrard said, "These matters are usually kept secret."

"But," Sibby said, puzzled, "I know I don't understand everything. Still I do know that it was Vazdz who destroyed Treglad, and separated Arbytis from his Lady, and it was Vazdz who made the Karabdu powerful and had them conquer everybody in the early days. So how can Arbytis be one of them?"

Herrard rubbed his forehead a moment and sighed. "I have studied the religion of the Karabdu for many years, making many translations and commentaries, and the more I study, the more I see that when they worshiped Vazdz as he told them to do, they did not truly prosper. Yes, yes, they had a great city, and power and wealth, but this was not what their souls craved. They needed to live with the desert and move with the seasons. And it seems that when they returned to this former life, they returned to the spirit of the days before Vazdz, even though they recognized not this change. But Arbytis saw it and knew it for what it was, so he freely became one of them by blood, although the name of Vazdz he would not speak."

Dastra broke in petulantly, "I thought you were all in a hurry. And yet you sit here and talk about the gods! If we must leave, we might as well leave soon."

Herrard pushed himself up from the table, nodding gravely. "Your highness speaks truly. We should be on our way."

Sibby followed him out into the sunlight and squinted her eyes. The air smelled even better outside, and in the short grass all around there were little yellow flowers like dandelions and buttercups. Her colt had been fed already, but she carefully rubbed him down before she saddled him. She was mounted and letting him stretch his legs when the others came from the hut.

As she watched, Herrard whistled and a big yellow dog came leaping up to him from among the grazing sheep. He leaned over and talked to the dog for a few minutes, then patted him on the head. "Fortunately, my dog is a better shepherd than I," he said, "and he will tend my flock for me while I am away." He helped Dansen saddle the other horses and load the packhorse. He then brought up his own, a heavyset chestnut with bulging muscles. "Ajjibawr would give me a finer steed," he said, "but I am a heavy man and need a heavy horse. The steeds of the Karabdu like not to have me ride them." And he pulled himself up and led the way down along a narrow track worn in the grass and the flowers.

Their way led them up into high, rolling pastureland, toward the mountains in the distance. Herrard's sheep had long ago shown him a narrow cleft through which a man might pass, and into this he led them. They were two days going through the mountains. During this time Herrard would not let them touch the stores the Karabdu had given them, making instead wonderful stews and soups from the wild vegetables and roots that grew along their path. To Dansen he spoke concerning some of his discoveries about plants useful for food and medicine. Dansen, delighted, made copious notes.

Two days further on, they were clearly nearing Tredana. Cultivated fields appeared around them, and farmhouses standing singly and in clusters. Sibby had become so accustomed to silent emptiness that the sounds of men ploughing, roosters crowing, dogs barking, and cows mooing in the field seemed very crowded. By the second morning, they could smell the sea, and before noon the towers of Tredana, standing high on cliffs overlooking the sea, were before them. The city had long since outgrown its walls, and a tangle of shops and houses and winding streets covered the surrounding hillside. Part of the castle was on the very edge of the cliff, and overlooked the quiet blue bay below where small fishing boats sailed in and out or peacefully bobbed at anchor. It was serene but alive with crying sea gulls and people selling things loudly in open market squares.

When they were near the foot of the hill, Herrard drew rein. "I need go no farther," he said, but Dansen disagreed.

"You have not known the prince as I have," he said, "but Arbytis was your blood brother. We may need your help."

Herrard considered. "It was for my brother I meant to leave. But two may do what one cannot. I can no longer bear city life, yet I will wait for you one fortnight before setting out myself. You know the Circle Inn on the road to Villavac? You may find me there." And with a brief salute he turned away from the city and rode west.

As they rode into the city, they had to push through crowds of people. In every open area, foodstuffs and various goods were spread out for sale, and there was hardly any room for travelers. It seemed very lively to Sibby, but Dansen was puzzled. "I cannot think why the city is so grim," he said at length. "It may be some tragedy has struck and we know it not." The castle gates confirmed his fears, for where the royal banners were usually hung, there was draped a black pall instead, and no flags flew from the many turrets and towers. Sibby felt uneasy, but as they rode into the large windy courtyard, she squeaked with surprise and jumped off Leron's back, dropping the reins behind her. Dansen looked to see her being swung up into the air by a tall black-bearded man: Gannoc. He laughed out loud with delight and jumped down also. Only Dastra sat rigidly on her horse, her pale cheeks flushed with embarrassment.

"Gannoc!" cried Sibby. "You're here! Oh, is Mara here, too?"

"Indeed she is, and to see you safe will make her happier than she has been for many a week. We believed you dead in the flood."

"We thought the same about you, and after the Karabdu rescued us they went and looked for you, but they didn't find anything."

"We were saved by trappers from Villavac—real trappers this time. But enough talking. You must come and rest and eat. Mara will not thank me for keeping you out here." Gannoc nodded courteously to Dastra and took her horse's bridle. "I can see you have been among the Karabdu. These are the finest horses in the city."

Dansen collected his wits. "But what tragedy has struck here in our absence? Why the mourning and black drapery?"

Gannoc looked into his eyes with sorrow. "Could you not guess? It is for the prince. Mathon's council has proclaimed him dead." He hushed Sibby's anxious questions. "No, we do not know anything further than what we all saw with our eyes by the lake. It is a political decision, made for sundry reasons. But we shall wait to speak of that privately." And he led them down a brick passageway into a maze of alleys, all part of the castle. By a large gate, he halted. "I live here now, in surprising state. The king has been more generous to me than I fear I deserve. But it is good for Mara. My grooms will take your horses." Even as he spoke, two boys came up and led their horses away. "They will bring your things in. Come; Mara will be overjoyed to see you."

To Sibby, his house did not seem very large, six rooms perhaps, which overlooked their own stableyard in front and an enclosed garden in back. This connected with passageways leading to the rest of the castle complex. Before they had crossed the front yard, the door opened and Mara came out, still holding the flagon and the cup she had been pouring when she saw them from the window. These she dropped, hugging Sibby to her breast. Mara even kissed Dastra, but the princess unbent very little. They were all talking at once as they went inside.

While they were sitting in Mara's long, low kitchen, Gannoc disappeared. He returned presently. "The king will see us tonight directly after supper," he said. "He thanks Vazdz for your safe return, and offers the princess that refuge and home which Leron promised her."

Dastra tossed her head. "I should hope so! I had expected to be brought to the king at once, but I suppose this will have to do." Gannoc looked at Dansen with sympathy.

Over cold meat pie and wine, they told their stories to each other. Sibby and Dansen learned that Gannoc had been struck senseless and had lain two days asleep while Mara, battered but uninjured, did her best to shelter his body from the sun and find food for herself. Gannoc took Mara's hand and laughed. "She almost killed the trapper who found me. She returned to find him bending over me, and had he been a second slow in turning, she would have had his brains out with a rock."

Mara blushed and tried to look angry. "You were being no help to me! And besides, he did turn and identify himself, so no harm done."

Gannoc and Mara in their turn listened with great interest to Dansen's narrative, in particular when he told of Simirimia's visit. They would have talked on further, but Mara finally hushed them. "There will be much time to talk later. Now we must rest, so to be fresh when the king commands our attention tonight." And she led them to their rooms, Gannoc and Dansen still talking as they went.

When Sibby awoke later, it was dark, and for a moment she could not think where she was. The door opened and a soft light was cast upon the walls. Mara was standing there, holding a candle. She came over and touched Sibby lightly with her hand. "Time to get up," she said. "The king expects us in half an hour." She put the candle down on the plain wooden dresser and helped Sibby wash and dress and fix her hair. Mara exclaimed at the Karabdin dress and looked at her critically. "My little girl is growing up," she said, and Sibby just nodded, remembering the face in the mirror. She was glad there wasn't one in this room.

Downstairs in the house, lamps were lighted and the curtains drawn, and it looked cozy and peaceful. The warmth from the fireplace felt good. It had seemed chilly for spring-time until it occurred to Sibby that of course this house had no heating except for fires. Dastra had dressed with great care and looked a princess in truth. Mara eyed her and nodded. "The king will approve of you, there is no doubt." Then she gave them heavy cloaks to wear against the evening air, and they stepped out into the garden and through it to the passageways beyond. Gannoc led them swiftly through the maze to a small door set in a featureless high brick wall. It gave on a corridor hung with tapestries, and at the end two guards stood holding spears. They saluted Gannoc and stood back for him. He gathered his party together, then opened the door and ushered them in.

"Your majesty," he cried in a clear voice, "here we are as I said."

Sibby wasn't sure what she had expected: probably an old

man who looked something like Leron. She was not prepared
for what she saw. Mathon Breadgiver was immense, not
grossly fat, but tall, and soft and plump all over, with a long
white beard and hair and shaggy black eyebrows. He was
sunk in a large padded chair that had gilded scrollwork forming a little canopy over his head. His large feet, in velvet
boots, were propped on the low fender of a blazing fire. He
held his arms out to Dansen and shouted, "Come here,
m'boy. God's blood, it does m'heart good to see you! Can't
get up, the gout you know." Dansen hurried up and tried to
bow, but Mathon insisted on hugging him to his massive
bosom. "Damme, but you scholars are a tough lot. Let me
have a look at you!" And he held Dansen back at arm's
length. "Hmmm, yes, older and thinner I've no doubt, but
Dansen unmistakably. These nine months past have been dull
indeed without your readings at breakfast—What? And
who's this? Ah, the little princess in the tower." And he held
his hands out to Dastra, whom Mara had led forward.
Mathon grasped her slender white hands in his pudgy ones
and kissed her cheek loudly. "Most, most welcome, m'dear.
Life here's been devilish slow without m'son. Do us good to
have some young blood, eh?" He was beaming at Dastra as
he spoke, but Sibby could hear the tremble in his voice.

Then Gannoc had his hand on her shoulder and was gently
leading her up to the king. As the king embraced her, she
found he smelled pleasantly of lavender water, and that his
beard was very soft and silky. His plump hands were surprisingly strong. She looked up shyly and found his dark eyes
twinkling at her. "Here's the child I've been hearing of from
Gannoc! Just turned up on the beach, eh? Well, well. You remind me of someone, child, eh, Gannoc? Look at her eyes—
black, ain't they? Puts me in mind of Armon. I'll wager you
have the temper that goes with them, what?" Sibby
blushed—at home she had lost her temper a lot, although
since she came to the new world she'd been too busy or too
tired most of the time. "I thought so, never fails. 'Hazel eyes,
can surprise; eyes of brown, never frown; black regard, be on
guard!' That's what my nurse used to say."

Mathon suddenly reached down into his gown and, pulling
out a large handkerchief, blew his nose. "I knew Armon'd
burn himself out, but Leron!" He blew his nose again and
rubbed his eyes. Gannoc hastily went and poured out wine on

the sideboard, first for the king and then for the others. They drank in silence, but Dastra could not keep from yawning behind her hand. Mathon, who'd been staring into the fire, with his handkerchief dangling from one hand and his silver goblet held limply in the other, roused himself. "I'm sorry, m'dear. Didn't mean to keep you up. Just like someone to talk to sometimes."

Dastra smiled at him and touched his hand. "I'm sorry, sire, but I am fatigued. If you could have someone show me to my room, I will try to be better company tomorrow."

Mathon beamed at her and pinched her cheek; he did not notice her flinch. "Gannoc, call me nevvy here. Bound to be somewheres about—can't get rid of him now he smells the throne in his future. Me new heir," he explained to the others. "M'dead brother's one and only. Younger than Leron, but makes no odds—acted like a damned careful old man since he was a babe in arms. King Ddiskeard indeed! Splendor of god!" He swallowed his wine in one gulp as Gannoc reappeared with a languid young man at his elbow.

Ddiskeard was carefully dressed in black, and he had a pointed black beard and skinny moustache. Sibby was reminded of Mathon's nursery rhyme as she looked into his light hazel eyes. "May I be of service, uncle?" he asked, bowing smoothly before him.

"Make yourself useful for once around here. This lady," he gestured to Dastra, "is the princess Dastra, daughter of Treclere. Leron's girl. Well, she's here if he ain't. Might as well take her to her rooms and introduce her to her servants. Promised Leron to take her in. Liven the place up."

"Indeed," said Ddiskeard, bowing to Dastra with a smile of appreciation. She smiled and held out her hand. They were both smiling to themselves as he led her out of the room.

Mathon looked kindly at Sibby. "Suppose you'll want to run along, too." She shook her head.

"I'd like to stay and talk if you want to."

He took her hand and patted it. "Good girl, Mara told me you were a sweet child. She said she missed you as though you were her own." At the thought, he paused and blew his nose again. Then he looked up. "Gannoc, bring up chairs. No need for you all to stand around like a damned bunch of courtiers. We're all friends here, thank the gods." So they sat in a ragged semicircle by the fire, holding newly filled wine goblets, and the king gave a sigh of content and settled deeper into his chair.

"It's good to see friends. Yes, yes. Especially when you're king. Another day spent with those scurvy dogs in m'council and I'd abdicate and go be a hermit. Yes, by the fire of god!" And he straightened up and pounded his fist on the edge of his chair. No one seemed surprised by this; Sibby realized that Mathon, too, had black eyes. "But no sense in telling you my troubles. It's your stories I must hear, yours little lady and yours, Dansen. Which reminds me, Gannoc told me of the loss of your records. I'll see you have m'library undisturbed, aye, and as many scribes as you need to take down your notes."

Dansen was touched. "Your majesty is too kind. But before we speak of that, there is news I would beg of you. How comes it that the prince is thus treated as one dead? We saw him taken, it is true, but taken not slain. And that which we saw in the camp of the Karabdu makes us suppose him even now a prisoner of Simirimia. He needs a rescue, not eulogies!"

Tears gathered in Mathon's eyes, but he did not turn his head away. "I know," he finally said in a very old voice. "I know it well. But how shall I save him? Shall I move this bulk of mine to the back of some draft horse, and make m'way to Treclere, and beg for my son? Will that rescue him, think you?"

Dansen was distressed. "But sir, your armies! Leron was ever a popular prince!"

"Aye, but Armon's foolishness these seventeen years since has spoiled their stomach for marching on Treclere. M'poor wife's brother was not the only one who paid for that expedition with his life. They will protect me here, right loyally; they will not attack Treclere. The rogues in council are right in this, for if I order and the army refuses, the throne will be like a chair with three rotten legs. You have another heir, they say— or, mayhap Leron will return as he went, with no help from us. The dogs!" And he covered his eyes with his hand, making his seal ring flash in the firelight.

Sibby burst out, "Won't anyone try to save him? I don't mean the army, I mean some friends. Maybe they could sneak into Treclere or something. You can't just leave him there! You can't!" Her voice broke in tears, but she was too upset to feel embarrassment. "He's your son, he's the prince! Doesn't anybody care about him?" As she stood in front of the king, shaking with rage and tears and terrible sorrow for Leron, Mathon began to cry also, grotesquely, not hidden behind his handkerchief but openly in the plain firelight, his full face crumpled up and his chest heaving. Gannoc went up and stood by him, a hand on his shoulder, and Mathon took his hand.

"I'm an old dog, Gannoc, with nothing left but my bark. I cannot save my son." He shook his head slowly from side to side, then put one hand out to Sibby and squeezed hers gently. "I know you love my son, and I love you for it. But we are powerless. You saw Simirimia among the Karabdu, and she was a woman. But in her own city she is power itself, and has been for a thousand years. Poor Armon learned that to his cost, and two thousand men with him. Young, I might have fought her though I lost; old, there is no chance at all."

Mathon turned, looking again into the fire, and Gannoc signaled the others to leave. "We will not keep you further, sire," he said. "Our stories can wait until tomorrow." The king blew his nose again and nodded blindly.

"We hold a banquet tomorrow in memory of my son. I shall see you then."

Sibby looked back once more as they went out and saw Mathon sitting forward in his chair, his head buried in his hands and darkly silhouetted against the roaring fire.

From THE SONG OF ARMON
by Arbytis

Ms. in the private collection of Prince Leron, son of Mathon Breadgiver

They who went to Treclere were strong and young
they all were heroes famous in many a story
Armon the prince, his brave blood brothers with him but of
        two thousand only two returned

They who went to Treclere were strong and young
but their beds were made in the earth with no arising
They lay with wolves who thought to lie with maidens and
*   of two thousand only two returned*

Two thousand marched but only two returned
My brother and I, a poet grey with years:
Weakness and age make mock of strength and youth for
*   they who went to Treclere were strong and*
*   young*

Chapter Fourteen

Dansen spent that night with Gannoc and Mara, because his own quarters in the palace would not be ready until the morrow. There was no question about Sibby: Mara would not let her stay anywhere else. After breakfast, Dansen explained to Sibby about Armon and his armies, as she had asked him. Leron had sung of these things to her long ago, but she remembered the story only vaguely. Dansen reminded her how Simirimia had seen Armon in a vision and desired him for herself, sending him fair messages how they might ally themselves together against Mathon and rule Tredana and Treclere as one realm. And she also promised him lasting life. Armon, quick to anger, had brought the armies of Tredana under his own leadership to attack Treclere and humble the queen. But his armies did not return, and the body of Armon was never found.

"I see what the king meant about having a temper! In a way the whole disaster was partly Armon's fault. It's different with Leron—he wasn't attacking."

"No, that would not be Leron's way. Mathon would say it is because his eyes are brown. But whatever Simirimia's reasons, she has the prince and will continue to keep him unless forced otherwise, and force it seems is something the Tredanans will not use."

"I don't understand why the queen wants him. I know she has some sort of feud with Arbytis, and of course she's an enemy of Tredana, but what good does it do her to have Leron? She hasn't asked for ransom, or threatened to kill him, or anything."

Dansen mused quietly. "Her reasons may be personal. Prince Leron resembles his uncle greatly." Sibby looked up, startled.

Dansen went on, "An alliance between herself and the prince would give her a rightful claim to the Tredanan throne, without having to fight for it. This may be her intention."

Gannoc spoke up. "The same has occurred to the king's council. For this reason they proclaimed Leron dead, thinking that if he be dead in law, Simirimia must fight to prove her claim in any case. And this they feel she is not prepared to do, since it is widely held that her powers decrease the further she removes herself from her city. Many think Ddiskeard the true heir in any case, since only Leron's premature birth made him the elder. And thus Ddiskeard now becomes true heir whatever we or Mathon may think of him."

He spoke to Sibby gently. "Think you child, this measure may well be the saving of Leron, for it renders him useless to the dreaded queen."

"Or it might kill him! She won't need him now. And besides, even if he escapes, he'll have to come back and fight with Ddiskeard."

"Not if Mathon is still alive. He is old, but his wits are sound, and his heart is with his son."

Sibby bit back the argument that was on her tongue. It had suddenly come to her, with immense clarity, that it was up to her to save the prince.

As she dressed for dinner, she continued to turn the new idea over in her mind, examining it from every angle. Rianna had said something about enlightenment and attainment; what could be a better achievement than the rescue of the prince? Sibby could understand that it was better to lose one man than a whole army, but this particular man was someone she liked. It was certainly worth risking herself. She began to get so excited that her fingers shook as she fastened her dress. This could explain why she had been sent. She had been sure there must be a reason. It was her own special destiny. And so easy. At least at first. Herrard would be waiting to leave for Treclere because he was bound to Arbytis. She would travel with him. All she had to do was get suitable clothes, gather a few supplies, and ride away. Simirimia herself had given her the excuse for coming to Treclere, when she invited Dansen. She would just say that something had happened to him on the way.

Mara was pleased to see Sibby in such good spirits, and once more exclaimed at how grown-up she looked in her long white dress. This time Gannoc led them down a different route, to one of the main gates, and they were passed through with much ceremony into a small enclosed garden. The grass was brilliantly green, there were flower beds, and through two angled windows in one wall they could see the harbor far below, blue and sparkling in the morning sun. They stood a moment looking out and smelling the fresh salt air, and then went in through a tall glassed door and down a corridor into the great hall.

At one time the hall had been brightly painted inside, with murals depicting the glories of Tredanan heroes covering the walls and ceiling. Later kings had carelessly opened new windows and boarded up old ones, made two new fireplaces, and changed the position of the doors. They had also let the painting fade with time and dirt and black smoke from their fires. The walls still retained a dim feeling of presence, however, a feeling of people, horses, and trees lurking almost out of sight wherever one turned. In the center of the hall a long table was spread; and at it Mathon was already seated, in a canopied chair as before. His wine steward was carefully dipping a long white feather into the royal goblet; Dansen explained to Sibby that it was a specific against poison.

Ddiskeard sat on Mathon's right hand and Dastra on his left. Other notables were ranged along the sides in descending order of importance, but Gannoc and his party had been given special seats opposite the royal group. Mathon looked quite jovial as he beamed at them across the table, bending now and again to hear what Dastra said softly in his ear. From time to time Dastra would catch Ddiskeard's eye and they would smile at each other. She did not look very bereaved. In fact, as Sibby looked around, she noticed that most people did not look particularly sad. They were chatting with their neighbors and drinking wine and picking their bread until the meat arrived. At the far end of the hall, there was a small forlorn group of musicians trying to be heard; she could only see that they were playing.

Silence fell during the meat course. The music could be heard faintly. When the meat had been removed and new wine poured, everyone looked at the king expectantly. Mathon did not rise, but he straightened in his chair and placed his hands against the table to brace himself. In a controlled voice, he announced that his dead brother's son was now his heir and that they should consider Ddiskeard their host. Then he relaxed back into his chair and tried to put on a cheerful look without great success. Sibby recalled that Leron had said the Tredanans were poor at pretense.

Mathon's announcement was obviously not news to the throng, and all eyes turned to Ddiskeard. He was still dressed in black, with silver embroidery, and the rings on his hands sparkled. He bowed graciously right and left, and it struck Sibby that his response was greater than the ovation. If the people did not look distressed, they did not look overjoyed either: Ddiskeard's reception was polite, no more.

"Lords, ladies, and gentlemen," he said, "dear fellow subjects of King Mathon, I regret having to speak to you on such a melancholy subject. As you know, my cousin Leron has been cut down in the flower of his youth, and I now stand, all unworthy, in his stead. I humbly accept the honor my uncle has conferred on me, and I can only hope that someday I will hold a place in all your hearts as warm and revered as did my noble cousin." There was only a slight response to this, and it seemed to Sibby that a shade of annoyance passed across Ddiskeard's face. "I have one pleasure this sad day, and that is to present you with an exiled princess who claims asylum in our kingdom." He gestured, and Dastra rose with a pretty blush and lowered eyes. "Her highness, Princess Dastra, the affianced bride of my royal cousin. Her rescue was his last brave deed, and to protect her he gave even his life. His last wish was to see her safe in Tredana, and I know you will welcome her as heartily as I do." The response to this was far more enthusiastic, and Dastra sat down smiling, shaking her head at requests to speak. This final shyness quite won everybody's heart.

Sibby was puzzled and whispered to Dansen, "How come they're all pretending Leron's dead? I thought it was just a legal decision, for politics."

Dansen answered, "Gannoc has explained to me that the decision was made by the council in closed session. They thought it easier than telling the full truth to the people, and felt Ddiskeard would command more respect in this way."

Sibby said, shocked, "That's terrible! They have the right to know!"

Dansen sighed, "I agree. But Ddiskeard has many friends in the council, and his opinions carry weight whether he or some other expresses them. I wonder, though, if Mathon will be able to carry the secret for long."

Sibby looked up and saw that Ddiskeard was looking at them. She flushed guiltily, but he was smiling at Dansen. "I would introduce to you a companion of the prince whom we thought lost, Dansen the Learned. He has an interesting tale to tell." While Dansen told of their sojourn among the Karabdu, Sibby's attention wandered, and she began refining her plan. She noticed, though, that Dansen did not speak of Simirimia's visit; it was probably another state secret that the council wanted to keep to itself to ponder. Thinking of the Karabdu and her stay there gave her an idea: she would ask Mara to help her get new riding clothes after the Tredanan fashion, so she could exercise her horse. That way it would be easy to leave without anyone's noticing.

As she was thinking this, Dansen finished and gestured to her. She realized he must have mentioned her, so she rose and bowed and sat down again very quickly. It looked like a lot more people when you were standing up and they were all looking at you.

After the speeches, it was time for the bards. They sang their poems rather than reciting them, accompanied by harp in sort of a random way that was different from Leron's playing and singing. Dansen explained that the difference was real: Leron had not been a poet, but a singer, a maker of short songs and airs. These were professionals who remembered long stories in verse that could go on for hours and also made up new ones about different events. There would be a new one someday about Leron, too, he said and sighed.

Sibby began listening with interest, but the first poet, a favorite of Ddiskeard's, was just terrible. He sang a hymn in honor of the new heir to the throne. The next poet was no better, and after a while Sibby began to feel uncomfortable. At least the first one had been short: this one went on and on. An hour had gone by, and the bard was still chanting, his lines interspersed with soft thrums on the harp. Then it was an hour and a half. She looked around and saw that except for Mathon, who was frankly asleep, everyone was listening with great attention. Even Dastra. It was incredible. She whispered in Mara's ear that she had to leave, and Mara, guessing a more obvious reason, led her out quietly. When they were back at the house, Mara admitted that she was tired, so they both sat down in the kitchen and waited for the others to return. It was almost an hour before they came, so Sibby was glad of her lie.

Next day, Sibby put her scheme into effect. Mara was glad to help her find new riding clothes, a woolen kilt like the men's traveling outfits, with a long skirt to go with it, and new boots. That same day, Sibby smuggled some cheese from the dinner table and packed it in her saddlebags along with a few odds and ends of clothing. She also had a Karabdin knife that had been given her by one of the tribe's young men. She put her saddlebag under the bed, near the wall. She wasn't worried about warmth, because her fleece saddle blanket was big enough to roll up in at night, and she also had the long Karabdin jacket.

That day she rode for about two hours, out of the city along the Villavac road, and returned in good time for supper. She meant to leave secretly, but this would be her alibi in case she was discovered. So she told everyone how much fun she had had, and how much she looked forward to the same next day; and when Mara kissed her good night, she hugged her hard in return, feeling mean and ungrateful.

Next morning, Sibby wandered about the city for a few hours. With some money Gannoc had given her, she bought a few things she thought she might want, and a bird made out of blue glass as a present for Mara. Then after lunch, when she should have been resting, she got up and dressed very quietly. She put Telyon carefully into her bag and set the bird on the bed. She tried to write a note, sitting at the little writing table by the window, but she hadn't written anything for a long time, and she was clumsy with the feather pen. *"Dear Mara and Gannoc, Thank you very much for everything. You have been very kind to me. The bird is a present for Mara, because she likes blue. I am going to try and save Leron. I hope I will see you again. Much, much love, Sibby. xxxxxxx (these mean kisses)."* She knew her fifth-grade teacher wouldn't have approved of it, or even her fourth-grade teacher, but it would have to do. She picked up her saddlebag and crept out.

Out in the stableyard it was warm and silent, and the grooms were also asleep as she had hoped. Leron was glad to see her and was very noisy while she saddled him and strapped the bags in place. She had to put her hand over his nose while she led him out through the yard, but she got through the gate undiscovered. Then she was off. She picked her way through the drowsy afternoon streets and market-places, coming at length onto the road to Villavac. Somewhere ahead was the Circle Inn, and Herrard would be waiting. She began humming, and Leron lengthened his stride into a canter, tossing his head and pretending to snatch at the bit and enjoying the bright spring weather. She was on her way at last.

HYMN
by Kybberus, Bard by Appointment to Prince Ddiskeard

Grant me, O gods, a tongue as honey sweet
To pour my praises at great Ddiskeard's feet.
For when black sorrow gloomed the weeping land
His sun dispelled these shades on every hand.

When that the flowering branch of Mathon's root
Fell all up-wrenched, a dry and withered shoot,
Who calmed the troubled people's stormy tears
By pouring oil on their tumultuous fears?

Who smoothed the way before their stumbling feet?
Who led them as a shepherd leads his sheep,
Out of the dark and pain of sorry dreaming
Into a pasture green and pleasant seeming?

Ddiskeard it was, that great and glorious prince
Who heralds with his rise (but few days since)
A new and prosperous time for all the land,
Scattering blessings with an open hand.

THE GREAT QUEEN

Chapter Fifteen

It was a great deal further to the Circle Inn than Sibby had supposed. As the road led away from the city, it became rougher and more rutted. Near Tredana, a smooth surface had been built up with sand and stood some few feet above the surrounding fields, but out among the farms the road had worn into the ground leaving a steep bank on either side. Roots of trees and hedges had been left exposed where spring rainstorms washed down. Sibby pulled her colt back to a jog because of the stones and uneven footing, and he fretted impatiently, hopping with his hind legs and trying to lengthen his stride out into a canter again.

Because she was paying attention to the path in front of her horse, Sibby did not notice when the cultivated fields were first left behind. By standing up in her stirrups she could see over the bushes that lined the road and into the fields beyond; when she did this she found herself in the midst of rough pastureland. The landscape was very uneven, streaked with green and brown, and sheep moved over it slowly in small clusters and by ones and twos. Above the shelter of the sunken road, it was very windy.

Later, a fog moved in from the far distance, darkening the sky and carrying a promise of rain. The wind became chilly and began finding its way through the bushes and along the road. Slowly the horizon closed in around her. The fog was condensing into rain about her when Sibby saw what must be the inn about a mile ahead of her, dark against the dimly lit western horizon. The road had come out almost level with the land and was climbing a long gentle slope; the inn was at the top. It grew suddenly quite wet, and Leron sprang ahead as she set him free at last. They made the top of the hill in great style, galloping flat out.

Gravel sprayed out behind them as they dashed into the roofless courtyard. The inn was built like a large square C, with rooms in back, kitchens on one side, and stables on the other. In front of the entrance, the inn sign stood on its post, creaking back and forth in the increasing downpour. Sibby jumped down and handed her reins to the stableboy who had come stumbling up. She tried to sound self-confident and grown-up. "Please rub down my horse and bring my saddle-bags inside for me." She gave him a coin, one of the last that Gannoc had given her to spend; the memory made her feel guilty. Then she hurried to the main door, hoping that Herrard had waited.

Inside, she gave a sigh of relief. It was warm and dry, if a little smoky, and Herrard's long length was stretched out in a chair by the fire, asleep. A mug of ale was set down, half full, on the floor beside him. Eagerly she ran up and put her hand on his shoulder. He surprised her by coming to as quickly and completely as a wild animal. He sat up, shook his head once, and said, "Good, you are here soon. How many have come?"

Sibby, taken aback, said truthfully, "I'm the only one. It's kind of a long story." She suddenly felt little and foolish, and waited for him to laugh, but he only looked at her closely and nodded.

"I must hear it. But first, dry yourself and put some food in your stomach." He motioned her to the other chair by the fire and went to find the landlord. She was shaking her wet hair loose in the warmth of the flames when he returned, carrying the cold remains of lunch on a wooden plate in one hand and a mug of weak ale in the other. The landlord followed after, with a small table, which he set by the chair and briskly wiped clean with the edge of his long greasy sleeve. He would have stayed on hand, but Herrard dismissed him with a nod and a coin.

Sibby found she was ravenous, and Herrard watched with satisfaction while she ate. She was wiping up the last bit of cold gravy with her bread when he spoke. "Now, child, perhaps you have strength to tell me what has transpired in Tredana and what plans have been made for the rescue of our friends." He stood leaning against the mantel with one foot on the raised hearth, and Sibby could see no expression on his shadowed face as he listened to her description of the past few days. When she mentioned Ddiskeard, he muttered something under his breath, but he told her to go on, so she also mentioned some of her own ideas and a little of what the Lady of the Rock, Rianna, had said to her.

Herrard thought for a few minutes. "It may well be you are right. I cannot say. It mislikes me to risk a child on such a journey as this, and yet I can see you are determined whether I accompany you or no. And I am equally determined to go for my brother's sake." Sibby looked at him hopefully. "I say, let us wait another day and see if any others appear. It will give you time to reconsider, and today is a poor one for setting out in any case."

"But what if Gannoc comes to take me back to Tredana?"

"You are a child, but you are not his child. In this world no one has the right to command you. Whether you like it or not, you must henceforth make your own decisions." He smiled down at her. "You may find this new estate quite trying in some respects, albeit exciting in others."

Sibby nodded. "I'm afraid that you'll have to take one responsibility for me."

"And what will that be?"

"I don't have much money left. Would you mind very much paying for my room tonight? Because otherwise I'll have to set out this evening even if you wait until tomorrow."

"I think that I can manage this once," said Herrard, and put his hand lightly on her shoulder.

That evening was very quiet, for there were no other travelers at Circle Inn. While Herrard mused in front of the fire, his legs stretched out before him, Sibby wandered restlessly about the room, examining the glazed plates on the heavy oak dresser, fingering the pewter platters ranged along the mantel, and trying out the various hard wooden benches and chairs for comfort. The ceiling was low and raftered, the plaster between the beams dark with years of smoke, and the windows had been made out of many small bits of distorted glass. "How can they make a living with his inn if there aren't any guests?" asked Sibby, after checking to make sure Herrard was not asleep. He spoke without looking up.

"At certain seasons they have many guests, bringing produce from Villavac to Tredana, or returning to the countryside, money in hand. Also, travelers commonly stop here for refreshment whether or not they stay. The inn has been here all my life, and long before. And if the Players arrive tomorrow, then you will see a bustle indeed."

"Players?" asked Sibby. "Oh yes, I remember. Leron talked about them. They tell fortunes, don't they?"

"More than that," replied Herrard. "The Players are those who live not in one place as do the Tredanans, nor yet do they follow the seasons. Rather, they travel from town to town, and from village to smaller village, performing acts of skill and trickery, playing out scenes of passion and buffoonery in courts and innyards, winning thus a meager livelihood in money and food."

"That's right," said Sibby. "I remember Leron said that the Tredanans were never good at acting, because they couldn't compete with the skills of the Players."

"Indeed, their skills are many and varied. I have found them to be good friends in trouble, but then I have many strange friends. I hope they do come tomorrow, for they are oddly gifted concerning the future, and may tell us something of use concerning the trip to come."

Soon afterward they went to bed. The landlord gave them each a very small candle, and Herrard explained to Sibby that it would just give her time to get into bed before it went out. It was to keep guests from wasting time and candle wax. Her room was opposite Herrard's in the crooked low-ceilinged upstairs hall. There seemed to be only six or seven rooms, but Sibby did not get much of a look at hers before the candle guttered and she had to scramble into bed.

The sun coming in strongly through the uncurtained window woke her up. Her room was small, and she was surprised to see it had several beds wedged into it besides hers, which was closest the door. The walls and sloping ceiling were white plaster, the floor bare wood, but outside the little window were beautiful scarlet geraniums in a window box. She ran over and looked out and smelled the fresh morning air. The view stretched bare and lovely as far as she could see across rough rolling pastureland, with occasional trees in small bent-over clumps. A tiny dot of color caught her eye, and she leaned out to see what it could be. Far down the road, where it was sunken and hidden beneath hedges, bright colors flickered and sunlight flashed on metal and she thought she could hear faint music on the breeze. The Players were on their way. She hurried into her clothes and went down to breakfast.

Herrard was already by the fire, and breakfast had been ordered. He brought out a leather pouch and began making

Karabdin coffee in a small pot begged from the landlord. "This is one vice I cannot shake," he said. "Will you join me in it, or was your stay in the desert too brief to accustom you?"

"We drink coffee in my world too," said Sibby, not feeling it necessary to add that children usually did not. She had become quite fond of Karabdin coffee. She added, "I think the Players must be coming. I could see something on the road from Villavac, and I think I heard music."

"Yes," said Herrard, "they are on their way. I went out to meet them this dawn and found they were an unfamiliar sept, although kin to a group I know well. Their leader is named Ginas, and she seems a wise and able woman."

"Woman?"

"Of course," said Herrard. "Among the Players it is said men do three things well: carrying, quarreling, and casting quoits." He suddenly grinned. "I have often noticed in my wanderings that those in authority, whether for good or for ill, can give the most excellent reasons why others are not." And he shrugged his shoulders.

It was easy enough to tell when the Players arrived. The quiet innyard was suddenly full of animals and people. There was hammering and banging as they set up their carts along one wall to make a sort of stage. Horses neighed, dogs barked, donkeys brayed, and ten or twenty chickens flapped in and around everybody's legs. Despite the babble of voices and seeming confusion, the stage and several small booths were quickly set up and decorated with wooden signs and carved symbols. Within an hour of arriving, performers were up on the platform dancing and singing. The landlord looked pleased. "Soon the inn will be full to bursting. It is well for your comfort that you leave tonight, for I doubt not that I'll be sleeping them four to a bed before midnight."

Herrard laughed and nodded. "Of that I have no doubt. It played a part in my plans, you may be sure."

Sibby didn't know how the word was spread, but it wasn't long before the first farmers began arriving. They set down their baskets of vegetables and eggs on the cobblestones and watched with open mouths as the Players skillfully mimed various scenes, from time to time breaking into song and dance. Sibby watched, as fascinated as the rest, for about twenty minutes, accepting a handful of nuts to eat from a motherly woman standing by her. She looked around at a touch on her arm and saw Herrard standing by her.

"Ginas has read my future for me; she will do yours if you come now." Sibby followed him through the crowd to an enclosed wagon standing alone near the entrance to the inn. Herrard smiled encouragement. "I will wait for you here. Heed well what she says."

Sibby's heart beat faster as she stepped up into the wagon and the faded dark velvet curtain fell to behind her. The inside was lit only by a small lamp on Ginas's table and by the sunlight that outlined the dark curtained windows. Ginas turned the lamp up and the room brightened. The Player was as old as Sibby had expected but still quite beautiful, dressed simply in a plain black sleeveless robe with her white hair hanging loosely down her back. There were silver chains around her neck and waist and a big glassy ring on her left hand. It glowed blue as she beckoned Sibby to sit down. Ginas looked into her ring a moment, and then, with greater intensity, at Sibby.

"For you, child," she said in a low voice, "I will read the cards of my people that was the Book of the Temple Ornat, the one and twenty-one images and the four truthful suits. We will spread a lamp and see what kindles it." As she spoke, she shuffled a pack of large cards between her hands with a smooth rippling gesture; she had Sibby cut them three times, and she quickly laid them out on the dull red cloth. "The three of your past, the oil in the lamp," she murmured, and then continued, "the one of your present state, the wick, and above igniting by two influences the three that stand for future. And here is the flame, the one above all forever. But where is the spark? Here, one and two and three." And before Sibby's eyes, the cards were set out in the shape of a lamp, in five rows centered above each other. The last three were put down separately on the left side.

The backs of the cards were plain, and Sibby was struck by their beauty and color as Ginas turned them over. The images reminded her of something she had seen once, long ago. The bottom row showed a wheel, a broken empty tower, and a figure that was two women in one. Above a beautifully moving picture of the sea stood by itself, and above that two people with their arms entwined and a woman like Ginas walking along with a lion leaping beside her. Above these were three cards, a flowering bush that seemed rooted in a dark, dead human figure, a cold white moon shining above a dark tower by a black river, and a dragon pierced to the heart, blood flowing. The most beautiful card was at the top, a white bird wreathed in golden flames, crying great tears like crystal while its wings curved gloriously above its head. Sibby gasped at its beauty, and was surprised to see Ginas start also as she turned it over. The three other cards were plainer but still strange to Sibby, six silver ships, eight golden rings, and a spear.

Ginas took Sibby's hand in her own, her forefinger pressed against the leaping pulse. "There is much to be seen here, much to be read. It is a fierce lamp to burn for so young a woman. Fate has spun you around on a wheel and spoken to you in the dark. You have seen the destruction of hopes you thought were well founded, and been led astray. Now you are changing as the sea changes, bringing together three of the four, the breath of air bringing water upon the earth. It may be that what I say today will influence your thinking, for the Player stands on your right hand here. Yet stronger than I is the card on your left, the contract of one with another. For this you will face peril, witnessing the destruction of innocence and the deception of the moon, and yet the final outcome will be resurrection as from an opened grave. This is a strange reading for a child, but strangest of all is that the Kermyrag should be your flame, for he is rarely to be found though I should spread the cards for a king or high priest. In him all elements are united, his house is in the five winds, he stands for truth and will and sacrifice and the mingling of forces to a positive end. Let us see what has sparked this reading." Ginas turned to the last three cards. "The six of ships. Here I see vanished childhood, the past put away, and new surroundings. The eight of rings signifies learning of new skills to some larger purpose than simple knowledge. But here is the best sign, the single spear showing the triumph of hate and love to an unguessable degree." Ginas paused and held up her left hand before Sibby's eyes. "Look now into the stone, and tell me what is imaged there."

Sibby, entranced by Gina's soft speaking, the dim light, and the beautiful images, did so. It was blue as water and deep as the sea, drawing her into its depths. A cold wind cut through her, and she seemed surrounded by ice, ice that glittered gold and white in freezing leaping flame around her. Tears fell and steamed on the ice before her as the graceful bird was consumed in curling feathers of fire, and she cried to see its pitiful dark eye. "No, no!" she cried and stretched out her hands. Suddenly she was back in the wagon, and Ginas was looking at her. "He's burning," she cried. "We must help him!"

Ginas let go Sibby's hand and sat back in her chair. "Indeed," she said, "he burns in agony and none of us may save him. But it may happen he will be your help."

In a shattering change of mood, Ginas leaned foward and turned up the lamp to full brightness. "I have read for you, but the meaning must lie in your heart. Consider what I have said. There is more than I can understand, but some advice I can give you. If you come to Treclere, wait for a weak new moon before you act, for in the moon's full light no one can see clearly. In time all meaning shall be plain, but do not forget, even though you do not understand." She made a gesture of dismissal, and Sibby walked slowly to the curtain. She stumbled down the wagon steps into blinding noonday sunlight, and stood a moment gathering herself together before she went to find Herrard.

He was standing a few feet from the cart, waiting as he had promised. He was watching the Players on the stage, and he turned as Sibby came up, some laughing comment on his lips. When he saw her face, he did not speak, however, but silently gestured that they should step out of the crowd to where they could talk. As soon as they were by themselves, Sibby spoke. "Ginas knows we are going to Treclere! Did you tell her?"

"I spoke nothing of our purpose. But such as Ginas often know much without being told."

"Will it be all right? I mean, they wouldn't tell Simirimia, would they?"

Herrard shook his head. "The Players have no love for the Deathless Queen, and she no love for them. It is said they have knowledge of some special mystery, which they use for purposes of divination, a mystery they learned when they served long ago in Treglad in the temple Ornat. Simirimia envies them their powers of foresight. Yet it may be this is but a story to explain the Players' dislike of the city, for I have never seen any such special skill with my own eyes nor yet heard Arbytis mention it."

Sibby looked surprised. "But that's how Ginas told my fortune! With cards, that she called the Book of the Temple. And I'm pretty sure she did the same for Leron once."

"This is most interesting. She only read my palm." He looked at Sibby with a new awareness. "You are the first I know to have seen them. I recall now what you told me, of the Lady in Treglad speaking to you apart with Leron and Arbytis. I think your intuitions are correct. I will have no further qualms about your accompanying me to Treclere. It may be," here he laughed, "that in truth it is I who accompany you."

BALLADE: HOME SONG
by Dorlion, Prince of the Tredanan House, who being taken prisoner at the age of eighteen by Dzildzil, during the third battle of Villavac, was hostage among the Karabdu for twenty-five years in their desert capital, writing in that time many poems and songs.

Freely translated from the Old Tredanan by Leron, he being in the first month of his captivity in Treclere.

One day as I sat looking to the east,
in cruel Treclere built high above the shore,
I thought of how we laughed and sang at feast
home in my castle, and my heart was sore
to think of my fair city, and much more.
Then would my longing heart give me no rest
to see Tredana, which I love the best.

I told myself that it would ease my heart
to close the window and look out no more.
I told myself this prisonment might start
the sweet return of Peace, all good in store,
rebirth of fortune, and the end of war.
But still this cruel heart pained my aching breast
to see Tredana, which I love the best.

Come, load the strong-winged hopeful Firebird
with all my wishes, asking him to fly
across the weary miles. Then would no word
of mine be broken, yet I might espy
through him, my home again. Sweet Peace, I cry
come quickly, grant my humblest request
to see Tredana, which I love the best.

O Peace, I would not lose you, dearest treasure,
for war is hateful to me beyond measure.
Yet wrong or right, my heart tears at my breast
to see Tredana, which I love the best.

Chapter Sixteen

Sibby knew that Herrard was anxious to learn more of her talk with Ginas, but he would not stay to discuss it then. The day was fair and the hour had advanced to noon, and they must be on their way. She went to see the horses saddled while Herrard paid the landlord and had a bundle of provisions put up. And, like a dream, the vision of the burning bird receded in Sibby's mind. The two horses were hardly groomed and saddled when Herrard reappeared, carrying Sibby's saddlebag and his own leathern one. He strapped them in place, tipped the stableboy, and they mounted up.

It took a few minutes to push through the crowd in the yard, since most had set down various bundles on the ground, and when they got to the road Sibby set her colt forward into a canter. Herrard brought his chestnut up level with her. "It will save us no time to spend our horses quickly," he said. "The secret of a long distance quickly covered is to change pace often and rarely go too fast, lest short speed be paid for with long lameness." Sibby pulled her colt back into a fast trot, and they went on in this manner, alternating periods of trotting and slow cantering with stretches of walking and only occasional brief gallops. She found that in this way the horses barely sweated and seemed almost tireless.

The road continued poorly surfaced as it had been between Tredana and the inn, but it was not sunken into the ground. It wound along across the rolling open country in a changing and yet strangely featureless way, unmarked except for occasional roads leading to small villages hidden among the far hills. That night when they made camp some few hundred feet from the road, Herrard remarked it was another three days' journey to Villavac. He built a small fire, and Sibby helped him mix a kind of simple dough after the Karabdin fashion to be baked into flat bread on the stones by the blaze. She looked up at the immense black sky, bright with stars and

a waxing moon, and listened to the emptiness of the wind.
Herrard filled her cup and poured a little ale for himself.
"Can you tell me," he asked hesitantly, "anything of the
cards you saw this afternoon? I will understand if you prefer
not to say anything, of course."

Sibby shook her head. "No, I'd like to tell you; it's just that
I do not understand too well myself. Let's see . . . she said she
would use the twenty-one images of her people, and the four
suits. I know what suits are at home, but these weren't like
them, they were different. I saw some ships, and rings, and a
spear. I don't know what the other one is. They weren't as important as the picture cards. The pictures were beautiful."

"What were these pictures? Can you remember?"

"I saw . . . ten of them, yes ten, and the funny thing is I
just remembered where I saw pictures like them once before.
It was at home, back in my own world. Just before I came
here. I was in this big house, and there were pictures like that
on the table. But that doesn't make sense, because how could
they have anything in my world that comes from Treglad?
Anyway, she put them down in a special way and said they
were a lamp. She called the top one the flame and said it was
an unusual card. It was very beautiful, a burning bird, with a
crown between its wings, crying big bright tears. I saw it again
in her ring, when she told me to look, only it was different,
like I was really there. It was an icy cave, and the bird was
there, burning. She talked about it being a help or something,
but I didn't understand." She stopped, surprised to see how
shaken Herrard was, remembering Ginas's similar reaction.

"You have seen the Kermyrag? Seen it with waking eyes?"

"It was just a vision in her ring, but it was different from
the card, much brighter and—and, well, more terrible. Is the
Kermyrag something important here?"

"Of greatest importance, although few believe his true existence." Herrard's eyes turned inward and he thought a long
moment; then he added slowly, "He is said to dwell in the far
north, attended by the hermit who is called the Zenedrim. If
you have seen him, then I am sure some great power is working on your future. What of the others?"

"Uh . . . there was a wheel at the bottom, a red wheel
standing up in a green field. She said something about fate
spinning around. I guess that would be coming here in the
first place. And there was a card like the one I saw before, an

empty tower, that made me think of Treglad, because it was all broken and in ruins. I think she said it was the destruction of plans or something. And there was a really strange picture, sort of two women in one. One looked like the Lady of the Rock and the other like Simirimia, and they faced away from each other but their bodies were melted together. She said the truth had been spoken to me and my duty made clear. And then there was this card that looked as though it were moving, showing the sea coming up in a big wave on the land, and she said it was me now and that I was changing. And . . . oh, yes, there were two people, a man and a woman, with their arms kind of twisted around and their hands clasped, and she said it was a contract with someone that was influencing me. And this was funny, but there was a picture of a woman who looked just like Ginas, only with a lion by her, and she said this meant she was influencing me, too, by talking to me! What else? . . . Oh, there was this bush growing out of a man, that she said meant rebirth, and a dragon with blood coming out that was the end of innocence. That was the future, that and a card that was all dark and scary, a moon shining over a black river with a black tower above it. There was a snake in the water and a big cat and a black bird sitting by the edge of the water looking in. That meant some kind of lies. And I told you about the bird on the top."

Herrard listened to all this intently. "And when did she mention Treclere?"

"At the end she said, 'If you come to Treclere, do not act when the moon is full, for by its light none can see clearly.' It made me think of the moon on the card."

Herrard rubbed his chin with his hand, considering. "This is all most interesting. I would dearly love to see these images sometime. I would say that the pictures themselves have meaning for you as well as their interpreted meanings. That card of the moon is most obviously a representation of Treclere, for it is well known to be above a black river, and the moon is the sign of Simirimia. And that card was in your future, you said? No doubt there are other meanings in the rest, if we could but find them."

Sibby thought a moment. "I can guess one. The dragon. Just after we rescued Dastra, we saw this big animal, a dinosaur, like a lizard only bigger. I tried to tell them it wasn't dangerous, but they wouldn't listen. Dastra said it was a demon sent by her mother, and Leron killed it with his sword. And it never fought back or anything. It just died, and then Leron felt terrible, because he knew it didn't mean any harm. It really looked like the dragon on the card. Only that already happened, and the card was in the future."

"What did the Lady Rianna say in Treglad? Her words might explain some of this."

"She told me some things I didn't understand about my name, about speaking the truth and being . . . sib? to someone."

"Sib means a sort of kinship. This is strange, since you cannot have any relatives in this world. Did she say anything else?"

"Yes, she told Leron there would be three times he should listen to me. And she told me that she could promise 'enlightenment and attainment, but not happiness.' "

"Strange," said Herrard, "for if we accomplish our purpose, then you must be happy, I would think. What of the other prophecy? Have you spoken as she said?"

"Yes, when he killed the dinosaur. I tried to tell him not to. I don't know about any other time."

"It is a good sign, then, that we shall find him, for other times must remain to you."

This had not occurred to Sibby before, and when they were curled up in their blankets a little later, the thought comforted her and she fell quickly asleep.

As Herrard had said, it was three days before they came to Villavac. The road led them winding up into the mountains, skirting pleasant little green valleys and wandering along the edges of rocky chasms, until it finally came down in easy stages to the large valley where Villavac stood, surrounded by the fertile fields and green pastureland. Herrard would have avoided the town but for his sheep. There was a farmer there might buy them, so they went into town to find him.

As far as Sibby could see, Villavac was nearly as large as Tredana, but there was more open space between the buildings, and these themselves were smaller and lower than those in the city, mostly small shops and private homes. As they rode in, families were beginning to cook their dinners on charcoal braziers set outside in their courtyards, and the pleasant smell of smoke and meat hung in the narrow streets. Sibby and Herrard aroused little comment as they rode past.

In the center of town there was a large open space with an ornamental pond in the middle and grass and flowers around it. The building that overlooked it was the governor's palace, and Herrard explained to Sibby that Leron had been by birth heir to that position through his mother Leriel's line, becoming governor when his uncle Armon died. As they rode past, Sibby looked up at the blank brown front of the building and wondered if Leron would ever see it again.

Past the square, Herrard guided them through a further maze of streets until they were clear through to the far side of town. The noise and smell made it clear that there were stockyards here, and soon they were in a large area filled with small pens of sheep and cows and pigs. A boy ran up eager to hold their horses, and Herrard agreed, after a short dickering about price. Then he set out into the maze of animals and buyers and sellers with a long stride, and Sibby hurried after, stretching her cramped legs. Among the sheep pens, there was an old heavyset man with long sandy hair and a red beard, dressed in rough leather working clothes and thick boots. Herrard strode up to him and clapped him on the shoulder.

"What cheer, friend Glisser? I hoped to find you here."

"Herrard! By all that's wondrous! The surprise is to see you inside a town, and it neither snowing nor raining."

Herrard laughed, and introduced Sibby. Then he leaned forward and spoke more softly. "Are you through for the day? I would conclude a matter of business with you at your convenience."

Glisser nodded. "By all means. Let us remove to the Fleece Inn for a drink and a word in private."

He spoke a few words to the men he had been with and then set out rapidly, with Herrard and Sibby following after. The inn, Sibby saw, was on one side of the yards, a three-story wooden building with a board carved into the likeness of a lambskin hanging over the door. Glisser held the door for them and they walked into its cool dusty interior. As Sibby wrinkled her nose at the smell and looked at the filth on the floor, she understood why Herrard preferred to camp out of doors. Until the ale was brought, Glisser and Herrard discussed things of minor importance, but with mugs in hand, they settled down to business.

"You know I have two hundred head of fine sheep, such as

the Karabdu raise for the making of long-lasting woolen garments and carpets," said Herrard, and Glisser nodded. "And I have a dog whose skill you have often remarked." Glisser nodded again. "What would it be worth to you to add these sheep to your own, and Sweetmouth to your kennels?"

Glisser rolled his mouthful of ale around reflectively before swallowing. "In truth, if I could add Sweetmouth to my kennels I would cheerfully pay twice the market value of your sheep. I will not insult you by putting a price on the dog."

"Done," said Herrard, and clasped hands with Glisser. "I know you will treat him well. He is just now minding my flocks for me, in the southern pasture nigh to the desert's edge, by the old cottage. I will take half payment now and collect the rest when I return from my coming trip."

"Aye, and no doubt you will try and cozen me into returning the hound, but I warn you, Herrard, you will have to content yourself with one of the pups. I have a mind to put him to that spotted bitch of mine, the one with the red ear."

"I can see he will not be anxious to return to me, in that case! But I will stand by my bargain, never fear."

"I did not seriously doubt it. But we must eat on this. I will send a boy to fetch your horses here, and you must stay the night."

Sibby looked at Herrard and was relieved to see him shake his head. "We will eat with you gladly, but then we must push on."

Glisser accepted with good grace, muttering something about eccentric travelers, and went to get his strongbox and order supper. When he was gone Sibby spoke. "I'm sorry you had to sell your dog."

Herrard smiled at her. "Glisser will love him well and spoil him outrageously. I only hope he does not get too fat and unwieldy, for Glisser likes to see his animals feed. In all events, Sweetmouth will have a home whatever happens to us. And the pups should be fine beasts." He got up and stepped over to the fire, poking up the blaze, for with sunset the air had grown chilly.

Soon Glisser came in again, lugging a small box in front of him by two brass handles. It had several locks on it and a heavy chain. He set it on the table, and Sibby watched curiously as he unlocked it in different places, pushed panels and pulled levers, operating hidden slides and catches. It finally sprang open, and Glisser carefully lifted out the two small leather sacks it contained. He and Herrard counted the golden krahs while Sibby puzzled something in her mind. Finally she spoke, timidly. "What's the purpose of all the locks?"

"To keep out thieves, of course." Glisser looked at her as though she were crazy.

"But the box is portable. I mean, you can carry it. All you'd have to do is walk away with it and worry about the locks later."

Glisser scratched his chin and looked disconcerted. "I am ashamed to say I never thought of that." He looked at Herrard. "Why do you laugh?"

Herrard wiped his eyes and controlled his voice. "Because I have often thought of that, but your performance with it so amused me, I hated to spoil it."

Glisser began to laugh, too, reluctantly. "So, for your own amusement, you let me run the risk of being robbed. The gods save me from such friends! Here, child." He held a handful of small silver danyas out to Sibby. "Keep these for your own spending. I owe you something for your wise counsel." And he chuckled as he carefully locked the box once more.

Over dinner, Sibby asked Glisser about something that he'd put into her mind. "Are there many thieves around? Or are you just being careful?"

Glisser looked at Herrard and shrugged his shoulders. "All of us who travel far from the city fear robbers on the road. Few cases against them can be proven, though, for those they set upon disappear, and who can tell if they fell prey to wolves or men more savage than wolves? Herrard has had some narrow escapes in his years of traveling, and we all have heard tales to make us cautious. Some rumor has it," and here he lowered his voice, "that they even have spies here and in Tredana, who carry tales of travelers likely to carry great sums upon them. That is one reason I wished to transact our business here privately."

Herrard nodded. "I have heard this also. They are said sometimes to work for the Treclerans, also, when chance delivers some Tredanan of importance into their hands, for Simirimia is generous with her rewards. Yet with the goodwill of the gods I shall travel safely as always." Glisser nodded and touched his throat with a superstitious gesture.

After dinner, Glisser tried once more to make them stay, but Herrard was determined to take advantage of the full moonlight. Glisser followed them outside and, after they had mounted, he pressed an invitation on them both to visit him on their return, at his country house. Herrard thanked him, and they finally tore themselves away, leaving him standing there in the bright moonlight wiping his lips with the napkin that he had absentmindedly carried with him from the table. The streets were quiet and shadowy, and the moon rode ahead of them like a lamp. Once free of the buildings, they could see black distinct shadows and clearly lit trees and rocks everywhere they looked. The horses, refreshed by their long rest and good meal of grain, stepped out briskly, and Sibby felt as eager as they. She readily agreed that they ride as long as the moon shone clearly, to make up for their delay in town.

They did not talk much, but rode on pleasantly through the soft cool night, in and out of the shadows of trees. Yet even if they had been more on their guard, they probably would not have seen the rope stretched across the road in the shadow of a clump of trees. Sibby had hardly time to see Herrard fall when she felt its painful blow high on her chest and she was flung awkwardly to the ground, hitting her head. Her last thought was to hope that the horses would not run too far away, and then she lost consciousness.

An extract from Erlandus
OF NATURAL THINGS

. . . *It would not be possible to conclude this chronicle without some account of the mysterious northern waste and its fabled denizens. Some are familiar to intrepid hunters, bears whose fur is whiter than the snow wherein they dwell, and birds who cannot fly but walk upon their feet as does a man. These creatures eat ice for their sustenance, requiring neither meat nor vegetation. It is also well known that they die each year in the fall and wake again in spring, their bodies uncorrupted.*

In the uttermost north is the home of the Kermyrag. He is often reported to burn himself once in five hundred years, rising again from the ashes to new life, but this is a mistaken tale arising from the yearly example of the northern bear and other similar creatures. The ancients are most clear upon this point, that the Kermyrag burns forever, awaiting the sacrifice that will free him from his agony. But no man knows what that may be or who can work it out. . . .

Chapter Seventeen

When Sibby came to, she found she was crying, and her mind was so befuddled she did not know for some minutes that this was because of a blinding headache just above her right eye. She was sitting against a rock. Not far away was Herrard with his arms tied behind him; he had his eyes closed and his head was dropped back at a funny angle. There were rocks all around, and a few yards away a small fire had been built and some seven or eight men were sitting by it. They were counting out gold krahs into piles, undoubtedly Herrard's payment from Glisser. Each put his share into his own pouch.

One of them looked up and saw she was awake. He signaled the others, and they came over and squatted down on their heels, looking at her intently. "Who are you, child, and why do you travel with this man?"

"It's none of your business." Sibby was surprised at the loudness of her voice.

One of them, apparently the leader, laughed. "Very well. We can wait for the other to wake." Even as he spoke, Herrard's head dropped forward and shook from side to side. Sibby guessed his head must feel much the same as hers. The leader went and squatted by Herrard, looking into his face brightly lit by the moon. He himself was in shadow. "So, Herrard the traveler, you were well moneyed as I heard. My men and I thank you for your generosity."

Herrard's eyes were squinted with pain but his voice was expressionless. "I hope you shared the full five hundred evenly."

This shaft struck home, for Sibby could see the leader's mouth twist angrily, and she heard the men mutter something among themselves. The robber recovered himself well, however. "I hope for my part to share even more with them. It has long been rumored that you have a secret cache among these hills. I would appreciate your sharing its secret with us, as a

140

gesture of goodwill."

Herrard gave a small laugh. "I know that many foolish things have been rumored about my traveling, since no one can believe I merely wander for love of wandering. This is not the least foolish of these rumors. There is no cache, and no money save what you have from us already."

"I hope," said the leader, "that your tongue will loosen easily, for I hate to appear merciless. I would not like to be forced into cruelty." He hit Herrard very hard across the face and once in the pit of the stomach. When he spoke, it was as calmly as before. "You see what you have forced me to do? Please do not push me further. We have heard you speak of hidden riches here."

Herrard licked the little trickle of blood from the side of his mouth and shook his head. "There is nothing to tell. You waste your time and ours, Black Wolf. I spoke of only rare plants and strange animals."

"If you know my name, you must know my reputation as well," said Black Wolf. "I never trifle, nor do I waste my time. Plants, indeed!" He hit Herrard several times in the stomach and watched as he rolled over onto the ground. "You see to what extremes you push me? How much easier it would be to tell what I ask." And he kicked him as he lay there.

Sibby looked at Herrard lying in the moonlight, his hands bound behind him in shadow and blood dark on his face, and she suddenly became overwhelmingly angry. She looked up at the moon a moment and it was as though its light flooded her head and filled her with power. "How dare you?" she cried in a strange voice. "How dare you talk so? If you want to kill us then kill us, but don't keep on pretending it isn't all your own idea. Forced you? You're stupid and cruel, but you don't have to go on lying, too!"

Black Wolf looked at her with a strange expression. "So the child has a voice after all. You are right. I have been stupid." He motioned to one of his men, who grabbed Sibby by the arm and virtually dragged her up to where Herrard was slowly struggling up to a sitting position. Black Wolf stepped over to the fire and returned with a glowing brand, which he held up close to Sibby's face. She could smell acrid smoke and it was hot on her cheek and mouth. "See, Herrard," cried the robber. "See this child's face. I shall change it for all time unless you speak."

Sibby saw the anguish on Herrard's face as he tried to think what to say, and her anger at being so bullied took complete possession of her. It was as though the moonlight and her own fury were a sound ringing in her ears. She reached forward angrily and grabbed the smoldering end of the branch, holding it tightly. "See what good your threats are here!" she cried in a strange and terrible voice. "And how will you coerce me? With your pathetic fire?" And she opened her hand wide, seeing it blacken and swell up with a wild satisfaction. Black Wolf stumbled to his feet, touching his throat, and his men backed off also. He started to speak, then turned and ran ignominiously for his horse. Sibby found she was laughing loudly as she watched the robbers scramble onto their horses and ride away. She continued to laugh after they had gone, her head thrown back and her stomach aching with the convulsions, until finally after several minutes she became aware of the pain in her right hand and the throbbing agony in her arm. Her laughter turned to sobs, and she saw Herrard crouched over trying to undo his hands behind him. She reached instinctively to help him, and the pain in her arm made her giddy. Staggering over to the fire, she found her knife there in the little heap of their possessions, and taking it clumsily in her left hand she came back and began sawing at Herrard's bonds. As they parted, she fell to her knees and pressed her forehead against the cool rock, while sickness washed over her.

She was still retching from pain when she felt Herrard gently press a cold wet rag against her face. "There is a stream," he said hoarsely. "My stomach will not let me lift you, but lean on me, and we shall get there." He guided her through the rocks, and when they came to the water he had her thrust her hand deep into its current. "This is the best remedy for burns," he said, and then doused his head in the water to clear his own pain.

Herrard fast recovered himself, or seemed to, and he had Sibby lie by the water while he went and fetched a blanket from his bundle. This he folded and put under her so she could lie more comfortably but still keep her hand in the water. He scooped up handfuls for her to drink, then drank himself and sat down by her. "Are you cold?" he asked, and she shook her head. Her voice was trembling too much for speech. Nevertheless he went and got her fleecy sheepskin and tucked it around her. "Our horses are here," he said, "and all our things. We lack nothing but my money, and I think your small sum is still untouched in your saddlebag." Sibby nodded, vaguely glad. Herrard was silent a moment. "They thought you were a demon, or the agent of some god. It is no wonder they thought so. How did you do it?"

Sibby closed her eyes, feeling the coolness bathe her pulse and run through all her veins. She finally spoke, "I don't know. I was so mad. I didn't feel anything. And there was the moon—it was like someone else speaking, not me at all."

"It did not sound like you. I only hope your body does not pay too dear a price for this possession. Let me look at your hand." He lightly grasped her arm and brought her hand from the water, palm upward. All the inner surface was raw and exposed, swollen about the edges. "It will not hurt if you sleep the night with your hand in this stream. Tomorrow I will bandage it." He helped arrange her in a more comfortable position.

Sibby, still light-headed with shock, fell by degrees into a troubled state not quite sleep or waking. She was aware once of Herrard covering her with his own cloak, and she meant to ask him if he would be cold, but she could not wake enough to speak the words. Then she determined to awake and ask him, and found herself standing by the stream, but Herrard she could not see. Then she realized she was still asleep and this was another stream she stood by, in some dream. The water was black and mirrored a round white moon. She looked up at the black tower before her and then down into the water, and saw that there was a serpent in the depths, silver and green and very thick and strong. She looked down more closely, her face almost against the cold black water, and saw a young man stretched out in the deeps, submerged yet floating, his dark hair streaming out and his body limp and resistless. The serpent coiled about him lovingly and laid its flat head on his breast. "But I fear you are cold," she cried into the water, and the voice was not her own. Then she was awake, in the morning, her dream forgotten and Herrard bending over her.

As soon as she had eaten and drunk, she felt much better, although her hand ached in a steady pulsing way that seemed to sap her strength. It hurt more after it was bandaged, but she told Herrard it wasn't too bad and convinced him she was well enough to set out again. He agreed, but said they would stop whenever she felt the need. Of his own hurts he said nothing, and Sibby looked at him wonderingly. "Are you sure you are ready to set out yourself? He hit you very hard last night."

Herrard smiled briefly. "I have had worse hurt from my old horse when he is in bad humor. What pained most was not being able to strike back."

The grey colt was very good that morning about standing still to be mounted, and he moved along so gently he seemed to know Sibby was not as much in control as usual. Sibby noticed that Herrard's bruises were bad enough to make him grimace when he pulled himself up into the saddle, but he smiled at her cheerfully as they moved out. "We have our lives and our goods, at least," he said, "and all they took was money after all. With luck, we shall not need any more than what you have in your bag." Sibby smiled back a little tightly and they rode along in silence.

Herrard led them south and west at a slow pace, among the western foothills of Villavac, watching for a landmark he remembered from five years earlier. Before they came to it, there were three slow days of travel. Sibby's hand ached continuously, although it was obviously beginning to heal. Whenever they were near water, Herrard insisted that they wait so she could soak it, and this was the only thing that eased the constant pain. The third day out, it was so painful she did not even hear Herrard the first time he spoke to her. The second time she looked up and followed his pointing finger with her blurred eyes. "By those trees," he cried, "I am sure we will find a way through the mountains that will save us weeks of weary traveling. Five years ago I pastured my flock here and found the goats returning in the morning with wet feet and full stomachs, though this valley was parched and scant of grass. Yet on the other side of these steep peaks I know there is grass and water, and this they must have found. We shall look now."

They rode up to the trees, and then Herrard turned his horse's head toward the mountain and let it pick its way along with a loose rein. The chestnut stopped once or twice, then ambled up to some boulders and found a faintly worn path behind it. It snuffed the ground, tore up a small mouth of grass, then at Herrard's prodding heaved a sigh and began walking along, weaving between the stones, moving steadily, if slowly, upward.

By evening, they seemed to be climbing no longer but following some level ridge raised narrowly above steep sloping declines on either side. Herrard was worried as they turned slowly back toward the north, and he halted finally, declaring they would go no further that night. For once his chestnut disagreed and pulled resolutely to continue on his way, hurrying a little further and then plainly indicating his intention of scrambling down the western slope to some unknown destination. Herrard said that they had followed him thus far and they might as well continue, so in the thickening dark they began a cautious descent, sliding and recovering themselves down what appeared to be a very long and steep hillside. They were beginning to doubt the old horse's judgment when they came out level on thick green grass. Herrard was surprised. "We cannot yet have crossed the range. This must be some high valley unknown to men. I hope this is not the end of our shortcut."

Sibby hardly heard him. She was slumped with exhaustion on her colt's neck, her arm dangling and burning in its bandages. When they stopped at last by some trees, she was too tired to eat, but lay down in her blanket, falling once more into a strange uneasy dreaming. She saw an old man walking along, carrying a lantern, and when he was closer she saw it was Arbytis. She was going to ask him why he carried the light when he raised it so it shone on her face, and in its light she could see he was still blind. Yet he knew her, and smiled, stretching his other hand to her saying, "Thanks be you are not yet too late." Then the bars of light from the lantern changed into bars of metal and he seemed a prisoner behind them. She was still disturbed much later when she awoke.

The valley was too beautiful to allow any depression to linger. As the sun came up, birds began singing all around them in the grass, and a white mist rolled off of the steep encircling hills. Around them the grass was deep and green, and they could see both horses some way off standing knee deep in the lush pasture. Something glittered in the near distance: a lake.

Herrard breathed deeply. "This is true paradise," he said. "Let us make breakfast by the shore, so you may bathe your hand once more." He picked up a few things, and they began walking through the tall wet grass toward the water. Sibby almost stepped on a bird's nest hidden in the grass before her; she looked wonderingly at the mother bird who regarded her in turn with a steady eye. Timidly, she stretched out her good hand and laid a finger on the bird's throbbing breast. It did not flinch. Sibby looked at Herrard. "Paradise indeed," he said.

Around the blue lake there was a narrow beach of white sand, and here they sat and built a small fire. The water was pure and clear, and in it Sibby was able to open and close her hand for the first time. The two horses waded out breast high into the water and drank noisily, thrusting their noses in deeply and tossing their heads. Sibby suddenly laughed out loud as her colt turned to look at her, his white mane tumbled rakishly about his neck and eyes peering out from under his long thick forelock. She laughed again, and he suddenly exploded with good spirits, kicking up his heels and biting the old chestnut on the neck. Herrard's horse bumped him with his nose, and the two suddenly went bucketing off, leaping and snorting like foals. Sibby turned to see Herrard smiling broadly. "This is a wonderful place," she said. "I don't think anything bad could happen here."

"I think this must be the place of which Arbytis once spoke to me. Here he once came to rest when he thought he could go no further. And here he found strength to go on again, his only wish being to stay." The first part of Sibby's dream came back to her indistinctly, and she nodded. Then she started as the grasses near her parted and a large spotted kitten came clumsily out onto the sand, followed by two others. As the mother leopard followed, she looked at the two humans calmly, and Sibby held out her hand. She had always wanted to stroke a wild cat. The leopardess sniffed Sibby's fingers, then rubbed the side of her face against them, and Sibby felt for a moment her curved teeth under the fold of her mouth, her prickly whiskers, and the velvet of her fur. Then the cat went to join her cubs who were rolling around clasped in each other's paws on the clean sand, growling in high-pitched voices. Sibby looked again at Herrard and saw to her surprise that he was looking serious. "There is one danger here," he said, "this peace is not for us. We are not on our journey to rest and be happy, but rather to rescue our friends. We cannot stay."

Sibby found she had almost forgotten that they must leave. "Yes," she said, reluctantly, "we must go."

She pulled her hand from the water, and they could see that the swelling was much less, and even the bandage did not chafe as much as before. They quickly packed their things and Herrard caught the horses with some difficulty. All around, the birdsong had been getting louder and now in the full light of morning it was almost deafening. As Sibby stood in the grass, watching Herrard lead the horses toward her, a small antelope poked its head around a nearby bush and looked at her, its large ears twitching. Sibby went to it and put her hand on its neck; it turned and lipped at the edge of her cloak. She cried out, "I don't want to leave here. We can't! This is the best place in the whole world—listen to the birds!"

Herrard looked at her with understanding. "Can any place be truly happy if your friends are prisoners?" And the light seemed suddenly to harden into bars around her as she remembered the past part of her dream, and the joy was gone.

"No," she said, "I was forgetting." But she pressed her face against the antelope's warm neck for a moment before she turned away to help Herrard by holding the horses as he saddled them.

The horses were as reluctant as they to leave the valley, and climbing the further slope they cast longing glances backward. At the top of the long hill, Leron almost turned back, and Sibby had to push him hard with her legs to keep him going forward. Then she drew her breath sharply, for before them on the other side of the hill was a vista of rocky peaks, rising high above them and plunging far below. The way down seemed impossibly sheer. She looked at Herrard. "We have come thus far," he said. "We might as well continue."

They did go on, and somehow the horses always found a way. Only in a few places did Herrard advise that they dismount and go on foot, leading their mounts. By noon of the third day, they were out of the mountains and beginning to cross the wide plateau where, further north, Sibby and Dansen had been separated from their friends by the flood. Herrard explained that such floods were common enough in early spring but unlikely in the sixth month of the year. "In no more than another month," he said, "we should reach Treclere." They had stopped for water and Sibby was bathing her much improved hand. She looked up at his words, half startled. She was beginning to wonder seriously what they would do when they got there. Time would tell: and time was nearly gone.

THE BALLAD OF BLACK WOLF

as sung in the streets of Villavac

Near Villavac as I rode out
So early in the day
Oh there I spied a fat farmer
Come weeping on his way.

Refrain: Oh brave bold Black Wolf
Oh bold Black Wolf

Oh are your houses plundered
Or is your family slain
Or robbers driven away your sheep
Or with your daughters lain?

My houses are not plundered
My family is not slain
No man has driven away my sheep
Nor with my daughters lain.

But I have been in Villavac
And seen a doleful sight
They say they have three lads there who'll
Not see tomorrow's light.

They say this evening they shall hang
For robbing on the way.
Not so, not so, cried Black Wolf then,
This thing I shall assay.

He gave the farmer fifty krahs
Which made him leap for joy

No power on earth, said Black Wolf then,
May lightly me annoy.

He dressed himself in ragged clothes
And walked into the square
And not a man who stood by him
Knew Black Wolf was there.

And when his three lads were led out
He threw them each a knife
And back to back those robbers four
Stood battling for their life.

Ten men, ten men, were wounded then
By one, by two, by three,
And many another fell down dead
As they did fight for free.

Oh many talk of crossing streams,
That never wet their feet
And many sing of bold Black Wolf
That never did him meet.

But I have been into the hills
And seen the robber band,
These three, their brethren, and Black Wolf
The bravest in the land!

Chapter Eighteen

Sibby and Herrard entered the fens at the narrowest point. They were impatient to get through the uncomfortable marshlands, yet not so impatient, for these lands marked a clear boundary between the empty lands and the territory of Treclere. Twice they encountered fishers in the fenland, simple folk from whom they bought fish and eggs with Sibby's small store of money. With this and wild game and Herrard's vegetables they fed well, yet as their journey grew nearer its close, they found themselves constantly uneasy, unable to eat or sleep in comfort.

Having crossed the fens, they continued due west through level farmland, aiming to reach the great sea inlet where Treclere was built, thence north to the city itself. The further they rode, the more cheerless and sinister appeared the land, for the rich fields were unsown and farm houses stood open to the sky. In the little towns, they saw no living creatures but the birds flying up in startled crowds from empty windows. Herrard was puzzled. "Once I came this way, in a spirit of adventure, some twenty years ago. Then the fields were teeming with grain and the villages full of life. I cannot think what could have caused so great a change." Sibby found it hard to imagine the region as prosperous and lively. Its stillness was far emptier than the peace of open wilderness. She and Herrard began avoiding the towns, not because of danger but because of the way their horses' hooves echoed against the walls of the empty houses. In one overgrown field through which they passed, they heard a regular creaking noise, which proved to be the long wooden handle attached to an open stone well. The bucket had rotted away, but the handle swung up and down in the wind, as evenly as breathing. It was very grey and weathered.

A little more than three weeks after they had crossed the mountains, a west wind brought them the smell of the sea, from the great ocean inlet ahead. Open pasture stretched ahead of them in a long rolling sweep for about ten miles, to end in overhanging cliffs. Beyond this they could see the sparkle of water. The horses cantered down the seemingly endless slope, and the sun was so bright and the grass so sweet it was hard to believe that Treclere stood only fifty miles or so to the north of them. Something in the grass caught Sibby's eye; then she saw some other curious dark objects and pulled Leron to a stop. She leaned down from her saddle and looked harder, not wanting to dismount because the stiffness in her hand made it hard to get up again. "What do you see?" asked Herrard, bringing his horse around a tight circle and joining her. She pointed into the grass.

Herrard swung down and lifted one of the objects. It was dark green, shiny in places, and shaped like a bowl with something stuck on the bottom. He turned it over in his hands, and there was a hard unhappy look on his face. "The bronze helmet of a Tredanan foot soldier. Its like has not been made for twenty years." He stooped and thrust aside the grasses. The soldier lay where he had fallen years earlier, his armor dark and discolored, now scarcely covering his huddled bones. Sibby gasped and tightened her hold on the reins as Leron sidestepped, ruffling his nostrils with distaste.

"Why is it here?" she cried and Herrard looked slowly around him before he answered.

"I fear me this soldier sleeps in good company. Two thousand rode with Armon seventeen years ago; this pleasant plain is watered with their blood. Look you how uneven grows the grass: there a man fell, there a horse. This is their only monument." As Sibby watched, Herrard stepped a few paces further and once more leaned over. For a moment he looked down into the tall grass, then shook his head sadly and backed away. "They never reached Treclere, except for Arbytis and his companion."

He quickly pulled himself onto his horse and turned once more seaward. As they went forward, now more slowly, the ground was littered with armor and weapons and human bones; flowers grew up toward the sun through the empty open hands of skeletons, and pieces of armor had incongruously become part of the plants and bushes that had grown through and around them. There was not a square yard of the field that did not bear witness to the slaughter.

Even when they finally came out onto the head of the cliff and looked down onto the wind-ruffled water far below, they could not escape, for on the beach far below were the round-ribbed skeletons of several horses who had plunged with their armored riders over the side, escaping battle but meeting death all the same.

Miles north of those grim fields they finally camped, on the stony upper reaches of the narrow beach. For a while they sat silently by their fire, thinking of the next day, which would bring them to Treclere. Herrard spoke first. "We have seen the answer to the mystery of those empty villages. That was more than two thousand on the plain. Armon must have raised the countryside as he rode, bringing them to share his luckless fate."

"But what about the people who stayed at home? They wouldn't all fight."

"No, for their fate we must look to the queen. Doubtless their homes are left as warning. I doubt if any who dwelt therein still breathes the air. She is very powerful. Child, reconsider. I will go into the city and report back to you. Stay safe outside." Sibby shook her head.

"My story's better. She did invite Dansen. I'll say we were attacked, that's why I came on alone. My hand is proof." Herrard shook his head but said nothing further. Presently they rolled up in their blankets and fell into a sleep of a sort.

Just before she woke, Sibby suddenly found herself mounted on a strange horse. She was dressed in armor, and the horse was a dark streaky blue in color, with a black mane and tail. There was a man riding near her, holding before him a large square banner, yellow with a white band down the middle and a blue sun on it. The silk tassels around its edge shimmered in the wind. The day was clear and fresh, and the people seemed as sharp and distinct as a picture. She looked over her shoulder and saw an army assembled behind her. So she stood up in her ornate stirrups and motioned with her hand. The army cheered at this and began to walk forward. Then other images blurred this one, and soon after she was awake.

After breakfast, as they set out once more, some little motion of her horse reminded Sibby of her dream. She mentioned it to Herrard, because it seemed so pointless a vision. He looked at her with narrowed eyes. "Are you sure no one described that scene to you?"

"Of course not. How could they?—I just dreamed it!"

"You may have just dreamed it, but I saw it, years before you were born." He paused, looking inward. "The stallion was named Blue Sky, and he was Armon's favorite mount. Naturally the prince rode him when he left Tredana on his doomed expedition. A noble of the realm carried the banner of the prince's family, which has not been used since the death of Queen Leriel, his sister and wife to Mathon. And she died soon after Armon left. You could never have seen it."

Sibby looked at him, and finally said in a small voice, "You're not joking are you?"

"Joke? Hardly. I had forgotten, though, until you mentioned it, how he stood in his stirrups and waved his men on, not waiting for the marshals. They were all so sure of themselves."

After this they rode on in silence. Other strange memories mixed themselves in Sibby's mind, but she could see nothing clearly. Only impressions remained, and soon, too, even the sunlit image of her most recent dream began fading.

They had ridden only a few hours when the towers and roofs of Treclere began to rise above the horizon. The city rose sheer and abrupt, towering above the dusty plains on the one side and the cliff-overhung inlet on the other. It was entirely surrounded by walls, tall, smooth and black, glittering in the sun. The south gate, which they were approaching, was pointed at the top and at least thirty feet high, and although it stood open, it was not welcoming. Sibby thought they should wait to enter the city after dark, but Herrard was afraid that the gates might be closed at night. So they boldly rode straight up and passed within, and no one called to them or blocked their path. As they rode through the gates, Sibby's head swam and she found it hard to breathe. Under the shadow of the wall it was as cold as if the sun had never shone there, and the smooth polished stone seemed icy. The horses made dull clanging sounds on the cobbles.

Within the city there were many people busy at various tasks. But there was little speaking and no buying and selling. No one looked at them. Even so, Herrard suggested that they dismount and lead their horses to appear less conspicuous, and this they did. They walked along through the crowds, looking for hostelry. As time passed and nothing dreadful happened, Sibby breathed more easily and looked around with interest. The buildings were of dark stone, for the most part, their windows shuttered or unlit. Everywhere large numbers of mournful birds were clustered on ridgepoles or windowsills or huddled in small patches of sunlight on the uneven ground.

As they passed one shadowed alley, Sibby nearly jumped, for a tall man stepped out of it and came up to Herrard, laying a hand on his shoulder. He cried, "Rassam!" in a low whisper, and Sibby saw to her delight that it was Ab'Bakr.

He saw her, too, and smiled at her, as Herrard cried, "Ab'Bakr! As I hoped, you are here before me! Where is my brother?"

Ab'Bakr frowned and shook his head, drawing them aside. "A week since, he went to the palace, and has returned thence four times, speaking little and seeming not himself. And each time he has been the more anxious to return. The queen has sent fair messages, inquiring after our comfort, but I would rather see my master as he was."

Herrard frowned. "Where do you lodge? I would speak privately."

Ab'Bakr took Sibby's horse by the bridle and led them quickly down a maze of streets to the Palace Inn, where a groom took the horses from them. He showed them up a back staircase to his small dark apartment. The others of the Karabdin party were not there, so Ab'Bakr closed the door and stood by it, motioning them to sit. He remained standing and alert.

Quickly Herrard told him of Sibby's plan, and Ab'Bakr objected to the risk. Finally he was convinced, although reluctantly, being most anxious to learn of affairs in the palace for his own reasons. At least their meeting solved one problem, for it would give Sibby some chance to leave the palace, on pretext of visiting her Karabdin friends. All assumed without quite saying it aloud that Ajjibawr would not carry messages for her. They agreed that only after a week had elapsed without news would they try anything on their own and make new plans. For now, Ab'Bakr would take Sibby to the palace saying he had met her traveling alone.

She got ready to leave at once. Before she left, Herrard took her hand and squeezed it encouragingly. Then, surprisingly, he kissed it lightly and smiled at her. "Remember, if you become furious in the future, direct your wrath at others, not yourself. Then must you surely prevail against all comers." Sibby smiled back a little shakily and went out.

Ab'Bakr did not waste time with words. He led her swiftly through the city streets to the main avenue where the palace entrance was. The palace was another city within the city, walled itself, with its own massive gate. Like the city walls, all was smooth and shining and black, but this gate was shut. As they approached, a small door in the gate swung open, scraping on the cobbles, and a guard in armor stepped out. He stood, spear in hand, and waited for them to speak.

"I am Ab'Bakr, of the Karabdin party. Ajjibawr my chief is already within. I bring to the queen an invited guest, a child from Tredana."

Sibby could not see the guard's face under his helmet, which shadowed his eyes and came down in a beaklike curve over his nose, but she did not feel there was any reaction or change of expression. He merely stepped back to let her enter. Ab'Bakr made to follow her, but the guard brought his spear shaft down on the ground with a sharp thud. Before Ab'Bakr could protest, Sibby silenced him. "It's all right," she said. "Thank you for showing me the way." And she followed the guard across the high-walled, windy courtyard.

The far side of the courtyard was marked by a line of massive pillars, each thicker than the height of a man, supporting a flat roof carved along the edge into strange symbols, picked out in gold. They walked between the columns into a high and shadowed room, as bare as the outer yard, with a smooth polished floor. There was a tall rectangular door in the farthest wall, flanked by taller statues. Sibby craned her neck and squinted her eyes against the gloom to make out what they were. One seemed to be an enormous cat, the other a bird with a hooked beak. It was hard to tell. The whole place smelled cold.

Still without speaking, the guard gestured that she should wait, and he walked away as unhurriedly as he had brought her. She had hardly turned back from watching him go when the door began to open slowly on a silent pivot. She stepped up hesitantly and looked in. This room was also vast and high-ceilinged but smaller than the outer room. Pillars marked off a corridor around it on three sides, and the walls behind them were bright with red and blue and green and yellow murals. The floor was bare, and a great fire burned at the far end, leaping up into fantastic and ever-changing shadows. Before this, in a gilded chair, sat Simirimia.

Sibby bowed, very awkwardly. The queen's voice rang out clearly in the room. "The Tredanan child. This is an unexpected pleasure. But where is your learned guardian?" Sibby had no trouble making her voice tremble, as she told of robbers and separation. The queen listened, unmoved. "What tragedy," she said at length. "Be assured you shall be well attended here. Approach me." Sibby walked slowly across the distance, until the fire was hot on her face and arms. Simirimia lay back against her cushions and looked under her lashes. She was whiter than Sibby remembered, almost as white as the thin linen gown that fell in narrow pleats to her feet. There was gold at her throat and ears and all around her arms, but she no longer wore Leron's brooch. As she spoke, her green eyes slowly examined Sibby, passing over her like a small shiver. "I have another guest whom you know. Ajjibawr of the Karabdu is here."

Sibby moistened her lips. "I met one of his men in the city. He took my horse for me and led me to your palace."

Simirimia nodded and slowly turned one of her bracelets around her narrow wrist. "Of course." She smiled. "You will join us tonight at dinner. I would hear news of Tredana. Now you will be shown to your apartment."

Sibby looked up in surprise to see a girl standing by her, who had come in noiselessly while they were talking. She was delicately made, with long brown hair tied back in a ribbon and a plain expressionless face. Sibby tried to speak to her, but she gave no sign of hearing. Simirimia dismissed them, and Sibby's last sight was of the queen sunk back into the chair, gazing sleepily into the fire.

Leriel the Queen
Privately to her JOURNAL

. . . Now that Armon is on his way indeed, there are certain things I feel I must set down here, things I have not been able to confide even to my dear lord Mathon. I fear the dream I

first dreamed five years since at the time of my son's delivery is about to work itself out, and I further fear my brother and I are so closely linked I cannot long survive him. O that I had not this wretched gift of my family, to see the truth in dreams. But this has been the way of our women for untold generations.

I will set down that which I never dared write before. I have seen my brother Armon dead on a plain above the sea, surrounded by dead to the number of thousands, all scattered in the grass. And I have seen his body taken to a black city, secretly by night, and there raised by sorcery. And I have seen him in the arms of her who had killed him, and I have seen him dead indeed, and all my hopes with him. Ah Armon, my dearest brother, we who were in the womb together, shall we meet also in death, or must you wander a lonely spirit in the streets of that most alien city?

Chapter Nineteen

Sibby was led up several shallow flights of stairs and down a labyrinth of corridors to a bare brown room. It was furnished with a table, a small oil lamp, and a hard narrow couch that had gilded serpents encircling its frame. The far wall had a tall window through which Sibby could see only the sky. The girl who led her there went out and returned with a bowl of water and towel, which she set on the table. She then withdrew, in silence.

All the long afternoon Sibby sat there, looking out at the darkening sky, and no one came. There was no handle on the inside of the door, and no other entrance to the room. So she sat on the couch and tried to order her thoughts.

A little past sunset the girl came again, and Sibby followed her in silence down the dark passageway, in and out of the light of flaring torches fastened beside occasional doorways. By one door, indistinguishable from the rest, the girl stopped and motioned Sibby in.

The room was small and luxurious, with carpets and tapestries and inlaid furniture. A long low table was spread with a white cloth, and a cheerful fire burned in the fireplace. As Sibby stepped through the door, she heard a familiar sneeze. Ajjibawr stood by the fire rubbing his nose. Before she could say anything, he looked up and it seemed that his eyelids dropped a moment in warning. Then he spoke with polite indifference. "I see we meet again. Where is my friend Dansen?"

Sibby, a little uncertainly, began repeating the story that she had told Simirimia, and he interrupted only once, to ask how she had hurt her hand. Even as she spoke, the queen walked in and sat down slowly in the chair at the head of the table. "I see you have found one another." She indicated their places at the table. "You shall have much to talk of, but first we shall have food and wine." At her words, two quiet girls appeared and poured wine for them from tall silver flagons. The white tablecloth was soon covered by bowls of fruit, cheese and bread, and meat cooked in honey. They ate delicately with their fingers, in silence. After the food had been removed, Simirimia leaned forward on her elbow and twined her hand about her goblet's stem. Her other hand, Sibby noticed with surprise, lightly caressed Ajjibawr's palm.

"Now, child, tell us of Tredana. How goes it in that city?"

"When we left, the city was in mourning. The news had just come that Prince Leron was killed while on a journey." She looked at Ajjibawr to catch his reaction, but he was leaning back in his chair expressionless, his heavy eyelids dropped. "So they proclaimed his cousin Ddiskeard heir, since he was the next oldest in that generation. Dansen didn't like Ddiskeard, so he said it was a good time to leave." She stopped, feeling Simirimia's attention wholly on her. She felt that she could scarcely breathe.

"Leron was killed? The young prince? And how did that occur?"

"I—I don't know. His party brought back a princess, though, that they said he had rescued. Her name was Dastra. She's very beautiful."

"Dastra!" cried the queen in a terrible voice, and the torches flickered and flared up. "You must have mistaken the name."

"No, it was Dastra. She had been in a tower or an island, or something. No one knows the whole story. It seems pretty strange."

"Dastra!" said the queen again, and the silver goblet bent slightly in her hand. She breathed heavily for a few moments. Yet when she spoke again, it was coolly as before. "So there is a new heir to the throne. But what if the old one should still be alive?"

"Dansen explained to me that it wouldn't make any difference, now that the official proclamation has been made. He said there were some thought Ddiskeard should have been heir anyway, since he would have been older if Leron had not been born early, before his time. And anyway, the old king isn't very strong."

As she spoke, Ajjibawr had leaned forward with new interest, and now he spoke. "Whether alive or dead, the prince has paid a heavy price for his daring. What of the princess whom he rescued?"

"I don't know. They say that Ddiskeard welcomed her very warmly, though, and that they got along very well together."

Ajjibawr nodded appraisingly. "I see." He clasped his hand more firmly over the queen's and smiled into her eyes. "This news must affect our plans. We seem to have lost a weapon. But no doubt you will have other ideas."

Simirimia looked at him as though from a distance. She removed her hand from under his. "Doubtless I shall. I suggest you leave us now and spend this night in the city. I have much of importance to discuss with this child, and questions to ask." She turned her head slightly so that her hair fell between them and hid her face. Ajjibawr rose, and bowed and left without another word. Sibby watched him go wonderingly.

As the door closed behind Ajjibawr, the queen observed Sibby through narrowed eyes. She seemed newly composed and was apparently absorbed in eating grapes one by one from a full purple bunch in her hand.

"How old did you say you were, child?"

"Almost—almost twelve."

"I remember, yes. Describe to me this princess. You did see her?" Sibby nodded, and as she described Dastra a frown grew on Simirimia's face. Without warning she threw down the grapes, stopping Sibby in midsentence. "Silence!" she hissed. "I will test this matter for once and aye!" She looked deeply into Sibby's eyes and Sibby felt suddenly very removed, as though she were watching a picture. As from a distance, she watched the queen with a small gesture make the torches dwindle to a dull blue glow and then, with a flick of her hand, cause the fire to blaze up. Simirimia leaned forward in her chair clenching the edge of the table with her hands, and her face was contorted as she muttered strange words between her teeth. Small rents appeared in the tablecloth by her hands. Her heavy perfume filled the small room, and made Sibby sleepier. Her mind began to wander among its mixed memories. As she drifted, an image began to form in the fire, a woman dressed in thick grey robes with a veil wrapped around her head and neck. Her hands were lifted in terror, but she seemed unaware of the flames enveloping her.

Simirimia spoke in a penetrating cool voice. "So, Verissa, you do not love to see me. Speak, worm, where is my daughter?"

Dastra's maidservant cried out, and fell to her knees. "O Queen," she sobbed, "do as you will with me, but do not touch my family. It was my fault, mine alone. I slept late, and when I awoke she was gone. I do not know how, truly!"

"Do you not?" said the queen. "We shall see." Her lips curled with anger and her face became dark with effort as she muttered some last words and made a tearing gesture with her hands. Verissa screamed, and then the image had become real, and the old woman stumbled forward and fell to her hands and knees by the fire. Her robes were singed around the hem.

Simirimia stood up and suddenly seemed very tall. The firelight cast a huge and billowing shadow behind her. In a motion smoother than walking, she came round the table and stood before Verissa. "It is true, then! It is true my daughter is gone! For this your village shall burn in torment; as for you . . ." She stooped and placed her hands on either side of Verissa's tear-stained face, staring directly into her eyes. There was silence for a moment, then Verissa's face became calmer and she stood up silently. At Simirimia's signal, she left the room quietly, her face unchanging as Simirimia completed her sentence, ". . . as for you, oh, you shall pay at length."

Silence followed, and Sibby's head suddenly cleared. The torches once more burned brightly, and Simirimia sat by the table, eating another grape. A fluttering, bumping sound made Sibby look up and saw a little grey bird flying about terror-stricken in the room. As she watched in puzzlement, a girl came in silently and caught the bird without much effort. Simirimia did not look round, but said quietly, "This one is to stay within the palace." The girl went out with the bird, and Simirimia looked at Sibby as though nothing had happened, and nodded. "You were speaking of Tredana. Pray continue. I would hear more of Leron's death and the new heir."

Sibby tried to speak, but her tongue stumbled and her head was dropping with sleep. In a few moments the queen had interrupted her.

"I did not mean to keep you so late. We shall talk again tomorrow." Sibby had meant to ask about visiting the others of the Karabdu who were in the city, but the words dried in her throat. She merely nodded, and found, as she half expected, a girl waiting by the door to guide her.

Sibby's head was still clouded as she followed the girl back to her room. As they went in, she was aware first that the lamp was lit and that there were blankets on the bed. Then a strangely familiar voice behind her spoke a few words, and the girl stopped so suddenly that Sibby almost bumped into her. Sibby turned and saw the son of Meddock carefully closing the door behind them. Sibby suddenly awoke. The girl remained motionless as though turned to rock.

"Lelu?" she cried softly. "Small! It is really you?" And she grasped his outstretched hands tightly while he smiled up at her amazement. "How come you are free?" He held up one hand for silence, glancing at the frozen servant girl and the closed door.

"Be careful," he said. "Dangerous. I escaped. But Arbytis is captured. Leron is captured. I try to help them. Now you help, too. Come."

"But what about the queen? And the girl?"

"Girl will stay until I speak. I have learned words. The queen is busy now. We see Arbytis."

Small touched the door lightly with a cunning gesture, and it opened for him. Sibby followed him cautiously out into the corridor. "I want to see Leron," she said, but Small shook his head with a worried look on his face.

"Later maybe. Now not good time."

"Why?" asked Sibby, but Small shook his head again without answering, hurriedly leading her down the dark hallways. He was virtually invisible in the shadows, and Sibby did her best to slip along silently after him. She followed blindly up to a small door that led them into a series of ever more cramped tunnels until they came at last into a small round chamber, lit with moonlight through a tall narrow slit in one wall. Here Lelu muttered and moved a few stones with his hand. A panel swung back, exposing the wrong side of a tapestry matted with loose and dangling threads. Moonlight shone through all the little tears and slits and holes. He looked past this carefully, then took Sibby's hand and brought her around the edge of the hanging into a small room. She almost cried out at what she saw.

In a shadowy corner of the chamber, there was a golden cage about five feet high and four feet wide. A white-haired figure sat huddled in the corner, and Sibby knew it was Arbytis. Small crossed the room silently and gently touched the old man's hand. His head rose from his knees, and he spoke calmly. "Lelu?" He was very thin, his hands clawed like a bird's, and the moonlight seemed to shine through his skin, like sun through porcelain.

"Arbytis!" said Sibby softly, and reached through the bars for his hand.

Arbytis's face wrinkled with concern as he took her hand and held it firmly. "Thanks be you are not too late. Yet I fear for your safety." .

"I came for you, for you and Leron. Don't worry about me. But this cage!"

Arbytis seemed to smile. "Cage? My body is a worse one. I am not uncomfortable. But how came you here?" Sibby knelt by the bars and in a low whisper told him of what had happened. Arbytis listened intently, still holding her hand lightly. When she had finished, he spoke musingly. "I would not fear overmuch for Ajjibawr. The queen has power, but he has strength and experience as well as loyalty to his brothers. Though he may weaken somewhat, I do not think he will betray you. And it is good to know Herrard is so close. Yet for all their strength and loyalty, the burden lies on you, child."

Arbytis paused. "Child, it is not force that will rescue Leron now. He is truly a captive, more so, perhaps, than you can understand. Remember what my Lady spoke in Treglad. Trust in the truth as you see it. Speak the truth when it has to be heard. Leron has need of your ears and eyes just now."

"I don't understand."

"You will begin to understand, once you have met with the queen again and seen the prince. You have the gift of watching and listening, child. Use that gift now. The queen is easily angered. If you amuse her instead, you may learn much." He raised his hand slightly. "Do not be impatient. There still is time. Leron may yet return to his home unscathed, in triumph." He looked so solemn as he spoke, Sibby felt uneasy.

"Do you really think so?"

Arbytis reached through the bars and touched her cheek lightly, as exactly as though he could see her. "Child, I do not know. But the queen approaches, and you must leave. That I can see clearly. Go now in safety. We will talk again."

Lelu returned Sibby to her room quickly and silently. The girl still stood just within the door, one hand slightly raised. Lelu stood in the doorway and spoke once, softly, to Sibby. "Go to bed. I will come back tomorrow." Then he said the words he knew and closed the door. The girl finished stepping forward and quietly spread Sibby's bed, leaving with untroubled eyes and no awareness of what had occurred.

After the door closed, the room was quiet and dark outside the circle of the lamp. Sibby found she was very tired, and she washed quickly, blowing out the light and lying down in the lonely dark. She turned uncomfortably, trying to adapt her bones to the hardness of the bed. At last she settled on her back, her head dropped at a wakeful angle, feeling strange currents in the air grope across her face. She closed her eyes against the unfamiliar shadows of the room and saw instead vaguely frightening flashes of irregular light on her eyelids. More and more sleepily, she watched the shifting shapes inside her head. Then it seemed she was looking at the room where she lay, but from a distance, and the couch was empty.

Simirimia was standing there by the window, flooded in moonlight and holding an apple in her hand. She was dressed in black and was very beautiful. The door opened and she looked up triumphantly, stepping aside for the four soldiers who entered heavily, bearing between them on a litter some shrouded form. This they laid on the couch and then withdrew at Simirimia's impatient sign. Simirimia walked over and drew back the sheet, and Sibby was almost startled awake, for the body revealed looked like Leron, only thinner and older. He was horribly disfigured with blood and dirt, his breast gaping open with a terrible wound, and his gashed arms and bruised head limply dangling. The queen looked at him with a strange expression, then turned and lit the small lamp, holding it so the flickering light licked over his face. Then she set it at the couch's head and, taking the apple she held in both hands, tore it in half with a quick gesture. She bit out the seeds and spat them into her hand, leaving the fruit to fall on the floor. All this Sibby could see clearly, but there was no sound at all, even though Simirimia had begun to speak. As she spoke over the seeds, sweat gathered on her face and her eyes shone like lamps themselves. Finally she closed her hand and pressed it with the seeds to her lips, and afterward placed them in the dead man's half-open mouth. Again she spoke strange soundless words, and the sweat gathered until it ran down onto her neck and breast, staining her dress at the shoulders. She moved her head back and forth, clenching and unclenching her fists as she talked, in an even, rhythmical motion. Her breast heaved with effort, and her face was dark with blood. Finally she screamed aloud and knocked the lamp over with her foot so the oil spread out on the floor and flamed and died. She tore at her own face with her fingers, leaving red streaks, still clenching and unclenching her fists, and blood dropped from her face onto the face beneath her. Her head dropped forward with exhaustion and as she sucked in her breath and watched, fresh blood welled up in the corpse's wounds and a little jet began to spurt rhythmically from the great hole in his breast in time with the motion of her hands. Smiling, she leaned over him and closed the wound with her fingers, calling aloud for attendants.

Then Sibby heard her words, clear and distant and real. "Dress these wounds, wash and anoint him." As the dead man's fists opened and closed convulsively in a mimicry of Simirimia's movements, light began pulsing through Sibby's head and she awoke in terror listening to her own heart beat. She pulled the covers over her head and tried to forget what she had seen. It was as though the corpse and she shared the same bed, yet she did not dare leave the protection of her covers. Outside her bed, the air was cold and unfriendly. As she lay there terrified and awake, more visions began unrolling in her head, and she was helplessly watching a small room like the room where they had eaten. Simirimia was there still dressed in the green gown that she had worn at supper. She sat by the fire and a young man knelt before her with his head in her lap. This time Sibby knew that it was Leron. Simirimia held his hand in hers and slowly traced with one finger the long scar which followed the line of the vein on his bare right forearm. She lingered at the wrist and then, lightly touching his palm, pressed his hand against the side of her dress above her heart. Leron raised his head and put his hands on her shoulders, and the green dress slipped slightly down on her arms. There was a small scar on her neck just below her right ear, dark against her white skin. As Leron tried to take her in her arms, Simirimia pulled away and stood above him, her head thrown back and her face contorted with laughter. As she laughed, Leron bent his head again and covered his face with his hands, and Sibby knew it had something to do with Dastra. Then she fell asleep and there were no more dreams.

LYRIC

by Leron, prisoner to Simirimia, in the second month of his captivity

Cruel and Fair One, let me die
O do not slight me yet again
Who once upon your breast has lain
Alone content no more may lie.

Cruel and Fair One, let me die
Within your arms all pain is bliss
Without you joy is meaningless
O do not let me longer sigh.

Entangled in your hair I cry
No one is dearer to my heart
Though I have all, if you depart
Then Cruel and Fair One let me die.

Chapter Twenty

Sibby was awakened by the girl bringing her breakfast the next morning. The sky beyond the window was very blue, and the events of yesterday were oddly remote. After she had eaten, she dressed quickly, expecting the queen to call for her, but no word came. The girl who took her empty dishes said nothing, and left as silently as she had entered. When the door opened again, Sibby looked up expectantly. It was not the girl, it was Small.

Again he warned her to silence. "The queen sleeps late this morning. Arbytis sent me. We go see friend in city." Sibby followed him unquestioningly. Shadowed and dark by day as by night, the palace corridors unwound confusingly before them, thick with smoke from the torches. Finally, a steep narrow staircase led them down into a service passage that gave onto the stableyards, and Small kept them skillfully in the shadows as they crossed to the outer wall where a small door stood ajar. Beyond it was a crooked street, empty of people.

Sibby knew it was just her imagination, but the air on the far side of the gate smelled different, and her head seemed to clear as she left the palace compound behind her. But as they hurried down back alleys, in and out under the leaning shuttered buildings, past small empty courtyards, the strange stillness of Treclere depressed her spirits. The only sounds were the sighing of birds huddled together in the sun and the wind vibrating between the buildings. Small brought them through these featureless streets to the back of the Palace Inn, but, instead of going upstairs as Sibby had the day before, he led them to another door, where the steps led down into the cellars. A smell of damp earth and water-slimed stone was cold on their faces as they felt their way down. Soon Small came to a stop and scratched on a wooden panel; it opened to reveal Herrard sheltering a small lump of candle in one hand.

"Sibby!" he said, his face lighting with relief, and he nod-

ded courteously to Small. "Welcome again, son of Meddock." He brought them into the room and closed the door
silently behind them. The chamber was low and vaulted, apparently quite deep in extent, with huge pottery vessels
ranged seven or eight deep along the walls. They were sealed
in butter that smelled strong and rancid. Near the center,
there was set a rough table where Ab'Bakr and another man
were sitting, glasses of tea before them. Ab'Bakr spoke.

"Most welcome. We were relieved to hear of your safety
from this friend of Arbytis. He came to us in the night and
said he would bring you if he could. Our other friend is Qayish, the keeper of this inn." The other man stood and nodded
at this, a small thin man with a nervous face and strong
gnarled hands.

As they all sat, Sibby looked around and said, "Is this
place really safe?"

Herrard smiled, but Qayish almost jumped. "I hope so
with all my heart," he said, and picked up his glass with a
trembling hand.

Ab'Bakr smiled at him and Herrard. "Fear not, friend,"
he said. "I am sure we must all prevail in the end."

Sibby looked from one to the other. "Did Lelu tell you
about Arbytis?"

Small answered her, shaking his head. "No, cannot explain. You tell."

So she quickly described what she had seen and what had
been said. As she spoke, Herrard's mouth tightened. His
hand hit the table. "By all that is holy," he cried, "this queen
shall pay a heavy reckoning."

Again Qayish started and looked around fearfully, and
Ab'Bakr looked on him with pity. "From all I have heard,"
he said, "she has much to answer for already to her own people. They have little cause for loyalty."

"Loyalty?" said Qayish. "What loyalty can a parent feel
when each year this he fears will be the time his child is called,
taken into the palace, never to return. Each year they come,
the faceless guards, on the first day of spring, making it a season therefore to be dreaded rather than welcomed. Twenty
youths and twenty maidens return with them to the palace,
never to be seen more. Five daughters I had, and now there
are two, and I cannot say if they will be with me in another
year's time." He covered his face with his hands and Sibby

looked at him with sympathy.

"Why does she take them?" she asked.

"No one knows for certain. Some say—some say there is a great monster hidden in the passages of the palace, a great snake or a beast of prey. And thus she appeases it. But no one knows."

"But couldn't it just be the way she gets her servants? There are all those girls in the palace, they must come from somewhere."

Qayish looked up, startled. "Girls? You have seen girls in the palace? Perhaps you have seen my daughters. They had light brown hair, fair as the Karabdu, and the oldest had a mark beside her mouth."

Sibby shook her head. "I don't know. There are so many. But I'm sure there isn't any monster or anything like that. I saw . . . why can't I remember! I saw something with birds, and a fire . . . something about what she does with people. I don't know how I forgot, but I do know she has a special way of controlling people. Lelu knows some of the words to use."

Small nodded. "Arbytis told me. I speak, they stop and do not move. I speak again, they move but do not know."

Qayish breathed deeply and bit the knuckles of his right hand. "I wonder if I dare hope," he said at length. "There are so many stories. Can you remember no more?"

Herrard interrupted him. "She will remember nothing the queen chooses she forget. Tell me, what have you learned of the prince?"

"Nothing. Lelu won't tell me. I don't know what's happened to him."

Herrard looked at Lelu, who dropped his eyes unhappily. "The queen keeps the prince," he said at last, unhappily. "She has power."

Herrard met Ab'Bakr's eyes comprehendingly, and Sibby, although not quite understanding, made a connection in her mind. "Do you mean he's changed, like Ajjibawr?"

"I fear they mean more changed than that," said a familiar voice, and Sibby whirled to see Ajjibawr by the door. She squinted her eyes against the dark to look at his face, and she saw something there she had not seen last night. Impulsively, she got up and went to him, and he took her hand for a moment. "I think this is a happier reunion than last night," he said, and smiled down at her. By the table he clasped Herrard's shoulder for a moment, nodded to the others, and sat down. Ab'Bakr set a glass before him, and the rest waited for him to speak.

First he turned to Sibby. "I am sorry, child, if I seemed strange last night, but truly I was not myself." With a sense of comfort, Sibby watched him casually flick open his snuffbox and take a pinch in his fingers. "I went to find my brother Arbytis and found something quite different, as poor Ab'Bakr can testify." He smiled at his companion, and Ab'Bakr flushed. "In truth I have sorely tried my friends, but I am relieved to report they need fear no more. When I saw you last night," he nodded at Sibby, "and then returned to find my other brother here, I saw that too much time had already been wasted. You have learned in one evening what I could not in six. Much though I dislike to see you return to the palace, I fear it is the only way." He paused to sneeze, and rubbed his nose in silence. "Lelu will bring us any news you need to send, or bring us to your aid should you require it. When you have learned more, we can plan, no sooner. Do you agree?"

Sibby looked around at their faces. "Yes," she said, "and I think I better get back as soon as possible, before the queen sends for me."

Ajjibawr nodded. "We cannot linger. But first," he raised his hand to his throat, "I pledge the death of the Deathless One."

Qayish shook his head despairingly but pledged hesitantly with the others. Ajjibawr looked at him with eyebrows raised, and Qayish muttered in an embarrassed voice, "The way you said it put me in mind of the rhyme they speak. 'Not man nor woman shall be the one, that shall bring death to the Deathless One.' That's what is said."

Herrard laughed. "Mayhap an eagle will drop a stone on her from above, as they say one did long ago in Vahn, bringing death to the mad architect in the desert. Prophecies were ever made to be circumvented."

Ajjibawr smiled at this, and as they rose Qayish went to the door and listened for a moment before opening it. Lelu took Sibby's hand, but before he could lead her out, Ajjibawr stopped her with his hand on her shoulder and, leaning down, touched his lips to her cheek. "Courage," he said, and she could feel that he smiled. Then she followed Lelu into the blackness, and up into the eye-dazzling light of day.

They returned to the palace just in time. It seemed only a moment after the door had closed on Small that it opened to admit one of the queen's servants. The girl led her quietly along the upper passages to a gallery Sibby had not yet seen, a long vaulted corridor lit by narrow windows cut deep into the stone along its outer wall. At its farthest end, the hall was filled with harsh white light, where a tall door opened out into the lead-tiled roof. There, by a low parapet, stood Simirimia, overlooking her city. Birds were clustered about her feet, and the wind lifted up her heavy long black hair. She turned very slowly and looked at Sibby without expression.

Sibby halted a few feet away and waited for the queen to speak. For a long moment, Simirimia only looked at her, then turned to look down at the city and sea inlet far below. Finally she spoke. "Describe Tredana."

Sibby searched for words, then began to talk hesitantly about the hill, and the harbor and the castle above it.

"How great is the city?"

Still uncertain, Sibby was trying to answer when the third question came, not a question really but a statement.

"It is not greater than Treclere." Quietly the queen continued, "Not greater, and not truly his. And yet he wished to die for it. Foolish, foolish one."

Finally she seemed to notice Sibby's presence, and motioned for her to approach. Sibby cautiously did so. She looked resolutely at the queen, uncomfortably aware of the spinning distances just visible in the corner of her eye. "Child, tell me of the new prince."

Sibby spoke, and as she did so there was amusement in Simirimia's face. She did not interrupt Sibby, but as she listened she bent over very slowly and took one of the birds in her hands. It did not move, but its eye was bright and terrified, and Sibby could sense the anguished squeezing of its heart under the ruffling feathers. With one finger, Simirimia stroked it, listening, and as Sibby haltingly finished her description, the queen's fingers tightened their grip on the bird, and another question was asked. "Child, tell me of this princess, this—Dastra."

So Sibby spoke of her beauty, and her charm, and how the rumor was that Dastra was intended to be the wife of Leron. At these last words, she was surprised by the queen's laughter.

She looked up shyly and saw not the rage she had expected but a proud amusement.

Looking at the bird she held in her hand, the queen said, quietly, "They will not prevail!" And walking to the parapet, she flung the bird over the side, high into the wind. It fluttered a moment, then began flying strongly, lifting toward the sun. Simirimia watched for a moment, then gestured with two fingers only, her hands still relaxed on the stone balustrade. The bird fluttered and turned in the air, then fell turning over and over, to disappear in a small brown spot on the street far below. "They will never prevail. The power is mine." She dismissed Sibby with a gesture and did not turn to watch her departure.

That afternoon, Sibby decided that in some ways being bored was much worse than being frightened. No one came for her, not the queen nor any of Sibby's friends, and there was nothing to do but sit. The girls who brought her meals were silent as ever, and Lelu did not come that evening. Next morning, however, she was not left long in suspense. Small came while she was eating breakfast and took her urgently by the hand. "I want to see Leron," she said, but he shook his head.

"Hurry. Must see Arbytis. No time." He almost pulled her out into the passage and along the route they had taken two days before.

As they stepped in behind the tapestry, Lelu stiffened, and Sibby heard footsteps in the further room. Lelu cautiously put his eye to one of the many small tears in the fabric, and next to him Sibby did the same. Simirimia stood in the center of the room, looking at Arbytis, her head thrown back and her nostrils flaring. She was dressed in white. "So, my priest wakes." She touched the cage lightly. "These bars become you, Arbytis, as do your infirmities. Have you reconsidered?"

Arbytis looked up wearily and clasped his hands on his knees. "You must know that my answer cannot change."

"I only know that it must. Once in this very room I bent you, years ago, and so I shall again."

"Through me once you gained your desires, but even then you found you had gained more than intended." Arbytis smiled slightly as he spoke, but Simirimia, with narrowed eyes, made an impatient gesture with her hand. Fierce pain flitted across Arbytis's face.

"There shall be worse than that if you think to anger me. It is because of Dastra I must use you now."

Arbytis shook his head. "Have you not yet learned? My powers are my own. They do you no good. Now Dastra is in Tredana, what will you do? Your men took us too late, I think, and missed the most important one."

The queen gestured as before, and Arbytis recoiled as though from a blow. She leaned forward with an angry languid movement and hissed, "You laughed to see me gain my desires, knowing the words spoken so long ago for me. 'Death is the child of the Deathless One.' " She made a contemptuous gesture with her hands. "But you are in my power again, and there are certain others hostage to your fate and mine. Until you tell me what I wish to know, your blood shall run in your veins like fire!"

Arbytis's face contorted in agony, and he fell back against the bars. Yet even as he writhed in pain, he managed to gasp out, "And what then? If I do not speak, will you kill me?"

Simirimia almost spat with frustration, yet she stopped Arbytis's torment. "You shall wish for it more than ever you did through all the weary years. Though my child should destroy me, yet shall I destroy the hope of the Tredanan house. And you shall see it all, though I now keep your eyes."

As she began to pace about the small room, she came near the hanging, and Lelu hurriedly pulled Sibby back, closing the panel behind them. He was shaking with helpless anger.

"Can't we help him?" asked Sibby.

"You must stay safe," said Lelu, and hurried her away. At her door he paused only a moment. "I will come when I can. Remember. Be careful." And he vanished down the corridor.

Left alone, Sibby was so angry and frightened it was some time before she could control herself. She kicked the hard, unforgiving wall and pounded in frustration against the heavy glass window. Finally the tears came, and she sat on the edge of the bed with her face in her hands, furious and shaking. Why had she come? There was nothing she could do to help anyone. She did not even look at her food when it came but lay back on the hard bed and tried to figure out all the things she had been seeing and hearing. If only she could see Leron and talk with him, so they could make plans. She stayed under the covers until late in the evening, when a serving girl came quietly in to fetch her. Sibby gladly followed her out.

Their way led down several flights of stairs, coming at last to the great audience hall where Sibby had first been brought. Simirimia was seated as she had been before, and she looked at Sibby closely but did not signal that she sit. At length she spoke. "I have had a curious revelation." Sibby said nothing. "I have spoken with one who is acquainted with you. Stand forth, my wolf. Is this the child?"

And to Sibby's dismay, the robber known as Black Wolf stepped from behind the massive colonnade that encircled the room. He was shaggier and older than Sibby had realized, with a hard brown face and long untidy grey hair. "It is she," he said, adding, "and more than a mere child."

Simirimia beckoned, and Sibby was compelled to walk up and stand before her. "Show me your hand," said the queen, and Sibby held out her right hand, palm upward. It was thickly scarred, and the fingers were partly bent. "Demons do not burn," said the queen.

"But I tell you," said the robber, "she showed no pain. She laughed at us, and spoke in a mighty voice."

Simirimia looked at him coolly, and slowly nodded. "I believe you. You shall be rewarded. Go now."

"But what of her companion?"

"Do not try to think for me. You may become unable to think at all. Go." And the robber backed hurriedly out and left the room.

Simirimia looked again at Sibby, this time through slitted eyes. "You have not been open with me. Who is this Herrard, this traveler?"

Sibby thought quickly, her eyes avoiding the queen's. "He—he was a friend of Dansen's. He agreed to bring me here after Dansen disappeared."

"Where is he now?"

"I—I don't know."

"You must make me better answers. The Wolf met you by Villavac. Why not turn back there?"

Sibby stared at the ground, feeling foolish. The blood drummed in her ears and she could think of nothing except that she was trapped. Something forced her to look up. The queen was smiling slightly, without warmth.

"I wonder that you told your fabric of lies about Tredana.

Perhaps you had some purpose in coming here. You must be examined further."

"I wasn't lying. Ddiskeard is the new prince, and Dastra is there."

"It is the other heir interests you more. I should have known when I saw your eyes. You are some cousin of the prince, thinking to deceive me. Well, I shall take you to him. Come." And Sibby found herself following Simirimia out of the room.

The room to which she was led was familiar, although she had never been in it, for it was the room of her dream. The chair where Simirimia had sat stood by the fire still, and Leron sat by it on the floor. He was looking into the fire. When they entered, he turned eagerly and got to his feet. Sibby had forgotten how handsome he was. "My lady," he said happily, and then he noticed Sibby. "Sibby?" he said slowly. "What brings you here?"

Tears had come into her eyes and she couldn't manage her voice, but finally she said, "Leron," adding ridiculously, "you're alive."

"Of course," he said and turned from her to go down on one knee before Simirimia.

"I did not dare hope you would visit me today," he said, and Simirimia let him kiss her hand, smiling slightly. She sat down in her chair, and Leron settled himself at her feet. "You are not entirely forgiven," she said, but she dropped her hand caressingly upon his neck, and smiled at Sibby who was watching with wide startled eyes. "Tell me, prince, who is this Sibby? Your cousin, perhaps?"

Leron shook his head. "No, a stranger who joined us on our misguided expedition."

The queen's brows lifted slightly. "Then she is known to Arbytis as well?"

"Assuredly."

"Curious. I shall require an explanation from him. You will accompany us." As she spoke, she stood up, and Leron followed obediently. He did not look at Sibby or speak to her, and she thought she felt empty because she had not eaten dinner.

An extract from Skotla
A COMMENTARY ON THE THIRD BOOK OF DZILDZIL

*. . . some feel they can trick their fate and live comfortably
hedged by reassuring prophecies. Little do they realize that
the True Light, Vazdz, knows all and sees even unto their
hearts. Thus it fell out that when Shubar of Vahn fell in love
with the Moon, and promised to build her the greatest and
strongest palace in the world, stronger even than the citadel
of Vazdz, he fell into grievous error thereby. Fearing the
righteous jealousy of the One, he sought and found a prophecy, telling him the Goddess would be true to him as long as
the building stood complete, and furthermore that the stone
would yield to no man's hand nor yet to weather, and that he
also would endure so long as his work stood whole. Vain and
foolish man! He turned his back on Vazdz, building to his
own glory and that of the inconstant Moon. She had been un-
true to him more than once before the last stone was set, and
as he wandered mad with grief, a great bird caught up the
topmost block and flying past him dropped it on his head.
And thus the prophecy was fulfilled according to the plan of
Vazdz, and not as a mere man had read it.*

Chapter Twenty-one

The room where Arbytis was kept was dark and quiet. The queen must have stayed after Sibby and Lelu fled, for Arbytis was sunk in an exhausted heap, red marks like burns showing clearly across his pale face. Sibby looked at Leron, but he was curiously unmoved. "How can you stand to see him caged?" she cried, but he looked at her with bewilderment.

"I see no cage," he said, and turned once more to watch the queen.

At Sibby's words, Arbytis had roused himself, and he sat in the corner of his cage supporting himself on the knuckles of one hand while he smoothed his beard with trembling fingers. Simirimia spoke quietly. "I bring two visitors. Both I think are known to you."

Arbytis nodded gravely. "You are welcome, Sibby. I hope your trip has not unduly taxed you."

Sibby shook her head, then remembering he could not see, said in a small voice, "No, I'm fine."

Arbytis nodded again, then turned his strangely open face in Simirimia's direction. She answered his unspoken question. "I have come for an explanation. Tell me of this child. What are her powers? From where has she come?"

"She is Sibby, come by an accident of fate, and her powers are the usual ones of locomotion, smell, taste, and the like."

Simirimia clenched her left fist, and Arbytis whitened with pain. "This is not a place for wit. I have no time for it."

"Truly, you have no time left. The end which began with your child's birth comes ever nearer, and the wings of the Yinry are beating on the wind. Do you hear them, goddess? Even you must answer for the breaking of the law. It was not your place to create life, and that life once created may not be tampered with. Even you may not escape the Yinry."

The queen's nostrils flared with anger. "The Yinry sleep still as they have since the world was made. Do not think to scare me with priest's cant. The wheel is turning still. This prince whom once you persuaded to interfere in our affairs may now undo what has been done. He will shortly march on Tredana with a great force at his back, and Dastra I think will trouble us no more."

Sibby looked at Leron in amazement, but he was still watching Simirimia. Arbytis only smiled, a little sadly. "A great force? Where are your thousands? Was it five hundred years ago or six that you stood here, and the numbers of youths glittering in silver mail was so great that it dazzled the eye. But they are sealed away in gold and lapis lazuli and agate, and their red mouths are dust. Where are these thousands now?"

There was silence for a moment, then Simirimia answered softly, "I have no need for panoply. The Karif is mine, and the Karabdu will ride at my command."

Arbytis said only, "They are mighty warriors. But no victory was ever assured."

Simirimia walked up to his cage once more and grasped the bars with her hands. "It is for this I require you to light me a lamp. Stay. Do not be eager to refuse. Whatever this child may be to you, she is less than nothing to me. She is my hostage." As she spoke, she tightened her grip on the metal and Sibby fell to her knees with a small cry, feeling as though a band had been drawn tightly about her head.

Arbytis spoke out hurriedly. "There is no need for this. I will read for you. Will the lamp content you?"

"It is all I require for the present." And she released the bars. At a gesture, Leron fetched for her a small casket from a niche in the wall. He never looked at Sibby where she still knelt, her hands pressed to her head.

Within the casket were cards painted in gold and green and red and blue and yellow. In Arbytis's hands they seemed to waver and shift of their own accord, and after he held them a moment in silence, he spread them on the floor of his cage, making a lamp as Sibby had seen Ginas do. There were many familiar cards, some even in the same places they had held for Sibby's reading. Arbytis pressed his hands against his empty eye sockets, then spoke.

"Three things sparked this lamp, the single star, the queen of ships reversed, and the Player, also reversed. These signify together the triumphs of hatred, depravity, and perversion, of vanity and negligence. A wrong road was chosen, a mortal error made." Simirimia said nothing. "First in the past stands the wheel, reversed; that is an ill act of fortune. The three of stars shows faulty judgment and the seven rings are imprudence. I think you understand to what the cards refer." Arbytis was speaking without passion, and Simirimia continued silent. "The ten ships reversed mark your present state. This is a deadly strife between blood relatives. An influence on your future is a card you do not need to have read, the Double Goddess. But the wisdom of her unity is denied by this other, the six of stars, deceiving, leading to no solution. And I see in the future the five spears of desire ever unsatisfied, the star-child, which is perception come too late, and the four rings, which are selfishness. The flame: Calab stands reversed, and positioned thus he means no hope, no new road of escape. This is a true reading from the great book itself." Arbytis fell silent, and Simirimia looked on the cards, pale with some unguessable passion. At length he spoke again. "I could have told you this without the images, as I could have told you my sight did not lie in my eyes, thus saving us both pain. The book is mine, and I am still high priest, whatever my circumstances. Eyeless or whole I am still the Seer."

Simirimia suddenly drew herself up, and her power could be felt in the air. "High priest, I charge you, alter your cards. Look again and see what changes there may be. Listen for my future victories."

Arbytis shook his head. "I have listened for your victories and heard only silence. I have looked down the passages of your future and seen them empty but for dust. I have smelled the air to come, but the blood reek drowns all other scents. The cards will not alter. The Yinry will not be stayed. Take Tredana if you must, dispose of men and things as you please, but the end will not change. The blood is there. Can you not smell it? How it sickens the heart!"

"If you smell blood it is your own, priest!" She made a savage downward motion with one hand, and Arbytis fell forward, his hands still pressed against his face. As he fell, she turned to Leron and took his hand in hers. "Prince," she said, and her voice was changed and soft, "in this hour you would have been of greater use to me had you been born a woman." Leron looked startled, and the color rose in his face. She smiled. "I mean no insult. But the women of your house could dream true dreams, descended as they were from the readers of Ornat. I have need of true prophecies, and this priest whose one duty should be to serve me mocks my need and seeks to turn my purposes aside with warnings of destruction."

Leron spoke haltingly. "But he should do as you command! He is your priest!"

"Yes, but I may not trust him. Prince, you cannot dream as your mother did and see the future for me. Yet you may serve me in this need. There is a vessel in Vahn that shows all manners of truth. I have often thought of it. Bodrum the king will send it to me out of loyal respect and awe, but I must have a faithful messenger, one beyond temptation. Will you fetch this for me? Our future together depends upon it."

Leron bent and kissed her hands. "I will hurry that I may be back the sooner."

Sibby looked at Arbytis in anguish and saw him smile a little. Simirimia also saw this, and she shook her head slowly. "Priest, I know your thoughts. You think he will not be half the distance to Vahn before he passes beyond my guidance. You are thinking I will never hold in my hand the great cup of the Zenedrim, the Jawmir itself. You are thinking the prince will return to his own city and not wait for any desert force. But I am not without skill in these matters. I, too, have thought, and now I will forge the ancient bond."

"No. Only consider!"

"I have considered. It is not difficult."

"It is not lawful."

"Your laws do not concern me, priest." She turned and beckoned gently to Sibby. "Approach me, child."

Sibby stepped forward, and as she did so Arbytis, dragging on the bars, half managed to rise within the stooping confines of his cage. "No!" he cried, in a surprisingly great voice which filled the room. "There is no need for this!"

Simirimia's eyelids drooped, half veiling her bright green eyes; she smiled, and her breathing was slow and pleasurable. "In one thing you spoke the truth, priest. Soon we shall see the blood of which you lately spoke. Leron, fetch to me my lamp."

Leron nodded his head and hurried from the room, and as he left Simirimia slowly stretched and began to walk about the room. Suddenly she halted, her head thrown back and her

nostrils flared. Then her black brows drew angrily together
and she gestured with her outer fingers at the tapestry. The fi-
bers fell apart, and it settled in a dusty heap, revealing Lelu
frozen in the hidden opening, bread and wine in his hands.
She gestured a second time, and the jug and plate fell to the
floor and broke. Lelu did not move, but his hands dangled
uselessly as Simirimia slowly turned back toward Arbytis.

"I fear you will wait long for this supper, Arbytis. So yet
again you come into my realm strangely accompanied. The
high priest of Ornat, friend to dwarves and desert tribesmen.
How the years change us. But I am not angered. Now I need
not spend my resources entirely." She flicked her hand at
Sibby, pressing her back against the wall. "This child shall
stand hostage still, until I need her again."

Arbytis shook his head despairingly. "Release the boy, goddess. He has done you no wrong."

"No, he does me service. He brings me what is needed for
the ceremony. He is a vessel filled with life." She smiled at
Lelu, and he stepped forward into the room, resistless. When
she lifted her hand, he fell to the floor as though his legs had
been struck out from under him. Only his eyes remained alive
and moving in his head, and when Sibby tried to reach for
him she found her own hands too heavy to lift and her tongue
dead in her mouth. Under dropping eyelids, she looked up at
the queen in terror and felt her head wavering on her shoulders.

Simirimia almost shone in the moonlight. She stepped over
Small as though he did not exist and pressed her body against
the bars of Arbytis's cage. "He will serve me well, do you not
think? In this matter a silver brooch would not be enough.
But the ancient bond, well forged, should prove the distance
to Vahn and the space of a month, should it not? Should it
not? Answer me, lying one."

Arbytis got painfully onto his knees and bent his head
humbly before her. "I supplicate, I plead . . ."

"It becomes you, Arbytis, in its uselessness. See now the
power you have mocked. Despair to prevail against the
Queen of Treclere."

She turned away from the cage, unclasping the warm bull-
headed snakes from around her naked arms. She let them fall
to the floor, and with them her heavy golden belt and neck-
laces. As she walked in a circle about Small, she began mur-

muring to herself, and taking the small dagger that had been at her belt, cut through a long plait of her hair, half the width of her wrist. When Leron came into the room, she met him at the door, still murmuring under her breath, and burned the hair through in the center as he held the lamp up for her. These she then crossed and laid in an X upon the floor, while Arbytis's desperate words went unheeded. At her bidding, Leron placed the lamp where the hair crossed and it burned up brightly in the small room. Simirimia's shadow stooped above her, and her warm scent filled their nostrils.

"Prince," she said quietly, "place him by the lamp." She gestured, and her shadowy hands loomed on the walls above them. Leron dragged Lelu's slight, wiry body across the floor and placed him between the hairs, his head by the center. "Prince, kneel by the lamp and place your hands on his forehead." Leron did so, and the flame leaped up between his arms, illumining his face and casting strange shadows on his familiar features. As Leron's long fingers pressed against his head, Lelu opened his eyes and looked up helplessly. After a moment, he shut them in resignation. The queen bent over and opened the throat of his tunic, exposing the great vein. This she touched lightly with her fingers, then took again the small gold dagger, looking into Leron's face. "I shall bind you to me with the bond of blood." Leron looked straight into her eyes, nodding. "It cannot be broken except by death. As long as you live you are mine." And she held the blade to the flame, until it glowed red.

Arbytis was still on his knees and had his face in his hands, his white hair dangling about him in disorder. "It is unneedful," he cried, "a wanton act. . . ."

Simirimia interrupted him. "The wheel has spun around as it must, and the words you spoke to me seventeen years ago have brought us here tonight. Remember that throughout your ceaseless future."

As Sibby struggled and drifted in her mind, she saw the queen's arm rise, the lamp flame hard and bright along the blade. It seemed to her that the arm was raised through light and shadow very slowly, and she watched it lift and watched the play of light on Leron's unfamiliar face for many minutes before she realized what was about to happen. Her mind was as slow as the minutes had become, and she could not speak or keep her head from falling forward under its own weight.

Then it seemed she was at the bottom of a long sweep of high uneven steps, and that the queen and Leron and Small were all assembled at the top, far distant. She was to go up and speak to Leron, but the steps went reeling around her and she could not tell up from down or one side from the other. So she grasped at the slippery surface and pulled herself up by painful inches, clinging to them as they spun round and round and almost let her fall into the unguessably deep darkness. She shook her head from side to side as she struggled, trying to free her heavy tongue, and at last her mouth fell open. As she came within distance, the blade was beginning to fall, slowly, through the immense distance. One word was forced out.

"No." Choking on her own dead tongue, she still managed to speak. "No. Leron. Listen."

Impatiently Simirimia brought the blade down in a shining arc, but at the last moment Leron flinched, jerking Lelu's head to one side while he looked at the queen with startled eyes. Lelu opened his eyes also, looking up into the prince's face, seeing perhaps his own blood there. For the queen had struck a second time, before Leron could take away his hands.

Blood arched up. The lamp was extinguished in its flood, and Arbytis fell forward on his face. His hands grasping the bars before him were spattered. Sibby slipped to her knees, knowing she had spoken a second time to the prince, a second time too late. The floor around her was wet with blood redder than the dragon's and as unneedfully spilled. But Leron knelt unmoved in the darkness, as Simirimia placed one dripping hand on his throat and stroked her own bare throat with the other. Their bond was forged as the great queen had intended.

An extract from Brydeni
OBSERVATIONS ON THE CUSTOMS OF LESSER TREGLAD

Uncatalogued ms. found in the library of the Royal House of Tredana by Dansen the Learned

Concerning their Rites of Passage

When a child is born to them, a wooden figure is carved by certain elders of the tribe, and this they inter with special ceremonies in a cave hidden in the ruins. Under one circumstance only may this image be seen again, as hereinafter described. It is their belief that so long as the image stands fresh and clean, so too stands he for whom it was cut, but with the latter's death the figure begins to decay. When it is dust, they say no longer does the spirit of that man dwell on the earth, and he is forgotten as though he never were.

For one reason only will they examine the image of a living man, which would be thought an outrageous act else. When that one of their number has been absent more than thirteen months, and no word heard, the chief will go alone to the cave to prove if that one be still living. And they all agree that those whose images were found to be crumbling never were known to come again to Treglad.

THE WHEEL

Chapter Twenty-two

Toward morning, Leron half awoke, strangely puzzled in mind. For a long moment he could not think where he was. It seemed he was at home in Tredana, yet in an alien bed. The window faced east as it did at home, but there was no friendly smell of sea and no blue sky. Instead there was only an incredible red light as the sun rose swollen and dark beyond the casement; the room throbbed with dawn, and pools of scarlet light puddled on the coverlet and seemed to stain his fingers. He thought he moved his hands away in distaste, but they did not move, and he realized he was not yet wholly awake. Even as he realized this, he was awake indeed, and it was much later in the morning; the sun was high in the blue sky, and it was round and yellow.

Leron got up and began to dress quickly. Now he remembered that the queen had asked a special favor of him the night before, a favor she would not entrust to anyone else. Her priest had betrayed her, and it was he, Leron, who was to go to Vahn and fetch the Jawmir. As he washed his face, he shook his head from side to side, but the cloudiness there would not go away. The strange gaps of memory that had been vaguely troubling him for several weeks now were even larger. The night before, Simirimia's words, the priest's refusal: it was all so unclear in his mind. But he could still feel her soft touch upon his throat, and such warmth and happiness spread through him thinking of her that the uneasiness had no power over him.

Even as he thought of her, the door opened and the queen stood there, smiling gravely on him. She was dressed in thinly pleated linen that fell to her ankles, her arms were bare, and in her left hand she was holding a heavy collar of silver. Leron hurried over to her and knelt down. As he kissed her hand, the warmth and closeness of her body dizzied him, but she raised him to his feet and held him steady with one strong hand.

"Good morning, my prince. Today is the day appointed. Today you will set out, my emissary, to fetch home to Treclere an ancient treasure. You will do me an extraordinary service. But first, I have a gift for you." With one hand she loosened his tunic at the neck and gently slid the silver collar into place, murmuring under her breath as she did so. The weight of the collar was smooth, warm, and comforting.

"As long as you wear my gift, you will never forget me." She checked his protest with a slow smile, and touched his lips with her fingers. "I jested only. I do not doubt the— power of your attachment."

She took his hand and led him to the room where breakfast had already been prepared. Leron was touched to see that she had ordered his favorite fish, fried crisp with their tails in their mouths and awash in butter, but he found to his wonder that he could eat no more than a mouthful. Feeling sick to his stomach, he set down his knife and fork, accused by their calm round eyes.

"Not hungry?" she poured out the wine and touched his hand to the goblet. "I am glad to see you do not leave me too easily. But drink, at least; you will need all your strength." She herself ate easily and with seeming relish. As Leron drank, his strength returned, and he felt more easy both in heart and stomach. He sat back and tried to memorize the queen, glad to serve her, yet in despair to think of leaving. He watched how her eyelids veiled her quick green eyes, how her hair seemd to move with a life of its own, wreathing around her stark white shoulders. How narrow her wrist was to enclose such strength. How secret her mouth and how warm and comfortable her body. As he thought of her body, her eyes slid sideways and met his own, quiet and amused. "You will not be long away from this—comfort. Be glad, my prince. Your efforts will bring our destiny into full flower. Together we will rule a united kingdom. Is a few weeks' journey a high price for eternity together?" Numbly, Leron shook his head, and Simirimia laughed silently, her head back and her throat arched against her dark hair. "Ah, you have learned your lessons so well." Suddenly she leaned over and kissed him on the mouth, deeply, and as suddenly pulled away. "You will find your things prepared for travel. Meet me in the audience hall

when you are ready to leave. There are messages I must give
you and certain instructions. Now go."

It was almost in a dream that Leron returned to his room
and found clothes laid out for his journey, the hunting knife
and flask and heavy boots, his own sword freshly oiled in a
new scabbard. As he buckled it to his belt, a fragment of
memory came to surface in his mind, some great beast with
black shiny skin suffering and bleeding, a feeling of guilt and
pain. The memory sank from sight as quickly as it had risen,
but even as he left the room with all his gear he could still hear
faintly the words of this strange vision, a child's voice crying,
"No!"

For a moment after he had entered the great hall, he
thought he was still dreaming, for the child of the vision was
there, her eyes the same as when she had cried no in that surprisingly loud voice. Then his head cleared and he recognized
Sibby, but she did not return his smile. Behind her stood the
Karif, attentively to the right of Simirimia's chair, light from
the small windows in the roof picking out his pale and arrogant profile. When Leron entered, the Karif had been looking down into the queen's face with a bold intimacy, but he
turned and nodded politely, one eyebrow slightly twisted in
recognition or impudence.

"So we have met only to part," he murmured formally.
"Vaźdz attend your going as he did your coming, and may the
Light illumine all your future paths." Leron looked past him
to the queen, who smiled and rose and took his hands in her
own.

"A double throne awaits your return, prince of the house
of Tredana. Soon the Karif will set out on his campaigning,
and the army he raises will be ready for your return, to march
at your back on the long journey home."

She let Leron keep her hand in his after he had kissed it,
and she touched his neck lightly, just above the collar.

"We are bound by blood, and need no trinkets to link our
souls, but the powers of the circle are many and may prove
useful. You know your task, that is, to ride to Vahn and demand of Bodrum proof of the fealty he has sworn. Since the
days of Sembath, loyalty has been sworn to Treclere, but this
is the first proof ever required. When you give to Bodrum the
papers and the messages I send, he will give to you the Jawmir

and you must come straight back. But I do not think you have it in your heart to linger." She smiled, narrowing her eyes, and Leron nodded. Gently she took away her hand and lifted a packet of papers sealed with red ribbons, that was lying on the broad arm of the chair. "I will look to see your return in one month's time. Now bid farewell to your young friend and leave. The horse stands at the door, your escort is mounted and waiting."

Leron took the packet and kissed it, and tucked it safely away in the breast of his tunic. Then he turned to the child to say a friendly word of farewell and saw she was crying. He smiled kindly at her.

"Do not weep for me, child. There is no danger in this. I will soon be home again."

She made no answer, turning her head aside, and Simirimia's mouth twisted slightly. "Departures must ever sadden. Go quickly, my prince, that you may return the sooner."

There was an unmistakable note of command in her voice. Leron nodded once more to the child, puzzled by her strange behavior, and murmured a brief word of parting to the Karif. Ajjibawr nodded courteously in return; he was standing offensively close to the queen. Leron tried to take her hand again, but she drew gently back and shook her head. As Leron left the room, his last sight was of the Karif standing next to the throne, his hand on the arm. He could not see the child.

The courtyard was in full sunlight, and there three mounted soldiers waited, his own laden horse beside them. He mounted in silence and followed his escort out through the gates, hearing, although he did not turn to see it, the wooden gates bolted shut between himself and Simirimia. He set his horse forward at a slightly faster pace, and the soldiers matched his speed without comment.

Their way wound through the city's silent streets, past open, quiet courtyards and somber alleyways. Beyond the western gate, the road became an obscure streak across a level dusty plain, and along it they continued while the sun slowly moved down into their line of vision, blinding them. Mid-afternoon they halted. The captain of the soldiers did not speak, but pointed straight ahead into the setting sun. Then he wheeled about and his men followed, cantering back along the road they had come, a glittering armored blur on the darkening eastern skyline. The meaning was clear, and Leron pushed his own horse on into the sunset.

An hour later, Leron made camp, strangely tired. He had not ridden for months, and his whole body protested the new exercise. At first the wood he gathered would not light, but finally he managed to encourage the blaze into a small but steady flame, and by it he sat and reflected, too tired and too lonely to think of eating. At first he did not even move when he heard a horse's hooves, thinking his own horse was wandering in search of better grass; then he recognized the sound of a rider and got to his feet as a stranger rode up, halted, and swung down from off his bony, lathered horse. It was an ugly chestnut and had obviously been ridden hard, for it stood with trembling legs and dropped head, its lower lips loose and quivering. The rider patted its neck and turned to Leron with a smile.

"I crave your pardon for this disturbance. When I saw your fire, I pushed on in hopes of companionship, for I felt I could not bear another night alone in this wilderness. May I keep your company here?"

Leron nodded uncertainly. The stranger was a big man, taller than himself, with a brown beard and eyes. He looked to be strong, and it occurred to Leron he might be a robber. As he thought this, the man smiled, and touching his throat lightly bowed courteously.

"I am Rassam, called the Traveler, presently on a journey from the desert peoples to Vahanavat. I would consider it an honor to break bread with you."

Leron nodded, feeling ungracious. "I am Leron," he said at last, "also on a journey to Vahanavat. You are welcome."

Rassam smiled. "First I must attend to my poor horse. I will return in a moment."

When he came back, he was carrying two bundles. The first was an array of foods unfamiliar to Leron, strange vegetables and herbs that were soon simmering in a pleasantly steaming stew. The other, a triangular case of canvas, reminded Leron of something long ago. He put out his hand hesitantly. "A curious shape," he said at last. "May I ask what you carry?"

Rassam looked up from stirring his dinner and smiled.

"Only my harp," he said. "An ancient instrument for which I have much fondness. It even bears a name, though why an object should require such, I do not profess to understand. It is called Telyon."

Leron fell silent but the longing to see Telyon itched in his fingers. Finally he spoke again. "May I—may I see this harp?"

Rassam motioned with his hand. "Open the case, friend. You may look and play also if you like."

For some reason Leron found his hands were shaking as he unfastened the case. Inside was a harp gleaming with deeply polished wood and glittering in its inlay work. He touched the strings, but the sound was disappointing, dull and unresonant. Embarrassed, he put it back with stammered thanks.

Rassam said nothing but handed him a plate of stew. While they ate, he commented, "It is a difficult instrument. But to the right fingers it can be remarkably responsive." Leron nodded.

The stew was delicious. Soon the food and the fire's warmth completed what the ride had begun, and he stretched out by the fire, his suspicions of his new companion forgotten. He looked into the flames a moment, then touched his collar and fell asleep with Simirimia's name upon his lips.

Warming her own hands by the great fire in her chamber, Simirimia heard him and smiled slightly. For a moment she watched him sleeping there, then an unfamilar restless urge seized her and she paced the room, aware of a chill in the air for the first time in centuries. The Karif had gone back into the city, and now she regretted the loss of this pleasant diversion. Almost she considered sending for him once again, when her hand brushed against a carved wooden box set on a low table. Although her treasures gave her little joy now, she took up the dried bit of leather that once had spoken words of prophecy. She fondled it with her fingers, then made a small motion with it in her hand, calling to herself he whose tongue it once had been. In the deepened shadows of the room, a dark figure slowly formed and stepped out into the dwindled torches' light—manlike, featureless. The Great Queen smiled.

"Speak as I bid, answer as you must." The figure nodded. "Tell me again of the Zenedrim. Speak of the Kermyrag and the Jawmir. Speak the old words."

Softly, like wind in a reed pipe, the words sighed from the mouth of the Tongueless Speaker, and Simirimia listened with half-closed eyes. But she frowned as he finished speaking, for the closing of the old words were these:

> Petitioner, late and soon
> you follow the dog down and
> you drink the water of the underworld.

"Always the same! Priests! Doom and long memories. Just so did you speak in the temple, Hartun—was it a thousand years ago? No matter. A hundred thousand spring rains washing down on your buried body can not erase your presence here, not while I hold the bond. Ah, Hartun, why did you resist me? Think what rest would have been yours by now, and what powers first. But you are useful in your fashion. Be gone now." She pushed lightly with her fingers and Hartun was gone, broken up into shadows once more.

THE PROPHECIES OF THE ORACLE OF ORNAT:
An excerpt concerning the Kermyrag

> You have seen him burn in the north: a thousand suns
> are not more beautiful than his flame.
> You have looked into the cup: a thousand wells
> are shallower than its hollow deeps.
> Speak to the Zenedrim, behold the flame,
> Look in the cup, pluck the immortal harp;
> Even so is the great price not yet paid,
> As the sea is emptied not in years but ages.
> Will you buy from him, O Petitioner?
> Will you buy truth of him, the Zenedrim?
> Will you buy life of him, the Lord of Fire?
> Who hears these words, heed and consider well:
> even the Great One, even the Bird of Fire,

even the Winged Lord of the changing air,
even His Excellence shall not escape
The Yinry.
    Petitioner, late and soon
    you follow the dog down and
    you drink the water of the underworld.

Chapter Twenty-three

The road to the mountains was flat and uneventful. During the next few days the travelers rode and camped, from time to time fording the broad shallow rivers that wandered across their path. Leron grew slowly to trust the stranger, Rassam, although they spoke together very little. His chief companion was Simirimia. The queen's necklace comforted his body with its warm heavy weight about his neck; it was as though he could still feel her hands laid soothingly on him. He did not ask to see Telyon again.

In less than two weeks they had reached the mountains. The road rose along easy inclines, doubling back and forth as it climbed the pass. At the very top, it entered a gorge where only one horse could walk at a time, and this was true for almost three miles. This was the famous Karseni pass, Vahn's chief protection from surprise attack. Rassam explained that in the legends of Vahn it was said that the evil Yarum's team of monstrous horses had dug the gorge with their restless pawing, as Yarum waited to surprise the daughter of Anith and carry her off to his hidden kingdom. But, he added, it was more likely that it had been caused by some great river long since diverted to another route. The wind booming between the high stone walls did sound like horses, though, and Leron could understand the reason for the story's having lasted so long.

Another four days' traveling brought them to the coastal plains. The white, flat-roofed buildings of Vahanavat showed clearly against the green land; and many strange-looking ships lay at anchor in the harbor beyond. As they rode nearer and nearer, there was a pleasant smell of the sea and a stronger smell of fish. Leron was vaguely reminded of Tredana, and it moved him in an obscure way. Rassam stood up in his stirrups and breathed in noisily. "Although I am no sailor, I have ever enjoyed that salty smell, and

195

missed it in its absence."

Leron smiled and touched his necklace with one finger for reassurance. "I also," he said softly. "Now we are arrived, friend, can you direct me to the palace? I have a duty to discharge there, and seek as I told you before an audience with the master of Vahn."

"Unless matters have changed since my last visit, it is too late in the day for you to go to the palace. Come with me to the inn, and we will find at what hour the gates are opened and at what time you should be waiting there. You have a letter to show the seneschal?" Leron nodded, and touched the front of his tunic. "Then there will be no trouble for you. Without such an introduction your wait might be long indeed."

The streets of Vahanavat were narrow and cobbled, high in the middle with open drainage ditches along each side, and they wound in and out among the low, apparently windowless buildings. Through gateways, Leron could see that the houses all faced inward upon their closed courtyards, turning to the streets a blank protective back. At one of the many crowded stalls, Rassam stopped for a moment and showed Leron a fruit he had never seen before in Tredana or Treclere. It had a thick, rough, sunny skin, and when he tried to eat it the sweet juice ran over his chin and spotted his tunic. Rassam did not laugh at him, though, for he was too busy wiping his beard dry with the back of his dusty sleeve. Fascinated, Leron would have also bought some smaller, similar ones, a beautiful yellow in color, but Rassam smiled and shook his head, rebuking the vendor who assured Leron that the small ones were even sweeter than the large. "They are good for cooking," he said. "But more acid to the tongue than vinegar." Leron reluctantly let the fruits go, and they went on their way again.

The inn was easy to locate. It was called The Ship and was built out over the water on one of the principal wharves. Grey-green water lapped past the windows of its public room, and everything in it was slightly damp to the touch. Rassam was greeted as an old customer, and the host confirmed his suspicion that the palace gates had closed for the day. He counseled Leron to be waiting at sunrise the next morning. To Rassam he added, "Tonight even you will not regret having to stay indoors in such mild weather. Lord Baradel is holding a feast with singers and other entertainment, and has paid for a roast pig as well."

Rassam grinned. "Truly, one misses the taste of pork in the desert. Tonight will not be a loss despite its being spent indoors. Now if the singers will not be too noisy and let me eat in peace, all will be well."

Leron frowned. "Why do you carry a harp if you do not care for song?"

"A harp?" asked the host, and Rassam motioned him to be still. "I enjoy my own music," he said easily, "but not that of others. It is a great pity Odric must ever be in the north, in Mindo'ila; were he here, you would hear real singing."

The host smiled. "But he is here! And he will sing tonight and play his baraka. Tomorrow he sets out for Mindo'ila, but he has been here this month or more. If you visited us more often, you would know he returns to Vahanavat every six months or seven. You came in good time."

Rassam nodded. "In good time indeed. I have not seen Odric for two years. This evening will assuredly be a pleasant one."

Alone in his room, Leron washed and dressed in clean clothes. Rassam had arranged for their traveling garments to be washed, and Leron was relieved to strip off his filthy linen shirt and dusty tunic. The new clothes from his bundle smelled faintly of the herbs used in the presses of the palace of Treclere, and it made his longing for the queen even greater. He threw himself down on the bed, his face buried in a clean shirt, and tried to pretend that the familiar scent came from his sheets instead. He was still lying there half asleep when Rassam tapped at the door, and he hurriedly pushed the shirt out of sight as he got up and called, "Come in."

Rassam stood in the open doorway, with clean clothes and water-smoothed hair. "Are you ready? Does not your mouth water already? Smell the pig fat crackling!"

Leron sniffed and smiled. "Ready indeed," he said and followed his companion into the hall.

Downstairs, many of Baradel's friends had already gathered. Rassam did not see Ordic, so he sat down in a corner with Leron, and they ate as soon as the meat was done, their travel-starved stomachs too impatient to wait on the probable coming of an old friend. While they ate, Rassam told Leron some of Vahn's history, of which Leron knew only the vaguest and most legendary bits.

"You know they trade with the Karabdu, bringing them coffee beans and silk cocoons in exchange for fine wool, carpets, and finished silken fabric. Trade is the life of Vahn. The ships in the water ply to all known lands and discover still others, taking the goods of our world and exchanging them for new, unknown, and valuable items." He wiped his greasy fingers on a hunk of bread, ate that, and continued. "But perhaps you are not aware that legends link the early history of Vahn with that of Tredana, through the destruction of Treglad. It is all because of Arleon."

"Arleon? Yes, I remember. They say—they say he fled the destruction of Treglad and, wandering the world, came at last to Vahanavat. That was before he founded Tredana. I remember Dansen saying. . . ." Suddenly the necklace seemed tight, and he could not speak. He pressed his hand to his eyes. "I don't really remember any more," he said in a strained voice.

A strange voice broke in on them. "Arleon?" it said. "Do I hear the name of that blackguard spoken here?" Leron looked up angrily, but saw only humor in the bearded face confronting him. The stranger was not a tall man but strongly built with a barrel chest and a magnificent chestnut beard curling over it. He wore the tight conical cap of Vahn and a sailor's gold earring; there was a stringed instrument dangling from a strap over his shoulder.

"Odric!" Rassam got to his feet and clasped the stranger's hands between his own. "How that beard changes you!"

"It is not the beard so much as the good eating. Letha feeds me too well. I grew the beard only to cover my extra chin."

Rassam laughed. "Then you are appreciated in the north?"

"Indeed I am. I tutor the royal brats, eat at Letha's own table, and have two months of my own time every year. I am to return tomorrow, but now you are in town, I think I should stay another day."

"Make it two at least." He drew Odric down beside them and introduced him to Leron. Odric needed no urging to join them at meat. He was shortly interrupted, however, by several coming to him and demanding a song. He explained to Rassam that he had lost a wager with Baradel and his forfeit had been that he sing for him one evening as long as it should be required. So he put down his knife with reluctance and stood up, settling his instrument in a comfortable position across his stomach. Before he started he nodded at Leron. "I will sing first of Arleon," he said, "and you will see how fine he was."

As Odric told the story, Arleon seemed a blackguard indeed. Odric sang the lament of Queen Damari so sweetly, telling the story of her tragic meeting with Arleon, that all the room became totally still, listening.

> *Down from the hills, friendless and sick,*
> *Arleon came here so—*
> *I welcomed him into my city*
> *Healing my hands: my breast*
> *brought comfort: generously*
> *I gave of my peace and rest.*
> *Arleon, once I asked*
> *if you would stay or go:*
> *You looked and you smiled and said,*
> *"When the sun and the moon set together,*
> *then shall I leave." How I dread*
> *Sky and heart's strange new weather.*
>
> *Damari! Where shall she go,*
> *Burnt moth, passion's slave?*
> *Death-drawn what can she do*
> *but look for peace in the grave?*
> *My child shall not serve another,*
> *He who is Arleon's son*
> *shall rule for his dead mother:*
> *I that was Queen in Vahn.*

And Odric explained that as she had foretold it was so: Damari died and the present line of masters is descended from her son, who was a fearless sea captain named Sembath.

Leron listened to Odric with surprising emotion, and was pleased when he yielded to another man's request for a ballad. First Odric paused, however, speaking quietly to the two men who had asked for the first song. Then he bent down to speak in Rassam's ear. By now there were at least twenty young men in the room. "My friend Baradel was to have been here ere now. It is not like him to pay for an entertainment and then miss the food and the music. If he does not come soon, we may have to go looking for him."

Leron watched Rassam's face, then said, "Why so worried? What could befall one here?"

Odric looked up from tuning his baraka, and said briefly, "Men have been known to disappear and return later much changed. But we shall not speak of that here." Smiling broadly, he turned to the others in a room and bowed with a little flourish. "It shall not be said Odric does not pay his debts. The next song is a newer one, and in honor of my eastern friend." He indicated Rassam with the neck of his instrument. "It too concerns the people of the eastern lands, and a sad love story there." His fingers plucked a melody from the strings, and he began to sing:

> *A lady on an eastern shore*
> >   *Seasons pass and the seed is sown*
> *Two only were the babes she bore*
> >   *Sing, for all the singing birds are gone.*
>
> *The son has grown in strength and grace*
> >   *Seasons pass and the seed is sown*
> *The daughter fair in mind and face*
> >   *Sing, for all the singing birds are gone.*
>
> *The daughter now is queen and mother*
> >   *Seasons pass and the seed is sown*
> *Loving still her twin, her brother*
> >   *Sing, for all the singing birds are gone.*
>
> *To battle now he rides away*
> >   *Seasons pass and the seed is sown*
> *She with her lord and son must stay*
> >   *Sing, for all the singing birds are gone.*

As Leron listened he began to have difficulty swallowing. His stomach contracted and his palms began to sweat. Such was Odric's skill that he could see those two walking in the garden, deep in talk, while a small child followed unnoticed tugging at his mother's dress.

> *Two months are passed and the queen is ill*
> >   *Seasons pass and the seed is sown*
> *She moans and then at last is still*

Sing, for all the singing birds are gone.

Home from the wars a dark bird flies
  Seasons pass and the seed is sown
And at her window sits and cries
  Sing, for all the singing birds are gone.

Leron could see it all, as vividly as life. The queen pale and sick, sweating with fever and crying of death, crying for her brother's slaughter in a far land. And he could see the unnoticed child, the unnoticed father, standing alone in the shadows.

Sister, sister come with me
  Seasons pass and the seed is sown
And we shall fly beyond the sea
  Sing, for all the singing birds are gone.

Sister, leave the rest behind
  Seasons pass and the seed is sown
And we shall fly above the wind
  Sing, for all the singing birds are gone.

Sister, sister come away
  Seasons pass and the seed is sown
And we shall fly night into day
  Sing, for all the singing birds are gone.

Her maidens bar the window tight
  Seasons pass and the seed is sown
But she is gone that very night
  Sing, for all the singing birds are gone.

King and prince must weep alone
  Seasons pass and the seed is sown
For far away these two have flown
  Sing, for all the singing birds are gone.

Leron sat stricken at the table, one hand to his cruelly contracted collar, seeing for the first time in many years his mother's face and that of his uncle. There was a sickness rising in his throat, and he got up hurriedly to go to his room. But as he rose to his feet, the door opened and a small man seemed to bounce into the room. "My lord has been taken by the master's guards. Hurry. Everyone must go home. They will come here looking for his friends."

Odric took the man by the shoulder, and the others clustered around. Rassam touched Leron's arm. "We must go to our rooms. Remember we are here merely as guests. It was chance alone brought us to Baradel's celebration." He interrupted Odric, who was questioning the newcomer. "You will be safe?"

Odric nodded. "I will send you word tomorrow. Do not worry. There are many holes for hiding in this city."

Leron allowed himself to be led from the room, and as he did so he heard the small man telling his story in a low urgent voice.

"We were on our way when they stopped us. Six guards. They asked for my master by name and did not speak to me at all. I knew he would want me to warn . . ." Then the door closed between them, and Rassam was hurrying him up the stairs.

Confused as he was, there was a question he had to ask, a question that had nothing to do with Baradel or any of his friends. Rassam was trying to push him into his room, urging him to undress and appear asleep, but he insisted on having one question answered. "That song, the one Odric sang. You know it?"

Rassam nodded impatiently, then suddenly looked into his eyes with a strange awareness and almost a kind of pity. He answered slowly, "Yes, I know it."

"Does it have a name?"

"Yes." Rassam began closing the door between them. "It is called 'The Song of Leriel and Armon.' "

Leron undressed, but after he had gotten into bed he lay awake, still seeing those two in the garden. Seabirds shrieked and lamented outside, and the surf pounded in time to the rhythm of his blood. He was very tired, too tired to care for the tread of Bodrum's guards on the floor below or the hall outside. And after the guards had gone, he lay there still, trying to remember, wondering how long it had been since he had forgotten who he was.

Simirimia was aware of his distress, but she impatiently waved Leron's image aside, intent on a visit with Arbytis. In his chamber, the dried blood on the floor appeared black in the torchlight. The old man lay exhausted, his head slumped

forward on his drawn-up knees and his long hair in disorder.
For a warm pleasant moment she watched, then woke him
with a thought.

"Tell me, my eyeless Seer, what truths do you see tonight?
Do not try to fool me any more. You have seen my powers.
Leron, whom you so carefully nurtured to aid in the reveng-
ing of Armon, whom you led to Glass Island and whom you
aided in the releasing of my daughter—where is he today?
What does he remember of all your teachings now? He is
blood-marked and bonded and does my bidding. And now,
safe in Tredana, how will this daughter of mine cause me the
harm you prophesied? Tell me, priest, was it all lies? Was the
prophecy you spoke eighteen years ago another lie, another
part of the monstrous web of falsehood you have made, hoping to trap me therein?"

Arbytis lifted his face toward her, making no attempt to
conceal the pain that still was there. "Great One," he said,
and there was no irony in his voice, "I see your death as I said
before. The keepers of the old order stirred when you raised
Armon and made life from his death. It was a great offense,
but the first, and the Yinry stayed their coming. A second offense, and even the daughter of the Great Mother, even you,
O great Queen, shall not escape the Yinry. Is the cold age you
feel now a lie?"

"The cold is in your bones, not mine. I shall not offend the
Yinry. They may sleep on undisturbed. They need never have
awakened had it not been for your tricks. Perhaps when they
come, it will be for you. Who told me what words to say?
False priest!" Her knuckles whitened as she held the bar, and
the pain of her anger brought blood up into Arbytis's white
face. Not until he dropped forward again in exhaustion did
she release him, with reluctance. "You cannot lie to me forever. Some things I have already guessed. You planned to pro-
voke my power against my daughter, did you not? The second offense. I know the old laws. I will not harm Dastra.
And now all your plans are so awry, I need never even see
her." At the door to his room she looked back and smiled
again. "Poor priest. Old man. Perhaps you should turn to
my sister for strength." As she laughed, the door swung silently shut and Arbytis was alone with the smell of blood sick-
eningly strong in the air about him.

An extract from Brydeni
THE VARIETIES OF THE HUMAN RACE

*Many prominent authorities assert that the seafarers of Vahn
may properly be considered a variety of the human race sepa-
rate from the five others above mentioned. It is common
knowledge that this people first dwelt not on the continent
but on a far western island, having no contact with other
lands, but fishing and tilling the earth. They had their own
gods also, and when Vazdz appeared demanding homage
they refused him, so that he destroyed their island in fire and
smoke as a lesson to other obdurate peoples. Many fled in
boats to settle on the continent's fertile western coast. Their
homes, however, they did not forget, and once they had new
ships built, they sent in every direction looking for their island. Thus were they led gradually into their present ways of
seafaring and commerce, but their old home they have never
found. In appearance like unto the people of Treclere, they
are, however, a strong and luxury-loving people, frequently
given to barbarous cruelty with respect to their enemies.*

Chapter Twenty-four

That night, Leron dreamed he was standing before a great fire, smoky in his lungs and hot on his face and hands. He put his hands into the flame, and the pain burned through his wrists up into his shoulders, and one great flame broke free and seared him on the throat. The pain was so great he could hardly breathe, but as he wavered on his feet, the flames became a wide cool lake, with grass-green serpents coiling in the depths. They came wreathing up onto the sand, caressing his ankles, and everywhere they touched was suddenly quieted. Lovingly they came up onto his neck and wreathed his arms, and he gave himself to their embrace and finally slept in comfort.

It was not yet light when the host tapped on his door. Looking up through his high latticed window at the greyish sky, Leron thought of sleeping again, dismissing the tap as a mistake, but then he remembered his audience with Bodrum. The water in his basin was chilly, so he washed briefly and dressed quickly.

Downstairs in the big raftered common room, it was quite dark, and mist beaded the dull metal plates ranged along the walls. A few embers glowed in the fireplace, and as he warmed his hands by their vague heat, he almost remembered his dream, but it eluded him.

After a few minutes the host came in from the kitchen with some cold meat and wine. He was followed by Rassam, who looked absurdly alert for such an unfriendly hour. Rassam carried a brass pot in his hand and a small cup. The odor of the coffee was pleasant and unfamiliar to Leron, but the taste was a great disappointment, and he let Rassam finish the entire pot. They sat in silence, eating, until Leron spoke.

"Last night, was Odric in danger?"

Rassam shook his head. "No, the warning came in good time. The guardsmen found an empty inn. But there is fear

205

for Baradel."

"Do you know him?"

"No, I have heard of him only. He is a friend of many in Vahn; for some, the only one. Bodrum is jealous of power, and friendship is a kind of such."

"Can none of his friends help him?"

"Not easily. You will know better after you have visited the palace. And you had best go at once, despite your letter. The line may already be a long one."

It was. When Leron reached the palace at dawn, the gates were just being dragged back and pegged into place for the day. Already a crowd of some thirty or forty people had gathered, mostly women with children. Leron found they were wives come to plead for husbands who had been arrested or pressed into government service. At first he had only curiosity, but as he looked into their faces and heard them talking among themselves he felt an interest that was almost pity, even though they were only common people.

The sun drew the mist off the courtyard where they waited, and as the grass dried, the air became warm, then hot. The servants of the royal household were sumptuously and inappropriately dressed in heavy velvet, despite the gathering heat of the day, and soon sweat ran down their dark faces. They hurried about, telling people where to wait and what to say; and as the hours passed and the heat increased and no one was admitted, their tempers shortened and several in the crowd were rudely pushed away.

Finally, midway through the morning, an inner gate opened and the seneschal appeared. Leron would never have fought his way through the supplicants clustering round him if one of the lesser servants had not noticed the letter from Simirimia he was carrying rolled up in his hand. With his short staff of office, he made a clearing in the crowd and pulled Leron by the edge of his tunic to stand face to face with the seneschal. The seneschal saw the mark of the great seal of Treclere and his brusque words faded in his throat. He signaled two of the guards to come and accompany himself and Leron into the palace, bowing with new respect to the Great Queen's emissary.

"Your pardon, lord," he said. "We did not know you were waiting here." He pushed an old woman aside who was kneeling, her skinny hands and fleshless wrists raised in appalling supplication. "My master will see you at once. He is always pleased to receive a message from Treclere." And he motioned for Leron to precede him into the palace.

Within, it was arched and light. Their way led not to an audience chamber as Leron had expected, but through into the center of the palace compound, where there was another courtyard much larger than the one by the gates, overlooked by the countless windows of the palace rooms and encircled it. At one end of the courtyard, a small group of men were playing music on an assortment of instruments. The melody was pleasant and apparently had words fitted to it, although at that distance Leron could not distinguish what the singer was saying. In any case, his attention was drawn to the nearer end of the yard, where a group of fierce young horses were being held by a few stableboys. From time to time the horses reared and flashed their feet forward, straining at the ends of their taut lead ropes and whinnying. What excited them was a rider, galloping furiously past them round and round in circles.

The ridden horse was silvery grey, much lathered about the mouth and darkened with sweat. The rider's large belly lapped onto the horse's neck, and his robes obscured much of its body, so that only its long, sweeping tail, thin legs, and restless head could be clearly seen. A small dark object lay in the dust, and apparently the rider was attempting to reach down and seize it as he galloped past, but each time he attempted this the horse swerved away, nearly unseating him. On the fifth try he succeeded and, whirling the horse around on a sharply tightened rein, came galloping full speed up to the seneschal and Leron, brandishing what Leron could now clearly see was the severed head of a goat.

"Truly was it written," he cried hoarsely, "that one may look to the desert for virtue as one may look to the sands for flowers. These horses the Karif sends are more ox-clumsy every year. Did you mark how near he came to stumbling? If Our team is to be victorious, Our horses must have finer balance. Remind Us to write the Karif tonight, indicating Our grave displeasure."

The seneschal took the horse by the bit and held him as Bodrum dismounted. "Truly there is no one more skilled at Zir-i-bala than yourself, Great One. Much training will be necessary before an ordinary rider can hope to compete on such an animal. But the horse is fast?"

"Fast, yes, but speed alone does not make Zir-i-bala, no more than one tree makes a forest. A horse must combine the spring of a panther, the lift of a hawk, and the tenacity of a bear, as his rider must show the fortitude of a lion and the poetry of a champion. Who is this youth?" Bodrum turned on Leron suddenly, and Leron flushed because he had been covertly examining the man's face. Bodrum's small pink mouth pursed irritably as he waited for the seneschal's reply.

"A messenger from Treclere, Great One. He bears a letter from the Queen."

"From Treclere? From the hand of our Gracious Lady? It is no wonder that the light of his moonlike countenance fills Our poor yard with the reflected glory of her noble presence. Come into Our chambers, if you will. We must consider her gracious words in seclusion." He swept in ahead of them, and Leron followed with the seneschal, who left them alone in Bodrum's small, high-ceilinged office.

Leron stood by awkwardly while Bodrum read the queen's letter. The Master of Vahn walked over to the window, where he stood holding the parchment close to his face, his lips moving softly. Then he let the letter fall to the table and sat down in his velvet-hung chair. He smiled. "The message is as fair as the hand that wrote it. Our respects to her and Our fondest welcome to you, royal cousin of Tredana." He nodded his head, indicating that Leron might be seated. "Cast off the natural humility you must feel in Our presence; remember, you, too, are a prince." Startled, Leron sat and waited for the Master to speak again.

"Our gracious lady writes that you will explain all in Our presence. We are, as Vazdz himself would publish abroad, a most loyal servant to her majesty. Tell Us, therefore, what do you require?"

Leron began to speak, at first hesitantly, then with increasing confidence and detachment, the silver collar suddenly tight about his throat and seeming to shape his very words. He said or heard himself say the purpose of his journey, he heard or saw himself hear Bodrum's surprise and pleasure at

Simirimia's interest, his surprise and concern at his inability
to comply—it was the unexpected note of concern that
brought him fully awake. Bodrum was speaking with his
head slightly bent, a fleshy droop of hand and wrist concealing his mouth and softening his words.

"For the Great Goddess, the most Noble Simirimia, how
could We refrain from doing whatever she might graciously
command? The chief treasures of Our realm would not be
enough to express Our humility and gratitude toward her.
The Jawmir We would gladly give, were it still in Our hands.
But, alas, it has been absent from Our realm these thirty years
or more." There was a plate of life-sized fruit cast in solid
gold and studded with red gems on the table, weighing down
some papers. Bodrum took up an apple and fondled it in his
hand. To Leron the gems looked like monstrous sores on the
fruit and he could almost imagine it splitting open in the master's grasp into rotten flesh and worms.

Caressing the fruit, Bodrum continued. "In truth, it was
more than thirty years ago. A moment of the Great Queen's
time, but long enough for Us despite Our many godlike at-
tributes." He spoke without irony. "We were young then, passionate perhaps, and there were difficulties with Our people.
The old men of Our council, whom We could not properly instruct owing to Our youth and inexperience, decided on some
false religious mummery: gifts to the Kermyrag in the utter
north, a request for guidance from the Zenedrim. They had
their way and the journey was undertaken, the Jawmir going
as a gift returned to the Zenedrim. Truly is it written that once
the snake of deception nests in the brain, one may look for a
host of little serpents to hatch there, folly and imprudence,
deceit, falsehood, and outright lies. Thus it was with Our
council, and thus We caused them to be removed from their
high offices. We rule alone now, except for the guidance
of Vazdz. But the fabled Jawmir is lost with those who carried it, buried deep no doubt in the snows of the pathless
north."

He tossed the apple an inch or two and caught it as it fell
back, his eyes on Leron's face. "As We read this new situation, We are not unaware of your unenviable position. You
must steer a tight course. Failure to return with the Jawmir
might even arouse the Great Queen's august anger. But We

are mindful of the needs of others. We will help you to steer north yourself. Perhaps it is written you will find the Jawmir there."

There was a rap on the door. Bodrum frowned, then cried impatiently, "Enter!"

The seneschal appeared in the doorway, bowing low. "My humblest apologies, O Great One . . ."

"Speak up, tell Us quickly, why do you burst in upon Us?"

The seneschal coughed. "It is a matter concerning the— your late champion's son."

"Yes?"

"Our methods having proven fruitless, and the time being short, I thought it necessary to address my ignorance to your worthy Omniscience, risking this interruption and hoping for your sun-eclipsing mercy."

Bodrum waved his hand impatiently. "Fruitless, you say? No word at all?"

"Not one. He laughs at us!"

"Let the prisoner find that this should rather be a place for tears. Apply the full force of the law. He may shorten a painful hour as he wills. Truly it is written that the fate of the unrighteous rests in their own unclean hands. We will come shortly, and inspect your progress. Now you may depart."

The seneschal bowed deeply and backed out, closing the door behind him. Bodrum smiled again on Leron. "We have had an idea worthy of Us. There is one in the city who may provide you with the guidance you need to fulfill the Great Queen's bidding. We will summon him and send him to you. His name is Odric, and he shall do your bidding."

"How—how long is the trip north?"

"No man can say exactly. Two months should bring you back again, if all should prove successful."

"Two months. I must send a message to the queen."

"Of course, of course. One of Our own men shall ride to Treclere. Write now, if you wish." He hesitated, then murmured in a low, tactful voice, "If you would prefer a scribe, We will send for one. . . ."

Leron smiled and shook his painful head. "No, I prefer it thus. I can write a fair hand." Seated at Bodrum's table he hesitated a moment, then began carefully making the smooth round letters his old teacher had shown him. The image of his teacher troubled him for a moment, standing between him and the parchment; then as he finished making the proud shapes of the name Simirimia, the image vanished and he could write more freely.

SIMIRIMIA:

Leron, Prince of Tredana, Governor of Villavac, and heir to the houses of Mathon and of Leriel, sends you this greeting by the hand of a friend. Know that in the pursuance of your gracious wishes I am forced to journey north even to Tremyrag, and will not return to Vahanavat for two months from this date. Look for me then in three months' time, bearing that object you desired of me, and know that I am your most devoted and obedient, Leron.

He signed the letter carefully, folding up in it his hopes of happiness and rest for another three months' time, setting on it with a seal of wax the finality of his separation from the Queen.

Bodrum took the letter from him and laid it on the table. "We will take good care of this. We understand in Our benevolence that you will want to set out as soon as possible. We would invite you to stay here for the night, but We understand you will have many arrangements to make." Grasping Leron firmly by both shoulders, Bodrum kissed him on each cheek, calling for the seneschal almost at the same moment. "Travel in health and safety," he murmured, his bright eyes uncomfortably close to Leron's and his hands lingering on his shoulders. As the seneschal entered, Bodrum stepped back and, taking up Leron's letter, passed it into the servant's hand, closing his fingers over it. "A message to Treclere," he said. "It must leave immediately."

The seneschal bowed, "I shall attend to it as you wish, Great One."

Bodrum smiled, and clapped Leron on the shoulder brusquely as he left.

The full afternoon heat struck Leron in the face and filled his lungs as he stepped out of the palace corridor into the light. His collar was still too tight, his head ached unbearably, and he had failed to complete his mission. Three more months. He was not even sure of finding the Jawmir. The queen might think he had betrayed her. He stumbled up the steps into the damp, cool inn parlor. It was empty, and Rassam's room stood open at the top of the stairs. He managed to get into his own and shut the door before falling face forward onto his bed. If only he could have said more in his letter. Would she know he had wanted to say more? He shut his eyes, but the pain behind them sickened him and would not let him sleep.

LETTER

By Private Messenger from Bodrum VIII
at his Summer Palace to Madam Letha
at her residence in Mindo'ila.

Royal Madam and Dear Sister:

It is Our Melancholy Task to inform you that the Stinking Rot and Corruption which festered lately in Our Reign has once more burst out to spoil Our Summer Content. The Son of Our Late Champion has proven the Truth in that old Wisdom, that what is bred in Bone must flower in Flesh. Last Night We questioned him straightly on these matters, and although We do not have a Clear Answer as yet, We have already decided in Our Wisdom to send Odric Northward to return to your House.

Consider him closely: Mark his Words and Manner; do not permit that he should leave, except to journey North as We have required. For with him travels a Young Man, some Vassal of Simirimia of Treclere, who styles himself Prince of Tredana. We do not choose to interfere with Simirimia's plans, but if Odric indeed accompanies him, it may be a Most Useful Solution. For although he is both Idle and Ignorant, Able Tools have been made from Less.

Our Affectionate Regards to the Boys.

BODRUM VIII
Given under his hand and seal at Almond Island, on this the 12th day of the 7th month of the 39th year of his reign.

Chapter Twenty-five

Well in time for supper, Leron rose from his bed and washed his face and hands. As he dried his face, he could feel his slight beard rising along the edges of his jaw and his hands automatically took out and sharpened his iron razor. The soft pull of the razor across his face was soothing, and now he could see it was far better to journey north for the Jawmir than to return empty-handed to Treclere. Three months might be an eternity for him, but Simirimia was wise and would understand.

Downstairs, the inn parlor was nearly empty, except for Rassam and another sitting together with their backs to the door, near to the sluggish fire. Leron recognized the chestnut hair and the instrument lying half-strung on the floor. Bodrum had wasted no time.

They turned at his approach, and Rassam smiled. "Supper is already ordered," he said. "We thought you would be down soon. I disliked to disturb you when you have such a heavy journey before you."

"Take this," said Odric briefly, and handed him a mug, which he filled from a jug of wine standing by their feet. He poured it neatly enough, but his hands were shaking, his face was pale, and his mouth was tightly compressed, absurdly pink in the depth of his wild brown beard. Leron nodded cordially and drank. The wine of Vahn was sharp and musty, and he made an involuntary face. Odric smiled halfheartedly. "The poetry of Vahn does not lie in its vineyards. Nor I fear in the grace of its government. I stand before you at royal command, to accompany you north: we leave tomorrow."

He spoke shortly, and Rassam laid a hand on his sleeve. "I am sure this is no plot of our friend's. Why I doubt he has even heard of Tremyrag and the Zenedrim."

"I do not care what myths and fables he knows or does not know. But to be forced from the city when my friends have need of me, to chase after legends and fantasies, distresses my soul."

Leron felt the blood rise in his face. "It is not the matter of some foolish fantasy. We travel on behalf of the Great Queen of Treclere, on whose service no man might better put himself in danger."

Odric raised his eyebrows. "This puts me in mind of all those tedious tales they tell in the villages, wherein the hero is sent from village to farm to court to castle, round and about again, all to fulfill some trifling request. I prefer to sing these songs and not to live them."

Leron threw down his mug. "I do not need your help. Set me on the right road, and I will leave tonight if necessary. I never asked your help."

Rassam shook his head. "This is not a good beginning for your trip. Peace, friends, peace. You, Leron, will do well to avail yourself of Odric's companionship and knowledge of the north. And you, Odric, have no choice in this matter. Be thankful you are merely dismissed from town. Would you rather follow your friend's fate?"

"His fate. That's the heart of it. How can I leave, not knowing his fate?"

Rassam smiled reassuringly. "I am not unskilled in these matters. I will help as it lies within my power." He turned to Leron again. "You must pardon our friend, who is distraught over a personal matter. Now let us sit and eat, and speak of your forthcoming journey."

While they ate, Odric and Rassam began a friendly argument concerning the north, and Leron listened closely. He had some fleeting memory of these stories, of an old man teaching him the tales, years and years ago. Odric maintained that north of Mindo'ila there was ice and snow only, but Rassam swore he knew one who had been to Tremyrag and spoken with the Zenedrim there. "What, your deathless priest? You are too honest, friend Rassam, too easily tricked."

"When you meet him, then you will believe."

"Possibly. But it will take more than an old man with a long white beard to make me believe in Tremyrag, and the Zenedrim its guardian, and the great Kermyrag burning for all time. Good songs—but songs only. What, Rassam, why look so grave? Do you think the Yinry will come and take me away for my blasphemy?"

Rassam smiled, but his shoulders moved in a slight tremor. "No, the Yinry do not come for ordinary men. For gods and goddesses and maybe kings, but we are safe. They are keepers of the old laws, and we are less than nothing to them."

Odric laughed, relaxed for the first time that evening. "Rassam, Rassam! I cannot credit what I hear. You are a believer."

Rassam shrugged his shoulders and nodded. "I believe," he said simply, and Odric did not press him further.

After supper they sat for a while in silence. Odric sprawled in his chair, one dangling hand plucking at his instrument, which lay on the floor beside him. The notes reminded Leron of a harp. Suddenly, he turned to Rassam. "I would have liked a chance to try your harp further. I think it is a sweeter instrument than the baraka."

Rassam grinned, with an odd look like relief in his eyes. "Try it now, then. It had been in my mind that you might want an instrument to help you pass unnoticed with Odric. There may be suspicious villages, unfriendly people, between here and your destination. Try it again, and if you like, take it as a parting gift from me."

Leron felt an absurd uprush of pleasure. "I cannot thank you enough—it is too much—"

Rassam shook his head. "Consider it yours. I will fetch it now. I fear it is sadly in want of tuning."

Leron flexed his hand as he waited for Rassam to return. At some time he was sure he had played a harp, but he could not think what the notes were or how the strings were struck.

When Rassam returned, Leron carefully undid the wrappings and stroked the glossy, oddly familar wood. There was a crack in its side, but it was tight and well-mended. The harp fit comfortably to his hand and rocked into an easy position on his knee. As he adjusted the pegs, he could hear the notes it should sound ringing in his head. He grinned at Rassam and stroked the harp. "Telyon. I think this is the best present I have ever had."

"It gives me pleasure to hear you say it."

Hundreds of melodies were suddenly jostling for attention in Leron's memory. His right hand, dropped against the strings, found the tune for him and slowly plucked the clear sweet notes, strange and familiar at the same time. Odric smiled. "You have a good ear to remember my tune so well."

Under his breath he murmured, "Seasons pass and the seed is sown. . . ." As Leron realized what he was playing, he paused, stricken. Unnoticing, Odric reached forward. "May I see this harp?" He took it clumsily, and in his hands it seemd an awkward shape. He ran his hands over it, trying to coax forth a melody, but the sound was discordant. "I will teach you the baraka," he said, "if you will help me with this."

Leron nodded, forgetting the cruel images of Odric's song in his eagerness to explain. "It is not so difficult. Here . . ." He took Telyon and placed the harp properly against Odric's knee. "You hold the instrument thus, and the playing hand like this . . ." He rippled his fingers in the air. "Always remember the hand's position. My old teacher always said the instrument was no better than the hand that played it." As he spoke, he struck the strings, and Telyon trembled with an ugly, dull resonance. He pulled his hand across in a simple run, and the notes plinked sullenly like pebbles on sand. His smile faded, and he put the harp away from him on the bench, tugging with one hand at his silver collar, suddenly tight and heavy. "It seems—it seems I must teach myself before I teach another." Suddenly afraid, he took up a freshly poured mug but in the firelight the wine looked like blood and he set it down, sickened.

Soon afterward they all retired; and as Leron lay waiting for sleep, the taste of wine in his mouth was the taste of blood. And Odric's ballad would not leave his head. Indeed, as he finally slept he could almost feel the black bird on his windowsill, singing so cruelly, so very, very sweet.

That night he slept with one hand on his collar, to feel Simirimia's presence the better, and he awoke much happier. As he packed his saddlebags, he found he was looking forward to Odric's company. He would learn new songs and play the harp, and presently return in triumph to Treclere.

By the time Rassam came down, Leron had already eaten and was leaning out the window. He smiled at Rassam. "The weather is fine for traveling. We have a good day to set out."

Rassam nodded and sat down to his breakfast. "You will find Odric a good comrade and a cunning traveler. When he comes here, you will find he has already purchased the supplies you need, at half the price you would have paid. He has a special trick of going to the market early in the morning, just as it opens. Odric will bargain for this item, and that, until he has a group together, and for these he offers one price. I am a poor man, says the merchant; I would not cheat you. Liar! says Odric."

Rassam paused to whack the top off a boiled egg with his knife. "He says liar but he smiles, and there is no malice. He shows them the money he has offered, and they are tempted. But they will wait. They think he will come back later and pay a little more. So he makes ready to go, as he goes, he says, it is a pity I cannot buy from you. This afternoon I must be on my way to walled Luntar. In six months' time, or more, I will be back. Well!" He set down the empty eggshell delicately, smiling. "They cannot wait six months. He gets his price, they all drink tea, everyone is happy. And yet, if you or I went there that same hour, we would pay twice as much for the same things. I must confess, I do not understand merchants."

At that moment, Odric pushed open the door, his arms laden with foodstuffs. Leron laughed delightedly, and Odric grinned in answer. "Has Rassam been telling tales on me?"

"Only good ones." Odric set the things down on the table. There were two fur cloaks, and done up inside them was a hunting knife, a new tinderbox, a string of onions, tea, sugar, a large lump of animal fat in a clay pot, a chunk of salt, and other staples.

With Rassam's advice, they made three piles, one for each of their own riding horses and the third for the pack animal that Odric had bought.

"Truly," he said, "I may have been cheated in this, and the merchants laughing at their long-awaited revenge, but my curiosity was such I could not pass the beast by."

"What manner of beast is it?" asked Rassam.

"I do not know. They have no name for it and said some smugglers had it. Talaat, from whom I bought it, I have long suspected of receiving stolen goods from robbers in the east. It is some sort of northern animal and I hope well suited to our trip. Its fur is very long, and its hooves are in two parts. They said it will carry twice the load of a horse, but then, they would say the same of me if I were theirs to sell into slavery." He laughed and sat down to eat.

Rassam watched him for a moment and replied, "You eat twice as much, at any rate."

"My frame requires sustenance." Leron looked at their modest supplies, wondering how long they would last, and

Odric caught his glance. "Do not fear to starve, lad. We will be in walled Luntar within the week, and food is cheaper there."

To be exact, it took five days, five days of constant traveling beginning with the first light and continuing until somewhat after the late dark. The road led through long, rising fields, which spread treelessly from Vahanavat to the mountains in the north, then up into the hills. As the road climbed slowly into the barren, folded foothills, the night became colder, and they left the villages behind. Less than one day on the road was enough to show that Odric's fears about the pack beast were unfounded. It was a willing if not very rapid walker, and for Leron it showed an especial fondness, following him about the campsite at night until he was forced to tether it, and even then resting its head against his breast and slobbering its green cud lovingly down his front.

The second night out, they camped in the lowest range of hills, where the air was already much cooler. Telyon came easily into Leron's hands, and he was able to play a few melodies for Odric, although he could not remember the words clearly. Odric tried a few tunes, berating his clumsiness, then tuned his own instrument with a sigh of relief and idly pulled a sweet air from its strings. And so it went the following evening also. Odric was working on a new ballad, and Leron listened idly, lost in his own thoughts.

But the night before they came to walled Luntar, things changed. It started trivially enough. He was brushing the pack beast's matted hair into pleasingly glossy shape when it inadvertently leaned upon his foot, and there it continued to lean despite his words and blows, for it was sleepy and not very intelligent. Odric had to throw his whole weight upon the halter to shift its bulk, and Leron found that the pain and annoyance had spoiled his mood. After dinner the harp came awkwardly into his hands and its strings fought him, refusing his touch. As he savagely tightened the upper notes, the top two strings snapped, raising a welt across the back of his hand. Odric tactfully kept silent, so Leron was denied even the small pleasure of an argument. Finally he slept, to wake in a misty, drizzling dawn with an aching head added to the pain of his foot and the smarting of his hand. They set off in silence, broken only by the pack beast's surprised bellow when Leron rapped him across the shoulders to make him move more quickly.

Shortly after midday, they came to the city. Luntar was the ancient northern outpost of Vahn, well fortified and set commandingly high upon the edge of the mountains. Its outer walls, once carved with intricate representations of Vahn's glorious past, had crumbled, but the defenses of brick and mortar still stood, repaired in places. A small city had grown up around its outer line of defenses, and shops and huts and stockyards straggled up the hill and leaned against its walls. There were surprising numbers of beggars in the streets; many seemed to have been branded and some had only one hand. Odric explained it was the sign of a convicted thief, which made it surprising to Leron that he should stop and give a coin or two to most of those who barred his way. There were even beggars clustered by the door of the inn where the two intended to spend the night, just within the walls, and Leron pushed past them embarrassed as Ordic stopped to speak in a friendly way and give out a few more coins.

That night at dinner, he intended to bring up the folly of kindness to outlaws and thieves; but before he could turn the conversation, a loud drum interrupted them, muffled at first, but increasing as it seemed to come nearer to the inn. They were eating in a private upstairs room, meat and vegetables burned black on an iron skewer but strangely delicious, when at the sound of the drum Odric looked toward the window with a grimace of distaste, dropping his food onto the table.

"What is that?" asked Leron, and as he spoke the sound boomed directly below their window and he could hear the sound of a crowd also, and laughter. Torchlight flickered on the inner side of the window casing.

Odric wrinkled his nose and took up his food again. "There is no cause for alarm. It is merely a signal for . . . amusement, such as has become popular under Bodrum's patronage."

Leron stood up and moved to the window. "What amusement? Is it that game—Zir-i-bala or whatever he called it?"

"No, Zir-i-bala is a court pastime. This one is popular with soldiers and the poorer sort of tradesmen. Bear-baiting."

The words meant little to Leron. He had seen a bear once and was curious to see one again from a closer distance. Perhaps it would lift the black humor he had been carrying since last night. "Good. I had been getting bored. Where is the entertainment held?"

"In a hall built for the purpose, not far from here. But I assure you it is nothing you would enjoy. It is very rough."

Apparently Odric felt it was up to him to make all the decisions. Leron moved resolutely toward the door. "Do not wait up for me. I have long been curious to see such." He closed the door with a snap and went lightly down the stairs, pleased with his resolution.

ODRIC
Ballad fragment

The Lady rose up in the morn
and she's left her Lord in bed,
and she's away to the gay green hills
to follow her heart instead.
And she's not ridden a mile, a mile,
a mile but nearly three,
when she's met her True Love in the road
and she's kissed him heartily.

Well met, well met, my own True Love,
but we must not tarry long,
we must be in your castle high
before they find me gone.
And they had not been a week together,
a week but nearly three,
when this Fair Lady's begun to weep
and cry most bitterly.

Why do you weep, why do you mourn,
why do you sigh so sore?
Do you regret your palaces,
your silks, and golden store?
I do not weep for these, she said,
nor for any golden store,
but I do weep for my own little son
whom never I shall see any more.

A year, a year, a year ago
I held him to my breast,
but they took him from his mother's arms
and never now shall I find rest.
Her True Love's kissed her on the lips,
cried, Love, be of good cheer.
We shall away to the False Nurse's gates
and bring your son back here.

Then he has mounted on his grey,
the Lady's up before,
they ne'er did stop until they come
to the King's own sister's door.
And as those lovers rode along
little did they guess
that never sun would rise again
upon their happiness. . . .

Chapter Twenty-six

In the street outside the inn, it was dark, and Leron picked his way carefully along the rough road in the general direction of the drumbeat. Not far ahead, the road opened out, and in a small square stood a large building made of heavy wood timbers. From time to time the door would open and throw a long yellow oblong of light across the square, loud with the talk and laughter of the men inside. The drum now sounded from within. As Leron approached, the door opened again, making him blink with the brightness of the torchlight within; one hand came up instinctively to cover his nose as well. The smell of the place was strange and strong, like a stable, only more sour. Jostled by other latecomers, he went inside and looked around curiously.

The building was a large hollow hall, open to the roof, with a pit in the center. Ranged about on benches or in small groups were perhaps two hundred men, in light armor or drab cotton shirts and trousers. On most of the soldiers the mail hung loose and unfastened. They were talking and drinking, and a few lay stretched out on the floor or huddled sick in the corners—partly explaining the smell. But most were watching the entertainment in the pit, so Leron looked also, his hand still covering his nose.

There was a post in the pit, and chained to it from a leather strap around his heavy neck was a bear. He stood stoop-shouldered and bewildered, shaking his head from side to side as though to clear it, and his armored paws made futile little passes at the air. The thick rank fur of his coat was matted with blood, and in front of him stood a wiry young man, stripped and armed with a knife. The boy lunged forward and slashed the bear's side, and, pulling himself upright, the bear made an effort and hit with one dangling paw. There were a few scratches on the boy's white ribs; this blow missed him completely. A roar of laughter went up from the crowd

and bets were changed. More slowly this time, the boy
reached up and cut the bear's right ear open to the bone, and
this time the laughter turned to cries of derision, for the bear
did not retaliate. Its head fell backward under its own weight,
and it seemed to look reproachfully at the man, blood running darkly onto its collar. But this was in appearance only,
for its eyes had long since been dug out. Desperate to prolong
the show, the man circled behind the bear and cut through the
collar with two sharp tugs. At this, several sitting near the pit
moved back hurriedly, but most continued to watch as plac-
idly as before. As the collar fell, jingling on its chain, the bear
swayed forward, as though that chain had been its only support; but it recovered its upright stance and once more began
to shake its head, blinking and rubbing at its ear. Leron began
to feel sick. Suddenly confident, the boy in the pit sprang up
among the spectators and grabbed a cup of ale from the
nearest table, and also a long red cloak. Once more in the pit
he danced about the animal, fastening the cloak to it and arranging the folds in obsequious parody. The crowd yelled its
delight.

Like an old and bewildered king in an ancient legend, the
bear stood betrayed and helpless, ridiculous in its robes, surrounded by treachery. Its impotent eyes looked straight into
Leron's face, and he fell back before it, stricken with shame
and a curious pity, one hand trying to loosen the choking collar at his own throat. Then the young man held up his drink
to the bear and clowned at offering it, several times turning
his back on the bewildered animal. Finally, he tired of this
and threw the ale in its face. Snorting, the bear reared up and
growled, the cloak entangled in its front legs. It struggled a
moment there, heavy, clumsy, and foolish. Then it cast one
last blind look around the noisy bright lit hall and casually fell
forward. Before the man could beware, he was clasped in
iron arms. He screamed briefly.

There was a strange lack of violence about the man's death.
The bear's eyes were closed in weary resignation and its head
dropped forward lovingly on the man's bent neck. But his
clasp was final, and the crack of ribs was plain in the suddenly silent hall. It seemed a long time, but it was only a moment before several men with clubs had beaten the bear senseless and lifted his clean, unbloodied victim up out of the pit.
There was little fuss. And even as several men dragged the

bear's carcass out, two more brought in a pair of cocks, spurred and blindfolded, and were displaying them to the approving crowd.

Leron stumbled to the door and stood outside a moment, breathing heavily. Around the corner of the building another door opened, and he heard the men grunting and cursing as they dragged the bear out and left it with the other refuse there. Moved by something he did not understand, he waited until they were gone, then walked slowly over to where the midden was, stenching the air. As he picked his way through the rubbish, he saw a small figure move indistinctly through the dark to kneel by the shaggy carcass. Although it was very dark, and her back was to him, and there was no way she possibly could be there, he knew before he heard her speak that it was the child. Sibby.

Crying, she bent over and touched the bear's small fine face, where the hair grew close and shiny on the muzzle. About the mouth it was grey, for the bear had not been young. She was not aware of him behind her as she lightly stroked the rough hair, matted with filth as well as blood, following the line of the ribs, which stood up sharply angled in the bear's unnaturally huddled position. "Bear," she whispered, "O bear, I'm sorry." As she stroked its face again, a heaving sigh raised its ribs for a moment, and the lids twitched up from the empty eye sockets. It was alive despite the smashed skull. A distressingly small whimper came from its mouth, and the mangled head lifted slightly. Sibby leaned over and cradled the bear's head against her sheepskin tunic, whispering, "O bear, please die," and she kissed it. Finally, it did.

When the child made no move to get up, Leron put out his hand tentatively and touched her arm. He was still trembling himself, and he was not prepared for her greeting. "You!" she cried. "Here! I should have known I'd find you someplace like this! You probably enjoyed it!" Her lips trembled so much she stopped speaking and turned away. She was older than he remembered, but still very much a child. When she began walking away, he followed her silently, and when they reached her horse, he took the bridle still without speaking and they walked together toward the inn, the horse between them, in a painful silence.

Odric was alone in the upper room when they returned,

and his eyebrows lifted in surprise when Leron entered with the sullen, tear-stained child. When Leron spoke her name, his eyes lighted with friendliness and he bowed over her hand as though she were a great lady. "My friend Rassam, he whom you know as Herrard, told me of you. He thought you unable to leave Treclere, however, and I know he grieved for your safety."

"Arbytis helped me leave. He told me not to try to catch up with Herrard. He knew Leron would come here, and he told me the way to take. Ajjibawr helped, too." Her shoulders moved. "It was kind of scary. It was hard to get away, especially with the horse."

"Perhaps I will have to believe in Rassam's tales after all. So your friend the old priest sent you here, knowing that we would come. In truth he steered you aright."

"How is Herrard?"

"He was well when we left Vahanavat. But there are troubles in that unhappy city."

"Arbytis told me. He explained . . . as much as he could. And he said I would have to go with you—it's my fate. You have to believe him, even if you don't understand. I don't understand myself. But he really knows."

"Evidently." Odric saw how desperately she looked at Leron, still standing bewildered by the door, and he gently drew him over to the fire, urging him to sit.

"Little maid," he said to Sibby, "you must remember that our friend cannot forget the debt he owes the Great Queen."

For some reason these words made Sibby's expression softer, and she smiled a little sadly at Leron. "I know. Leron, I'm sorry. I didn't mean what I said before."

Leron was touched, but his pride had been hurt. "You are only a child," he said. "I knew that you spoke without thinking." He was pleased to see that the words hurt her, and soon she had gone to bed and left him alone as he wished.

Next morning early, when they went to the stables to collect their animals, there was another surprise. For Sibby suddenly looked up at him with her first real smile and said, "O Leron, how did you manage it? The ganoose! I never thought we would see it again!" And she ran to the ugly pack beast and threw her arms about its neck. Even as he began to protest that he had no idea what she was saying, the picture came into his mind of a frozen lake and two ganoose bellowing as he pushed and pulled them out onto the ice from the snowy shore. So, rather than admit this odd lapse, he merely nodded stiffly, avoiding Odric's eyes, and swung up onto his horse.

Upon leaving Luntar, they trotted in silence along the hard gritty road. Sibby suddenly squeezed her grey colt forward into a canter, then a dead run, disappearing around the bend ahead. When they turned the corner, they found her with the colt dancing in place, held back on a light rein but filled with exuberance and the desire to run again. She was caressing it with one hand as she waited for them, murmuring to it under her breath, and her black hair was as tangled and wild as the colt's arched tossing tail. Odric grinned at her. "Did that horse come from the queen's stables? It has a desert look to it."

"It is a desert horse. Ajjibawr gave it to me himself. Its father was his own horse, and this one is going to grow up to be just like him. He's nice, except he bites sometimes," she added truthfully. Odric laughed.

"A horse without some faults of spirit is good for nothing." He turned to Leron. "This horse makes a fine sight this morning, does he not?"

But with the mention of Ajjibawr, Leron's words of appreciation died on his lips. He recalled how insinuatingly close the Karif had stood to the queen when he left, pretending to agree to her plans. But if he were so friendly to the child, and to the false priest, what dangers to Simirimia might not appear? Ajjibawr might be a spy, an agent plotting the queen's downfall. "Truly," he said, "the Karif is justly famed for his horses. And likewise he is well known for his robbery and his deceitfulness, his raids and surprise attacks, his ruthless disciplining of the desert people. You were fortunate, child, to escape slavery in the desert and so come safe to Treclere. Though why you have left the shelter of the queen's protection for this journey north I cannot understand."

Sibby looked as though she would speak a sharp word of protest, then she shook her head with a funny little gesture of resignation. "The Karif was very good to me, and Dansen. He saved our lives . . . and Dastra's. But never mind." She turned and rode off ahead of them, more slowly than before, but too quickly for conversation.

That night after dinner, Odric took out his baraka and began trying to resolve his unfinished ballad. For a while Sibby watched and listened with her chin on her hands, then she went to groom her colt, leaving the two men sitting alone in the circle of firelight.

"The lady rose up in the morn and left her lord in bed . . ." Leron leaned his head back against the rock where he sat, trying to remember everything he could about Simirimia. The confusing memories of life before Treclere he firmly put away: they made his head ache, and since Sibby's arrival had become more constant an annoyance. The pulse in his neck was throbbing against the smooth, warm collar.

"She had not traveled a mile, a mile, a mile but nearly three. . . ." How many miles he would gladly travel. Well, she would be pleased, and thank him for his loyal services. . . .

"Well met, well met, my own true love, but we must haste away. . . ." How long would it be before they came again to Treclere? Then Sibby suddenly spoke out loud, interrupting Odric and his own comfortable reverie. She had her arms thrown about her horse's neck and her face buried in his mane. "How good he smells, just like grass and flowers!"

Odric would have ignored it, but Leron corrected her, kindly enough. "You have interrupted the song—you should ask his pardon." She looked up with surprise, and Odric shook his head.

"I was thinking out loud, I didn't mean to interrupt." Leron frowned, but she returned his look defiantly. Odric was smiling, peaceably.

"There is a story," he remarked casually, "of a princess who fell in love with a horse, thinking him a prince in disguise, and she made him her champion and escort. Wherever she traveled the horse must needs attend her, and in the end that prince who sought her hand in marriage had to challenge the colt and subdue it in fair contest." He was laughing as he spoke, and it was obvious to Leron that the legend had only just been made up for the occasion, but the result was not as Odric had intended. Instead of laughing, Sibby suddenly burst into tears, her face hidden against the colt's strong neck.

Odric immediately got up and went to her, placing his hand on her shoulder, but his words of apology were cut short. Sibby jerked her shoulder away and cried "Shut up," in a muffled voice. When he tried to speak again, she threw the brush she was still holding hard against his broad chest. It was very silly and childish, and Leron picked up the brush with a frown.

"Child, you should excuse yourself. You might have done our friend an injury." At this she turned and faced him.

"An injury? You—oh, shut up." She snatched the brush away from his fingers and went back to her colt. "Why don't you go kill something? They must have bears or something around here." She brushed the colt's sides with short strokes, wiping her eyes and nose from time to time with the back of her hand. At the mention of the bear, a wave of sickness made Leron suddenly sit down again by the fire, his legs gone limp. How could she possibly think he had enjoyed the pit? What had he ever done for her to think such things? He poked at the fire moodily with a stick, then rolled himself in his blankets in hopes of dreaming of Treclere.

The full moonlight suddenly flooding out from behind the mountains made him feel curiously exposed, and for a long time he lingered on the edge of an uneasy sleep. As he stroked the smooth round of silver about his neck, he saw slowly form behind his eyelids the image of Simirimia's warm firelit room, and he nestled more deeply into the softness of his blanket. There was peace in his vision, and great comfort. He smiled and slept, soundly at first, and in Treclere Simirimia rolled over in her great bed and smiled also, holding Leron as surely in her mind as she could hold any bird in her hands. She lay as peacefully as he, but did not sleep, running the centuries through her thoughts like pleasantly smooth but unimportant beads on a string. Blood held him as surely as bars held Arbytis.

Alone once more in his small room, Arbytis also had composed himself to sleep, his head leaning against the cold bars of his cage. His thoughts turned inward down the long tunnel of his life, time flowing backward, stopping, moving on, eddying around some memories, covering others, polishing bits of knowledge, and dissolving unimportant events. Back, far back at the beginning, it flowed out into the day, and there was his first life like a deep pool yellow with sunlight. It was so beautiful there that he surrendered his mind to it, refusing to be pulled back into darkness, and the sun of that day younger by a thousand years warmed his cold bones. He had been proud of the respect of young priests and readers and the casters of fate. The smell of Ornat was still the most beautiful thing he had ever smelled, water-washed stones and warm-breathing lamps of oil. And each day he had spoken with the goddess, vibrating with her answers like the great bell hung in the tower before the temple. "Arbytis. Arbytis." The memory of her speaking made him feel cold; clouds had come between him and the sun. "Arbytis!" He was being drawn back into the dark, away from the light. "Arbytis." Suddenly awake, the old man clutched at the bars, listening and unmoving. It was not a memory. The goddess was speaking, so faintly it could not be heard above his quickened breathing and painful heart.

Time passed, and there was nothing but his own blood pulsing in his ears. He dismissed his hope as the vain wishes of an old and hopeless man. But even as he relaxed, he heard the name again and knew he had not imagined it. "Arbytis." It echoed faintly within his head as it once had strongly within the dome of the temple and, as in the old days, Rianna spoke to him, and he obeyed, amazed but unquestioning.

Simirimia, suddenly wakeful, listened also. Nothing now. But before? Uneasy, she set her mind more strongly on her obedient champion, clenching her fists as she tightened her will about him. Leron stirred and muttered in his sleep. The pleasant blankets muffling his body had become bonds, and he was suddenly drowning, choking, smothering in a warm salty sea that pressed in on his helplessness. He struggled to wake, but the bonds dragged him down, the water stifled his breathing and choked his utterance. Fingers tightened about his neck, and his eyes began to press outward from his face. He could not raise his hands. Images of pain and terror grew great and shrank again in nervous profusion, steel cutting into flesh, and blood billowing out like silk, while helpless eyes looked calmly into his. He could not look away. Then the pressure eased for a moment, and it was no longer a sea that stifled him but soft arms clinging to his body gently as seaweed and as inescapable. His thoughts began to dissolve into a mindless sweating stupor, but he fought the pleasure as he had the terror. He managed to speak, or seemed to. "I must wake up. I shall, I shall." A great cry of determination broke from his lips, and the relief was indescribable. Over him bent Odric, anxiously, and Sibby was holding his hand tightly. He smiled weakly at them both.

"Your eyes were rolling so," said Sibby, "we thought you would never wake up."

Odric nodded in agreement. "You were wrestling mightily, yet it seemed you would not win." He got up and poured a flagon of small beer. "Drink," he said, and Leron obeyed, still shaking slightly. He took it in only one hand, however, for he had not released Sibby's. Her hand was strong for a child's, very warm and reassuring.

After Leron had drunk and lain back, Odric returned to his own blankets, but Sibby continued to sit by him, holding his hand, the chilly wind ruffling her long unbound hair and whipping the edge of her tunic. Her head was against the stars, and he could not see her expression. Leron broke the silence with an embarrassed laugh. "I fear to sleep again," he murmured, "as though there were something lying in wait, in some dream yet to come. I should have outgrown these childish fancies long since."

Sibby did not reply, but pressed his hand between both of hers, shivering slightly with the lateness and the cold. "You are cold," said Leron. "I regret having kept you up. Go back to sleep." He did not realize that this was the first concern he had shown.

Sibby shook her head, a dark movement against the stars. "I'm all right." But she did go and get her blanket and, wrapping herself in it, she sat down in the same place, once more taking his hand. "I'll be here until you fall asleep," she said. And when he did go back to sleep, his face was turned against her blanket-wrapped body and his hand was in hers still.

ODRIC

further ballad fragments

. . . *it was early, early in the night,*
the False Nurse soundly slept
her arms around the Lady's babe
when in this young man crept.
He's taken up the sleeping child
and kissed him tenderly;
The King your father needs you not,
come home to your mother and to me.

So he has mounted on his grey,
the Lady's up behind,
he's held her baby in his arms
and rode into the wind.
And late, late in the middle of the night
they rested under a tree.
This young man's held them both in his arms
and they've slept wearily.

And early, early in the dawn
when little birds do cry,
they did awake to find her Lord
the cruel King standing by.
The cruel King laughed a mighty laugh:
Revenge lies to my hand!
Take up your sword, unhappy youth,
come meet me like a man.

The young man, he reached out his hand
but he never touched his sword.
The cruel King struck him through the heart
and thus he kept his word.
The Lady kissed her dying love,
then she took up his blade.
But the King he got the better of her
and he struck off her head.

He set his blade to the baby's throat:
You come of traitorous blood.
I shall not kill you, yet of me
never shall you get any good.
Two graves, two graves, the King then cried
to lay these lovers in;
I'd never leave those two alone
without a wall between.

Chapter Twenty-seven

Leron woke with a thin strand of hair across his face. For a moment he thought himself back in Treclere. He was out of doors, in a clean grey misty dawn, condensed fog standing on his blankets in little drops; and Sibby was asleep beside him, so wrapped and muffled that only her long hair showed outside of the blanket. He smiled at her, his head feeling clearer than it had for many weeks. He got up carefully so that he would not disturb her. Near the little spring where they had made camp, the ground was soft and wet; everything was damp and smelled good. As Leron washed, he absent-mindedly removed the silver collar, splashing water on his neck and shoulders. After he had dried himself, he did not put the collar back on, for the skin beneath it felt rubbed and sore. Instead, he placed it in his saddlebags where it would be safe.

By this time the horses and the ganoose were plainly expecting attention, pulling at their picket ropes and whickering. One by one Leron led them to the spring to drink, then hobbled them loosely so they could graze. Before turning them out, Leron gave each a rough brushing, although Sibby's colt was spotless and gleaming. The two brown horses looked unkempt by contrast. He had not closely handled the Karabdin colt before, and he found the glossy coat and soft skin pleasurable to the touch. Looking into the dark brown eyes fringed with light lashes, he could feel the colt's charm and almost understand Sibby's infatuation. He gave the colt a friendly slap on the withers, and it turned and moved away toward the meager grass, walking gracefully despite its fetters. Behind him a voice spoke quietly. "Up early, my prince. I see my chores have been attended to already." Odric was smiling at him, his eyes still sleepy and his beard and hair magnificently disarrayed.

"Yes, I could not stay in bed. It is a beautiful morning."

Odric looked out over the bleak plateau, hung low with fog, and up at the grey sky where the new sun showed only as a lightening along the east. Then he looked back at Leron and smiled. "Yes, it is beautiful indeed."

While they were cooking breakfast, Sibby finally woke, and they were eating by the time she had braided her hair and washed. Like Odric's, her eyes were heavy with sleep, and her color was high. Leron smiled and handed her a plate. "I'm sorry to have kept you up with all my foolishness," he said. "I hope you have slept well since."

Sibby smiled and nodded shyly, and when, as she took the plate, their hands touched, she jerked a little and almost spilled it. "I'm still not quite awake, though," she said softly, dropping her eyes to her plate as she ate.

As they rode on that day, Leron no longer lagged behind, but pushed his horse to keep pace with Sibby. Two or three times when they reached invitingly open areas, they raced across them neck and neck, while Odric jogged after indulgently, leading the balky ganoose. Leron's long-legged brown horse had a turn of speed that more than matched the Karabdin colt, but he was weaker in his hindquarters and not so maneuverable, so when the ground grew rough or hilly he fell behind. When they stopped to rest, Leron began asking Sibby about her stay in the desert, and she told him about the horses there and all she had seen. He did not care to hear about the Karif, but details of desert life fascinated him, and he rememberd how, as a boy, he had longed to run away and become a desert brigand. Odric was also intrigued, for although he had been on several sea voyages, he had never seen the great desert. He was the one who noticed the glass ring, which Sibby wore on a cord around her neck. It was usually hidden in the folds of her shirt, but today as she leaned forward, talking, it fell into view and turned slowly, catching the light on its iridescent blue surface. He took it in his fingers and held it up. "This is Karabdin glass, is it not? It resembles the older pieces I have seen more than the new."

Sibby peered down at it and nodded. "It comes from the Valley of the Dead Kings, their old city. Ajjibawr gave it to me—he said that long ago they made all kinds of things, in glass like this that was really hard and lasted a long time, but now they've forgotten and can't make the things they used to."

"It is a thing of beauty," said Odric, letting it drop back.

"But it serves no purpose," said Leron, and he got up and brushed himself off. "I think we have sat and talked long enough." He walked to his horse and mounted with Odric, surprised, following, and Sibby last.

Except for an occasional heaviness in his head and a tiredness that made it difficult to think, Leron continued to feel better as they rode on. It was colder each day, and they were glad for their sheepskin tunics.

For three days they climbed higher and higher, daily at a more severe incline, and only on the fourth day did they reach a level plain. That morning there was a long slope ahead of them, ending in what seemed a gentle hill. Behind the hill northeast of them, the sky was brilliantly white and the air about was frosty. As they rode toward the hill, Odric smiled to himself, but he would not answer Leron's questions about the road ahead. As they slowly climbed to the crest of the hill he dropped back, so that Sibby and Leron reached the top together, to look down onto ice.

The glacier was smooth and enormous, a frozen swell that rolled motionlessly toward them out of the far north. Its breath was cold and dead and salty, and it breathed with strange rustling creaks and sighs as though some life stirred deep within. The sunlight skidded across it in a long yellow streak, and all the sky around was bright.

Leron looked back at Odric, who had stood up in his stirrups and was gazing intently across the ice. "Does anything that has life dwell herein?"

Odric shrugged, and settled in his saddle. "There are always rumors. I know of nothing for certain, but undoubtedly you will hear tales tomorrow when we arrive at the great house in Mindo'ila."

Sibby turned her back on the ice and looked at him questioningly. "How can anything live out here? Nothing will grow. And it isn't near a harbor or anything."

Odric smiled. "Wait, little maiden, and you will see more wonderments."

He led them down the side of the hill to a faint path, which took them along the western edge of the ice fields. They shivered in the wind that blew to them across the ice, yet the sun beat strongly down all the while, for it was summer still. Odric pointed ahead of them to the left. "Perhaps fifty miles hence in a narrow valley lies Mindo'ila, and there the great house stands where I had thought to spend the next few months. We should reach it by noon tomorrow, and thence we will be directed toward your destination. There is a man there I know can help us. Yes, you will find your welcome at Mindo'ila warmer than you suspect." And he laughed at some private joke.

Next day they had ridden five hours when Odric spoke. "Soon we shall be approaching Mindo'ila. Look over there."

Leron followed his pointing finger and saw a thin trickle of water coming down the irregular mountainside. Looking closer, he saw it was steaming in the glacial atmosphere, and, where it ran, the rock underneath was a most lovely coral color, formed into delicate crystals and lacy shapes. Odric put his hand into the water and broke off a bit of the beautiful formation; it crumbled in his fingers. He laughed at their puzzlement.

"New patterns are ever forming. The water makes these shapes in passing. And feel the water, for it is warm."

Sibby touched it gently and drew back her hand with a cry of surprise. "Warm!" she cried. "It's hot!" Odric nodded and motioned them on.

"This is only the beginning," he said.

As they rode on, they passed more and wider trickles of water, warm and steaming over fantastic mineral formations. Although the edge of the glacier lay less than a half mile to the east, the ground underfoot was warm and spongy. "If it were not for these warm springs," said Odric, "the ice fields by now would have covered this path, for, though frozen, still they flow. This warmth marks their boundary." As he spoke, the path turned abruptly to the left, leading them through a narrow cleft into a warm steamy passage through the mountain. A few hundred feet further on, it widened out into a small circular area, suddenly much warmer, for the glacier had been left behind a curtain of rock. The floor was covered with narrow cracks, through which steam rose in wavering walls, and Odric motioned them to a halt. "Watch that little pool," he cried, and even as he spoke the waters began churning, green and mysterious. A whirlpool formed, and suddenly with a convulsive thrust a great jet of hot water vomited up into the sky, spreading out fanlike and sinking back into stillness. Odric looked at their amazement and laughed delightedly.

"I promised you a warm welcome, did I not? We had best pass now, for the water rises every few minutes, and I should not like to be scalded." He set his unwilling horse to a canter, and the three pounded past just as the water began bubbling again. Safely past, they turned in time to see it heave skyward once more; the hot spray fell across their faces. Leron laughed.

"Warm indeed, friend! It has been a day for rare marvels." He smiled at Sibby; then, noticing her expression, said slowly, "I venture that you have seen such things in your own world."

Sibby flushed and nodded. "We do have them, but I'd never seen one close up. I think that where they are, there are volcanoes—mountains—mountains with fire and boiling rock in them."

Odric raised his eyebrows. "You are learned for one so young. There is a fire mountain here, but few know of it. You shall hear of it in Mindo'ila. Come into the valley!" And he cantered forward once more, leading them into a high narrow valley that wound its way before them as far as they could see.

It was green, piercingly green, overgrown with lush, dripping trees and enormous plants and vines, bright with birds and raucous with their cries. Leron looked around amazed, and then upward. He was surprised to see that the sky was hidden by vapor; there was no direct sunlight in the valley, only a brilliant, diffused illumination. As they pushed their way through the glossy leaves, Odric explained. "The sun never shines directly here, for the clouds are always with us. Yet growing things thrive, and the weather never varies. He would think himself in paradise who reached this valley during a winter of hard traveling as I have; and even in summer it is not too unpleasant." As he spoke, they reached a turn in the path and could see the great house ahead of them with the village sprawled about it.

The house was low and rambling, built of stone, with side porches and tall windows—almost a village of itself, of interconnected buildings and courtyards, all overgrown with heavy vines. They rode into the wide, square courtyard and saw the household gathered to meet them on the steps; the mistress of Mindo'ila stood on the top step, alone. Odric turned to Leron and murmured, "Quiet though this valley seems, it is not without defenses. One rides in and thinks one's self unnoticed, yet ever there is a party waiting, informed of one's arrival." Then he dismounted, sweeping a wide bow to the assembly, and ran up the few steps to kneel before the lady. She was small and squarely built, dressed in trailing yellow, and she raised Odric after he had kissed her hand. He gestured for Leron and Sibby to approach.

"Madam," he said, "I bring you greetings from your royal brother. My guest is your royal cousin, Leron of Tredana, the only son of Mathon Breadgiver, on a personal quest to the north as he shall tell you. The Master of Vahn has asked me to accompany him, and I carry his letter to that effect. The maiden is Sibby, also of the Tredanan party."

Letha took Leron's hand and pressed it warmly. "I see the style of cousin has startled you," she said with a smile. "I am sister to Bodrum of Vahn, and our house is that of Sembath, he who was Arleon's son, and thus there is kinship although slight indeed at this remove in time. You are welcome to whatever hospitality or aid my house can offer."

She led them into a vast shadowy hall, as filled with monstrous plants in pots as the valley was with wild ones. Chairs were placed together in intimate clusters and little low tables covered with miscellaneous objects stood scattered haphazardly about. There were also many cats. Sibby leaned over and petted one as she followed. They were taken up a low broad flight of stairs to a group of rooms which overlooked the courtyard.

"You remember your room, of course, Odric. Your friends may use these others here if they like. When you have refreshed yourselves and rested, we shall have a light meal downstairs." After the door had closed on her, Odric turned to Leron and Sibby with a grin.

"I hope you are both hungry. This is a land of light meals, and when there are no more light meals they serve dinners, and after that come the refreshments. I fear the good work of my trip is about to be undone." And he slapped his stomach reflectively.

If Leron had doubted Odric's word, a few hours showed him differently. After an interminable light meal, Letha graciously ushered her guests to dinner, and when dinner was concluded, they went into another room for sweets and a small course of refreshments. Sibby had given up entirely, but she caught Leron's eye as he tried to make a polite mess of the pastry on his plate and they both disgraced themselves with a fit of giggling, fortunately while Letha was talking to a servant. Odric, who had paced himself throughout the meal, fared better; but then he had had the largest appetite to begin with.

During their last course, Odric's two pupils came in, young boys aged eight and nine. The eldest was named Kerys, the other Varys. They were the sons of Bodrum, and Letha deferred to them as though they were grown noblemen and not mere children. At first they took no more notice of Odric than if he had been a servant; but as he began telling them of his travels, they unbent and soon were sitting by his chair, laughing and eagerly asking questions. Letha took another morsel of pastry and leaned toward Sibby and Leron. "Such dear children," she said softly. "A trifle spoiled, I fear, but so good at heart. I always feel that there is no better experience for the ordinary sort of people than to wait upon the noble. Dear Odric has improved so much since he first began to spend time with the children. One would never have thought a person of his background could become so—almost refined. I am sure you have seen the same transformation in your own body-servants."

Leron was at a loss for an answer, but Sibby spoke up quickly. "Odric is our friend." Letha smiled and took another bite of pastry.

"Of course," she said, "and a good friend, too. You must always make friends of your servants, so they will not betray you. Though in the city, it is different. One does not know whom to trust. That is why my dear brother in his extraordinary wisdom sent his children here, to be safe from traitors and assassins. But truly, I never thought that the son of such a mother could become the dear person Odric is. I have observed him most carefully, you understand, and no taint can be seen. It is remarkable."

Leron drew his brows together. "Taint? I do not understand."

"Of course, I was forgetting. Tredana would hardly know our little scandals. Why, Odric's mother was one of the worst wantons in the court. If it were not for my brother's generosity, Odric would have perished in infancy. Ah well, she paid for her crimes, as all must in a well-ordered and just society."

She plainly would have enjoyed gossiping further, but at that moment Odric crossed the room toward them, a child hanging onto each hand.

"Music has been commanded," he said with a laugh. "I have told them of a strange new instrument called the harp, and they wish to hear that as well as my baraka. If you will excuse me, I will return with the instruments." He turned to Leron. "You do not mind?" Leron shook his head with a smile.

In a few moments, Odric reappeared. Varys was struggling with the unwieldly baraka, and Kerys carried the harp gingerly against his breast. While Leron tuned the harp and tried its strings, the children clustered about his chair, reaching for the pegs and arguing. Leron motioned them back and began to play a simple tune, and the strings of Telyon danced lightly under his fingers. Odric smiled at Sibby, and she grinned back, listening with open pleasure. Letha smiled and nodded her head in time, and Leron, encouraged, began another tune, an old ballad. It was an old song and a sad one, of brother killing brother by mistake through jealousy, and as Leron played the music, it swelled and vibrated, ringing in the room. Astonished, he tried to lighten his touch, but the music would not soften. It grew in power, and out of the music a cold inhuman voice sang clearly. "Blood," sang Telyon as Leron's fingers still moved helplessly across the strings. "Blood," it sang again, and a sick feeling of guilt and revulsion swept over him. He was unclean, he could feel it. His fingers dirtied the harp, and it sang against him. As the strings shrank from his touch, he dropped the harp abruptly, and he looked up in terror at Sibby's face. But she showed only surprise at his sudden interruption, and he realized Telyon had only sung for him. "I—I'm tired," he stammered. "Perhaps tomorrow I can play more. I beg of you, Odric, to sing for us now."

Odric looked up from his strings. "Of course; it has been a tiring journey here. A short ballad, and then we must rest. Tomorrow we will play more."

The children made faces, but Letha nodded in agreement with Odric, turning to the princes. "It is late for you. You must not tire yourselves listening to Odric. One song more and then to bed."

As Odric sang, Leron laid a trembling hand on Telyon. He

could feel the harp shiver from his touch, and now he knew why it did not play for him. Memories were coming back, fragmentary, meaningless as yet, but they showed more pain than he would have thought it possible to bear, pain inflicted on those he loved, those who loved and trusted him and whom he had somehow failed to protect. He was sick at heart and needed to be alone. Letha's dismissal and gracious good night came none too soon.

From THE SONG OF ARMON

by Arbytis

fragmentary ms. in the library of Leron, son of Mathon Breadgiver

CONCERNING TELYON

Treasure of the Zenedrim
Taken for Armon's sake
Why are you silent under my hand?

Treasure of the Zenedrim
Speak to the dead man's sister's son
Why are you silent under my hand?

Why are you silent under my hand
Treasure of the Zenedrim?
Instruct us in this matter
  Armon dead
  and lost in a strange land.

Chapter Twenty-eight

At first Leron neither slept nor woke, lying in a trance, his mind open to the many images that presented themselves. How long had it been since he had forgotten himself, forgotten his home and his old father waiting for him? And Arbytis, his teacher and dearest guide. Somewhere he had dropped him, left him abandoned, and not even inquired of his fate until now. The old man needed him, and he had failed him. Gannoc, his faithful servant—had he returned safely to Tredana, with dear Dansen, loyal Mara? Even the princess he had dreamed of all his life—her safety, her escape, had meant nothing. He had killed the innocent serpent, abandoned his friends. Why had Simirimia not helped him do his duty? He wanted to get up and wake Sibby. She might answer some of his questions. But no—she was under the power of the Karif. He could not risk it.

As he lay sweating in the humid night, a light appeared on the balcony beyond his tall, lead-shrouded window. It shone bright and clear against the milky sky, orange ringed with yellow. The light grew, and in a trance he found himself standing by his bed, then walking out onto the balcony to meet it. It flared up into a perfect spearhead of color, then dwindled until he could see it was nothing but a lamp, held high in the air by a dark-dressed figure. The face was hooded, but he could feel that it was old. "Why are you here?" asked Leron, and as he spoke the lamp flared up and broke like a feather into little curls of light. The mist made it seem they were together in a small stone room or rocky cave, not on an open balcony. "Why are you here?" he asked again, and the figure raised one long-sleeved arm and pointed north.

"Ask rather, why am I here?" The words spoke quietly in the air around him and Leron started with surprise. "Ask rather, why do I suffer these questions and yet not look for answers? It is very nearly time for your petition to be heard.

Remember Arbytis and come to me." The flame rose up once again, then broke off at its base and fell, light as a leaf or feather, to curl and burn and die out at Leron's feet. But even in its fading, it seemed to send a great light northward and as Leron looked in that direction the sky seemed suddenly filled with light, patches of rich unearthly color lighting the near distance, while behind them, more beautiful still, taller pale lights seemed to waver and walk along the horizon. For a moment he was alone, and then he heard a step behind him.

The balcony outside his window ran under Odric's also, and it was Odric who stood beside him, naked except for a sheet pulled around his waist. He spoke dreamily. "They say that when Anith went looking for her daughter she had no light, because this was before fire, so she could only search by day and spend the dark nights weeping. But it was cold then, in the days before fire, so her tears froze on the ground around her and mirrored the stars and the moon by night, and the sun's own light by day. And these lights were like torches, so that wherever she walked throughout the world there was always light standing about her."

Leron turned to him, slowly awaking from his trance. "Did she find her daughter? Why was she missing?"

Odric smiled sleepily and rubbed his eyes. "That is another story. I will tell you sometime. For now, it is enough to be one of the very few who has ever seen the Torches of Anith."

Leron stood silent for a moment longer, leaning forward to rest his hands against the tough stone railing. Then he spoke slowly, not looking at Odric's face. "I have seen more than the Torches of Anith tonight. There was a man here, or some spirit, with a message I cannot fail to heed. It is time for me to go north, and to go north alone."

"I will accompany you if you wish. Not for any order of Bodrum's but out of friendship."

Leron smiled, still without looking up. "You have been a good companion and guide. But there is much you do not know. Some things I have not said . . . and some things I do not understand. Even if it were not for my mission on the queen's behalf, still I would have to go north. There is some sickness in me, Odric, and even if it kills me I must try to burn it out, in Tremyrag."

Odric said nothing further, but clasped Leron on the shoulder, briefly, then turned and left him alone on the dark balcony.

Next morning they breakfasted privately in a room adjoining their apartments; Leron did not sit down to eat until his few things were repacked for the journey, and he came to the table dressed for travel. Odric was already started upon a second course of fish, carefully arranging the little bones along the edge of his plate as he licked them clean one by one. He greeted Leron comfortably and poured out a pale yellow wine. In the Karabdin blue glass goblet, it took on a strange acid hue, but it was pleasant on the tongue and throat. Leron had just begun to eat when Sibby appeared, like himself dressed for travel. She looked at him very seriously and spoke quietly.

"I dreamed last night that we had to leave today. I guess you did, too. Are you all ready?"

"I am ready. But I will go north alone. You must stay here and be safe with Odric."

"Odric isn't safe. He's going to have to come, too, or leave here, anyway. That was in my dream, too."

Odric looked at her, curiously. "Is it because of Bodrum's orders, that I was to guide Leron north?"

"In a way. Only now it's worse. They're on their way here, to take you back to Vahanavat. I saw them in my dream. Ten soldiers, and a captain with a broken nose. They're riding very fast."

Odric looked startled. "There is no way you could know of that captain, unless you have been in Vahanavat."

"I'm trying to tell you, it was my dream. I've never really met him. But it was clear as anything. They'll be here soon, I'm sure of that."

Odric reached across the table and put his hand on her arm. "Why are they coming for me? Did your dream tell you that?"

Sibby dropped her eyes. "I—I think so."

"What do you mean?"

"I don't know—I mean, maybe it's not true, or maybe it happened a long time ago. There was this man, and they killed him, the soldiers I mean. They tortured him and he died, and he was a friend of yours and now they're after you."

Odric pushed back his chair and got up, suddenly pale. "What did this man look like, the one that was killed?"

Sibby's lips trembled. "He looked very nice," she said softly. "He had reddish hair and a dark beard, and he looked very kind. But he was all bloody, and he died." All of a sudden she was crying, and she turned her back on the two men so they couldn't see her face. "I don't know why I'm here," she said. "Everybody's so cruel, and people get hurt or killed or something horrible happens. No one ever died at home. No one I knew."

Leron moved to comfort her and she turned and hid her face against his chest. As he held her, he could see Odric shaking his head with disbelief.

"This is the end of life as I have known it," Odric said. "I had no dearer friend than Baradel." With a sudden frustration, he picked up his goblet and smashed it against the table, cursing. Then he shrugged and wiped the bits of glass from his hand with the napkin. "Wait here," he said softly. "It will take me a moment to pack. Bodrum's letter to his sister stressed the urgency of our journey. She will protest our going but not hinder us."

The house was still quiet with early morning when they gathered by the entrance. The great front doors were open to the sun, and a few cats sprawled in the light while others trotted in and out. While they waited to say farewell to Letha, one of the cats stretched and opened its mouth in a pink and surprisingly sharp-toothed yawn. It ambled over to meet Letha as she came with her servants, and wound so around her feet she had to pick it up and carry it. Her other hand she stretched to Leron. "I am saddened, so saddened, by this sudden departure. My royal brother told me of your desire to hurry northward, but still I hoped that you might rest for several days enjoying the hospitality of Mindo'ila. Perhaps upon your return from the north we may have the pleasure of a longer visit."

Leron bowed over her hand. "Be assured, madam, that we appreciate your kindness and will come again if events so order themselves."

She turned then to Sibby with a smile. "My dear, if you wish to stay and await your companion's return, you are more than welcome. Surely you cannot be anxious to journey into the uncharted north!"

Sibby shook her head, forcing a small smile. "Thank you. But I have to go, too."

Letha seemed to hesitate, then turned to Odric. "I have arranged for provisions to be readied, as much as that great pack beast of yours can carry easily. If you take him round to the kitchens, you will find all in readiness." Odric bowed, murmuring his thanks. "See that you discharge your duties well and do nothing that might displease the prince. I hope you will return soon and safely, for the children I am sure will miss your company."

Odric kissed her hand again, and they went down the wide shallow steps to where their horses and the unladen ganoose were waiting. While Odric disappeared around the back, Leron and Sibby waited. It was already very warm despite the early hour, and it was hard to imagine the cold that awaited them outside the valley. Finally, Odric returned, and they slowly rode out the way they had come, the ganoose greedily grabbing at leaves and grasses along the way, jerking so hard on its long lead rope that Odric's horse, to whom it was tied, pulled and kicked with irritation. Just out of sight of the great house, Odric signaled a halt.

"We must wait a moment," he said. "I spoke with one in the kitchens who can tell us something of the northern wastes. Yesterday I had thought to visit him in his home, but now if I am to be under suspicion, I think it better to meet him here. He is the only one I know who has ever returned from the far north."

They had only waited a few minutes when a man came slowly toward them from out of the heavy undergrowth. He was middle-aged and walked with awkward steps; his skin was leathery from long exposure to sun and wind and snow. To Odric he made a low obeisance, and Odric impatiently gestured that he rise. "Timar!" he exclaimed. "I am only a servant like yourself. Save this respect for others. We waste it among ourselves."

Timar shook his head. "Word has gone out to the kitchens. You are being sent north in the hope you will never return. The master does not dare kill you, but he knows you will never return and he will be safe. If you had not come to me, I would have followed you. The secret has been kept too long. It is time that you knew."

"Knew what? I only asked of the north."

"For the north, that is simple enough. One word will do it. Ice, or death. I followed an early spring north, hunting, and when the winter returned, I found myself where there was no land or sky, no north or south, nothing but cold and a whiteness too bright to see. I lost part of each foot, and all my fingers, yet I returned. But you are not a hunter. You have lived too much in town. I lost the use of my hands, but you will lose your life. If you go north, you will not even come back to turn the meat spit in the kitchens, as I do now. That is why I must tell you the truth, though I break the oath I swore so long ago, thinking to protect you."

Odric dismounted and, walking to Timar, clasped him by the shoulders, staring him in the eye. "What oath? What secret? Timar, the soldiers of Bodrum ride even now for my capture. What is this I should know?"

Timar twisted his face with distress. "I promised my lord Baradel. . . ." Odric flinched at the name.

"Timar," he said, "Baradel is no more. What did you promise him?"

Timar looked at him uncomprehendingly, then sank once more stiffly to the ground, taking Odric's hand between his own. "My lord," he said, "I promised not to tell you that you are the true heir of Bodrum's body. He did not hesitate to kill your sweet mother or her champion, Baradel's father, but you he did not dare destroy. Yet he took delight in seeing you serve in his sister's house, safe under his hand, no threat to the throne or help to anyone in need of it. I call on you in the name of the people of Mindo'ila not to sacrifice yourself as he has planned, but stay and be the saving of all Vahn."

"This is a cruel jest, Timar. What nonsense is this? Why is it given that you should be the one to know and reveal my sudden royalty?"

"The Lady Maric was rightfully married to Bodrum, and I served in her house. I served her still when they took her son away and put him to nurse in Mindo'ila. And I served her when she first began to meet with Baradel in secret. And I serve her memory now, ever since the day the Master came home in the early morning with blood on his coat and left the Lady Maric and Lord Baradel dead in the fields. And when young Baradel returned to court, I swore to him not to tell, for fear you would risk your life, too. He said in good time you would know. He planned to have things readied for you to easily take the throne. It was the only vengeance he could have, and he did it more out of love for you than from hatred

for anything. He was not a man to hate very well, even Bodrum."

Odric stood stricken, his hand still clasped between Timar's
deformed palms. Leron looked at him with new understanding and pity, but before he could speak Sibby broke the silence, very softly.

"Now you know how that song ends. The one you started
on our trip with the lady running away. Your friend told you
that story, didn't he? Only he didn't tell you the names, that it
was his father and your mother."

Odric looked at her with a bitter smile and shook his head.
"No, we do not know how it ends. I know that part one ends
in murder, but we will see if justice comes in part two. Timar,
I am at your service. Friends. . . ." he turned to include
Leron with a desperate appeal in his face. "Think not I mean
to abandon you, but our destinies now lie apart. I cannot
leave my people. Your future leads you north, but mine does
not."

Leron rode forward a few steps, and leaning over kissed
Odric on the cheek. "You are my cousin," he said. "If ever
my fate works itself out so that I return a free man and a
whole one, be assured I will grant whatever aid lies in my
power. Enough. My heart is with you."

He undid the ganoose's lead rope and tied it to his own saddle. Then he turned to Sibby. "Come, child," he said, and
there was no condescension in his voice. "Mysteries lie before
us, and the hour is getting late. It seems we share a fate."
Sibby nodded, then pushed her colt forward so she, too,
could kiss Odric.

"Sing me the whole song when I see you again," she said,
and he kissed her and promised it so.

Leron set his horse eastward, toward the valley entrance,
and Sibby followed. The sun was now high. When they
looked back, there was no sign of Timar or of Odric or his
horse. The soldiers of Bodrum would return to him empty-
handed.

THE QUATRAINS OF ODRIC SEMBATIOUN

from the oral tradition of Mindo'ila

The island of our birth is lost and gone.
We will not hear again sweet Telyon's song.
But strike the lute and sing; soon comes the day
when we will see the end to an old wrong.

In old Luntar the snakes and lizards crawl
where glories once were carved into the wall
And in the citadel a creature hides
where once the great Sembath was lord of all.

If it is true the loveliest flowers spring
where some great hero died, or some great king;
then in the depths of our great citadel
the dark will flower with blooms that blood can bring.

I write this verse in memory of the slain
Lord Baradel: he will not rise again.
But if the dark is scattered into flight
then, Baradel, you are not dead in vain.

THE KERMYRAG

After the tropical warmth of the valley, the cold of the glacier struck them to the bone. They followed again the way between the glacier and the mountains, headed north. The cloven hoofs of the ganoose spread and held with each complaining, grumbling step, but the horses slipped and trembled, taking stiff, cautious steps and often refusing to go forward. For much of that first day, therefore, they walked beside their horses, and for part of the second also, holding to the stirrup leathers for support. The afternoon of the second day led them away from both mountain and glacier. The foothills gradually slipped away westward, and the curving bulk of ice turned east. Due north, straight ahead, there was a level stretch of snow, as hard-packed and even as desert sand.

By evening of the second day, they had moved onto the snowfields. At first Leron wondered to be so tired; then, as the twilight lingered, he realized that the dark was falling much later than before and that they had been traveling for an hour at least beyond the usual time of making camp. The ganoose lowered himself and slept soon after they stopped, and Leron and Sibby, wrapped in blankets, huddled next to his shaggy bulk for warmth. Hidden by the continuing half-light, the growing moon rose upon them as they slept.

Although he was asleep, Leron could feel the moon's clear light looking as deeply into his mind as a pair of dark green eyes. And as he felt the eyes upon him, he knew that he was trapped. Wings fluttered darkly in his ears, and once more he found himself cunningly and cruelly bound, bound and drowning.

He tried to call for help, but his body would not listen. For a long, terrifying moment he saw blood before his eyes, tasted its salty thickness in his mouth, and smelled it in the air about him. Despair and nausea seized him, and as he rocked in agony, his throat began to burn with a terrible fire, and in his dreams he thought that he beat at it with his hands, but the flames leaped up and crackled about his face. When he thought that there was no escape left but death, suddenly the flames died down a little, the smoke wisped away into the air, and he felt in his hands something heavy, wet, and smooth, wonderfully soothing. He raised it to his eyes, and it avoided his gesture and slipped sinuously through his fingers to wind lovingly about his neck, and although he knew it for some kind of serpent, he let himself fall back again and relax into blissful slumber. For the touch of the serpent was healing and cool, and he was once more at peace within himself.

Next morning after he got up, Leron was aware of a heaviness in his head that he had not felt for many weeks. As he folded his blankets and smoothed his sheepskin tunic, he realized that he was once more wearing the queen's necklace, and for some reason he could not quite fathom he was a little embarrassed about it and pulled his shirt together at the neck so that Sibby might not see. He did not remember his dream, yet when she asked him how he had slept and he answered, "Well," he felt ashamed and was dimly aware of a lie. He was relieved when they mounted up and set off, for it released him from the need for talking. His memory was more confused than ever, and he was not sure what to say to Sibby.

The snowfields were less piercingly cold than the glacier's edge had been, and yet more wearing in their monotony. Snow, crisp and dry, crunched under their feet, spreading out evenly to meet the sky in all directions. The sky was like an inverted porcelain bowl, dimming by night and glowing evenly by day. Occasionally the straight line of snow was broken by a cluster of frozen ice slabs or the lips of a jagged crevasse, but these interruptions were rare. The strangest thing was the stillness. The air was as calm and as clear as the sky was unchangingly light. There was no sound except what they made themselves, and that was deadened by the vastness of the region. As they continued further north, it seemed to Leron that the sky pressed down upon them, heavy and heavier: the pressure on his entrapped, tangled mind made him want to cry out, but to speak was too great an effort. He was aware that Sibby looked at him strangely, but her pain was more than he could comprehend.

How many days they numbly continued on, Leron could

not tell, but finally the line of sky before them was obscured by a rising vagueness, which gradually revealed itself to be a wall of mist into which they must walk. At first the air was only a little less clear than before, but with each step the mist grew denser and it was harder for them to see. They were forced to dismount and went forward leading the animals. Strange snapping sounds came out of the growing fog, and the ganoose hung back on its rope, uneasily bellowing. One moment they were walking on level ground, then a crevasse opened just behind them, nearly under the ganoose's feet. The terrified beast cried out and lurched forward, hind hooves scrabbling at the pit's edge, then slid forward into safety and stood trembling with heaving sides. Sibby said nothing but hugged her colt's head against her breast while he pulled unconcerned at the edge of her tunic. Leron touched her arm. "We must stay close together." Sibby nodded, and in a few moments they started forward again, still leading their horses.

When once again the ice opened, it cut directly across their path just as Leron was looking back to call to Sibby, who had fallen some steps behind. The ground shook, and he lost his balance and began falling down into the fissure. So great was his surprise, he dropped the reins he held; and his horse, frightened by the noise and movement, bounded several paces away. Desperately, Leron grasped at the uneven edge of the crack, his feet already dangling in a space fully three feet wide and unfathomably deep.

Sibby jerked cruelly at her colt's mouth and ran as close to the edge as she dared, throwing the flimsy reins down to Leron. He managed to grasp their ends and to wrap them about one wrist, but the colt obediently stepped forward in answer to the pressure, and Leron slipped back further into the fissure. The mist was so thick he could barely see the shape of Sibby's horse just above him, but he knew that Sibby had grabbed the reins next to the bit and was pulling hard, trying to fight the terrible drag of his weight.

After a long moment, the horse began to back slowly, confused by the conflicting signals reaching his mouth and ears. Sibby talked to the colt eagerly, encouragingly, and inch by inch Leron was pulled up out of the crack, scraping his belly against the hard, jagged edge. At last he lay full length on the ground above, gasping for breath. His hand was swollen from the pressure of the reins about his wrist, and Sibby ran forward to undo them.

No sooner had she loosened them and flung them aside than a second crack sprang open, radiating outward from the first. Leron cried out as he felt himself slipping back, and at the same moment the colt shrilled a high-pitched stallion scream. Ignoring her horse, Sibby threw herself forward and caught tight hold of the edge of Leron's tunic; he rolled no further. But the crack had sent an opening line almost under the grey colt's legs, and it was too late to pull him away. In a moment he had plunged from sight, still screaming, and as they watched where he had been, the ice snapped together as unexpectedly as it had opened.

Even in his numbed state, Leron thought that Sibby would cry out or weep, but after running to the crack and seeing it closed indeed, she only sat for several moments with her face hidden in her hands. Leron sat down beside her, massaging his bruised wrist, and when she did not speak he finally broke the silence. "You saved my life."

She looked up into his eyes, then down at his neck, where the silver collar showed through his ripped tunic. "Yes," she said simply, and a few minutes later they rose to their feet and went on, Sibby with one hand buried in the thick fur of the ganoose's neck.

A little further ahead, the mist grew so thick they were compelled to walk hand in hand. The stillness was intense. Leron could not even hear their footsteps. Only his heart hammered loudly; everything else was more still than a dream. Then Sibby's hand was almost pulled from his grasp as the ganoose plunged forward and dropped its head. The sound of its lapping tongue broke the silence.

They were at the edge of a quiet pond or lake, thick with mist, for the water that touched against the snow was warm. Leron's horse also pulled away and began thirstily drinking. A moment only and Leron and Sibby had knelt by the water between the two animals. Leron drank from his cupped hands and saw that Sibby was crying at last. He turned away so she would not feel him watching her, and saw in the heavy fog beyond his horse's head a dark shape approaching.

It came very slowly and in complete silence, and only when it had bumped against the shore could it be plainly seen. It was a small boat, carved of wood and richly painted. It moved without oars or sails, and there was a bench in the middle, emblazoned with the arms of Tredana. Leron rose stiffly to his feet and, bending over, gently took Sibby's hand in his own and lifted her up. He helped her into the boat and, pausing only to pull off their animals' bridles and to undo their girths so they stood unencumbered on the quiet shore, he stepped in after her. The boat moved slowly into the thick white mist.

There was no motion on board the boat, no sound to be heard, and the mist veiled their expressions from each other. Leron began to feel drowsy. At first he fought it, then seeing Sibby already asleep, her arms crossed on the gunwale and her head hidden in them, he gave in and settled down beside her.

When they awoke, the bright blue sky was ringing with larks. The water behind them was clear and quiet, the sunlight scattered across it like bright stones, and under their boat's square prow a grassy shore sloped gently up from the lake. A short distance away, across a lawn of thick green grass, grey stone walls rose up. The tall wooden gates stood open.

Slowly they got out of the boat, and it did not rock under their shifting weight. As they stood looking up at the gates, there was a sweet silver sound of trumpets, although they did not see anyone. Sibby looked at Leron. "I guess that means we're to go in." Within the courtyard, there stood a long low building with a gently angled roof. Its doors were also open, so Leron and Sibby walked across the short thick grass and went inside.

Torches flared along both walls of the windowless hall, and massive candles were ranked along the back. There was a long narrow table down the middle with a heavy wooden chair on either side, close to the far end. And here, at the head, sat an old man, dressed in dark robes. His brown hair fell over his shoulders, and in his thick heavy beard his lips were red and moist. He did not rise, but gestured widely with his hands.

"Welcome, most welcome, to my hall, Leron of Tredana and Sibby Barron of the Otherworld. I pray you of your courtesy be seated here and dine with me."

Leron touched his chair with his fingers, then drew back, for emblazoned on the chair as they had been on the boat were the blue and yellow arms of his city. "By what means did you bring us here?" he cried. "How do you know our names, and who or what are you?"

The old man chuckled and nodded his approval as Sibby sat down on his left hand, unafraid. "I am called many things, young man, but for now you may know me as Yoseh, lord of Tremyrag, your host. Sit; eat; drink; fear nothing."

Leron sat down, and despite his wonder, he ate well, for the food was delicious and a welcome change from the fare they had carried in their packs. It was Sibby who noticed the great curiosity of the table: no matter how much they ate of anything, when one looked at that plate again there was no less food than before, and the level in the jugs of wine stayed constant.

Yoseh followed her eyes and smiled. "You are observant, my dear," he said. "I have other such wonders—see!" He drew a small pouch from the bosom of his gown and held it up before them. "It is small, is it not? Yet were I to open it a thousand times, or more, each time should a handful of yellow gold reward my search." He pulled open the strings as he spoke and poured a heap of heavy golden coins out on the table. The pouch seemed empty, yet when he poured a second time, he made another heap as large as the first. Sibby shyly picked up a coin and examined it, and Leron did likewise.

Watching their interest, Yoseh let the purse slip through his fingers and it fell with a thud before Leron. He took it in his hand and tested its weight gently, then handed it back to Yoseh with a shrug. "It is very curious," he said politely, but with little interest.

Yoseh looked at the prince through narrowed eyes. "I have many other curiosities as well," he said. "If you have finished, I will show them to you." He cleared a place on the table in front of him and picked up a long narrow chest from the floor by his chair. When he threw back the lid, a motley collection of objects was exposed. He showed them ornaments of precious metals that reduplicated themselves, and this aroused little more interest than the purse. A salve good for all manner of wounds piqued Leron's interest, and he turned it over in his hands while the old man tried to display for him the wonders of a short supple sword, invincible against all comers. Leron yielded at length to his pressure and set down the ointment. He tested the blade's suppleness and made a few passes at the air, then returned it. The old man seemed crestfallen, and Leron spoke to him kindly, while one hand tried to ease the increasingly tight collar at his throat. "It is a lovely blade, well-made and true, but I cannot be sure invincibility is so great a virtue. It is so easy to confuse success with being right."

"Success is power."

"To what end?"

Yoseh shrugged and poked a moment among his treasures. "Of course," he said, "it is futile for me to tempt you. You little need strength or riches when the power to play the birds from the air and the fish from the sea has been given you and you have idly tossed it aside."

Sibby looked up, startled, and Leron frowned. "I do not understand."

"For more than twenty years I have been without one of the chief ornaments of my collection. The great maker of music has been gone, used by you as though it were a toy or common instrument. But now my Telyon is home, and it shall not again go forth." And to their great astonishment he drew forth from the chest a familiar triangular case and loosed the harp from its coverings. He ran his hands across the wood frame in a loving and familiar gesture. "It has been mended, I see—but no matter, the job was done with skill and affection." He plucked the strings and nodded, entranced. "For many days Arbytis pleaded with me for the loan of this. He hoped it would teach you that which he could not. But you dropped it on my lakeshore as easily as you dropped the saddles and blankets, and now I will not risk its loss again."

Leron reached impulsively for the harp, but Yoseh shook his head with a stern gesture. "It is too subtle for you. Arbytis trusts too well the strength of your inheritance. You come of a noble line, prince, but this harp is nobler. And how can you think to touch it here, while your hands yet stink of blood?"

"Blood?"

"Smell your hands," Yoseh thundered, and, like a little child, Leron found himself obediently lifting his hands to his face. Such a reek met his nostrils that sickness rose in his throat.

"Why are you surprised, prince? Feel of your neck. Do the innocent wear the chains of a criminal?"

Leron touched his collar, swept with pain and confusion,

and as he touched it he heard Sibby cry out in his defense.

"He can't help it! If you know so much, you ought to know that! Why don't you help him if you're so great? Arbytis told me that you would help. Why don't you help him get free?"

Yoseh looked less stern and smiled a little sadly. "Child, you do not understand some things, wise though you are beyond your age. The prince has been given overmuch. With the virtue of his bloodline, the powers of Leriel and the strengths of Mathon, with the High Priest of Ornat his tutor and Telyon to play, with the words of our Lady Rianna and the love of his companions, to what great future has he come? The destruction of that innocent beast in the swamps was a prelude merely to the terrible murder of a friend."

Suddenly reaching down into his box of treasures, Yoseh pulled forth a great shining goblet, silver on a tall stem. "You came for the Jawmir, here it is. Look in and see yourself."

Unwillingly, Leron placed his hand on the Jawmir's cold and shining side. It was filled with some strange liquid, piercingly cold, and at first he could only see his own face, wreathed in mist. Then, deeper in the cup, behind his eyes, the story of his last few months played out in rapid agonizing detail. Helplessly he began to cry, and Yoseh watched him sternly. "Your tears are too late. If you will make amends, you will need more than a child's remorse."

Once more Sibby interrupted. "There must be some way I can help, too. Please!"

"What have you left to give? The creature you loved best is dead in the ice fields. You let him die to save the prince. What else do you have to give?"

Sibby shook her head helplessly. "I thought I was able to help before. The Lady of the Rock told me. But I spoke to Leron, and he didn't listen. So it really wasn't much help at all."

"Perhaps you should try again. Three times you spoke and he listened not. What would you say to him now?"

"I—I'm not sure. But—Leron, even if it's true what Yoseh says, about your having so much help, that isn't true any more. Simirimia is planning to attack, and now that Ddiskeard is the heir to Tredana you won't even be welcome at home. And we have to help Odric in Vahn, and that won't be easy either. Whatever was true before isn't any more.

There's so much to do and it's going to be terribly hard and can't you pay somehow with what you will be doing? Nothing'll change what is over. Lelu would've wanted you to save Arbytis, not just be punished for his death. He understood about Simirimia's powers. I'm sure he didn't hate you."

Yoseh raised his eyebrows consideringly. "What do you say, Prince of Tredana? Will you give up an easy future in payment for your past?"

Leron bowed his head, still clasping the Jawmir in both hands. "I would give my life itself. But I would rather pay at length, and hope to do good by it, than pay quickly with a useless sacrifice. I am the only one who can profit by my death, and I have profited too much already."

He looked up at Yoseh, trying to keep his lips from trembling, and saw for the first time a grave approval in the old man's face. "Well spoken, prince. Arbytis was not perhaps entirely misled. There is much work for you to do. At last you have listened to the child, and perhaps it is not yet too late. First, remove that shameful collar."

Leron tried to undo the clasp, but it would not yield to his fingers. Angrily he pulled at the metal, and it began to constrict about his throat. The harder he pulled at it, the more it tightened, but he did not give up. If he failed, he felt he would lose everything. He pulled again, and the room grew dark; the blood thrummed in his ears. The torches along the walls began to dwindle as he struggled, and the candles died down to a bluish nub of flame. Yoseh stood up and raised his hands above his head, crying aloud in a great voice.

"Back, O Queen, go back, go back. You have no powers here. It is the Zenedrim who speaks, lord of Tremyrag. Back, I say, into your proper body and begone!"

A dark shadow lifted from the hall, and a wind whirled all around them. Leron thought he would die, but before he had fainted quite away, the pressure suddenly relaxed and the collar slipped from his neck, slithering across the table with a horrible life of its own. But it was not quick enough. Yoseh snatched it up from the board, and, saying a few words in his beard, flung it into a nearby torch. There was a loud sound, and the room trembled, filled for a moment with a nasty smell; and then there was nothing.

Leron rubbed his neck and took a mouthful of wine from his unemptying glass.

"I am free," he said at last, "but she is still strong. I do not understand how to defeat her."

Yoseh smiled. "The weapon is with you. Only the understanding is not there. Arbytis can tell you what you need to know."

"Even if I were to return with the Jawmir, she would imprison me. She knows that I am free."

"Armon was her enemy, yet she would have raised him to a throne. You will have to use your wits and not your passions. No one is truly invincible. You were wise enough to reject the purse and sword, because you knew that for those who so dearly desire such things there can never be enough money or enough power. No power is infinite. Some things the wealthy cannot buy. Even the Yinry, the keepers of the old order, even they are not infinite in their power. They are answerable to higher powers, even as the gods are answerable to them."

He looked at Sibby's questioning face. "What is it, child? What would you know?"

"This place is Tremyrag. Is this where the Kermyrag is?"

"It is the place of the Kermyrag."

"Ginas showed me his picture. Is he a god? Is he answerable to higher powers?"

"He is answerable only to the rest of creation. Child, you have asked for very little. Here, look into the cup and see for yourself."

Timidly, Sibby looked into the Jawmir and, as she looked, her long lashes fell and veiled her eyes from Leron's sight. But the light from the cup played on her face. In silence she looked, and tears of sympathy rolled from her eyes although her face was calm. Reluctantly, she tore herself away and looked at Yoseh. "May Leron see?"

He nodded, and she passed the cup across the table. He took it as timidly as she had and looked. At first there was nothing but the dark shining surface of the liquid; then some small lights formed deep down, sparkling and leaping like flame. It was flame, flame dancing on ice, the icy rock ribs of a domed cave in which he was standing. He was looking at the ice floor by his feet, watching the colored lights change and flare and die down again. Reluctantly he looked up, very slowly, and saw before him the great firebird whose reflection filled the frosty air around them. The Kermyrag writhed in pain, and yellow flames ran all along its glorious, white-feathered wings which curled up over its head. From its great dark eyes fell tears of blood, steaming on the ice floor of the cave. Leron reached out his hand to comfort it, but the heat was too intense.

He saw that somehow Sibby had joined him in the cave, and she, too, was stretching out her hand. But it was already scarred and twisted with flame, and it seemed she could bear the heat. Leron cried out for her when she touched the bird's white breast, but her tears were only for the Kermyrag. He lifted his great head slowly, and one dazzling bright bloody tear fell onto Sibby's deformed hand. She drew it back with a silent cry and touched it to her lips. As she did so, Leron looked up into the wings, which were suddenly bursting into greater and more golden flames than before. Among the arched and curling feathers of fire, he could see Tredana, his city, burning also. It seemed his whole future life was drawn on a small scrap of paper, which turned up at the edges and flamed and crumbled into ash. As he thought this, the fires around him dimmed, and they were alone in a dark room remote from the Kermyrag.

Leron looked up from the table. It was empty. The Zenedrim and his treasures were vanished; there was no food or wine. The torches were black and unlit along the walls, and the candles had burned out in their sockets. Sibby's scarred hand was still pressed against her lips as she met Leron's gaze, then they both turned to where Yoseh had been sitting. His chair was empty, and the dust in its seat and on its arms was thick and undisturbed.

Dansen
Privately to his JOURNAL

It is now a week since those terrible events occurred which still burn as fresh in my memory as though but an hour had elapsed. I have found a safe place here among my records in the palace library and thus I dare commit to paper my recollections.

That afternoon, Gannoc came to me worried, asking if I had seen the child Sibby. He showed me a note she had left and we decided she must have written the truth and be even now on the way to Villavac, intending to meet with Herrard at the Circle Inn. Gannoc prepared to set out immediately and reason with her to return. He left a message with me to give his Majesty, who was napping after dinner as was his custom, yet before he had left the room the door burst open and several of the palace guard appeared, carrying their spears. They knocked over my papers and notes heedlessly, and two of them took poor Gannoc by the arms as he had been a common felon, saying he must come at once to attend his Majesty. I followed them unnoticed.

In the king's room, what a sight met our startled eyes! The old king lay groaning upon his bed, red-faced and sweating and mouthing unintelligible syllables. His physicians were nowhere in evidence, but two doctors I had never seen before were there, speaking of paralytic strokes, and incapacitation, and a regency. I was not surprised to see Ddiskeard arrive soon after, and he did not conceal his feelings well, though he pulled a long face for my benefit.

Since that time, Gannoc has attended his Majesty constantly, but the doctors do not leave him alone and we have our suspicions of their cures and potions. Ddiskeard has the council under his thumb and will soon have the crown upon his head. But only yesterday he spoke with me of a new history to be written, and his hints have resolved me to be careful. The child did well to get away when she did, I think. I wonder how it fares with our poor prince. . . .

THE EXILE

Chapter Twenty-nine

Simirimia once more tried to call Leron back through her enchantments, but there was no answer; and at last she realized her serpent must be destroyed, victim to the older powers of the Zenedrim. Angrily she swept back and forth in her chamber, flexing her strong white fingers. Never before had the bond of blood been broken. She paused before her fire, feeling her own blood run thin and cold, and read out a futile curse in the old language of Treglad. She had not thought ever to lose Leron.

Leron, Armon's mirror image. Armon had died in battle rather than submit, but his sister's son had not been so difficult. She could not believe he was gone. She brought the flames up with a flick of her hand, but no images were there. Leron did not answer. At length, past anger, she sat in her chair still looking into the flames, her chin resting on her hand, turning the history of Armon and his city over and over in her mind. Before Armon, she had not noticed Tredana, except in contempt. A cluster of houses built upon the cliffs, producing nothing of interest or value. The centuries passed for her in pleasant profusion, and nothing contested her supremacy. In Treclere all her desires were answered, and she watched with careless pleasure the steady dwindling of spirit in the ruins of Treglad, as Rianna slowly faded in memory and power.

Then, a hundred years was nothing. The lives of others, fragile as moths or butterflies, flashed across her awareness and disappeared again and still she continued, still unchanged. Until she had seen Armon of Tredana, eighteen years ago.

She had seen him in a vision, and she had spent that night and many more in a strange discontent. By her various arts she watched him, and he was beautiful. For a month she watched him in Villavac or in Tredana, walking in the garden with his arm about his sister, arguing with his sister's husband, the king. And after a month she could bear it no longer, and she sent to him secretly an offer of alliance and un-dreamed of power.

Simirimia shook her head slowly, and her hair curled restlessly along the arms of her chair. In her infatuation, she had forgotten the lineage of Armon and Leriel, descended as they were from the readers of the Temple of Ornat. Never the possessors of power themselves, still they were ever too proud to accept the gift of it from others. Angered, Armon would have ridden against her had she been twice as great. A small triumph curled her lip as she remembered how Armon had been brought in dead from the fighting, and how by her arts she had raised him for a day and a night. Arbytis, her priest, had shown the way. He had bent once, and he would again. She rose slowly, savoring the heat of the fire on her body, then went to put a new task to the captive high priest.

North of Treclere, where the hills came steeply down to the long sea inlet, Leron awoke. The boat of the Zenedrim was beached on the pebbly shore, and within it Sibby was asleep beside him, her face hidden in her crossed arms. He watched her for a while before waking her, for he was not sure they would ever have such a quiet moment again. The afternoon air held the bitter dry tang of late summer, and he wondered how long they had been in the seasonless north. At last he touched her shoulder, and she woke and smiled at him.

Reluctantly, Leron got to his feet and stepped out onto the shore. Sibby rose also, then exclaimed with surprise and reached forward under the boat's prow where it curved back and covered their feet. On the wooden floor lay a dagger small and made of gold with an ivory handle. They had seen it among Yoseh's treasures in Tremyrag, but he had not mentioned it. Sibby took it gingerly and drew the blade a small way from the leather scabbard. It was covered with black scrollwork, like writing. She looked at him questioningly. "It must be for us, don't you think? I mean, it wouldn't be here by accident."

Leron nodded and helped her from the boat. "I think it is for you. I did not see it. The Zenedrim does nothing without reason, of that at least I am sure."

Sibby nodded and paused for a moment to fasten the dagger securely to her belt. Then they walked up the shore to the hilltop. From there they could see Treclere in the distance, no more than ten or fifteen miles away. As they began walking, Leron felt a heaviness descend upon him, increasing as the city darkened and grew on the southern horizon.

Before they came to Treclere, there was a small village in their path, empty like the villages Sibby had seen before. Among the buildings, it was yellow dusk, long-shadowed. In a darkened doorway, some birds murmured to each other. Sibby started and looked around her with surprise.

"What is the matter?" asked Leron, and Sibby looked around again, listening, before she answered.

"I—I thought I heard someone say something."

"But the streets are empty."

"I know, but—there! Didn't you hear that?"

"Hear what? The wind? The birds?"

"The birds . . ." Sibby put her hand on his arm, distressed. "Leron, I can understand them! Can you? The birds are talking. . . ." She put her hand over her mouth as though she were tasting something unbearable.

Leron put his arm around her shoulders. "Sibby, there's no one here but us. It's all right. . . ."

"But it isn't all right; I can hear them. Oh Leron, the things they say!" Leron turned, following her glance, to where some birds were clustered, muttering, in a doorway. "Listen—she's crying, 'How long, how long, how long? Twenty years, twenty years. Family gone, body lost, spirit taken, twenty years, twenty years, twenty years.' And then that other one's saying, 'She's dead, she's dead, she's dead, cannot follow, cannot follow, days follow, months follow, years, years, years . . .' And those two there—" she pointed to a crumbling window ledge—"they were brothers. Can't you hear them? It's so plain. 'Brother, brother, hope no more, no more hope, no more hands again, no young girls again, only birds, only birds, only birds.' " Impulsively, she ran over to the shadowed window casing. "Tell me," she cried, "are you . . ." but her words frightened them, and they all scattered in an uprush of wings, for all the world like ordinary birds.

Leron followed her and again put his arm around her. "They cannot understand you," he said. "How do you understand them?"

"I think it's because of—of him, the Kermyrag. I can still

taste his tear. It was like blood. I'd forgotten, but when the birds spoke I tasted it." She looked at her scarred hand as she spoke, but there was no new mark to be seen. Leron took her hand in his and turned the palm upward.

"If anything could grant you such a power, the Kermyrag could. How did you thus come to scar your hand?"

He listened to the story of Herrard and Black Wolf, and it was plain to him that Sibby did not herself understand the forces driving her. "Perhaps Arbytis will be able to explain this to us. You burned yourself in anger to protect a friend. Surely one must earn the right to touch the great firebird. You did, as I, alas, did not." Thinking of Arbytis, he drew Sibby on, away from the village. "As for these birds, it is plainly a matter to do with the Great Queen. If we are successful, perhaps their pain also will end."

Sibby turned a backward look at the shuttered houses and empty street. "Yes, I hope so. But I wouldn't want to sleep here in any case."

Leron agreed. "We will be more comfortable in the open. And tomorrow we will come to Treclere."

It was chilly inside the queen's palace. The strong joists and beams and careful masonry were still firm around her, unseamed by age or weather; but a cold had settled into the passages of her palace that would not go away. And the high narrow windows were shadowed also. No longer did the morning light come in as before, and Simirimia kept great fires burning in every room; but still she felt the change and wondered. She had not been so uneasy since that desperate time nearly eighteen years past, when she had known herself to be with child. Centuries ago, Hartun had read a verse for her, "Get she daughter, get she son; so death is got by the Deathless One." And she had laughed because there were no gods left by whom such a child could be got, and she knew she would never have to fear for the ending of her existence.

How Arbytis had thought to trick her! He yielded to her and read the words that raised Armon, never telling her that a child would be got by virtue of those same words, thinking to sow her death with Armon's seed. At first she had tried a great sending, across the barrier to the shadowy Otherworld, an exchange with one of those who waited there and from time to time sent messages. But not since those of the Broken

Circle in Treglad, the renouncers of Ornat, had made the long journey themselves, a thousand years since, had any crossed over. She was not successful. Visitors still might come, but for her the door did not open outward. The child in her womb remained, the craft did not work; the monstrous burden stayed in her body, prophesying her death.

Once Dastra was safe on Glass Island, Simirimia had again found her content. And Dastra in Tredana, as long as Leron was obediently to hand, bothered her little more. But all was altered, and she brooded as she had during that dark time years ago. If it were not forbidden for one of the Great Mother's race to kill its own flesh, how easily all would have righted itself. But she could no more kill Dastra than she could see how harm lay in her, and the question fretted her while she shivered in her palace. The only pleasure she could see was Leron's return and the forging of a permanent bond, unbreakable even by the Zenedrim.

Halfway through the next morning, Sibby and Leron stopped to rest a few miles north of the city. They sat down by a flowering thorn where two blackbirds were beautifully singing. But the blackbirds were joined by a third, whose song was bitterly intelligible to Sibby. She put her arms about her legs and dropped her head on her knees, not offering to translate. Leron spoke up hurriedly, trying to drown out the bird's thin lament.

"Do not forget to be careful when you go to the inn. If the queen thinks you slipped away on your own, she will not be too anxious for you; but if she connects you with me or finds you in the city the same day I return from the north, you might be in deadly danger."

"Qayish will hide me, in the cellar. I talked with him before I left. He even gave me provisions. I stayed there until one of Ajjibawr's men could bring out my horse from the stable." She choked up as she remembered her horse, but at least the birds were forgotten for a moment.

"Good. I do not know what will happen when I return, but I must trust to Arbytis's guidance and the words of the Zenedrim. But Sibby—if we do meet again, and I am not myself but changed by the queen, I beg of you, please. . . ."

"What, Leron?" She looked him in the eyes levelly, not at all like a child.

"Sibby, I would rather be killed outright than ever do harm

to anyone again."

She leaned over as he said that and, putting her arms around him, hugged him hard. "Leron, don't worry about that. You will be all right this time. I know it."

As they entered Treclere, Leron saw Sibby grow pale; there were gentle bird murmurs and rustles on every side and it was plainly a terrible weight of grief for anyone who could understand it. His own feelings were simpler. The thought of returning to Simirimia's palace clutched at his belly and made him sick and weak. He could never trust himself again. Numbly, he watched Sibby turn away among the houses and disappear; then he walked as boldly as he could along the main street up to the massive wooden gates.

He did not hesitate, but struck the door loudly with his closed hand. "Open up!" he cried in a mighty voice. "Leron of Tredana requires admittance." The bolts were pushed back, and then the door shuddered open across the uneven paving stones. There were four guards waiting inside, armed with spears. Leron pushed past them, and they stepped back out of his way. "Take me to the queen," he said, and he walked between them toward the low, pillared building. The guards walked with him to the door of the great hall, then stood back as it swung open on its silent pivot. The chamber leaped with firelight, and seated at the back Simirimia waited to receive him.

"Welcome from the north, prince," she said. "Come in. We have much to discuss." Silently, the door swung to and they were alone together.

THE PROPHECIES OF THE ORACLE OF ORNAT:

An excerpt concerning what must be

Is there anything that lives without hope of death?
Is there anything built which will never crumble?
Does not the dragonfly think his hour in the sun a
  lifetime?
Does not the great tree wither as surely as the wildflower?
Are you so different, O Petitioner?

Run if you will, but none escape the Yinry.

You have seen the man with seven sons, how is he served?
He has followed the dog down and drinks the water of the
*   underworld.*
You have seen the barren woman, how is she served?
She has followed the dog down and drinks the water of
*   the underworld.*
You have seen the Great Mother, how is she served?
She has followed the dog down and drinks the water of
*   the underworld.*
You have seen the First Father, how is he served?
He has followed the dog down and drinks the water of the
*   underworld.*
Are you then greater, O Petitioner?
Run if you will, but none escape the Yinry.

Even the deathless ones of high descent
Even the daughters of the Great Mother
Even these Goddesses of most excellent respect
Even these shall not escape the Yinry.

The law binds all from lowest to most high
The sun is bound by day, the moon by night
Bound in their dance the stars and wandering planets
Bound are the seasons to their turning wheel
O Petitioner, even you are bound
Run if you will, but none escape the Yinry.

Chapter Thirty

The firelight behind Simirimia's chair threw her features into shadow, but Leron could feel her bright green eyes upon him as he approached. She beckoned with her hand until he stood at her knee. From the height of throne and dais she looked down on him for a long silent moment. Then she laughed in her throat. "Your neck is bare, my prince. How did you lose my parting gift to you?"

He looked up into her face. "It was taken from me in the north. You said when you gave it there was no need of such trinkets."

"In the north. You were successful then?"

"Only in part. I learned in Vahn that Bodrum's council sent the Jawmir north many years ago. So I went north in search of it, even to Tremyrag, and there indeed I saw it and looked into its depths. But it was not given me. Nor had I the strength to compel its surrender."

"You had not the strength? Perhaps it was volition and not strength that was lacking."

Leron nodded, forcing his leaping pulse to calmness. "Perhaps, indeed," he agreed politely.

Simirimia's eyes flashed, and then were veiled. She gestured wearily with her hand. "You are much altered, prince. It was not thus you spoke when you took your leave of me."

"But it was thus I spoke when first I came into your kingdom."

The Great Queen pushed herself to her feet, gripping the carved arms of her chair. "Proudly said. So now the small cock crows. You are not even lord of the barnyard, little prince. Your future with me may not be as easy as your past."

"I do not intend to take my future here. There is blood between us. I have to avenge the death of my mother's brother, and that of my companion, the son of Meddock." Simirimia threw back her head and her hair lifted about her as though on rising water. "Blood," she said softly. "Yes, there is blood between us. 'By blood bind thee, by blood wound thee. . . .' " She moved her hand in a tightening gesture, and Leron fell forward onto his knees, his hands on his burning throat. For a few minutes he knelt there helplessly, his head dropped; then despite the pain he forced himself up onto one knee and then to his feet. Simirimia laughed, and released him slightly.

"Come, my little prince. We will talk with your old friend and teacher. Come see the changes these last weeks have wrought. Besides, I would have him see the efficacy of the ancient bond of blood." She swept past him and he was forced to follow, stumbling slightly, his hands still pressed to his constricted throat. It was impossible to speak, and his breath seemed to burn in his lungs.

The dark familiar passages were colder than Leron remembered, and he tried to suck in the dank air to relieve his lungs, but the burning pain continued. Before they had come to Arbytis's cell, Simirimia paused by a different door, listening, her head cocked on one side. As she listened, she seemed to waver in her will over Leron; the pain relaxed and he could breathe more easily. As the drumming in his head died down, he could hear beyond the door a murmur of birds, rustling and muttering and vibrating their soft cries: Simirimia heard more. "They are telling their stories," she said softly. "But who is there to listen to them?" The door swung open before her, she paused a moment, and then stepped softly in.

Leron stepped up behind her, and if he could have made a sound in his swollen throat he would have cried aloud with despair. As it was, the little groan he made caused Sibby to turn from the massed ranks of cages and see the queen in the doorway.

The room was large, high-vaulted, and dark, with no apparent windows. It was close, and stank with the smell of birds; the floor was deep in droppings and feathers. Some birds in the thousands of small woven cages were evidently dead, and the smell of their rotten flesh was heavy in the air as well. Cages were ranked out of sight into the shadows and up on all the walls; by the further wall Sibby stood startled, her hand on the edge of a row of cages, her ear next to the mesh. Simirimia laughed, this time with genuine pleasure. She smiled at Leron's stricken face.

"Why prince, this is fortunate. Your little companion

slipped away soon after you set out on your journey, and see, she is here to welcome you back. How pleased you must be to see each other."

As Leron watched, Sibby pulled herself up, raising her chin in defiance. Her unruly black hair was below her shoulders, and as she tossed it proudly back her gesture unconsciously mimicked the queen.

"I have been listening to your birds." Sibby's voice rang clearly in the room. "They've told me about what you've done. They were people, and you took away their bodies. But they haven't forgotten. They hate you."

Simirimia touched her left forefinger to her bottom lip and stroked along the line of her mouth, slowly. Under her dropped lids, the eyes gleamed and she was still smiling, but more narrowly. With the same finger she very slowly pointed forward with her wrist dropped, and a cage door fell open. The bird inside flew out, wildly beating its wings, and made a desperate circle above their heads. But she left her finger extended, and slowly, as the bird turned round them, it was drawn closer and closer, finally coming down onto her finger, clutching for balance. She looked at it a moment and her lips moved, then she flung it into the air and it flew at Sibby's face, striking with beak and claws. Sibby threw up her hands to protect her eyes and the edge of her open palm struck the bird a glancing blow. It fell to the floor with a broken neck, and Simirimia laughed as Sibby looked down at it in horror and pity, tears in her eyes.

"They are my obedient servants," said Simirimia quietly, "and so shall you be also. Come." But in the act of turning she paused, and suddenly stepped across to Sibby, taking her by the shoulder. The light of the torches had glinted on Sibby's dagger as she turned, and now Simirimia caught it up from her belt and drew out the blade. She turned on Leron with narrowed eyes. "You were not alone in the north, I see, or at least you did not return quite empty-handed. How does the dagger of Arleon come to be worn by this child?"

Leron rubbed his throat and tried to speak. "It was given to me," he finally choked out, and Simirimia looked down into Sibby's face, her fingers pressing into her shoulder.

"And you gave it to this child. But to what purpose?"

She touched the point of the blade against Sibby's cheek, and as she did so the room seemed darker and colder. But even in the lowered light, the mark the sharp point made was clear and red, a triangle not quite breaking the surface of the skin. Sibby said nothing, but her eyes glared at the queen in mounting fury, which Leron could see must be somewhat akin to what had happened when Black Wolf tried his bullying.

Apparently Simirimia did not notice, for she pushed Sibby ahead of her to the door, and the two of them were forced against their wills to proceed down the corridor another few steps to where a door opened before them. There was moonlight in Arbytis's chamber, and as they entered, an unlit torch against the wall flared into life at the queen's gesture. Leron was swept with guilt as they entered, seeming still to smell the blood of Lelu, and as he looked at Arbytis, he groaned again.

The old man lay in a heap on the floor of his cage, so shrunken and thin he seemed smaller than Sibby. Leron stepped hurriedly across to the cage, and, reaching between the bars, he gently took Arbytis's hand in his own. The old man half roused from his stupor smiling a welcome even before Leron could speak.

"Dear Arbytis, I have returned from the north."

Arbytis nodded. "You bring me the greeting of the Zenedrim, for which I thank you." His voice was very hoarse and weak. "Child, you are welcome also."

Sibby tried to pull away from the queen's grasp on her shoulder to go to him, but the queen held her tightly. She pulled angrily again, and her tunic twisted at the neck, exposing the Karabdin ring on its thong. The queen caught it between her fingers and turned it over in the light, twisting the cord painfully tight about Sibby's neck. "So. Arleon's dagger from the treasure of Tremyrag, and a token from the desert as well. Is the Karif also a part of your plot?" She paused in amazement as Sibby pushed her away and grabbed the ring back from her fingers.

"Take your hands off me!" she cried, and ran over to Arbytis's cage. She knelt next to Leron and held onto the bars, pressing her face against them. "Arbytis, I'm sorry. I wasn't going to come, but I heard about the birds. I know you understand. Oh, Arbytis, I want to help you." She stood up and faced the queen, almost spitting with anger.

"How dare you carry on like this. At home, they'd lock you up or have you killed. You're a murderer. I'll never do anything you say." Simirimia looked at her, and then at Leron still kneeling by the cage. At her gesture, Leron was frozen in place, but Sibby backed away angrily, her breast heaving, until she was against the wall.

Simirimia turned to Arbytis. "What new tricks are these, false priest? Is this some spirit raised by you and my sister to mock my powers? Is this a part of your plan to deceive me? Do not think I have not noticed. I know it is by some trick of yours that the air grows colder and darker every day. But it will take more than tricks to free you. You may help this child avoid me, but you cannot save her if I choose it otherwise." She spoke quietly and raised the dagger in her hand.

Arbytis shook his head. "Goddess, has pride so blinded you that I can see what you cannot? I do not need eyes to know what crouches on the roof, darkening the air around us. I do not need eyes to see whose breath it is that chills the very stone under my feet. I do not need eyes to recognize the offspring of your body or to read the fulfillment of Hartun's prophecy. Strike at your child if you must but the Yinry wait in the air around us. They are huddled on the roof and their breath is in our lungs already. Can you not smell their impatience?"

Simirimia dropped her hand, still holding the dagger. "Who is it talks of pride? Tell me how you control the seasons and make a child of twelve my daughter, born seventeen years ago."

"You did not entirely fail in your great sending. This child but recently returned from the Otherworld, and their time is not ours. The child you bore was not yours, but of an alien blood. Is the cuckoo a thrush because it is hatched in one's nest?"

Simirimia hesitated a moment longer, then shook her head. "You tricked me once in the matter of Armon. You shall not trick me again. Whatever the secrets of this child, she will be better dead, and Leron will come sweetly to hand never to break away again. Fool that I was to believe in your cards and mutterings. Fool that I was to think you were still high priest. Truly a cage becomes you better than any temple."

Arbytis clasped his hands before him. "Goddess," he said softly, "well do I know you cannot return. The Double Goddess is broken forever, and no man can put an egg back together once the shell is shattered. But think, why must it be thus? What profit has come to you from separation? Do not destroy yourself. Look for yourself; listen! Do you not hear their great wings beating the air down? They are waiting! And look at this child. Have you been so long without looking in a glass that you cannot recognize your own features?"

Numbed as he was, Leron looked again at Sibby while Arbytis spoke and wondered that he had never before seen the truth of what was said. She was only a child, but the straight dark brows and proud cheekbones were the match of Simirimia's. Only her dark eyes were markedly different, the eyes of Armon.

Simirimia pointed her dagger at the child, and Sibby looked angrily back. Energy crackled in the air, and Sibby fell to her knees crying out in a mixture of pain and fury. Leron tried to reach his hand to help her, but the queen's powers held him as heavily as though he were in chains.

Again Arbytis stirred in his cage, and it seemed the air grew darker and a cold wind came in through the narrow window. "Goddess," he cried, "could you not feel that in your own heart?"

Simirimia was white, and her lips trembled with passion. "I will prove your lies in blood, false priest. Come here, my prince, and show this old man what it means to meddle."

She pulled Leron to his feet as easily as lifting a puppet by its strings, and, when he stood before her, she placed the dagger in his right hand, closing the fingers onto the hilt one by one. Then she spun him around with a word, and to his horror, Leron found himself slowly approaching Sibby, the dagger in his dangling hand. He tried to tell her to move, but he couldn't speak, and she only looked at him with her anger turned to pity and concern. She even stepped forward to meet him, one hand upraised. "Leron," she said, "it's all right; she can't make you hurt me." He tried to shake his head, and the sweat ran down his forehead into his eyes. He could feel his hand being lifted, and a silent voice inside his head cried out in agony. Sibby would not move away. He willed her to move, but she came up close, touching her hand against his chest, looking him in the eyes. "Leron," she said, "remember."

As he looked into her eyes, he saw the reflected light of the torches, and for a moment he thought it was a vision of the Kermyrag burning in ice and pain. Relieved, he understood the answer, and as his arm struck, he somehow managed to turn the blow against his own body. The pain threw him to his knees, but he could feel the blade slip safely along the rib and would have laughed in double relief had any words been possible.

As he knelt there, feeling the warm blood run out over his belt and onto the floor, Simirimia released him so suddenly he almost struck his head against the floor. Dizzy with shock, he looked up and saw that Sibby had turned on the queen, and in a crazy anger would attack her with bare hands. Simirimia caught her by the wrists, but Sibby had a superhuman strength in her fury; for a moment they were poised in balance, and then Simirimia had the child pressed against the wall and was choking her by pressing her own hands against her throat. Sibby gasped and struggled, and as she choked Simirimia faltered, as though she, too, had been hurt. It grew darker, and the cold ached in Leron's wounded side.

Sibby gasped again, and Simirimia flinched also, but she pressed even harder, and her great strength told at last. Sibby could no longer resist, and Simirimia savagely applied more pressure on her stranglehold. The child went limp in her hands, and Simirimia laughed briefly in a breathless triumph. She would have twisted the remaining life out then and there, but the room went suddenly dark and a cold wind blew in at the door. She dropped Sibby onto the floor and whirled in anger, commanding the lights to rekindle, but they stayed dark. The cold wind continued to blow, despite her restraining hand and sharp word of power.

"What foolery is this, Arbytis?" She almost screamed at him and caused him such pain with her outflung hand that he was unable to answer. Gasping, he caught his breath and finally spoke in a harsh whisper.

"Their wait has not been in vain. Daughter of the Great Mother, you have brought your own end upon you. The Yinry are here. You have raised your hand against your own flesh, and now they have come to drag you down with them." He spoke not in triumph but with a peculiar sadness, and she looked at him, one hand pressed to her heaving breast. In the silence, he raised his head, and his lips and voice trembled with weariness and pain. "It has worked out as I planned it, eighteen years ago in this very room. Even the Great Goddess shall not escape the Yinry. Where will you meet them? They will not stand forever outside the door."

Her breathing calmed, and she turned to the door. "Priest, I will show you your lie," and she walked out into the dark hall. The brief silence was broken by a heavy beating of wings, shaking the walls and floors, and a sudden stench of cold that gusted through the room and disappeared. Moonlight streamed in again at the window and, as Leron pulled himself painfully to his feet, a tremor shook the building and almost knocked him down again. The wings were beating all around, and as they vibrated, dust sifted out from between the stones and the straight lines of the masonry began to shift awry. A crack began to open in the floor.

"Quick," cried Arbytis. "This palace was built by artifice. We must escape before it comes apart."

Leron staggered forward and pulled the flimsy cage door open. Arbytis was a fragile bundle in his arms as he lifted him out and set him on the floor. Then he tried to rouse Sibby. She came to slowly, but he somehow managed to push her to her feet and, taking Arbytis in his arms, he urged her from the room before him and into the corridors. Mortar was already slipping from between the stones, and the floor heaved slightly as they hurried out. So great was Leron's urgency to be gone, he did not feel his loss of blood until they stood in the courtyard safely beyond the pillared inner court. Then he sank to his knees, still holding Arbytis safely against him, and as he fainted saw the stones slowly collapse in an uprush of dust, and high above, spiraling against the moon, a multitude of birds flying free of the ruin.

LETTER

by private messenger from Madam Letha,
at her residence in Mindo'ila
to BODRUM VIII, at the Summer Palace on Almond Island

Most August Lord and Dear Brother:
When I received the Recent Missive graciously sent from your Hand, that which I read was Painful, but alas, it came as No Surprise. Often you have rebuked my Tenderness of Heart, and with such Tenderness I rejoiced to see Odric set out for

the North, where he might easily perish as Fate intends, and through no Word of mine.

But Truly, Intent without Action is a Seed without Rain. Therefore, I questioned Certain of my Staff and learned that this Corruption has spread even to Mindo'ila. I have cleared my own Company of it, and learned thereby that Leron of Tredana follows his intention North, while Odric takes his own Path. Look to your Men, therefore, Dearest Brother, and expect Odric to reach your Gates no later than Two Days after this Message. I pray for your Safety, and humbly beg you remain on Almond Island until this Matter clears.

Your Most Loyal and Affectionate Sister,
LETHA

The boys send also their Dutiful Regards, and pray you will send a Suitable Tutor, once Odric is Taken.

Chapter Thirty-one

There was still a clamor of birds in the air when Leron awoke next morning. Vaguely he remembered Sibby helping him staunch the blood from his wound and the slow painful journey to the inn. At first he had not thought he could push his way through the people crowding the streets, but suddenly several came forward to help, supporting him and Arbytis. The inn had been crowded, too, confusingly noisy, everyone talking at once and pointing toward the palace; but Sibby's friend Qayish had seen them and taken them to a room, bringing them food and wine and bandages.

He sat up carefully and grimaced at the way it caught his side. The door opened, and Sibby came in with full hands, kicking the door shut with a twist of her foot behind her. She put the food down by his bed, smiling wearily at him, and there were dark hollows under her eyes.

"Do you feel better?"

"I will be fine. The wound is painful but very shallow. How is Arbytis?" Sibby walked to the couch by the window where Arbytis lay and carefully pulled the quilts up around his neck, although the air was mild.

"He's sleeping still. He's so terribly thin." She rested her hand lightly on his white hair and then came back to Leron, sitting down on the edge of his bed.

"Sibby, I've been wondering as I lie here—what do the birds say now?" She cocked her head to one side, birdlike herself, and listened closely. She frowned with concentration and then smiled. "Nothing—I mean, not like before. It's just bird talk, dust and sun and nests. The people are free, I guess. At least, the birds are."

Leron nodded and broke off a piece of bread, smearing it against the thick hunk of soft butter that was on the plate with the cheese.

"Then it is as we suspected. The birds were vehicles only,

and now the souls imprisoned in them are free."

Sibby nodded. "But some of the birds were killed."

"We do not know entirely how this worked. Perhaps Arbytis will be able to explain. I still am not sure what happened with the queen."

He looked Sibby in the eyes. "Nor do I understand you entirely. Nothing is impossible with the goddess, yet I do not understand the words of Arbytis. You are of the Otherworld."

Sibby bit her lip and pushed her hair back with one hand, considering an answer, and the line of her face in profile was as distinct as Simirimia's. "Leron, what was that prophecy, you know, way back, that made you set out to look for Dastra in the first place?"

"It was that I would find the daughter of the great queen on a journey to the north."

"Well, you see—you just decided it was Dastra because you already knew about her being on Glass Island. But you did find me, too."

"But Sibby, this is madness. You never told us much of your life in the Otherworld, but surely you have a family! Things cannot be so very different in your world."

Sibby smiled. "Of course I have parents. But so what? Maybe it's like being adopted. I don't look like them. My mother looks like Dastra; I thought that soon after we rescued her, only it didn't make any sense. I mean, she's got blond hair and she's pretty and she likes to get dressed up. She doesn't like me exactly. My father's OK, except he's always busy. Leron, I never even missed them!"

Leron smiled and touched her hand. "If you are Simirimia's daughter, then you are also Armon's, and we are cousins."

Sibby didn't answer, sitting on his bed as she thought this over. Then after checking on Arbytis once more, she left him to get up and dress. Despite his wounds, Leron managed to wash and dress, cursing a little at the narrowness of the tunic as he struggled to push his bandaged way into it. Hearing Arbytis stir on his pillows, Leron helped him to sit up, and pressed a wet cloth to his face. There was wine and bread on the floor by his bed, and Leron helped him to eat. After a few swallows, Arbytis managed to speak.

"Thank you, my son. This is the happiest morning in many months, and the saddest in centuries."

"Why are you sad?"

"I was the high priest of Ornat, and I served the Double Goddess. With Simirimia gone, her sister cannot last. It is the end of my only purpose, yet I will continue."

After a short pause, Arbytis spoke again, even more haltingly. "You will understand that my grief is personal. To others, it is not important. It is so easy for me to look backward. Though I can read the future, it is painful and uses my little strength. I cannot be of further use to you." He checked Leron's protest. "There is no joy or strength left in me. Leron, my dear son, I was already an old man when Arleon came to Tredana! There is a valley east of here, and on our return I will beg of you to take me there. Though I cannot die, perhaps I can sleep there undisturbed by the whirling years."

Leron murmured agreement and helped Arbytis lie back again, the weight against his arms lighter than a child's. He kissed the old man on his forehead and, as he turned to leave, Arbytis spoke once more. "Leron, stay with your cousin today. She does not yet understand what was spoken last night. She is a true inheritor but very young, and it will be best if she does not think too much upon it yet." Leron agreed and shut the door softly behind him.

Downstairs in the common room there was a bewildered press of people, incredulous of their good fortune. Leron pushed his way through to the kitchens and found Sibby there with Qayish and his wife and daughters. She was eating a sweet bun and watching with satisfaction as the innkeeper kissed and hugged his restored family. Leron crossed to her and spoke softly in her ear. "Sibby, do you know much of Qayish's friends?"

"A little. Why?"

"Did they have any organization, any leaders? A council, perhaps? Treclere will not run itself. Today there is rejoicing, but soon there will be quarrels and disputes between neighbors, and litter in the streets. There must be some order."

Sibby looked astonished. "Do you really think so? I thought when Simirimia was gone, everything would be fine."

"Look around you. The people have lived as slaves for centuries. No one here even dares order his wine without support. How will they order a city?"

Sibby looked around with new awareness as Leron left her to talk to Qayish. The innkeeper, however, was too distracted by his unexpected fortune to pay attention. When he finally understood Leron's concern, his reaction was similar to Sibby's but much stronger. "Leaders? We want no leaders! If the queen is truly gone, that is enough."

"Matters are not so easy. Can you arrange a meeting with your friends? There are messages that must be sent, arrangements made. . . ."

"Tomorrow, come back tomorrow. Today we are all celebrating. Come again tomorrow, and we will talk. . . ."

Leron bit back his impatience. "Tomorrow, then," he agreed, and as he turned away, he blundered into a tall man who was forcing his way into the room, trying gently to push the crowd aside. The tall man cried out in surprise as Leron backed off, apologizing, then took him strongly by the hand. It was Herrard.

"Greetings. It does my heart good to see the son of Mathon whole." His quick eyes noted Leron's bandaged stiffness, and he smiled more broadly. "Or reasonably whole, at any rate. As I came through the streets, I thought what need there was of a prince to keep order, and lo, here I find one. There could be no more welcome sight." He turned to Sibby who had just seen him, and taking her hands, he kissed her on both cheeks. "Almost no more welcome sight. Child, when I rode away from Treclere after the prince, I did not hope ever to see you again."

"Herrard! Everything's turned out so well. Leron's all better, and Simirimia's gone, and Treclere is free again. It's so wonderful to see you here. Leron told me about your trip together. What happened in Vahn?"

Herrard's smile faded. "Much happened there, as you will hear. We were intending to travel into the Land and meet with my brothers, the Karabdu, when a pillar of dust rising up from Treclere pricked our curiosity."

"It is good you are here," said Leron. "Arbytis lies in an upper room, trying to rest against the journey home. He will be anxious to speak with you."

"Then the queen is truly defeated?"

"I do not fully understand, but she is gone from here, and all her captive spirits are released."

Herrard touched his throat and bowed his head briefly. "I

did not think this day would come in my lifetime. But I am forgetting my companion. He will be impatient. Come, let us bring him in."

With his strong arms, he swept the crowd back so Sibby and Leron could easily walk with him out into the courtyard. There stood a heavyset dark bay horse with Odric clumsily in the saddle. He was clumsy, as Leron quickly saw, because both feet were braced and bandaged inside his loose leather boots, and, under the folds of good humor in his face, there were lines of pain.

He smiled at their approach. "Sibby, little maiden! And Leron! You are safely returned from the north. Ah, if all is well with you, then I dare hope for my own tangled future. Here, help me get down." The problem was he could not set weight on either foot without considerable pain, and it was all Herrard and Leron could do to support him to a seat inside, for he was still quite solid in his build.

"I did not get away entirely free, as you can see. Back in Vahanavat I acted carelessly and broke my baraka over some scoundrel's head. It was good fortune I scarcely deserved that Herrard and some friends of mine were able to help me out of the palace not very long after my arrest. And also that the master was away on Almond Island. Although I was at the palace no more than a few hours, still I am unable to walk, and that was three weeks ago." He smiled at Sibby's questioning look.

"It is nothing very terrible, little maid. In Vahn there is a palace tradition of beating on the feet, and if one must be beaten, it is as good a place as any, and better than most in many respects." Then he shook his head and sighed. "If it were only a matter of my own pain I could laugh indeed. But things are not well in my city, and I see no quick way to change the order there."

Leron looked at him consideringly, studying the familiar face with new interest. "Perhaps," he said slowly, "perhaps you need a chance to learn the task to which you were born. By blood you are a ruler, but by profession you are not."

Odric nodded and shrugged his shoulders. "I have spent my life letting the days bring what they will. I have no training for what must be done."

"You need a place to rule and set in order. Treclere needs someone to order her. I think your fate has brought you here,

Odric of Vahn. What do you think, Herrard?"

"Indeed, it may have been more than mere curiosity that turned our course away from the desert. The more I travel and the more I see, the less I question fate." Leron caught Sibby's eye and saw her smile with satisfaction.

"It works out perfectly," she said. "Odric will stay and manage here while Herrard goes and finds Ajjibawr and explains the whole story to him. And we'll go back to Tredana and take care of things there."

Odric nodded politely. "I thank you for your confidence, my dear. But we may need a few more opinions before I am handed the control of this great city."

Sibby shrugged. "I'm sure it will all work out."

There, for that day, matters rested, for Leron found he could get no answers out of anyone on the first day of freedom. A great celebration had been roughly planned for that evening, and Leron hoped that by the next day some people would be willing to talk about the future. In the meantime, he and Herrard helped Odric as gently as they could up to the room where Arbytis drowsed, and at last Odric met the priest of whom he had heard so many times.

Herrard had already visited once, but again he went over to the couch and knelt with Arbytis's hand on his shoulder, speaking softly and rapidly in the Karabdin tongue. After he fell silent, Arbytis lifted his empty face in Odric's direction and nodded cordially. "Greetings, Odric Sembatioun. Your family is well known to me. You are more like your ancestor Sembath than any man now on earth can realize. I do not think you will find the management of Treclere beyond your talents." Herrard started, and it was clear he had not mentioned this to Arbytis earlier. The old man smiled. "Leron, my son, and Herrard, Rassam, my own blood brother, why does it surprise you that the High Priest of Ornat can read your thoughts? Once I spoke for a goddess."

He stretched out his hand. "Odric, approach." Clumsily, Odric did so, disregarding the pain in his feet, and he fell heavily to the floor on his knees by Herrard. Arbytis touched his shoulder lightly. "What I have to give, I freely grant to you. You carry the blessing of Ornat. Be wise, and if you cannot be wise, be considerate. Temper can turn to tyranny if too much power is there." Even these brief words tired him, so he fell back heavily against the cushions, and quickly they all took their leave so he might rest.

Later that evening, while the celebration flowed with wine and laughter and music in the rooms and yard below, Leron came softly up the steps to check on his old teacher. Sibby was sitting by the bed, dark against the moonlight, her hand on Arbytis for comfort as he lay asleep. Soft sounds of partying came up through the floor.

"Do you wish to join Odric and Herrard?" Leron asked softly.

Sibby shook her head gently. "No," she said, "it's time for me to think. But thank you."

When he came up again, much later, she was asleep, and he lifted her up and put her into bed and she did not awake. As he tucked the blankets around her chin, he gently leaned forward and kissed her on the cheek before he knew what he was doing. But she only stirred and squirmed like a sleepy child, finally turning over and burying her face in the pillow. He smiled and left, but two more times before morning he found he had to check and see that nothing had disturbed her sleeping.

THE SONG OF THE BIRD MAIDENS
(Inspired by the daughters of Qayish)

by Odric

Where we have wings we once had hands
Where we have claws we once had feet
Where we have bills we once had red lips
Careless of words we now think sweet.

Mourn, mourn, mourn O Sisters
Never, never, never shall we be young maids again.

Where we had warmth we now have coldness
Where we had parents we now have none
Where we had young men we now are lonely
Cold and mute, friendless, alone.

Mourn, mourn, mourn O Sisters
Never, never, never shall we be young maids again.

See how the walls are falling, falling
See how the wind now sweeps us along
See ourselves are waiting to greet us
See how our lips are round with song.

Joy, joy, joy O Sisters
Never, never, never shall the Great Queen come again.

Chapter Thirty-two

It did not need more than a night's celebration to demonstrate the need for government in Treclere. Next morning early, Leron returned to the ruins to see if the Book of Ornat could be found, and on his way he saw many angry faces and one fistfight. Quarrels and disputes had already begun among the newly governless. Within the palace walls, it was very still: as yet there was no scavenging, for lingering fear of Simirimia's powers. The greater part of the palace still stood, but dangerously twisted out of true, with floors spilling out through the walls like the entrails of a wounded animal.

Cautiously, Leron went in by the nearest opening, not without some lingering fear of his own. To be under any part of the palace roof was to be trapped in memories of guilt and shame, and he hurried more for that than for any reasonable fear of unsound walls and floors. The section where they had been together in Arbytis's room was most badly distorted and collapsed in several layers. A bit of wall, however, he recognized by the shape of the window still set in it, and there, untouched and waiting for his hand, the Book of Ornat stood in its heavy casket. He caught it up by the handles and hurried away, distressed by the twisted edge of Arbytis's golden cage, smashed under the stones.

Arbytis had not been able to wait even the short time since breakfast and was sleeping again when Leron entered. The old man's continuing weakness pained Leron, and he wondered how they would ever get him to the valley. He set the casket down by the bed and lightly ran down the stairs to join the others in the courtyard. Qayish was there, talking with Herrard, while Odric and Sibby listened. Leron listened to his complaints briefly, then broke in. "Decisions must soon be made," he said curtly. He described what he had seen in the streets, and Qayish added similar experiences that morning just outside the inn.

Then he bowed nervously to Leron, with an awkward deference. "Perhaps, prince, I was overhasty yesterday. If you could stay a few weeks and help us order things. . . ."

Leron felt a twinge of annoyance, and suppressed it with difficulty. "My own city has need of my return," he said. "But there is another prince here who might be persuaded to stay some months at least." Qayish looked around him, startled, his eyes passing over the shabby lame minstrel who had sung so sweetly the night before, and Odric laughed with his hands on his stomach.

"Be careful, dear Leron," he said. "You will give royalty a bad name if you are too free in your descriptions." Qayish looked at him puzzled, and Odric nodded his head, ironically. "Yes, landlord, you see here the displaced son of Bodrum, master of Vahn. I suppose that makes me a prince of sorts. I am prince enough at any rate to be most unwelcome in my father's kingdom!"

Once Qayish had been convinced this was no jest, he fell in enthusiastically with Leron's suggestion, hurrying away to gather his friends for a council to see if they would accept Odric as their temporary leader. At length, even Odric was brought to agree. Qayish's enthusiasm swung the decision of his friends, already made uneasy by the magnitude of the tasks confronting them in Treclere; and by evening Odric was no longer without a home, openly bewildered by the suddenness with which his fortunes had turned. That evening they celebrated again but privately, and Odric arranged for them to have provisions and fresh horses for the next day's departure.

Herrard left them first, just after sunrise. He bade farewell to Arbytis in private and took his message for Ajjibawr. It was necessary that the Karif learn of recent events as soon as possible, and Herrard was especially anxious to set his mind at rest concerning Arbytis. The parting was warm but brief. As Herrard turned his bony chestnut away from the inn gates, he spoke one last time, to Sibby. "Do not look so sad. We shall meet again soon in Tredana, and I will bring you the Karif's greeting." Leron watched her face light at the mention of Ajjibawr's name, and he felt a twinge of jealousy. He said nothing, but left to see to the ordering of their goods.

Odric had arranged well. The horses were already saddled, and in the queen's stables Odric had found a low-bellied smooth-gaited mare for Arbytis to ride, fitted with a special sideways saddle, like a chair. There was also a pack horse, well provisioned. Leron carried Arbytis downstairs and helped set him securely on his horse. The old man relaxed in the padded saddle and smiled approval as Leron carefully tied the casket holding the cards in a place where he could touch it if he wished. Then, although she did not need assistance, he swung Sibby up onto her horse as well and felt rewarded by her open smile. Before mounting, he turned to Odric and clasped his hand. Odric's eyes crinkled as he smiled and spoke. "Friends should always part as though briefly. I will look to see you back as my guests within the year."

Leron replied, "May the house of Arleon and that of Sembath remain as close as we two are today."

Arbytis broke in, softly and unexpectedly. "And may your houses be as secure as your friendship. Your futures are alike in their uncertainty." At that they both became more sober. Leron pulled himself onto his horse, and they slowly rode out into the fresh morning.

Soon after they left, Arbytis began drowsing, and within the hour he was asleep again, the saddle holding him firmly. Sibby spoke up, shaking her head as though something bothered her. "I just don't see how anyone could want Ddiskeard to rule. I didn't like him the first time I saw him."

"The first time I saw Ddiskeard I did not think much of him, either. We were both three, and his guardian brought him down from Sundrat on the north coast to come to my birthday feast. I think I remember emptying my plate over his head because I took exception to something he said. I believe he made some remark about my being older through some mistake, and I thought he cast aspersions on my mother. You know, a vision frightened her and she gave birth early. She would only say it had to do with Armon. I wonder now if perhaps she saw his fate. At any rate, I think I have always hated Ddiskeard since, though privately."

Sibby swallowed and played with her horse's mane. "You were jealous of her brother, too, weren't you, I mean my—my father?"

It was the first she had spoken of Armon, though Leron had sensed her curiosity. He answered her quickly. "Yes, I was jealous of Armon. They were twins, and it seemed they never even had to speak for each to understand. My father suffered also. But there was no unkindness meant. I was jealous, but I also loved him. Although he was very splendid, he was kind to me and did not treat me like a child."

"I wish I had known him. I don't really feel as though I belong. I feel—"

Arbytis interrupted gently; they had supposed him still asleep. "You do belong, child. Otherwise you would have opened that window and seen the trees beyond and not a Tredanan beach." Sibby agreed, but doubtfully still.

Sibby's memory for landmarks proved to be exceptionally good, and they retraced her path and Herrard's toward Tredana. After a week or more of travel, it was clear to Leron's watchful eye, as it was to Sibby's, that Arbytis was failing rapidly. From time to time he would amaze them with his strength and alertness, but this was illusory, like the leap of a guttering candle. As they rode into the fenlands, Leron began riding next to Arbytis, for fear he might slip from the saddle. It was, therefore, for his sake that they rode directly into one of the fenland villages rather than skirting it, for Leron hoped to find some sort of inn where Arbytis might sleep one night in a bed.

The village was small, perhaps ten houses with bulging thatched roofs standing starkly in the midst of flat marshy fields. A crowd of wagons, livestock, and people were gathered at one end, however, and it was clear some sort of market was in progress. The three travelers were accepted matter-of-factly and shown to a small inn that had two rooms to let. After Leron had spoken with the landlord, he left Sibby with the horses while he carried Arbytis upstairs, almost bumping his head on the low ceiling. The rooms were small, but well lit with large windows opening out in the thick sweet-smelling roof. Leron laid his light burden down on one of the beds and spread a blanket over him. Once more he thought bitterly how helpless were those who loved Arbytis: the best anyone could wish him was his death.

Leron had intended that they sleep late the next morning, but it was not quite light when a knock on the door aroused him. Before he was fully awake, Arbytis spoke. "Come in, my daughter, and most welcome."

Leron looked up, still on the edge of sleeping. A tall, white-haired woman stood in the doorway, dressed in black. As though he had been awaiting her, Arbytis was upright against the pillows, one hand stretched out in greeting. The woman bowed and spoke.

"I have heard your call and have come as you asked. Our race has dwindled, but the Players do not forget. We are the readers still, as you are high priest. . . ." She took his hand and, stooping, pressed it to her lips.

Arbytis smiled gently. "I have a further request to make, one you may grant more easily. The Book of Ornat is here with me, the true images; you must keep them safely for me and use them wisely as only you can." He indicated the casket with his hand, and Ginas lifted it by its handles, setting it onto the bed.

Slowly she opened it and took the cards in her hands, where they sorted themselves under her gentle touch. She did not look at them, but closed her eyes. "The true images, yes. I can feel them. Here is your card." She turned one over in her hand and spoke something quietly to Arbytis, which Leron could not hear.

Arbytis sighed and nodded. "Yes, I hope to go to the only refuge left. In the valley I will rest for a moment at least, until Vazdz turns me out onto my wanderings once more."

Ginas looked across to Leron. "Was it for the prince you called me here?"

"Yes, my daughter, I grow weary and I cannot trust my sight. Leron I love too well to be impartial. Read him his future. It is of great concern to me, the more since I may not share in it."

Leron felt he came fully awake at this, and when the Player stood by his bed he looked from her glowing ring up into her face. "Ginas," he said, "I have heard of you from Sibby, my close cousin. You read aright for her some months ago, at the Circle Inn."

Ginas smiled. "Greet her from me. I must be gone from here before she wakes." She bent slightly and spread the cards out smoothly on his blanket, making a lamp without any pause or hesitation, the cards running through her fingers like water. "The oil in your lamp is here, the Great Queen signifying your family and high position, the Dog reversed showing weakness and inertia, and the Flowering Tree which is renewal. For the moment this is you, the Contract; a personal bond is now of chief importance. Above stand both the Broken Citadel and the High Priest, known also as the

Bridge; time to come holds for you an overthrow of all you have known as secure, yet you will find a way. For in the future stand these three: the Lightning Thrower who enforces change; the Great Circle which is Ornat, movement as ordained; and the King reversed, which is lost patrimony. Yet I would not despair, for the flame burns clearly, the Karif which is ambition, willfulness, and accomplishment. I think you will not easily travel to Tredana, but there is a future for you in the old city; Ajjibawr you must trust; these are the personal meanings." Her finger lightly touched the covers three more times. "These sparked the reading, the single star, which is the beginning of enterprise, the four rings reversed, which are material loss, and the spear-queen reversed, which is opposition. Consider these things, O prince, and be wary when you approach your city, for things are not as they were."

Leron tried to lift his head and look at the cards, but his body was numb; he had only a glimpse of their bright colors as Ginas carefully replaced them.

Outside the window, in the small backyard, a cock crowed loudly announcing the dawn. Ginas went to Arbytis, bowing her head once more. "Farewell for now. Whatever the Players may do, never fear to ask it. I cannot remain out of the body any longer. But always I shall listen for your call, High Priest of Ornat. Farewell."

And as the cock crowed once more, she went to the door and disappeared into the shadowed hall. Leron meant to speak to her, but his eyes were heavy and he fell asleep before he could say a word. He did not wake again until much later in the morning.

As they sat at breakfast in the small room downstairs, Leron looked out at the empty street. Market day was over, and the small town was quiet in the hazy morning. "The Players have gone already."

Sibby looked up with surprise, but Arbytis only smiled. "They were never here. Their camp is many miles hence on the fringes of the desert below Villavac. It was a shadow that visited us this morning, Ginas in all but substance."

To Sibby he added, "Ginas of the Players has sent you her greeting. Out of the body she came this morning at my request, and through her Leron has been helped to see the future. You and Leron will see little of the peace I hope for in the valley."

Sibby thought a moment. "When we were in the valley, I dreamed of you a prisoner in your cage, and I saw an old man with a light that was also you."

"Myself, or perhaps the Zenedrim. Either reading would have meaning. Child, you are true to your inheritance. The house of Armon and Leriel was descended in a straight line from the temple at Ornat. All the women had the gift of true dreaming. It is a heavy gift, as Leron's mother proved."

Leron thought of his mother's suffering and muttered, "Too heavy a gift, perhaps," but Sibby only nodded, seriously.

Soon after, they set out, due east. The sun had burned away the mist, and it was a fine day for riding.

GINAS

She turns the card of the High Priest

Arbytis the High Priest, a long time tried
with wearisome living, forgets for a moment
pain and despair. The deepening quiet
of peace washes over his bent white head.
Turn to new conquests, O Vazdz with your fire,
your wrath, and your lightning, but do not forget
Arbytis the High Priest unbent by you.

Chapter Thirty-three

When Leron and Sibby rode into the valley of Villavac about a month later, leaves were falling thickly from the trees about them, and others were thrown up in damp clumps by the horses' dull-thudding hoofs. Since leaving Arbytis in the valley, they had made good time. Under the avenue of trees leading into town, Leron signaled a halt, and he pulled his horse back into the early evening shadows. Sibby drew alongside, her face a dim white circle looking up at him.

"Much though it irks me to say it, I fear we must heed the warning of the cards and proceed with caution. If any are pressing with questions, say we are looking for Glisser, and if we should be followed, we will prove our intent by riding away north instead of toward Tredana. But with luck, we should be able to look and leave without hindrance."

"I would have liked to stay and look around before, except we were in a hurry and you know how Herrard hates staying in town. It seems funny to think there could be any danger here."

"I hope there is none. Yet we may learn something of affairs in Tredana by keeping our ears and eyes open." They moved out into the lane, and Leron added with a small sigh, "And our mouths shut. A pretty homecoming."

The smells and sounds of Villavac as they rode in were pleasantly familiar to Leron: late roses blooming in many courtyards filled the damp night air with scent, mixing with the smoke from cooking fires and the many different spices being used. In the market, farmers were closing up for the night, watering their animals, putting their harvests into baskets and boxes and shutting them up into sheds. No one looked up from his work, but a man on a dark horse, wearing a cloak, called out to them.

"Hi! Hold a moment!" Leron looked up with surprise, then drew rein with Sibby beside him. The cloaked man cantered up, narrowly missing a pile of cabbages and two scratching chickens. "Strangers, are you not?"

"Yes, lord," said Leron in what he hoped was a humble yet self-confident voice.

"Ha, I thought so. Not much passes Griml without his seeing. On what rolls are you entered?"

"Rolls, lord? I have no property. I am a singer."

"I don't care what you are. The king's orders these three months past have been published throughout the realm. Can you not read? All must be enrolled. Where do you come from? And who is this with you?"

Leron felt his temper rise dangerously, but he made an effort and answered in the same tone as before. "This is my young sister. We have been away in the fenlands, performing. Our home used to be in—in Sundrat." Sundrat was the first place he thought of, probably because of Ddiskeard. It was also conveniently far away.

"Sundrat, eh? Well, come along, and step lively. We'll get you two enrolled and give you your paper. Now tell me straight, can you read?"

"A little, but—what paper is this?"

"Nosy, aren't you? Come along. You'll find out soon enough. The fenlands. . . . Sounds suspicious."

He whirled his horse, jabbing at its mouth, and led them at a trot toward the Fleece Inn; farmers scrambled out of his way. Leron gave Sibby an encouraging grin and they followed with the humility proper to their station in life.

Where the painted fleece had hung above the door, a wooden crown now dangled. Several soldiers with spears and short swords lounged by the entry. Griml threw his reins to one of them and ordered another to take the travelers' mounts as well.

The smell of the inn was heavier than before, sour with sweat and spilled beer, and the passages were crowded with men. Griml pushed his way through to a back room, once a small dining room and now an office. A heavyset man sat at the table there with two young soldiers, aides, nearby. He looked up and spoke, showing a coarsely hawk-nosed face.

"Greetings, Griml, what have we here?"

"Itinerants, sir, I found them in the stockyards and saw them for strangers. They have no papers. Say they've been in the fenlands, performing. Haven't heard the king's new ordinances." The officer frowned and looked up with annoyance as Leron spoke unbidden.

"We have heard nothing. When did Lord Mathon make this decree?"

Griml burst into laughter, short nasty barks like a jackal, then answered while the officer looked amazed. "Mathon? That witless old swine? The regent makes these decrees. You are either cunning liars or very ignorant." Leron's hand clutched at his dagger, but before he could make an angry reply he felt Sibby's hand cover his with a warning squeeze. He swallowed.

"What has become of the old king? He is ill?"

"No worse than always. He is secluded in the palace. I thought this was known even in the fenlands."

"It is."

The seated officer looked up under heavy curved brows. "A messenger was sent there two months ago and has returned. You have lied to Griml and that is a serious offense. False information given to a king's officer is an act punishable by confiscation of goods, imprisonment, thirty lashes, or all three, subject to the decision of that officer. Now tell us once more where you are from."

"I have said already. We are minstrels from Sundrat, who have traveled long and far, even unto Vahn, returning through the fenlands to here. We now seek employment on the estate of the nobleman Glisser. When last we were here, Lord Mathon ruled and we have heard no news since then."

The officer shifted his bulk around and, leaning over, spat delicately into a vessel placed on the floor. "Vahn? Might as well be the moon. If I put that on record, they'd have my head and I wouldn't blame them. Maybe a night in prison will clear your head. What a fine tale this is. Glisser!"

"I have told you the truth!" Leron, in his anger, felt that he had spoken truly, and his voice held a passionate conviction. Griml sneered.

"Of course, of course. And this girl's your sister! Better and better. Your kind really starts them young."

He laughed again and the officer's pursed lips twitched in an answering smile. This was too much. Leron didn't even hit him. He leaned his weight forward on one leg and dealt Griml a heavy, backhanded slap across the mouth, which knocked him against the wall and drove a tooth through his cheek.

Sibby gasped and the two aides, gaping in disbelief, caught him by the arms. Already cursing himself for a fool, Leron made no attempt to struggle, but it was hard for him to discipline the savage expression on his face into the chastened remorse and fright he knew was suitable. The officer had not moved. "Striking a king's officer, ten days' imprisonment. We'll see about your identity papers when you're let out. Maybe you'll have remembered some more information for us by then." He pushed himself up from the table by his hands and stood breathing heavily. For a long, considering moment he looked at Sibby, then returned to Leron. "Take him away. It's been a long day, entering the farmers and pig breeders and chicken merchants. And now itinerants." He raised an eyebrow at Griml, who was standing with one hand pressed to his bloody cheek. "There's a lot to learn about itinerants, I can see. Send the girl up to my room and I'll ask her a few questions over supper. And don't forget some wine." Griml bowed in answer.

Leron, his arms pinned behind his back, looked from the officer's flushed face to Griml's thin leering one and felt his gorge rise. He threw himself across the desk, dragging the soldiers with him, and yelled, "Get out of here! Run!" Then Griml grabbed him by the hair and gave him a sharp rap on the temple with a sword hilt, knocking him out.

At first, Leron thought he might be blindfolded. His hands were tied behind his back and his head throbbed with pain. It was pitch black. As he began coming awake, a dim shape grew in the dark, and he saw it was a small barred window with darkness beyond it. He was sitting with his back against rough damp stone, and some straw covered the equally damp stone floor. He had no idea how much time had passed. He leaned his head back against the wall, and it exploded into exquisite little pieces of sensation. What distressed him most was the thought that Sibby probably hadn't run, since she wouldn't have understood.

The minutes dripped past, and Leron tried several times to stand. Finally, he staggered to his feet, but his tender head hit the low, unseen ceiling, and he fell to his knees, giddy and nauseated. He found that his hands were loosely bound, however, and it was possible to force them down in back of his body and bring them forward under his legs. Once they were in front of him, he could use his teeth on the knots, and after a while the ropes gave way. On his hands and knees, he crossed to the window, where fresh air from outside helped to clear his head. But there was no more he could do. The bars were narrowly spaced and sound, and the heavy door proved well bolted.

No one came to see him except a sleek bold rat who arrived ten minutes after the breakfast bread had been shoved under the door and waited patiently for crumbs. The crack through which he had come was too narrow for Leron's hand, so the visit brought him nothing but a little company. And thus a whole day passed with intolerable slowness. That evening as he sat despairing, unable to think or plan, footsteps in the corridor stopped outside his door, and to his surprise the door was opened. "Ten minutes," said a man's voice. "Even for a whole crock I can't risk any longer. And no more tricks." The door closed again behind a ragged-headed grubby boy wearing clothes that were much too big.

"Sibby!"

"Shh, I'm in disguise, stupid. This is kind of fun, if it works. Are you OK?"

"You are all right?"

"Me? Of course. You're the one in prison."

"He didn't touch you?"

"Who? Now look, there's no time for talking. Here, take this." She pulled Leron's hunting knife out from where it had been hidden in what he now saw was his own sheepskin tunic.

"How did you manage this? The guards cannot all be foolish."

"No, they're really clever. They found your dagger right away, even though it was hidden in the bread. Of course, it wasn't hidden terribly well. Now when the guard comes back, you hit him with it."

"Kill him?" Leron looked at this new Sibby with fascination.

"No, with the hilt, the way Griml hit you. And—good, there's a rope in here. You can tie him up afterward."

Leron began to smile, reluctantly. "And then? Do we don cloaks of invisibility, or snap our fingers and freeze them in their tracks?"

"Don't be silly. There are only two guards on night duty, and this is one of them. We'll just have to sneak. What you do now is hide behind the door."

Leron took up the indicated position. "You seem very skilled in this."

"I've seen it hundreds of times. Not in real life—I'll explain later."

They fell silent as the guard returned. He entered unsuspectingly and only let out a little grunt when Leron hit him on the head. As Leron tied the poor man up, convincingly but not too tight, he heard Sibby breathe, "Perfect." Then she giggled with relief. "We'd better get back to Sherwood Forest," she added cryptically. "The sheriff'll be after us." And she giggled again.

The corridor was dark and empty, and they stepped out cautiously. "I came in the door up there," said Sibby, "Because of the bribe. It opens on a side street. Most of the soldiers are by the main entrance. I think we have a good chance, because the other guard said he had to go outside for a few minutes." Leron put his finger to his lips, and they crept down the passageway toward the door. Just as they reached it, they heard a step on the stairs, leading down from the main hall. But fortunately the door opened silently, and the next moment they were out in the street. The returning guard bumped into them as they rounded the corner, frightening Leron enough so he leaped on him and throttled him to unconsciousness almost without thinking, but apart from that they were unnoticed. Later, the feeling of the man's soft sinewy throat came back unpleasantly to him.

In the main street they paused. "Follow me," said Sibby. "I've learned a good way out of town." Leron took her hand and followed as silently as possible while she led them in and out of narrow streets, across gardens and fields and a few small orchards. Then Villavac was behind them. An hour more and they came to a grove on the mountainside where Leron's horse was tethered. "Good, they didn't find him," remarked Sibby with satisfaction. She sat down with a sigh. "I'm tired. How's your head?" Leron fell to his knees beside her and lay down with relief, his hands pressed to his pulsing forehead.

"It will be all right."

There was silence while Leron considered all that had happened. Finally he could not hold his tongue any longer. "Tell me, just how did you accomplish this?"

Sibby gave a pleased laugh. "Well, let's see. When you hit

that man, Griml, I guessed they'd probably punish you in some way, and when those guards grabbed your arms, I began thinking about escape. Not to save myself, exactly, but so one of us would be on the outside, for a rescue. So when you told me to run, and got their attention by jumping forward, I already had my hand on your dagger, and I pulled it out of your belt and took off. I ran into what used to be the main dining room, and the door to the stable passage was still there, the way I remembered. I ran out and practically fell over your horse, and was up and away before anybody at all had come after me. They were still busy with you. So I raced out of town and finally found these woods here. I knew I couldn't help you right away, so I started planning. I cut off my hair with your knife, that was in your pack, and put on your tunic and rolled in the dirt so I'd look like a boy." Leron laughed in spite of himself, but she silenced him with a wave of her hand. "This is my story. Shut up. Anyway, it was a good disguise, because when I came back to Villavac this morning, on foot, everyone thought I was a boy. I brought your silver brooch to sell, and your knife and dagger both. I kind of hung around and listened to the farmers in the market, and there was a couple there whose son had been thrown in prison because he had gotten drunk and hit a soldier. So I told them that my brother had done the same thing, and did you get good food in prison? And they said no, it was terrible, but there was this one guard you could bribe with ale, and he'd let you in to visit and bring food. That's Devrow, the man you knocked out. So I sold your brooch, because I figured you were more important—"

"Thank you."

"—and I got some bread and cheese and a whole crock of ale—"

"Was that all?"

"Of course not. I got a lot of money, too. Just stop interrupting. Anyway, I found out what time Devrow was on duty and brought him the ale like they said. I was afraid they'd find your knife, so I hid it in my tunic and put your dagger in the bread where they'd find it. Of course, I wept and apologized and said I'd been crazy to do it, and Devrow didn't dare kick me out because of the bribe. So he let me in and you know the rest."

She finished and took a deep breath, leaning back against

the tree. "I like this kind of adventure. It's simple. No one gets hurt. I bet we rescue your father, too."

Leron nodded, feeling very old. "I greatly fear it will not be so—so simple. But I thank you, cousin, for this rescue. Now I think we should sleep, and save further planning for the morrow."

Next day they fell into a disagreement. Stores were needed before they could go on to Tredana, and Sibby was confident enough of her disguise to want to go and purchase them herself in the market. "They won't be looking for a boy," she said. "Devrow wouldn't dare tell what really happened."

Leron looked at her hopelessly, knowing of no way to explain to her what he really feared, or to warn her of the danger she had recently been in. Finally she won out and set off happily down the road to Villavac, her money from the sale of Leron's brooch wrapped up in a cloth tucked into her belt. She intended to buy a donkey also, to carry what they wanted, and the prospect of choosing one and being able to buy it all by herself excited her as much as the adventures of the previous day. She had pointed out to Leron, quite reasonably, that in the crowded market a stranger was not noticeable the way they had been at night with no one about, but he could not feel convinced.

Leron spent the day in an agony of self-recrimination. He was sure she would come to harm, and had resolved for the tenth time to wait just a few minutes more before going in search of her, when he looked out and saw a small figure trudging up the road, leading a laden brown donkey. As they blundered through the bushes, Leron turned with a glad smile of welcome, which faded as he saw Sibby's white face and tears. He took her by the shoulders, and she fell on his chest, sobbing.

"Sibby! Sibby, are you all right? What has happened? Are you hurt?"

She shook her head. "No, I'm OK." Leron breathed deeply with relief. "But Leron, it's all spoiled. They've killed him, Devrow. They have this place right by the road, and his body was there, hanging. And they're going to leave his body there forever. There are bones there and everything. I thought this was just going to be like a story, but it's real. And I didn't mean it like that."

Leron held her until she stopped crying, too relieved that

she was safe to quite understand everything else she had said. It wasn't until much later he began to wonder what she had thought their adventure was, if not real. And by that time they were well on their way to Tredana.

SE'ENIGHTLY REPORT
from GROUP-LEADER SKARPA, Rural Office, Villavac Division to WAR-LEADER BELLISAR, Regent's Office, Western Counties . . . an excerpt

. . . Griml reported tenth hour, bringing in custody two itinerants found loitering in market after closing. Claimed to be brother and sister, minstrels from Sundrat, been in Fenlands, no papers, ignorant of Regency. No names given, but mentioned Glisser, outlawed under Act of Council in first month of Regency. Male: early twenties, six feet, twelve stone, dark; Female: mid-teens, five feet, seven stone, dark; descriptions posted and circulated. Initiated routine questioning, male struck Griml and was thus sentenced to ten days' imprisonment. Became violent and was subdued, in which time female escaped. Male imprisoned minimum security, disappearing thirty hours later. Appended is the confession of Devrow, the guard who planned this escape. It shows that both itinerants were spies, enemies of the Regent, in contact for many months with Devrow whom they bribed. I consider us fortunate to have discovered this traitor in our midst; Devrow has been duly executed and is now exhibited by the southern gate. The other two are clumsy impostors and should soon be taken; I intend to take a personal satisfaction from their capture and questioning.

The pig-breeders report that last season's farrowing has been less than . . .

Chapter Thirty-four

Again Sibby's sense of direction led them true, directly to Herrard's secret pass through the mountains. It was while they were camping in that narrow defile, one evening after supper, that Sibby managed to explain to Leron a little more of what she had felt about their adventure in Villavac.

"Leron," Sibby tossed back her shaggy hair and looked at him sideways.

"Yes?"

"When that man, Griml, asked you in Villavac if you could read, I had a funny thought. You don't really read that much, do you?"

Leron tried to puzzle the sense of this. "I do not understand what you mean by 'much.' I can read and write as easily as any educated man."

"But there isn't that much to read here. I mean, you have letters, and poems and histories and things like that. But you don't have all the books and stories the way we have in my world."

"What stories are these?"

"Made-up stories. Like bards, but different. You see, they have these machines there that can print books, hundreds of them. It's funny, but when I first came here I tried to explain TV and cars and stuff like that. But now I think I see I was wrong. That's not what's so different. Leron, we have so many books there. I don't know how to describe them. People just think up stories all the time and write them down, and they're printed into hundreds and thousands of copies, and people buy them and read them. Some people have just hundreds in their own houses."

Leron shook his head with a smile. "It is very hard to imagine." In his mind he pictured briefly the machine that could print hundreds of books. It seemed a tedious process to carve an entire wooden block for a page, for the letters would not be as fine as a scribe's writing, and the plate would be good only for the one page, which might lose value with time. But Sibby went on, interrupting his reverie.

"You see, the trouble is, all I've ever really done is read. You learn to read when you go to school, when you're five or six. Ever since then, I guess I've spent all my time reading, one or two books a day. Even when I'm watching TV, I have a book, too. That's how I knew how to rescue you. People are always getting out of prison in adventure stories. It's my favorite kind of story. But none of it was real. My whole life was really stories. When I wasn't reading them or watching them, I was making them up in my head. And then I came here, and now for a whole year, I haven't read or watched anything, everything's really happened. And I haven't missed books at all. At home I couldn't even eat breakfast without reading something, even the printing on the boxes the food came in. It's the first time I think I've ever really known people or done real things. And that's why it was my fault about Devrow. When I rescued you, I kind of forgot it was real. In stories you never have to worry about the guard; you just knock him out and get away. I forgot it was real life, and now he's dead. Just because I forgot."

"Devrow is dead because of Ddiskeard's regency and his new laws."

"But it is my fault, too. It was real for you. You were worried. I never thought that you might be stuck there, or that they could kill you. I was afraid before, of Simirimia, but this was like a story. Maybe I'll never know what's real. Maybe I really belong in the Otherworld, not here. I don't want to go back, not at all. But I'm afraid I may have to, whether I want to or not. It's where I've always lived, and it's where my parents are; and I know what's real and what isn't there, even if it's dull. I can't make such terrible mistakes. Oh, Leron, what if I have to go back?"

"Arbytis has said you belong. Trust him. Sibby, we want you to stay, too. You must belong to this world, or you wouldn't be here."

"I hope so."

"Believe so." Leron startled them both with the vehemence of his tone. And although Sibby fell asleep easily that night, despite her fears, Leron lay awake nearly an hour turning her words over and over in his mind.

Leaving the narrow valley next morning, they cut across country toward the highway very slowly, leading the horse and donkey and walking. And once they had reached the road, on Leron's advice they did not follow it exactly but went through the fields and woods and across moorland vaguely parallel to the highway, but safe from surprise by other travelers. Both feared that the Circle Inn might also have become a military outpost, so they gave it a wide berth. Soon they saw how wise was Leron's choice of route: looking down onto the road from a rocky outcropping they saw small groups of mounted soldiers ride past in both directions.

A few days' ride from the city, Leron decided they must take turns sleeping and standing watch, for even in the fields he feared discovery, if not by troops then by a farmer too browbeaten to keep a secret. The closer he came to home, the more impatient and bitter he found himself becoming. It should have been so easy, to ride home and greet his friends and his father, rather than skulking through the countryside like some hunted wolf. Two or three times he was unreasonably short with Sibby, but she seemed to understand and did not get upset.

At length they came to the forest that grew close up to the city on the southern side. Here Leron had often hunted as a boy, and he led them easily by familiar landmarks safe into its pathless depths. The trees were pine for the most part, with few low branches. The needles were damp and sweet underfoot, the spiky green branches high and cool overhead, rustling and letting through occasional shafts of moving sunlight. Ferns and seedlings blocked their way, but Gannoc had taught Leron cunning and woodcraft, so he knew how to move through the undergrowth. Parasitic vines on some trees had dried in colors of scarlet and orange: the chief sign of autumn in this evergreen palace. In they went, deeper and deeper for nearly three hours, until the glade was reached that Leron had chosen from memory.

Age or some infection had brought a great tree crashing down, and the path of its fall had cut a long narrow wedge out of the forest. Mighty roots at one end spread more than a man's height up from the ground, and this with the hole it had sucked out of the earth made a fine deep cave. Foxes had been using it, but Leron kicked in fresh dirt and soon had it clean enough for their own habitation. The horse and the donkey were loosely tethered, to crop the grass that had grown along one side of the massive trunk, rank and high in the exposed sunlight. A stream, which had helped to loosen the tree's hold on the earth, flowed sluggishly across one end of the glade. They washed and drank and sat resting a moment without speaking.

"Sibby, I am sorry to ask it, but I fear you must once more take the danger of going in disguise, to observe matters in Tredana."

"Well, of course. I don't think you could disguise yourself there."

"No, there I am certainly familiar. But there will be danger for you. They are sure to be looking for strangers, and checking the papers and enrollments and other documents they demand."

"I'll just have to do what I did in Villavac and go midmorning. I should be all right as long as there's a crowd. The only trouble will be getting to Gannoc and Mara, or to Dansen, to find out about your father."

"This first time, do not be hasty. Just watch and listen. I will show you the way through the forest tomorrow, and if you are not back by evening, I shall come and look for you. There must be yet some who are loyal to me and my father."

"Just don't be too hasty yourself. Something might hold me up. But I will be careful. I don't think I'll forget what's real this time."

As it happened, Leron did not have too long a wait the next day. He showed Sibby to the forest edge soon after breakfast, a ragged and dirty young boy to any that did not know, but to Leron uneasily and unmistakably a girl. He said as much, but Sibby replied that people generally see what they expect to see and he could only tell because he knew. The sense of her remark, once he considered it, surprised him. Back in the glade alone, he waited through the middle of the day, grooming the horse and the small brown donkey, which Sibby for some reason had named Trigger. Then he checked his snares for rabbits and bathed a second time in the stream, for it was as warm as summer. It often happened along the Tredanan coast that several weeks of autumn would be warm and close in weather: they called it Karabdin Summer, for no reason that Leron knew. He was lying on his back, looking up at the sun and wishing he felt sleepy, when he heard sounds coming through the underbrush. He had grabbed his knife but was still in plain sight when Sibby appeared.

"Boy," she said, "it's a good thing we're friends." Leron didn't answer, for he saw who it was she had brought.

Dansen came forward and knelt, bits of underbrush clinging to his robes, and breathing heavily from his walk. But Leron raised him, and they hugged each other strongly.

"Dear Dansen, faithful scholar. I had hoped to see you, but not so soon."

"My lord, my lord, you have grown so thin! You are as brown and ragged as a Player!"

"You insult the Players. But how do you come here? Sibby, however did you find him?" They sat down and Sibby curled her legs under her, looking pleased.

"I didn't really do it. I was in the market just listening to people talk—complain, mostly—when I saw Dansen arguing with a gooseherd about the price of quills. When he had gotten them, I followed and spoke as soon as it was safe. He was so surprised! But he was very good about not showing it, and he understood right away about following me and pretending we weren't together."

She grinned at Dansen and he took her hand affectionately. "The advantages of an educated mind. One is never surprised by anything. But my lord, this makes me happier than I have been for many a long month. You do not know what has transpired in your absence."

"Some of it I can guess. How does my father?"

"I wish I could tell you. The day this child left was the day he was stricken. For this reason alone, no one followed her. Gannoc had come to me because of her leaving, when we heard and were summoned to your father's chamber. But they would not let his own physicians examine him, in fact they both have been barred from the city. Gannoc has been a virtual prisoner in the palace, attending the king yet not allowed to do anything for him not approved by Ddiskeard. Two days after his majesty's stroke, Ddiskeard became regent, as you know is proper, and since that time a flood of decrees and commands and laws has come from the palace, all in the name of Mathon, yet drafted and signed by the regent. And now Gannoc and I fear for his majesty's very life. What plans have you?"

"None, as yet. Only determination. I was not sure how it

would be here. Sibby has told you something of our adventures?"

"Yes, in brief. Sometime I hope I will have the chance to take it all down properly, especially concerning Vahn and Treclere and your northern journey. To have seen the Kermyrag! But now, alas, even scholarship must be put aside."

"Dansen, I am sorry. I would not have had you say such a thing for all I possess."

"My lord, you shame me, as you did just now when you greeted me as loyal. There is something I must confess. I cannot keep it from you. I must tell you that at first I tried to work as though nothing had happened. Yes, I told myself that you would not return, that your father would not recover, and that my place was where it had always been, safe among the records of great scholars and thinkers. I had my histories to write, a Karabdin grammar to compile, and other projects of importance. But less than a week had passed when Ddiskeard came to me, most civilly, to see if there was aught he could do for me. And I thought we must have been wrong, and Ddiskeard an honest man. But my prince! I could not believe it! Soon he was suggesting how I might change the records here, put a different name there, and in sundry ways pervert the truth as I knew it!"

At these words he looked so indignant that Leron smiled. "I wish this were the worst my cousin has done."

"My prince, what infamy can be greater? Think a moment. If all records lie, where will our children turn for truth, in a world ruled by Ddiskeard and Ddiskeard's heirs? Already the laws are changed, and each regardless of his station has felt the altering of his daily life. In twenty years, who will know it has ever been different?"

Leron nodded and frowned. "Your point is well made. But continue."

"Ah, well, when I realized that even my books might be forced to bear false witness, I saw I could not continue blindly on. I have made records of all recent events as I see them, and these I have hidden in the library where I think they will be safe for many years. And I have met with Gannoc whenever possible to talk of an escape. Of course, he will not leave the king, and I would not have it otherwise, nor you. Yet to smuggle Mathon out, sick as he is, will be no easy task.

"You see then no chance of an overthrow, a restoration?"

"Sir, I speak to you plainly, with much heaviness of heart, on a matter I have considered long and carefully. If you could reach your subjects, there would be a chance. But you cannot. What you saw and experienced in Villavac is tenfold worse in Tredana. And Mathon is a prisoner, his very life at the mercy of your enemies. You cannot risk him, you cannot reach your people. I am as sure of this as I am of anything, that the only answer is to go into exile and rebuild there, to return again at some future time in a position of strength. The more time passes, the more unpopular Ddiskeard will have become, and the less you will be a supplicant and the more a savior."

Leron did not answer, but sat thinking with his head sunk in his hands. "Yes," he said at last. "I have known it already. You are right. We must consider how best to free my father from these villains."

"Maybe," said Sibby, "you should figure out where you will take him and who'll go with you."

"That is not so difficult. It is necessary that I return to Treglad, to tell Meddock of his son's fate. My ancestors came from Treglad; there it is fitting I should return, to build a new city. Dansen shall come, and Gannoc and Mara with my father. And you. Others I hope will join us, once the news has been spread."

"This is well thought," said Dansen. "But we must think how best to rescue your father. He is well attended." Sibby bit her lip.

"In stories—" she flushed, then continued. "In stories they do things like burn down a house for a diversion, and then when the bad guys are watching that, the good guys get away."

Leron raised an eyebrow. "And what of the people in the house?"

"That's the problem with its being real. I guess the idea isn't much good."

"No," cried Dansen, jumping up excitedly. "The idea is a fine one. My lord, you will not remember, but on the occasion of your birth, there were many bonfires in the city in celebration. A captain of the fishing fleet drank far too heavily that night and made a fire on his ship's deck. It spread across the harbor, beautiful and terrible against the sea and night sky. All the city gathered on the cliffs to watch, while others tried to save certain boats. Yet no lives were lost, for as you know there is not a fisherman alive would risk the bad luck of sleeping on his ship while it is in harbor."

Leron looked from Sibby to Dansen with hope and delight. "Dear cousin, dear friend, between you I think it is solved. Has the passage I found when I was little been discovered?"

"Not that I have heard."

"Then we shall risk it. I feel the success of this venture in my bones. Dansen, return to the city and speak with Gannoc. Between you, decide the best day for this, and that night I shall come to the king's room by the way I know. Is Sentell still free to come and go?"

"Yes."

"That is well. I know him for a faithful servant, and his wife's brother has four boats. Through him, arrange for the fire to be lit, three hours after sunset, explaining the great need but without details. I will try to bring my father out by the passage, and you may come also with Gannoc and Mara. We must go out on foot for safety. By the north road, Sibby shall wait with this horse and the donkey. Other ponies we can steal from my stud farms outside of Sundrat. Until that point we shall hide best on foot, in any case. The king may ride this horse, and the donkey shall bear our supplies. Dansen, what do you think?"

"I think it is a most excellent chance." Leron got to his feet, and Dansen seized his hand and kissed it.

"Tomorrow morning early I will bring Gannoc's decision. Until then, stay well hid, I beg of you."

"No fear," laughed Leron. "My neck is as precious to me as your scholarship is to you."

MISSIVE

From Ajjibawr Daryoziliman, Karif of Karabdu, to Odric Sembatioun, Lord of Treclere

To Odric Sembatioun, the Noble and Industrious, greeting from the Karif of all the Karabdu:

I have had from my true and sworn brother Rassam, known to you as Herrard, such news of events in your city as must make any reasonable man rejoice indeed. Know that you may always count me and mine friendly toward your policies. Therefore it is with a heavy heart I must refuse that kindest invitation which Rassam brought. There is a wind rising in the desert more terrible than the dreaded Lilsan, *the which when it blows leaves no trace behind of those it destroys, be they a hundred horsemen in full armor. Rassam came through the storm safely, in that it was not his appointed time to perish, as much as by reason of any craft or skill. Though it cover my head with shame to speak these words, still I must say them: trust no one of the Karabdu you may meet. A new zealotry and rebellion is abroad in the desert, and it may be many months before the sands are clean again.*

I send this word by the hand of the eldest son of Adaba Tayyib, one who is faithful to me after his fashion, and if you would reply, do not risk any of your own men but send back by him also. Only do not let him charge you for the carrying since he shall be well recompensed here as he knows.

May the sun illumine your way forever, and lead you to attainment and felicity.

Chapter Thirty-five

The streets were dark and empty. Leron followed their familiar twists and turns easily, meeting no one. It was two days since he had met with Dansen in the forest, and the plans seemed to be going smoothly. He found the old orchard near the castle walls overgrown and rank as it had been for thirty years or more. By some miracle, the gate still hung at the angle it had for as long as Leron could remember, its remaining leather hinge not yet rotted through. As always, he vaulted over it, steadying himself on the ornamental side post, and the rounded head of the stone carved demon was familiar under his hand.

He had first come here soon after his mother's death, finding in the old orchard a place to play, away from his nurse's eye. He had never told anyone where he went, and no one had ever found out, not even when he discovered the tunnel and following it surprised Mathon napping in his room, where he was said to be in conference and not to be disturbed. Feeling his way through the dark along the brick wall behind the trees, Leron laughed as he remembered that meeting. Mathon had explained to him how the tunnel had come to be built, for the king's escape during the Karabdin wars long before. It was supposed to have been blocked up. Despite its danger to him, Mathon had kept the secret so that his son's amusement would not be spoiled and his orchard retreat discovered. Under Leron's fingers, the brick gave way in a familiar pattern. He ducked below a branch and into the low entrance. The passage angled sharply to the right, so if it were seen at all from in front it looked more a niche than a tunnel. It was lower than he remembered, but then he had not been in it for nine years or ten.

Slowly and confidently, he went through the slimy dank dark. In places he stumbled where tree roots had forced their way up through the tunnel floor, for it skirted three sides of

the orchard before climbing up through the castle walls. At
last it began its ascent, larger here with a vaulted roof and
cobbled floor, but still completely lightless. Through three
different levels it climbed, then turned to come out in a corner of the king's room, under the stone-carved window seat.
Light from Mathon's chamber shone very dimly into the corridor's end, for the seat was carved like a garden bench surrounded with ivy, and the ivy was cunningly done in pierced
sculpture, concealing the panel that covered the tunnel entrance and at the same time letting in light. Leron crept up
softly and put his eye to one of the tiny holes.

The light was dim because there were only two candles
burning in the room. Mathon's curtained bed was in shadow,
but Leron could hear his heavy irregular breathing. There
was no one else there. Leron could not be sure if the harbor
fire had started, but he was too impatient to be entirely careful. He pushed the panels apart and pulled himself up into the
room, carefully closing the panels behind him. There were
curtains to hide behind if necessary, or he could even go under the bed. He crossed the room quietly and looked down at
his father.

Mathon had lost weight, and the skin hung loosely on his
face and hands. His beard and hair seemed dirty and tangled,
and his face was red, damp with sweat. He did not lie easily,
but murmured things under his breath, his face twitching
while his hands opened and shut on the sheets. Leron bent
over and touched him gently.

"Sire, are you awake?" Mathon's eyes came open all at
once, and they looked straight up into Leron's.

"And who the devil are you?" he said distinctly, then, muttering, turned his head on the pillow, looking toward the
door. In a soft hoarse voice he went on, "Away, give me some
light. Light! Lights! Candles! D'you want we should drown?
The dark is rising, light's the thing." Voice and expression
were intense, yet he did not speak above a whisper.

Leron leaned closer, and touched his hand. "Sire, dear father, it is I, Leron. I've come back. It's your son."

"Son, son, son, son? Ha! You lie. I've got no son. I had a
son, but that was long ago. He's gone, they're all gone, everyone gone. Traitors! They want me to drown." One hand, surprisingly strong, came up and grasped Leron's tunic. The old
king raised himself partly from the bed and spoke in Leron's

ear, with a shrewd expression on his face. Close to, he stank as though unwashed for months. "I'll tell you what, I've got a good son. Brave and strong and handsome in the sun. A prince, yes, a prince, a prince and popular, aye. He'll make a good king. But he's dead and rotten." Mathon fell back on the pillows and his eyes closed wearily.

"Away," he said in a firm voice. "You smell, you reek of mortality."

Tears burned in Leron's eyes, but he leaned forward again and took both his father's hands in his own. "Father, dear father, you must know who I am."

Mathon sighed and opened his eyes again. "I am an old man," he said. "I will tell you straight, my eyes are not what they once were. I do not know you now, whatever they may have told you. They tell all sorts of lies behind my back, I know they do. They said perhaps I know you, it's a lie. A damned lie. Fly, fly, fly O sweet black angel." His eyes closed again and his hands went limp in Leron's grasp.

At that moment the door began to open, and Leron flung himself behind the curtains—in good time, for it was not Gannoc. Two strange men came in, one carrying a flask. "You can see the flames all over town," said the first. "Give him his draught, and we can leave him safely for a few minutes."

"Don't rush me. The fire will not be out before we get there. You know he should get the full amount." He walked to the bed and jerked Mathon by the shoulder. "Wake up!" Mathon opened his eyes, and even from behind the bed curtains Leron could see the anger glittering in them.

"Lights!" he said. "The dark is too deep in here."

"Drink this and we'll see about lights."

"He'll get me lights. Away, away, away! He'll bring me lights."

The doctors looked at each other. "Who'll bring the lights?"

"Who? The raven will, the crow, the kite, the blind and hungry worm. Peace, peace, peace!" Mathon put his hands to his ears and shook his head from side to side as though at a great noise. "The raven bellows for revenge. Croak not, black angel, I have no food for thee."

One of the doctors laughed and thrust Mathon back against the pillows. "Stop shouting; there's none to listen."

He turned to his friend. "Phew, he stinks."

"I'll shout, I'll cry aloud. You stink of life, I smell of clean corruption, sweetest death. World, world, O world." Still snickering, one of the doctors took Mathon by the head, trying to force his jaws open as one would a sick animal.

"Be ready," he told the other. But as he spoke, Mathon flung him off with sudden strength.

"Whoremasters, cowards, sons of bitches! Begone, sirs, begone." He swept them back and one hand struck the medicine, dashing it to the floor. Behind the curtains Leron relaxed, for he had been ready to do the same and take his chances wrestling with the two. One of the doctors cursed and struck the king across the face.

"Now what? We'll miss the excitement. Old fool!" The other looked at the spilled liquid and then at Mathon writhing and talking deliriously. "He's mad enough as is. One dose can be safely missed. We'll bring him another before morning." At the door he paused. "More lights did you say? Of course, your majesty." And he knocked over the two candles as he shut the door behind him.

In the dark Leron came out from behind the curtain and stooped over Mathon. The king's eyes were open. "You have returned again, again. Ah my head. These dreams and fancies grow too strong I fear."

Leron took his hands firmly and, bending over, kissed him on the mouth. "Believe it, father. It is your son. I am no fancy, and I have come to take you away to safety with me."

Tears began rolling out of Mathon's eyes, and he turned his head away, weak and ashamed. "Go away, go away. Taunt me no more. Vision, spirit, fancy! O, I beg, I beg of you, have mercy. I am an old man, and I fear I am not in my perfect mind."

Crying himself, Leron bent his head to Mathon's and spoke to him softly. "You will be well, you will be. Now you must trust me awhile." His emotion was such that he did not hear the door open, but it was no enemy. Dansen came in, then Gannoc, and with him Mara.

There was no time to waste in greetings. "Gannoc, help me lift him. Where is his robe?" Without pausing to answer, Gannoc went to the chest and pulled out a warm dark velvet robe, fur-trimmed. Together they helped Mathon into it, dazed and protesting, while Dansen barred the door from within to delay any followers. He looked around the dark chamber and chuckled.

"This should cause those ignorant guards some sleepless superstitious nights. The door locked from within and no one there!"

Then at Leron's direction he opened the panel and helped Mara down into the tunnel. As Dansen climbed in himself, Leron stooped and gathered his father in his arms. "No, Gannoc, I can manage. Do you follow after and see the panel closed tight behind us. I feel it may prove useful to us in who knows what future to have this secret still."

It was a difficult squeeze, but Leron made his way down into the shaft, and turning sideways he hurried along crablike through the passage, Mathon limp in his arms. Three or four times he stopped for breath, and Gannoc close behind him helped to bear Mathon's weight as they stood and rested. Even so, it was not long before they had come out into the orchard and were standing together in the tangled shadow of the trees. Beyond, to the east, the sky was bright and alive and red, great roarings filled the air, and the smell of burning came to them on the breeze. Mathon revived in the cold air and opened his eyes.

"Come, come," he said almost jovially. "I am the king. Tell me, you must, tell me, what is this?" The wind changed and a wave of smoke rolled over them, while beyond the farthest buildings a tall flame towered up and broke into colors against the sky.

"Bones!" cried Mathon, shutting his eyes. "Bones cry out revenge, revenge. Burn, burn, burn, burn, burn!" The last "burn" was a shriek, but it was lost in the roar and crackle from the harbor. Then Leron brought Mathon's cloak up around his face, and urging him to be quiet followed Gannoc out into the street.

In the streets they met only a few people, and these were all hurrying to the harbor to see what was happening there. A few sounded frightened, but for the most part there was a holiday spirit about them. One man did cry out to Leron that they were going in the wrong direction, but no one paid any attention to the remark. More easily than Leron had dared to hope, the north road was reached, and a mile from the city Sibby was waiting impatiently.

Together in comparative security, greetings were exchanged

at last. Sibby was hugged and kissed by Mara and Gannoc, as
was Leron. Mathon had fallen into unconsciousness once
more, so Leron mounted the horse and took his father up in
his arms before him. Into the woods they made their way, and
continued at a rapid walking pace until dawn, when a hidden
grove was found and they could sleep. Gannoc kept first
watch.

On foot, it proved to be a four days' walk to Sundrat. For
safety they continued moving at night and sleeping by day,
but there was no sign of pursuit. Outside of Sundrat they
made camp in the woods, while Gannoc and Leron made
forays into the fields of the king's stud farm. The horses had
been taken into the barns, but the ponies were still at grass as
Leron had hoped. In a few days, four had been quietly caught
by moonlight and taken away into the woods. They fashioned bridles out of rope, and Leron and Gannoc, still by
night, raided one of the sheds for grain and sheepskins. When
they finally set out again, they were almost as well provisioned as they had been the year before. What they lacked,
Gannoc stole on nightly side trips into the sleeping farms
about them. Leron protested this, but Gannoc explained he
only took where there was plenty. One morning, as they were
making camp north of Sundrat and only fifty miles from the
coast, he staggered in with a full wineskin in each hand, and
two more over his shoulders. As he fell to his knees under
their weight, Leron scolded him, laughing all the same.

"Gannoc, Gannoc, surely this is a family's entire winter
store? Would you have them freeze?"

Gannoc shook his head, chuckling. "If any freeze, it will
be Ddiskeard's soldiers. I took this from the stores of a garri-
son in the last village. They had barrels, too, but I am not Big
Belton, to carry casks in either hand. These skins were all I
could manage. I recalled how glad we were of the wine last
year, once we had reached the shore and had less food."

"I for one shall be glad of it even sooner," said Dansen as
he broached a skin. "Leron, your father's health. Shall I pour
him some?"

Leron looked to where his father lay and shook his head.
"No, he still sleeps. I drink to your toast, and also to the success of this journey. May it bring us greater luck than the
other."

At this Sibby made a face. "Boy, I can see where

I'm wanted."

Leron looked at her and shook his head. "Nay, I have no quarrel with the real princess we found. It was looking for the false one that brought on all this trouble."

Sibby suddenly looked up at Gannoc. "That reminds me. No one's said anything about Dastra. What's happened to her?"

Mara made an expressive clucking sound, with a little rude toss of her head. "That one! She has found true happiness."

Gannoc chuckled in his beard and looked at Leron commiseratingly. "So many things have been a shock to you, my lord, I hardly dare tell you that she has found another."

"I think I can guess this riddle. My cousin is the lucky man?"

"Yes, lucky indeed, married to the most beautiful lady at court."

Leron drank from the sack and wiped his mouth. "For once," he said swallowing, "I can almost pity Ddiskeard. Almost. I think that marriage was made by the gods, as the old saying has it."

Dansen looked up from his notes. "Brydeni has recorded variants of these familiar folk sayings, which extend back even to the Old Tregladan. I think I shall start keeping note of those still current in our speech."

Leron looked at him with affection. "Dear Dansen," he said. "In truth you make me hopeful of the future."

A HISTORY OF THE GLORIOUS REGENCY
Compiled by many Pre-eminent Scholars in convocation under the generous and benevolent auspices of the Regent himself (an extract)

. . . *And it was not long after those events of which we spoke that news began to come from every quarter of the land, showing how the hand of Vazdz was shown clearly in the doings of men. Everywhere was his triumph to be seen, not just in the blessed regency of the pious Prince of Tredana. Our own near neighbors and cousins, the Karabdu, renouncing at last the many wickednesses of their tyrannical and bloody* chieftain, chose for themselves another, learned and skilled in council, and named by happy chance Dzildzil, thus bringing back to memory the days of the desert race's greatest strength and purest beliefs. And though it was many months before those rebellious tribesmen who had been led astray by the flattering tongue of their former Karif could be subdued and banished, yet this great work was accomplished, and now our two kingdoms rejoice in a friendship they have not shared for centuries. The desert capital is being rebuilt and there, as in Tredana, one may look for a golden age to commence—the felicity which can only be based on a strong and godly ruler.

Epilogue

Karabdin Summer was past by the time they came out onto the deserted beaches. The wind from the sea was chilly, although the sun shone brightly still and the weather remained clear. On the beach, nothing had changed, and Sibby almost looked to see their footprints from the year before, leading the way north. Many days it was possible to forget that they were moving into exile.

Mathon improved slightly. One night after he had slept, and also Gannoc and Mara, Leron sat up with Dansen and Sibby. He poked at the fire to keep it alight, while Dansen tried to read his notes so close to the flame the paper almost took fire. Sibby was also up, wrapped in her blanket but sitting forward, her chin on her hands. She interrupted the silence, speaking very softly.

"I wish I understood better."

Dansen looked up from his paper. "Understand what, my dear?"

"The way things happen. I mean, why does there have to be so much hurting? It's not just Simirimia, or Bodrum. It's like anyone who wants something just does it, or takes it, and no one cares if anyone else is hurt or killed. Even your mother—" she turned to Leron, "and my—my father, they weren't any better. It's as if everything's supposed to be simple, only by acting that way there's so much more trouble than if they stopped to think. Especially about other people."

Dansen smiled a little sadly. "You have touched the very heart of things, my dear. Since Mathon was struck down, I have thought so much about these various events, and further, considered the history of our city back for many generations. We have acted not as sentient beings but as figures in a ballad, playing out our lives in love and jealousy, in hatred, lust, brutality—mere selfishness, in short."

Leron was struck by the passion in Dansen's tone and

looked at him with startled eyes. "Prince, why so surprised? You have read this riddle yourself, though none of us perhaps have put the case in so many words. I have not been innocent either. My passion for my books was such I would have let all other matters go, had it been possible. My hands are not clean." He looked down at his fingers as he spoke, and laughed as he saw the ink stains there. "In truth as well as in image, I am stained indeed. Ah, well. Perhaps we all will profit from the need for a new order. Perhaps in Rym Treglad, the brain will rule, and help instruct the heart."

Leron poked the fire again, weighted with the requirements of the future. "What is meant by Rym Treglad?"

Dansen smiled. "In the old tongue, Rym means new. It is time, prince, that you began the study of Tregladan. My books are gone, but my memory is sound."

Leron smiled and nodded. "You are my teacher. I place myself in your hands." He stood up and stretched. "Ah, Dansen, if you can help me learn to rule by intent and not by mere reaction, then truly Rym Treglad may be a happy city."

One day, not long after, the sun shone more warmly than usual, and Leron decided they should stay and rest awhile, since there was nothing to be gained from hurry. Sibby took off her boots and ran through the cold green water, laughing like a little child, and soon Leron found himself running with her, laughing helplessly when she splashed him, first by mistake and then intentionally. Soon they flopped down onto the sand, and lay back weak with laughter. Leron clutched his stomach.

"I cannot sit up. I think the muscles are torn." For some reason this set them off again, and it was many minutes before they could speak. Leron reached over and took Sibby's hand. "My lady," he said, and the term came naturally to him, "my lady, I am glad that you are here."

That noon they were calm enough to help with the cooking, and Leron washed the dishes while Sibby dried them carelessly. Dansen was writing and talking to himself, Mathon drowsed, and Gannoc and Mara stood together, looking out to sea.

"Come," said Leron when they had finished. "We shall go explore the terrain." He led Sibby up into the hills on their left, and there on a rocky ledge they sat companionably. Below them the waves rolled in, making irregular rushes at the sand, while seaweed wandered back and forth indecisively in the foam.

Leron looked at Sibby and his mouth was dry, and for some reason he had to press his hands against his knees to keep them from shaking. Her hair fell down in front of her ears in curls and she was making faces as she turned some thought over in her mind. Suddenly she shattered his mood, jumping to her feet and saying, "Let's go look for rabbits. I want to catch one for a pet. I mean, not for food." She ran up into the bushes and began looking for signs of burrows, and Leron joined her; but soon their morning mood betrayed them and they were seized with laughter once more.

Leron cried, "Oh look!" to Sibby, and when she turned, he pretended to be a rabbit caught in a snare, bounding about. Sibby laughed and began skipping away into the brush. Suddenly, Leron ran after her, chasing her in earnest, and he caught her by the arms.

"Sibby," he said, and then stopped. He had no idea what to say. For a minute he looked down into her black eyes, while she looked up at him with patient curiosity. Then he bent his head and touched her lips with a kiss.

Sibby did not move when he released her, but she looked at him uncomprehendingly, and then, as he leaned forward once more, she stepped back. He reached out, and she stepped back again, not frightened but puzzled; and as she took that second step, she seemed to stumble and fall. Then she screamed with real terror, and for a long sickening moment Leron thought it was because of himself. As she began growing dim before his eyes, he understood and threw himself forward into the bushes, trying to grab her hand. "Oh no," he cried, "oh no." But his hand found nothing there to hold, although it hit painfully against something too hard and too smooth to be a branch.

The heavy window suddenly blew shut, and although she pushed and hit it with her fists, it would not open again. She saw, however, that it must have been some trick of light that fooled her in the hall, for the window was quite dark. The ivy tendril was still caught in it, the inchworm still engrossed in his first few bites. She wished she had been able to free him, but the window wouldn't budge.

As she pushed one final time, Sibby was guiltily aware of how late it must be. For some reason she felt very empty and sad. But they would be waiting for her at home. She'd better hurry. And what were those names she was going to look up? Oh yes, Sigerson and . . . and Tredana.

A clipping from *The Boston Evening News,*
September 29

SEQUEL TO STRANGE EVENTS IN MYSTERY HOUSE

While the police are still investigating the baffling disappearance of three people from a house on West Newton hill (Story page 2), the fate of the mystery house itself has been sealed. Wiliam Barron, of Barron, Leonard, & Esty, has revealed that his client, Michael Arleon of Jacksonville, Florida, will raze the recently inherited mansion and intends to develop the prime two-acre site for multiple dwellings. As soon as the police have concluded their investigation, there will be an auction of house contents, including a library of rare books dealing with spiritualism, mysticism, and the occult said to number in excess of six thousand volumes. A large and important collection of artifacts representing primitive culture and religion, assembled by the late Harris Arleon in a lifetime of research and travel, has been generously donated by his heirs to Harvard University's Peabody Museum as the Orlean Lodge Bequest. Meanwhile, the City Zoning Board continues to deny Michael Arleon's petition for a waiver, but William Barron is hopeful that his client will prove successful. "Our proposed development would be tasteful and modern, an asset to the entire area," said Barron to reporters today. "The era of forty-room houses like Orlean Lodge is past. Empty houses attract vandalism and pose a hazard to the whole neighborhood. Furthermore, quality town house units like my client's proposed Tudor-style village can provide older neighborhoods like ours with a badly needed face lift. Houses like Orlean Lodge were built for a different way of life and have long outlived their usefulness in twentieth-century America."

Airs, Ancient and Modern

Compiled from various sources,
Vahnian, Trecleran and Tredanan

ABOUT THE AUTHOR

Joyce Ballou Gregorian's father is an Armenian who fled Iran as a child, her mother a descendant of early New England settlers. She grew up entranced by tales of travel and adventure, some from her father's own life story. She is involved with the family business of buying and selling oriental rugs, and has traveled widely teaching and lecturing on the subject. (One reviewer compared the complexity of her plots and imagined civilizations to the intricacies in the patterns of the rugs she knows so much about.)

Ms. Gregorian lives on a farm in rural Massachusetts, and in addition to writing, singing, and working with pottery, she breeds Arabian horses. Her second book, the sequel to *The Broken Citadel,* entitled *Castledown,* will be available from Ace in the spring of 1983. The third book in the series is still on the typewriter, and is eagerly awaited by Ms. Gregorian's many fans.

Fantasy from Ace
fanciful and fantastic!

BEST-SELLING
Science Fiction
and
Fantasy

Stories
⤛ of ⤜
Swords and Sorcery

MORE SCIENCE FICTION! ADVENTURE